RENDEZVOUS

a vacation sports romance

by Sam Marie

RENDEZVOUS

To the man who puts book boyfriends to shame – I'm still looking for you. Call me?

Being deeply loved by someone gives you strength, while loving someone deeply gives you courage.
—Lao Tzu

1

David

THIS FUCKING PLACE. I swear to God, I will lose it if one more person comes up to me and says *Buenos diàs, señor*. It's not a good morning. No morning since my arrival has been a good morning. Yet, everyone here is so happy. I want to be silently served drinks while I brood on the beach. Is that too much to ask? Instead, everyone is trying to vomit their happiness onto me. I don't drink the Kool-Aid – never have, never will.

It was a stupid idea to come on this vacation, but I was running out of options and I panicked. My agent says I should be saving face by running drills with the rookies. But doing so is too close to accepting my fate and ultimate demotion.

"Devon will be out there," Blake told me. *"After he filled in for you last season, he'll be giving a good show of support for the new recruits."* Blake is one of the best in the business. He gives sound advice, but it doesn't mean I have to listen. I don't need to go head-to-head with a second-string quarterback. Thirteen years as a starting quarterback with

multiple championships and accolades is enough to prove my value.

"Señor, buenos diàs. What can I do for you today?" a waiter asks, keeping a safe distance as I throw a dart toward the team photo that is pinned on the post of my beachside cabana.

Usually, I feel bad for being rude and standoffish to wait staff. The man is just doing his job, but I've been here five days and my mood has only soured. Nothing can pull me out of this funk, and the repetition of daily events is further fucking with my head.

I toss another dart, aiming for the faces that threaten to end my career, before answering. "I'll take a bottle of Glenlivet single malt, oldest year you've got, and a six-pack of Modelo." The waiter nods and flinches as I throw another dart. "And bring it on ice," I call after him.

He conveniently keeps forgetting the ice. It's hot as hell out here – who wants to drink cold beer? I'm starting to think the waiter's silent opposition is a good approach. He's getting under my skin, one missing ice cube at a time. Eventually, one of us will break.

I pick up a fourth dart and keep my eyes on the target. With the precision of a veteran NFL quarterback, my aim strikes true – right in Devon's eyeball. It momentarily improves my mood, but the twinge of pain in my right shoulder evaporates any improvement going forward. Dismissing the old injury, I continue my dart assault.

Five. Six. Seven darts sink their way deep into the wooden post.

Laser-focused on the picture before me, I remind myself of the issue at hand. The end of an era is near. Am I ready for it to end? *Hell no.* Last season didn't end the way I'd hoped. This season is my chance to come back in a big way – to redeem myself from the hit that started this whole conversation. The word … The word makes me sick just thinking about it.

Retirement.

I may be thirty-six, but I am reaching the peak of my career. I can feel it in more ways than one. It's difficult to explain the feeling, but it thrums deep in my bones. While I dream of the field, developing plays and new routes that will crush the competition, my movements are slower than they once were.

No one believes I can continue playing at the level I used to – with the speed and agility of a receiver and the mind of a quarterback. What they don't understand is that I have worked my entire life to master the game of football. I'm not throwing away all that hard work because a minor injury.

Even if I don't run a four-forty anymore, my ability to see the field and perform under pressure is twofold what it was three years ago. My game strategy may need to change to account for my somewhat decreased reaction times, but I'm confident in my ability to do so. If only the people who decide my fate also believed that.

They think I'm too old, that my body will start wearing down, and I won't be able to keep up with the younger players. Picking a quarterback in the first round of drafts last year was telling enough. I can see the light leading me out, one first round draft pick at a time.

Every year I play, however, my skill level and confidence increases. Few quarterbacks have the experience and reliability that I possess. Some people call me arrogant, but it isn't arrogance. There is a massive difference between arrogance and ability, and I'll stick by my convictions until the very end. I won't go down without a fight.

I throw another dart and completely miss the paper as a sharp pain shoots through my shoulder.

Shit.

Getting angry about my situation seems to trigger the pain. Before coming here, my shoulder felt fine – there was no pain whatsoever. I've been throwing Hail Marys all day with no issue since therapy ended, and I've even continued my therapeutic exercises just to be certain I am fully healed.

"Easy there, killer," someone says behind me.

I turn around to find an older man, who looks to be in his sixties, walking up the beach. His footsteps imprint the sand in a long line down the shoreline. The waves washing ashore slowly erase any traces of his path.

"Care for some competition?" the old man asks.

His face is covered in a thick white beard that is the perfect balance between overly groomed and not trying too hard. He is wearing white linen shorts with a matching un-buttoned white linen shirt and Robert Downey Jr-looking sunglasses. There is no doubt in my mind that he's another rich asshole renting an obscenely priced bungalow at the resort – like myself.

I'm not good company, so I doubt he is either.

"Well?" he says expectantly.

"Thanks, but I'm not in the mood for company today," I reply. The man lowers his sunglasses, peering over the top edge to get a better look at me and the picture behind me.

My stomach drops. Here it comes – the recognition.

"Alright, son. If you change your mind, I'll be around." He turns and walks back toward the shoreline without even a single glance back.

I breathe a sigh of relief.

No matter where I travel, people recognize me. Even in Tulum, thousands of miles south of New York City, people have a way of finding me. If I were in a better frame of mind, I wouldn't mind posing for a few photos and giving out autographs, but my current state of mind will only paint me in a poor light. My publicists will be pissed if I offend some fans on their vacation. As a veteran, I don't exactly have an excuse for being a stuck-up jerk to people who idolize me. It isn't their fault I'm being pushed out of the league. Plus, there are expectations for someone in my position, being professional is one of them.

Fame and recognition is one thing I can't wait to give up in *retirement*. But my body and mind aren't ready to quit yet. The fake professionalism is worth every ass-kissing ounce when I am on the field winning games. There is no other feeling like it.

The rush of pre-game adrenaline, the build-up to each play, and the calm that comes over me as I call a play is a feeling that I will never be able to replicate in any other aspect of my life. It is like being alive and grounded at once – I feel as if I am in complete control of the world around me. And then the win – it's indescribable. It's as simple as the feeling you get as a kid when you finally take the training wheels off your bike. But it's as abundant and all-consuming as the jubilation you get from watching your own kids do the same thing.

I don't have my own kids, yet, but I've had a taste of that feeling from watching my nieces and nephews. Being present for those simple moments in their life made me realize how important it is to hold onto that feeling in my career. Because football is all I have. It is my entire life, and I am going to hold onto it as long as I can.

The owners want a young, fresh-faced quarterback to represent their team. I don't know what awaits me upon my return to New York, but I'm going to fight like hell for it.

Deciding to leave the punctured picture of my team-mates behind for the day, I tug off my shirt, toss it onto the daybed, and grab my goggles. It's midday – a good time for an ocean swim before I indulge in the liquor the waiter is bringing back. I quit being a big drinker when I hit my thirties. But I find everything about this trip to be an exception to my usual lifestyle choices.

I jog toward the ocean, pumping my shoulders and swinging them in circles to loosen the joints. My therapist encouraged me to keep swimming. The movement requires a full rotation of my shoulders and the water provides the perfect amount of resistance to slowly rebuild and repair the previously torn muscle.

As I step into the saltwater, a momentary calm consumes me. The water is cool compared to the blazing summer heat, and the sound of the waves washing ashore further soothes my soul. The ocean is one of the few places I love but don't get to frequent often. With the unpredictable New York City weather, there is a short amount of time I can enjoy the sea. With my schedule, there is an even shorter amount of time I can travel to warmer oceanside climates like where I am now. Nevertheless, swimming, surfing, and sailing will always be some of my favorite pastimes.

Tropical fish swim around my feet as I wade into deeper waters. The rocking of the waves deepens my relaxation. I dive under a shallow incoming wave and give myself over to the darkness and silence under the sea. It's peaceful. When I emerge for a breath, I feel a faint smile begin to creep across my lips for the first time in what must be weeks. Why have I waited five days to take a swim?

A buzzing sensation stirs under my skin. It is a signal of my need to fight the ocean currents, to compete with larger forces than I should. I adjust the goggles and dive again, using my arms and legs to move through the water, only coming up for air when I absolutely cannot hold off any longer. I relish in the taste of salt as it drips into my mouth with each breath. I watch the fish swim beside, under, and around me as I slice through the crystal-clear water. With each passing stroke of my arm, the tension leaves my shoulders, and my mind empties.

After exhausting my muscles, I head back to the shore. Saltwater drips from the tips of my hair as I pull the goggles loose and exit the water. The sting of salt in my eyes burns but I welcome pain in a different part of my body.

My hair has grown long in the weeks since the season ended and my impending downfall became all too apparent. Not having the energy nor the motivation to clean up my appearance, I unintentionally let it grow longer. With my naturally tan skin and newly untamed dark hair, I practically look like I am from some tropical place, not a city slicker who plays for the National Football League.

The idea of belonging to a place like this gives me a sense of imaginary nostalgia, like in another life I might belong somewhere like this. A place without worries, judgments, or politics. A place I can finally relax.

As I approach the daybed, I notice someone lying on it. My irritation stirs.

So much for relaxation.

A place without worries would also be a place without unwelcome guests, which is something I can't seem to avoid today. I take giant strides toward the daybed, hoping to make my irritation apparent. As I ready myself to berate someone for trespassing, I pull aside the sheer curtains flapping in the wind to face my trespasser. I didn't pay tens of thousands of dollars to be the rich asshole with a private bungalow and section of beach to have some stranger lounging about my area. The old man took his leave and continued on; he didn't overstay his welcome after I refused to give him an invitation.

This person – this woman – is a completely different story.

The woman, or trespasser, is sprawled across *my* daybed, between two empty beer cans with a third still in her hand. My attempt to intimidate and berate go unused because the woman is unconscious. She looks as pitiful as I have felt the past four days, and it makes the need to scold her a little more difficult, but she is on *my* beach, lying on *my* daybed, and drinking *my* beer.

I have principles, and some principles cannot be crossed. She is crossing all of those uncrossable principles – infringing on *my* space, drinking *my* beer, and wasting *my* time.

A snore slips through her lips as she exhales heavily, falling deeper into sleep. With her head turned to the side, waist-length matted blonde hair covers her face and most of her upper body. Her hair is a good reflection of how unkempt the rest of her looks. The woman's beach coverup leaves nothing to the imagination. It's sheer enough to see fully through and rests high on her waist, revealing very tiny, strappy bathing suit bottoms. I've seen underwear that covers more than her string bikini. Granted, she's curvy – curvy in all the right places; it would be hard to contain all that.

Based on what I can see, she's probably attractive, but I'm not about to let a woman's beauty excuse her actions or calm me down. I have dated plenty of fit, beautiful women, and they can be as deadly as they are gorgeous. Since I can't see her face, it's hard to gauge her age, but she is passed out before noon at an all-inclusive resort, so she is either a forty-year-old woman going through a divorce or a twenty-something who can't pace herself. Chances of her being some sort of gold digger who found out I'm at the resort are yet to be determined.

I can speculate all day about the mysterious woman on my daybed. But I don't want her to be in my zone all day. I look around for a beach attendant and curse when I realize I basically told him to *fuck off* after delivering the alcohol. He's probably hiding around a corner, laughing about my situation right now. This issue – a very unwelcome, inconvenient issue – is mine to resolve.

The last thing I need is to touch a strange woman and have her claim I am trying to take advantage of her

– especially since she is half-naked and drunk. Shockingly enough, men like me are targets for those types of publicity stunts, so I can never be too careful.

Hoping it will wake her, I decide to remove the beer can from her hand to avoid touching her in any way. I edge to the side of the daybed that puts the most distance between the woman and me, and reach across the far side to pluck the beer out of her grasp. I fully expect her to simply wake. Instead, she clings to the beer can and jolts up, keeping a firm grasp on the aluminum, causing it to crease. It is not the reaction I am expecting from such a small-looking woman, especially with hands as quick as mine, and I fumble the can, releasing it into her hand.

"Ow. What the hell?" the woman slurs sleepily, whipping the hair out of her face. It cascades down her back in a tangle of wild abandon. "That's mine, asshole," she curses at me. Her eyes don't seem to fully take me in as she refocuses on the drink and guzzles it.

All thoughts and attempts to be nice and subtle are off the table. Who the hell does this woman think she is?

"Actually," I say, snatching the beer out of her hand as she is still drinking it. The force of our equal resistance causes the remainder of the beer to splash onto her chest and soak through the sheer coverup, giving me a clear view of her ample cleavage. "It's mine, and you're on my beach." I drink what's left of the beer in a show of intimidation before discarding it in the sand. The move is a bit childish, but she is on *my* beach, and I don't want to be bothered with her antics any longer.

The woman scowls at me with a look that could incinerate lesser people. Those crystal-blue eyes are as sharp and deadly as an icicle hanging from a twenty-story building. Except I am not a lesser person, and I have seen much worse. I can play dominance games with the best of them. I cross my arms over my chest and stand my ground.

Let the shit-talking contest begin.

"Your beach? By the looks of you, I know you don't own this beach, so why don't you screw off? Like I said." She scoffs dismissively and lays down on the daybed, adjusts her see-through dress to cover her hips, snatches another beer from the ice box and pops it open. Her smile widens as she takes an overly long drink. Each drink draws out time to an achingly slow pace, emphasizing her point with each roll of liquid down her throat. She swallows three times before disconnecting her lips from the can and lets out a satisfied sigh.

My mouth moves, but no sound comes out of it. I don't even know what to say. The last few weeks of my life have been a beatdown. Yet, no one has said anything and in as much of a demeaning way as this woman just did. She tore me down in five little words – *by the looks of you.* Sure, I don't look my best right now, but I have a lot to offer. I do my best to steel my nerves and remind myself of the thirteen years and multiple championships I dedicated my life to.

This woman is not about to have the last word. It's time to change tactics.

2

DESTINY

THE STRANGE MAN PLOPS down on the daybed beside me and opens a beer, chugging half of it in one sitting. It shouldn't surprise me. He is huge; he probably has a massive lung capacity, so I shouldn't compare my drinking abilities to his, but the natural competitor in me does.

I meant to scare him away.

The old party girl in me gave me a pat on the back for holding down the beer during that chug. *God, it was awful.* As were the three beers before it, but I need a buzz. And this man seems set on disrupting my peace and quiet.

Normally a remark like I just made to him would send someone running for the hills. He has some nerve sticking around. I respect it – a little. There is also the possibility that he likes bitchy women and now this has turned into some fun game for him. I have run into quite a few men like that. They think I am a challenge, and the chase excites them. It's so cringy. Men, in general, are cringy to me, though. At least, lately.

Right now, I feel like tearing up this daybed and burning every last piece of it until there is only ash remaining – if only to spite the man who just woke me up and the man I am actively avoiding in the room next to mine. I have been a pent-up ball of anger since I arrived yesterday. All I can do is count the days until I can leave this resort and get back to my life – away from Will and his new girlfriend, Taylor.

Mister *I wear too tight swim trunks and think the beach is mine* is signing up for a lecture like he has never received before – not even from his mother. All morning, I have been on the hunt for a quiet spot to drown myself in booze and sleep away the day, and I swear to God that he is purposefully ruining it right now.

If he wanted this spot, he should've been here before me. Just because he wasn't, he has the nerve to wake me up and try to steal my spot. The sound of my ex and his girlfriend having sex in the room beside mine haunted me all night. Consequently, I barely slept ten minutes. This strange, overly large man has no idea how hard I am about to fight for some alone time. Size doesn't intimidate me. Never has, never will.

"I told you to go away," I say, drinking my beer and staring out at the ocean. I need to avoid eye contact with the bastard beside me. He seems up for a fight, and letting him see my willingness to engage will only antagonize him further. The proper way to win this battle will be to dismiss the shaggy-haired man who desperately needs to shave.

I bank that thought for a later insult.

"I told you this is my beach, so you need to fuck off," he says, shifting around and settling his impressive body weight into the pillows.

The weight shift causes me to slide closer to him, and I am forced to react, to look. I hate looking at him. As apparently as possible, I visually roll my eyes as I turn toward him. He is smirking. It unnerves me a little. Not only that, but it catches me off-guard. His smile, no matter how sarcastic, makes him look so arrogantly handsome.

I hate men like this.

He needs to leave. Now.

I need silence and relaxation, and I need to be as far from egotistical males as possible. They are bad for my health. I remind myself that he is just one more oversized, conceited male who needs to wash both his hair and his ego.

"Look, can you please just find another spot? No one was here, and I really want to be alone." I try another tactic – politeness – despite it taking all my effort to say please.

Unexpectedly, he rolls *his* eyes, mimicking my earlier expression and tone. "I'm not going to find another spot because this is my beach. Do you see that bungalow behind us?" he says, pointing behind his back without moving any other part of his body.

I follow the direction of his finger and see a small building with lush greenery that surrounds an enclosure I assume is a patio. A stone pathway connects it to the beach, then disappears into the sand. Although, the direction of the walkway is clearly pointing toward the cabana we are lounging on. As I look down the shoreline, I notice more bungalows. They would look like private residences if they weren't identically styled – clearly indicating their connection to the resort I am also staying at.

"What about it?" I ask dumbly.

"That's my bungalow, and this is my private section of beachfront. If you'd like to confirm, you can ask someone who works here. You …" he says, pointing at my chest next, eyes flickering momentarily on the beads of beer still dripping down the swells of cleavage, "aren't supposed to be in this area. So why don't you fuck off?"

His blatant vulgarity makes my stomach turn. "Oh …" I say, looking everywhere but at the cocky man beside me. I hate being wrong, and I hate looking like a fool. Currently, I look like both. It is an unfamiliar and very uncomfortable feeling.

"Yeah," he replies sardonically. His smirk grows into a full-on smile.

An ember of my previous annoyance reignites. Clearly, I made a mistake. The resort should have more obvious signs posted if this is a private area, and this jackass could have explained the situation, rather than going all barbarian on my ass – claiming he owns the beach. Technically, he is only renting this small section of the beachfront. Keyword being *rent*, not *own*.

I straighten my shoulders and adjust my swimsuit coverup. It keeps shifting immodestly, exposing every imperfect section of my body that he keeps looking at, and I cannot have my imperfections on display if I am about to make this man eat his words.

"You don't have to be so rude about it. Since you were, I'll be on my way, but I'll be taking this with me." I grab the bottle of Glenlivet and hop off the cabana daybed.

The man shoots up and rounds the bed in record time. I didn't think a man as large as him could move with such dexterity, but it doesn't faze me – I am quick on my feet, too.

"Oh no, you don't," he says, lunging for the bottle.

I shuffle out of his way, kicking sand in the air and forcing him to look away as I dodge his attempt to retrieve the liquor. I played soccer competitively for over half my life, and the moves are instilled in my muscle memory. He doesn't have a chance.

The man lunges again. I feign to the left with the bottle keeping my weight on my right foot. He follows the bottle, as expected, but I spin right. My shoulder grazes his abdomen as we swap places in the sand.

Getting around him feels like scoring a goal immediately after the other team has scored. There is no better comeback or way to knock the opponent down a notch. Thinking about the other team's face – the same look he currently has – when I pulled that kind of move makes me laugh unexpectedly.

It feels good to laugh, and soon, I am doubling over in laughter. I begin to forget what I am even laughing about as my thoughts spiral into the past. I laugh about my years of competitive soccer, my crazy twenties, the years it took to start a company, breaking off a relationship right before the proposal, and now, most hilarious of all, my current situation which feels like a collision of my choices in the last ten years.

Honestly, I deserve this.

I broke up with Will. I moved halfway across the country. I put my company first. He is allowed to move on, and he is allowed to stay friends with our friends. It doesn't even hurt my feelings that he has moved on. I'm not jealous, and I don't miss him. I'm simply sad and bitter because I want to find what he has found, too.

We are here to watch our friends get married, not skulk about, avoiding each other. I moved to San Francisco a year ago, leaving both Will and our friends in Chicago behind. This is my opportunity to spend time with them, something I haven't been able to do much of in the last year. While I've never regretted my decision to leave Chicago, when I arrived in Tulum and saw how happy Will and his new girlfriend were, I became unbearably sad. It's pitiful, really.

I figured a day alone in my room would be enough to gather my confidence and get over the despair, but when I checked in, I discovered Will and Taylor were in the room next to mine. They have yet to notice that our walls connect. I am certain if they knew, they would keep the sound of their screwing to a minimum.

I do not want to be reminded of sleeping with Will. It's not like it was mind-blowingly good, but I haven't had a good lay since him.

I really am pitiful.

Since seeing him and every other happy couple attending the wedding, I have been drowning my lonely sorrows in booze for the last day. As soon as I can return to San Francisco, I will go back to my work distractions and hope that online dating will eventually lead me to a supportive, independent man who challenges and loves me as much as I do him. I just have to get through this ridiculous situation first.

The frustrating man in front of me crosses his arms angrily. Catching my breath from the outburst of laughter, I straighten myself again.

"Are you done now?" He looks at me strangely and I stop laughing. "Just so you know, even though you got around me, you wouldn't have gotten far with that," he says defensively.

That's what he is focused on right now? This man definitely has an ego – an overly inflated one.

"Whatever you say, left feet. You fell for the oldest trick in the book." I notice him eyeing the bottle so I clutch it to my chest.

He lets out a frustrated sigh as he stares at it, his eyes glued to the space between my breasts, as he says, "Clearly, you're unhinged and on the verge of a breakdown. You need it more than I do. Take it." He steps aside to let me pass.

Unhinged. Unhinged?

Does this man have *any* manners? Does he not know calling a woman unhinged is the last thing anyone should do? He must have a death wish.

I can show him unhinged.

Out of pure defiance and the need to prove that I am not *unhinged*, nor willing to accept his pity booze, I storm back to the daybed, plop down, kick my legs up, open the bottle, and take a long swig. The amber liquid burns going down.

He follows me silently, laying down on the other side, but keeping a good amount of distance between us. His giant hand opens, palm extended to me, waiting expectantly. Wordlessly, I pass him the bottle. He takes a drink as large as I did. Probably larger, but I am not willing to admit that while the score between us is even.

"So, what's—"

"Let's not do this," I cut him off.

"Do what?" he asks.

"Small talk."

He arches a brow, but ultimately smiles in agreement. "Copy that."

We sit like this for a while, not speaking, just sharing the bottle, until eventually he falls asleep, and I wander back to my room.

3

DAVID

I WAKE UP AS the sun is setting. My head is feeling fuzzy from today's liquor consumption. The irritating mystery woman and I sat in silence for hours, passing the bottle of booze and chasing the potent liquor down with the remaining beers. I don't think I have ever sat in silence, next to a woman, for that long in my life. Maybe with my mother or sister, but that's doubtful – they talk a lot.

She didn't even pull out a phone to scan social media or take pictures. She just stared out at the ocean. She is debatably the oddest person I have ever met, and so unlike the athletes, their wives, mistresses, cleat chasers, free-riders, gold-diggers, and other people who constantly surround me. It was a nice change of pace. Unexpected, yet comfortable and uncomfortable at the same time.

When I called her "unhinged", I was being an ass, but after she sat down and got drunk on the daybed with me, I am fully convinced she is unhinged. Although, being unhinged may not be a bad thing. Her eerily comfortable silent company was a nice distraction. I found myself thinking more about her than my situation.

I don't, however, want to think about how she got around me with the liquor bottle. She fucking juked me like a pro. Granted, she wasn't fast. She just took me by surprise. I would've caught up to her after a few feet, but she did make it around me. It was impressive, which stung my ego and only heightened my desire to compete against her again. There is no way I was letting a crazy lady get the best of me. Although, I'll have to find her for another shot.

When she broke down in laughter and tears filled her eyes from laughing so hard, my competitive drive was doused. Then, after she sat back down on the daybed, I thought we might continue our arguing banter – that could be fun – but she didn't want small talk.

The entire thing was a confusing encounter. It made me doubt her intentions and sanity. But thinking about how odd she was distracted me from my own issues, and I found that, despite our crass words to each other, I felt a little satiated by her presence.

Selfishly, I wouldn't mind running into the woman again.

Standing up and stretching my arms over my head, I feel the weight of this useless day wearing down on my shoulders, and I decide it's time to be productive. It's been a long week, and after hearing those five little words – *by the looks of you* – I feel the urge to clean up.

By the look of me, I could use a haircut.

I go back to the bungalow and finally shave. While I am at it, I trim the sides of my hair. It isn't my usual style, but the shortened sides and tousled top make me look young and stylish, if I'm being honest. Satisfied with my renewed appearance and confident that the woman will be taking back her words next time she sees me, I jump in the shower and turn the steam on high.

As I scrub the lavender-scented body wash over my lower body, I stroke myself. It's been weeks since I touched a woman. And even then, the last woman I slept with barely did it for me. They're all starting be the same – the conversation, the meeting place, drinks at my condo, undressing, fucking … It's getting old and boring. The last one was hot, but she was dense and clearly only wanted me because of who I am. With all the stress I've had lately, it's been even harder to be interested in women that simply don't hold my interest.

Yet, I find myself continuing to think about the mysterious woman on my daybed. She is intriguing, in a bitchy, strong-willed woman type of way. Her sass and honesty is refreshing. I like how she doesn't hold back her opinion or try to hide her emotions – no matter how unpleasant and psycho they are. I want to be that way sometimes. She might be crazy, but crazy is helping me forget about the assholes back home.

Crazy is interesting.

Not only that, but she is undeniably beautiful. Those curves. I wanted to grab onto her hips and rock them on top of me. And no matter how many times I tried to stop myself from looking at her tits, I simply couldn't. It did something to me. That long blonde hair was a mess, but I imagined myself grabbing a fistful of it. And her mouth … Her mouth was constantly pressed into a thin line until she finally relaxed, and her lips became unbearably pouty.

They were utterly, perfectly plump.

I think about that mouth – how it pressed against the liquor bottle, how her throat rolled slowly when she swallowed, and how her tongue darted out to sweep the booze off her lips – as I rub myself. I want that mouth around me, licking the tip and swallowing my—

My cell phone rings, and it jolts me from my daydream before I can finish.

Shit.

I don't know why I find myself so intrigued by this woman, but I was on the verge of a much-needed release. My phone continues to ring, and I wish I could smash it against the wall. I wish I could disappear into my daydream and only come out when all my problems are solved. But reality is waiting. I need to get this mystery woman out of my head. I need to focus on my life.

I finish rinsing off the soap suds and grab a towel. Drying off, I hit redial on the phone. The resort concierge picks up. I silently loathe the concierge for interrupting me.

The only reason I got out of the shower was to check who called. Blake, my agent, should be calling soon.

"Hola, señor. Will you be taking dinner in your room tonight?" the concierge asks.

I think about it for a moment. I ordered food in my room the past four nights, but the room service menu is getting boring, and I have already tried everything on it worth tasting.

"No. I'll find something at the resort tonight," I say, deciding that I want to walk around the public area of the resort and see what the restaurants have to offer. There is always a risk of being seen, and a risk of my mood changing at the drop of a hat, but I think it may be worth checking out the scenery.

"Would you like me to make a reservation for you?"

"No. That'll be all, thank you," I dismiss her.

"Very well, call if you need anything. Have a good day," the concierge says.

I hang up before she can finish her goodbye. I am not in the mood to be nice, nor am I in the mood for someone to be nice to me. Maybe that's why I like the curt woman from the beach. She is the first person who has been rude to my face and not sucked my dick – metaphorically speaking, of course. Although, the latter might not be too bad either.

Back in New York, everyone talks behind my back instead of just being honest to my face. I would rather hear the harsh truth from someone, than to find out they are lying from someone else later. Blake kept things straight with me – that's why he is still my agent. The owners and coaches, on the other hand, are smooth talkers, never giving it to me straight and always saying encouraging words that make it seem like we are partners in the franchise. In reality, the players aren't partners; we are over-glorified, disposable employees – just like every other business.

Shoving the thoughts of betrayal aside, I dress in tan linen shorts and a matching white button-up shirt. The color pops against my tan skin, and with a fresh shave, I practically look like my old self – the one that was recently on the cover of *GQ*. The woman from the beach won't be saying *by the looks of you* again. I don't know why it matters what she thinks, but I feel the need to control something in my life. Fitting into the atmosphere of the resort and its guests by looking my best and dressing properly is one thing I can control; it's one way to prove to the woman that *by the looks of me* I look fuckable.

As I enter the public side of the resort, more people are milling about, headed out to watch the sunset, get drinks, or go to dinner. I am not sure what else there is to do here, so I assume everyone is doing something along those lines. I would typically find it relaxing as well, if I weren't feeling like a ball of unreleased energy, building in strength by day.

An oceanfront outdoor dining area catches my attention. The aroma of Spanish food fills the air as I near it. My stomach begins to rumble as I realize I haven't eaten all day.

I've only drank. The crazy lady distracted me so thoroughly that I forgot about my number one base need - eating. It's no wonder my head is feeling so fuzzy. I contemplate whether I even remember the woman properly – I hope I wasn't masturbating to a complete figment of my imagination.

In order to avoid the eyes of other diners, I request a seat at the end of the restaurant's bar top. The seat I take is placed behind a large wooden column. While it unfortunately blocks my view of the ocean, it also blocks others' view of me. It is perfect.

"What can I get you?" the bartender asks, placing a menu in front of me.

It takes little time for me to decide what I want as I scroll down the menu and list off my choices. "Double, tall tequila soda and water. Also, two orders of fish tacos, chips and salsa, and the carne asada burrito with a side of guacamole," I say, sliding the menu back to the bartender.

He gapes at me for a moment before snapping his mouth shut, nodding, and turning toward the computer to place my order. I am a large man, standing six foot five and two-hundred and thirty pounds, who works out constantly; I'm not sure why it surprises people how much I can eat. Especially after not eating all day. Later, I will likely order a round of room service for a second dinner.

"Guys, we have to get shots for the bride-to-be!" a high-pitched voice whines from the other side of the wooden pillar.

The sharpness of her voice makes my eye tweak. I hope she isn't at the bar long. But what else should I expect? It's Tulum. People are here to party and they have the right to do so. Not everyone, actually probably not anyone else, is here to escape their problems.

A squeal makes me plug my ears. "Dez! Finally, you made it, bitch. Where have you been all day?" the same woman says.

I am beginning to get annoyed, despite reminding myself that I wouldn't mind if I weren't being such a downer. Although, when you listen to a non-stop audience echo for hours every week, you tend to become sensitive to squealing. I suck down the tequila soda and wave at the bartender for another. The group becomes louder, and the continual chatter makes it hard to decipher who is speaking. The sound becomes like the crowd's echo, though, and the squealing woman settles down.

Eventually, the group leaves the bar, and I breathe a sigh of relief in the silence. My food is delivered soon after – it's a nice change from room service. I will have to come out for dinner more often. A change in food can do wonders for a bad mood.

Feeling a little better about the day and ready to hit the sheets, I pick up one more tequila soda on the walk back to my bungalow. Instead of going inside, I decide to lay out on the daybed, listening to the ocean as I finish the cocktail. I am a little buzzed, and instead of being angry like the days before, I feel okay. It was an odd day – there is no better way to describe it – but the absurdity is a refreshing change.

I have been stuck in my head about everything happening to me that I haven't been thinking about other solutions. I haven't been thinking about how to take back the control. It's no wonder the strange woman was able to best me in a foot challenge. I've been blinded by my own ambition.

4

DESTINY

"Dez! Finally, you made it, bitch. Where have you been all day?" Michelle squeals.

Her voice hurts my ears, not only because it is insanely high-pitched right now, but because I am hungover from my whisky binge-fest with Mister-silent-and-brooding. I plug my ears and take a moment to recover.

I fully expected him to say something, anything, while we sat and passed the bottle, but he was effortlessly silent. Granted, I cut him off by saying I didn't want to make small talk, but we sat there for a very long time. I almost started a conversation, but after telling him I didn't want to make small talk, I felt it would be stupid to then *make* small talk. More than once I caught him staring at me, as if he were studying me like some type of schoolbook.

It was odd. He is odd.

And clearly, he is as stubborn as me because he never attempted to make conversation, either.

I'm not sure if it is the similar competitiveness and drive that he possesses that I see in myself, or if it is the way he speaks to me. He didn't hold back his thoughts or opinions, even when most civilized people would. It adds a roughness to his demeanor that I find alluring. And I hate that I find it alluring.

He looks like the kind of man who could bend me over and screw me like I've never been screwed before. Maybe it has to do with his size – he has to be at least six and a half feet – and his body … His body is built like a Roman warrior, or what I imagine a Roman warrior would look like.

For a man of his age, he is in very good shape. I can tell he's in his mid- to late thirties based on the set of wrinkles around his eyes and mouth. He likely doesn't think he is as old as he is, or he knows his age and is overcompensating by spending too much time in the gym building that godly body. Call me a bitter woman, but a man without a ring on his finger and a body like that has to be a player. And, as stubborn as he is, I can't really be certain about anything he says or does. He seemed to change tactics with me mid-attempt to get the liquor bottle back.

A hyper-aware man is a dangerous man.

Figuring out people is my specialty, and he is a hard one to pin down. I didn't move halfway across the United States to develop an entirely new tool that identifies people's skill sets and personalities without knowing what drives them. Yet, he is disrupting my algorithm. My company gives Myers Briggs and other cognitive tests a run for their money. Not only that, but I've built it into a tool any human resources organization can utilize to assess their employees' strengths, weaknesses, and better align their abilities with roles to identify and retain talent rather than lose it.

I am branching out into other aspects of data collection and analysis as well, and my company's sales are growing rapidly. Moving to San Francisco to recruit top talent has been a game-changer. So, when this hot and cold man from the beach broke every mental algorithm I could run, I was at a loss for words.

Even now, I am at a loss for what to think, for what to do – for everything. I am truly dumbfounded, and intrigued, and frustrated by the man. Figuring him out has been my biggest challenge in a long time, and challenges are my crux. But this is a challenge I need to stay far away from.

"Earth to Destiny!" Michelle snaps her fingers in my face.

"Oh, sorry. I was … relaxing. At the beach," I say.

"Well, you better not ditch us tomorrow. We've missed you like crazy. I haven't seen you in months – there's so much to catch up on," she says with a pout.

"Of course, it was just the jet lag and the time change getting to me. I'll be ready to party tomorrow," I say, faking a smile.

Michelle places her hands on my shoulders. "Good! Let's do shots!"

She orders shots and I greet some of the other wedding guests, who are all old friends from Chicago.

Dale and his husband, Patrick, or Pat, are in attendance. I wasn't as close to them, but we often attended events together and found ourselves gravitating toward one another. We get along really well. Kat, and her boyfriend, Matt, are a little too drunk to talk to tonight, so I keep the greeting short and my distance far. Michelle's boyfriend, Javier, says hello, but I don't know him well – he is new to the group. They find their way back to the bar to continue ordering drinks while we wait to be seated. Lastly, I greet my ex, Will, and his new girlfriend, Taylor, and the happy couple getting married, Stacy and Ryan.

Stacy and Ryan's families are arriving over the next two days before the wedding, so it is only our small group of friends from Chicago who are here early to party and catch up. Normally, I would be thrilled about this opportunity to spend time with friends, but because it is just us and we are here for a wedding, Stacy has arranged a number of group activities that I will be forced to participate in as the only single wedding guest.

"Babe, it's so good to see you. We missed you today." Stacy pulls me into a hug before I am obligated to further talk with Will and Taylor.

"Thank you," I whisper before pulling away. "I was trying to catch up on sleep today. Jet lag. You know? Sorry for being MIA."

"Don't even worry about it. We have like six more days to catch up," she says as I give Ryan, her fiancé, a quick hug.

Michelle pushes between Ryan and me, holding two shots. "Pass them around; pass them around," she instructs, going back to the bar to retrieve more.

"Michelle, you're a terrible influence. You're going to have Dale and me puking on the bathroom floor tonight if we have another shot!" Pat whines while reaching for a second shot of his own.

"You guys did a lot of shots today?" I ask jokingly. Pat claims to hate shots, but we all know he loves them.

"You have no idea." Dale nudges my side and gives me a wink. I know what that wink means. His husband is borderline suck-dick-in-the-parking-lot drunk. Something he won't admit, but I also know he secretly loves.

"Oh, quit being a pussy, Pat," Michelle says.

"First off, that's physically impossible for me, and second, gross, I do not like my name and that word said in the same sentence," Pat retorts, cringing, and taking his first shot before the rest of us toast.

"Let's get this show on the road – the host is ready to seat us," Will says, walking up to our circle of friends with his arm around Taylor's waist. They both also hold shots of tequila – seeming completely comfortable with this situation.

I avoid looking at their close contact and his consideration of her. He was never publicly affectionate with me. It's clear he cares deeply for Taylor. I don't doubt that he cared deeply for me, too, but signs like this reaffirm my decision to decline his proposal. He and Taylor are meant to be; I am meant for someone else. Hopefully.

"Cheers to the happy couple and to all our friends for making it here this week!" Michelle says, raising her glass.

We clink shot glasses and I down the cheap tequila. It burns my throat but warms my belly, and the spiraling thoughts about my last unsuccessful relationship disappear.

The hostess leads our group to a long table near the backside of the restaurant. It has an amazing view of the sunset over the ocean. Since we are at an all-inclusive resort, everyone liberally orders food and drinks. I request two drinks at a time so I can get my buzz going again. Otherwise, today's earlier drinks are bound to catch up with me and make me feel like shit. Plus, I need to be thoroughly toasted in order to pass out and not overthink the sound of lovemaking on the other side of my bedroom wall.

"Dez, how is San Francisco? You just purchased a house, right?" Dale asks.

He and Pat are seated beside and across from me to provide a buffer from the unmentionable guests – Will and Taylor – on my right side. I appreciate their effort to keep me from having an uncomfortable conversation. Will has been careful to ensure Taylor is comfortable in my presence. Although, she seems to be taking the proximity perfectly fine and has been unbearably nice to me.

"Yeah, I did. Everything is going really well. Actually, I'm thinking about expanding and opening an office location in Los Angeles. We have a lot of clients and employees there, so it's a natural next step in expansion." My usual reply makes me feel like a robot, but there isn't much else I can say that would be considered socially acceptable. Such as, *I'm drowning in work,* and *I have no social life.*

Outside of spin class and networking dinners, I don't have a life in San Francisco. It's a fact. A sad fact that I want to change, but my company must come first. It's not like I haven't attempted to date. But every guy I date is either too nerdy, too needy, too broke, or a narcissist. The continual dating failures have basically driven me to work more, but I have found the success in hard work a worthwhile payoff in the end.

"Sounds amazing, girl. How's the dating scene out there? Have you met anyone interesting?" Pat asks.

I notice Will glance in our direction at that question, and I am tempted to lie, but that would do no good – unless my reply is laced with sarcasm, I am a horrible liar and everyone, especially Will, will know that I am fabricating the truth. Nothing looks sadder than lying about your happiness. "It's pretty bad, honestly. I'm currently coping with the fact that I may be single forever." I attempt to make a joke out of my pitiful situation. Not that it isn't obvious enough by the lack of significant other beside me.

"What?" Dale says. "That's crazy! You're uber-success-ful, stunning as hell, and the most loyal person I know. Men should be lining up for a chance with you."

"Honey, being single is the best. There are so many hot guys around here. I know you're with all couples, but don't let it get you down. Maybe there's someone at the bar for you right now," Pat jumps in, wiggling his eyebrows suggestively.

Dale shoots his husband a warning look and Pat laughs, reaching across the table to pat the top of his husband's hand. "No one is as hot as my husband, of course. But she can't have you, so you don't count, babe." By the answering grin on Dale's face, I know what those two will be doing tonight.

I look toward the bar, if only to confirm there isn't any hot and available men here, and my gaze snags on a wide set of shoulders hiding behind a wooden post. The hair is different, though, and the clothes are … actually nice. I might even go as far as saying stylish. The man from the beach looked like he lived on it, not owned it. This guy definitely looks like he owns it. It can't be *him*. But it could be another single, available man. My curiosity peaks.

The man stands and I quickly look away so he doesn't catch me staring. As he walks toward the exit, I peer over my menu to get a better look. It is *him*. Even though I can only see his profile, there is no mistaking him.

He is a giant compared to most of the people around here. Plus, there is no mistaking the arrogant sway in his shoulders as he saunters past the other guests. As he passes, their heads turn to gawk at him.

Damn.

He cleans up really well. I'm nearly breathless – because he's hot. Like smoldering hot. And I'm now feeling hot.

"Look at that – she spotted one, Pat!" Dale giggles like a schoolgirl discovering someone's crush. "Reel him in, Destiny."

"I didn't spot anyone," I hiss under my breath.

Yet, as dinner continues, I can't stop thinking about the man from the beach, the same man from the bar. He is clearly here alone, but who comes to Tulum alone and stays in an entire bungalow? Not to mention, who comes here alone and in such a foul mood? And who comes here alone when they are that smoking hot? I suddenly feel guilty for my cold behavior earlier as I start thinking about the more plausible reasons why he may be here alone.

Maybe he just lost someone – life his wife died. Maybe he just got a divorce – they cheated, or he cheated. The possibilities are endless, and they are all very dark and depressing. My current situation - having to sleep in the room next to my ex and his girlfriend, after I dumped said ex – is nothing compared to what he might be going through. Or maybe it is similar? The entire situation has me contemplating our earlier interaction.

And the warmth growing under my hairline is doing nothing to alleviate my spiraling thoughts.

As dinner ends and my group goes our separate ways, I find myself wandering toward the secluded bungalows again. It may be stalkerish, but I'm a little buzzed, and avoiding my room is becoming a habit.

5

DAVID

WITH A NEWFOUND SENSE of purpose, I called my agent early this morning and told him to explore trade options. New York is my home, but if they don't want me, there has to be another team out there who does. I can't believe I didn't think of this earlier.

I dress for a morning swim and run on the beach. When I reach the daybed, I absentmindedly toss my towel, phone, and shoes on the cushion as I jog toward the ocean to begin my swim.

"Ow!" the strangely familiar sound of a female shouts from behind me.

I turn around to find the crazy lady waking up on my daybed. Again. *What the hell?* My prior stalking concerns are starting to become more valid.

Her cheeks turn bright red as I walk back to the daybed, and I notice her scan my abdomen before returning her gaze to my face.

I arch an eyebrow and can't stop myself from asking, "Like what you see?"

"Let's not do this again. It's not about that," she replies groggily, smoothing out her dress – a dress that looks like it is meant for dinner, not a morning nap.

"I see." I am slightly disappointed her embarrassment is from her appearance, not because she was caught checking me out. "Did you sleep here all night?"

The woman quickly stands and starts walking toward the sidewalk that winds through the resort. Apparently, she is going to walk away with no explanation. If I didn't know this woman had a working larynx, I might think she just couldn't talk.

"Hey, wait!" I call, jogging barefoot after her. I fall into step beside her, but she holds her tongue. This woman is irritatingly quiet. "Are you stalking me?" I ask, half teasing, half concerned, and desperate to break the silence. I have run into my fair share of stalkers. Although her approach is a bit different than usual. She doesn't act like she recognizes me, but I can never be too sure. Plus, I wouldn't mind getting to know a little more about her.

"Get over yourself. I'm not stalking you," she says acidly.

Her tone carries so much bite. It isn't the response of a typical stalker, but I still can't be sure. This woman isn't like other stalker types I have run into. She is mysterious in more ways than one, and I think she has a bigger brain under that thick skull than most. Which may be a good thing or a bad thing.

"Do you watch sports?" I ask, digging for more information. This is a key question in figuring out if I have a stalker on my hands. They can never resist bragging about how much they know about football and how much they love watching the game. And of course, they pretend to only care about the game and the strategy; they claim to not really know who all the players are, but they know us all by name and they know how much money we make. There isn't usually much difference in stalkers and gold-diggers, other than stalkers latch on and gold-diggers find the next best thing.

She glares at me, exasperated. "I'm not interested in making small talk, especially about sports – of which I'm not a fan unless I'm playing or winning," she states matter-of-factly.

Well, that's the first time any woman has answered that question in that particular way. I concluded she definitely doesn't know who I am. Which makes this more fun. "Sorry, you just look like the sport-loving type," I say, recalling her agility while making an excuse for my random question so that I don't look like a total idiot who doesn't know how to talk to a woman.

"If you're recalling the way I juked you yesterday, then yes, I know what sports are and I have played them. It doesn't automatically make me a fan. I prefer to be the one performing, not watching. That way, I can control the outcome of events."

This is something I can relate to. It's the control freak in me. I briefly wonder if she is also an athlete by profession. Maybe she runs track? Although, the width of her hips suggests otherwise. And she really wasn't that quick.

"Are you an athlete?" I ask.

The woman laughs, but she stops when she looks at my face. It is a serious question, and I am not sure why she thinks it is funny.

"Do I look like an athlete to you?" she says, motioning to herself.

I take in her body for what feels like the thousandth time. With nothing but the ocean and her to look at yesterday, I might have memorized her shape. She is soft and curvy, but has the appearance of someone who used to work out a lot. There is muscle under a thin layer of healthy fat that contributes to her shape, and she likely focuses on maintaining what she has now rather than altering it. I fully approve of what she's got going on. Not that she needs my approval.

"Athletes come in all shapes and sizes, and by the way you moved yesterday, I'd say you have some sort of athleticism in your genes or background," I answer smoothly.

She rolls her eyes at my comment. Again. The same way she rolled them yesterday, and it somehow drives me crazier the second time around. A grown woman shouldn't be rolling her eyes. It makes me feel like I am saying something childish when, in reality, rolling her eyes is childish.

"I'm not an athlete, not anymore," she says.

I get the sense that she doesn't want to continue this conversation, which is soon confirmed by the way her pace quickens, and how she cuts me off when taking turns in the walkway.

"So why were you sleeping on my daybed again?" I decide to get back to my original question.

"I was walking around tipsy, saw a comfortable-looking bed, and decided to lay down on it. I guess I fell asleep. I've sort of had a lack of sleep lately." She says it so matter-of-factly, as if it's an everyday occurrence, which it might be becoming.

"Why is that?" The way this woman answers questions so curtly makes me curious to know more. She has me hooked, only giving me tidbits of information at a time. It isn't often I run into a woman who doesn't want to talk about herself all day.

"Because I work a lot," she replies, taking a hard right turn on the path that leads to a three-story building.

"What do you do for work?" I'm hoping to gain some traction in this conversation. We walk under the building's awning. The woman is failing to provide the answers to my many questions and I feel we're running out of time.

She stops at a door, room 315, and turns around abruptly. I nearly bump into her. I have barely been able to pay attention to my steps as I mentally replay our conversation, trying to disseminate the little information she has given me into something worth knowing about her. Ultimately, I can't be blamed for what happens. My hands fly up to brace against the door and barely stop me from slamming into her. Her hands land on my notably bare chest.

I look down at her, trapped between my arms and the door. Her face is still puffy from sleep and, in this position, the unusually strong-willed woman appears vulnerable. It feels like I finally gain some turf, and step inside her protective bubble, but it also feels like I did so uninvited. I push off the door frame and straighten myself, not wanting to make her feel uncomfortable after I have been so invasive.

It's not that I think she can't handle herself. It doesn't feel right to overstep her boundaries without permission, no matter the feeling of her fingers curling against my chest, as if she's trying to hold on, before I pulled away. While she might be frustrating as hell and continually loitering on my daybed, based on our limited conversation, I can tell she is an independent, stubborn, and hard-working woman. That deserves some respect. And appreciation.

I cough to clear my throat, and the uncomfortable silence grows between us.

"Look, I'm—" she begins in a soft tone.

"There you are, girl! I've been calling you all morning." A man with an immaculately groomed beard slides his arm over her shoulders and looks at me curiously. He's above-average height and a little plump around the middle, but he looks like he is probably considered an attractive man by most women's standards.

My gaze moves to the familiar hand he rests on her shoulder. It adorns a thick gold wedding band.

My stomach tightens. *God damnit.*

The woman glances between us as if she doesn't know what to say. It occurs to me that I've read this situation incorrectly. She is here with someone, and I have just been spotted escorting *her* – in last night's dress – back to *their* room.

This clearly looks suspicious, despite it being the exact opposite. I don't exactly know what to do, especially because the man looks happy in a crazed sort of way and I'm not sure what he might do to me after this discovery.

"Um … I'll get out of your hair. See you around," I excuse myself, giving the woman and man a salute.

A fucking salute. If he wasn't planning on following the man he thinks just slept with his wife, he surely is now after such a mocking dismissal.

I have never been more awkward in my life, but I have also never been caught following a married woman home like a puppy dog. It's no wonder she wasn't answering my questions. She was likely just about to explain to me that she is married. Although, if she is married, why is she not sleeping in her room?

There are so many unanswered questions that I know I should forget about, but they are like an itch in the middle of my back that I can't quite reach. Something doesn't add up with her; my intrigue is only growing. Part of me hopes the man follows me just so I can get some answers.

But when I turn around, no one follows.

6

DESTINY

"THANK YOU FOR SAVING ME," I say to Pat while unlocking the guest room door.

I rush him inside and shut the door quickly, leaning against it to keep my balance as a wave of the heat I had been ignoring rolls down my body. I didn't mean to fall asleep on his daybed last night. Again.

The walk back to my room felt like an interrogation. I would rather he fight me – verbally or physically – than make small talk.

Small talk is torture when you are trying to come up with an excuse as to why you keep sleeping on a strange man's daybed.

He asked me a million questions about myself. Does he not know what vague answers mean? They mean someone doesn't want to disclose any further information about themselves. He has no tact at all. Granted, I don't usually have tact when I want answers either, so I recognized his approach immediately. He thought his brute resilience would force me into giving him the answers he sought.

He is dealing with a pro, though. I don't cave easily. Except, when he was standing over me, standing way too close, I might have answered all of his questions then. Seeing his height from afar is one thing. Having his arms braced on either side of my head and looking up into his towering form is another. I felt tiny. But I didn't feel tiny in a scary, uncomfortable way; I felt tiny in a good, yet naughty way. Ideas of what a man that large could do to me flood my brain.

Usually, I don't like men trying to force dominance on me – trying to prove their manliness - but this man's subtle scent of domination is intoxicating. He's the type of man who doesn't need to tell you that he can pick you up and carry you a mile or screw you against the bedroom wall. He simply does it when he decides to, and you don't doubt his ability because you're too busy simply enjoying it.

It's been so long since I had a man in my bed and he is like a savory drink waiting to be consumed. He's like a tall glass of ice water on a hot summer day – a saying I never thought could apply to a person. He makes me sweat and gives me chills, two things that skin shouldn't be able to do at once. The man, the strange man, the man with no name, makes me believe we all have a kryptonite and he might be mine. He makes me feel so out of sorts. I think I should call him Achilles because that is what he is, in nearly every way – a Greek warrior in bodily form and my vagina's crux.

When Pat showed up, he scared him away as quickly as *Achilles* had been firing questions at me moments before. I don't know whether to be thankful or angry with Pat for the save.

"Details! I am dying to know why you are walking home in last night's dress with that … man," Pat gushes, digging through my minibar and pulling out two beers.

He offers one to me, but I decline.

"I cannot talk about this right now."

"Not happening. Spill, now! You know I won't stop. Is his you-know-what as big as I think it is?" Pat asks, plopping down on my couch and opening the beer.

I rub my eyes and slap my cheeks, trying to shake the feeling of *him* towering over me.

Get it together, Destiny. This is embarrassing.

"I don't know anything about his dick size, nor do I plan to," I lie, instantly thinking about what is under those tight swim trunks. I turn away from Pat, so he cannot see the lie written on my face. "He found me sleeping on his daybed and then followed me back here. Also, he's here alone. Like, who comes here alone? I think he may be some type of stalker or sociopath," I say, pulling off my dress and digging through my unpacked luggage for a bikini, while I try to steer Pat's mind away from the possibility of me and the strange man being in bed together.

"You were sleeping on his daybed and you don't even know the man's name? Scandalous!" Pat feigns shock.

"I was sleeping *alone* on his daybed. So don't judge me for not knowing him. And like I said – stalker. Sociopath. There's something wrong with him, I know it."

"Yep. I'm sure that's it. Well, you're only here for a week and may I remind you – you're also here alone. Stalker, sociopath, or whatever else he might be, you don't have to tell him who you are or where you live. You could just have some no-strings-attached fun. And then tell me all about it later, of course," Pat says with a shrug.

I stare at him indignantly. "I don't do that."

"Which part?"

"The no-strings-attached part." I roll my eyes without looking at Pat.

"Oh thank god. I thought you meant the spilling-the-details-to-your-most-cherished-gay-friend part." I ignore him. "You could try it. Never hurts to try new things," he counters. "How long has it been since you've been laid?"

"Not that long." I avoid his question because the last time I got laid was awful. Mister OCD, as I call him, was a massive disappointment. His biggest redeeming quality was his intelligence, but eventually, he just came off as disgustingly pretentious. I probably should have realized there was something wrong with him when I gave him the nickname, Mister OCD, weeks before ending it. Although it now makes me feel a little uneasy about giving the strange man the nickname Achilles. What does it say about my feelings toward him?

"Exactly." Pat sees right through me.

"Ugh." I hate that he is right.

"Okay. Last question. Do you really not know who he is?"

"No. Why would I?"

"It seemed like you two were getting quite cozy. I just thought you would have talked a little bit. You know – exchanged names, talked about your professions … Things like that." Pat sips his beer and eyes me over the rim of the can.

"Um, no. I'm not interested in making small talk with some guy who I'm never going to see again."

"Okay," Pat says with a smirk.

I don't know what has gotten into Pat, but frankly, I don't want to discuss, think, or see Achilles again. I grab my swimsuit and enter the bathroom to change. "Don't tell anyone about this. Okay?" I say loudly so he can hear me over the top of the bathroom door.

"I would never," Pat calls back, "except Dale – the husband must know everything."

"Right," I say under my breath.

The last thing I need is the entire group getting drunk and trying to hook me up with the only other single person here. From what I can tell, almost every person at this resort is with someone else. My chances of finding another single person are low, but I also didn't come here to find love. Or anything else, for that matter.

When I exit the bathroom, Pat is impatiently dangling my swimsuit coverup outside the bathroom door. I run into the dress and jerk it out of his hands as I pass. "Jesus! You scared the shit out of me."

"You've been god only knows where for two days. Michelle is driving me up a wall, and Dale is hungover so I told him he has the morning off. Which means you get to be my lucky partner in drunkenness today!"

I laugh at him. Pat and I don't hang out a lot – mainly due to our busy schedules and two thousand miles of distance – but when we do, it is like we are childhood besties. If I am forced to witness my ex groping his new girlfriend and listen to Michelle's high-pitched woo-girl voice all day, Pat would be my first choice of a buffer – distracting me with his wit and never-ending compliments.

"Okay, let's go," I say, slipping on the coverup and a pair of sandals by the door.

We walk out of the room toward the main pool where we plan to meet our friend group.

"Should we have a hand signal for when one of us needs rescuing?" Pat asks.

"Something like this?" I put up my middle finger sarcastically.

"You just can't stop thinking of fucking, can you?"

I smack Pat's arm playfully. "Stop!"

"Honestly, why did you not?"

We turn the corner and I see the main pool ahead. Our group is gathered by the swim-up bar. "It's not like that. I've just run into him a couple of times. There's no connection between us, and he hasn't even hit on me." I realize Achilles hasn't expressively shown interest, other than sneaking a look at my breasts. Most men would check out my cleavage, though – if they were interested in women at all. I have decent boobs. A lot of my recent weight gain went to my hips and my breasts. It's not preferable, but it's part of life.

"You don't think he's interested in you?" Pat asks as we stop at two open chairs.

"No way." It starts to make sense as I think about Achilles and me together. A man that looks like him doesn't go for women like me. He's tall, built, and gorgeous. His dark hair and green eyes pop against his tan skin. Angular cheekbones sit high on his face, pairing perfectly with his thin-lined lips. Next to me, he looks like the type of man who embodies women's daydreams. While I look like the type of woman who daydreams about such men.

"Guys! Over here!" Stacy yells from across the pool.

Pat eyes me and says, "We will continue this chat later. In the meantime, you seriously need to look in the mirror because you are hot as hell and that dude was eyeing you."

I blush, but ignore his compliment. I am not insecure about the way I look. I believe I am attractive, but not shockingly beautiful. My intelligence is slightly higher than most, and my drive and dedication are well above average. The qualities I possess that make me unique are certainly not my beauty though, I am realistic about that. Achilles on the other hand – his beauty, or handsomeness I should say, are astounding.

Pat and I take off our coverups and wade through the shallow end of the pool. We reach our friends, who are already giving the bartenders much to do. I give everyone quick hugs, even my ex, Will, and his new girlfriend, Taylor. We were introduced to each other when I arrived; not giving a hug to one person in the group, especially my ex's new girlfriend, would make me appear like a sour ex, which I am not, so that's how we greet each other now. It's lovely.

My friends like to drink, and being here to celebrate an upcoming wedding only seems to amplify their level of partying. Even though our hangovers are way worse now that we are in our thirties, it doesn't seem to slow them down. I think they just found better hangover remedies. I can't say the same for myself, but my misery and now frustration – with Achilles – is reason enough for me to party it up today, too.

"Can I get the spiked coconut water, please?" I ask the bartender.

"Make that two," Kat says behind me, wrapping her arms around my shoulders and hugging me from behind. She smells like tequila and salt. "How are you doing?" she whispers in my ear.

"Amazing," I feign excitement.

"Oh, don't give me that bullshit," she says as she sits beside me. "This is awkward. But you're being a champ. Could you not find a plus one? I thought you were dating some doctor guy."

Far from it. More like an obsessive-compulsive software developer.

The bartender slides our drinks across the bar, and I pull a twenty-dollar bill out of my swimsuit top to tip him. He thanks me before returning to wash dishes. I will keep the money flowing as long as he keeps the drinks coming and makes them strong. From the smell of Kat, I have a lot of catching up to do. And from the start of this conversation, I have a lot of forgetting to do as well.

"I had a plus one, but then broke things off with him. I let him sleep over a few times, and he was so specific about a nighttime and morning routine. It stressed me out. I couldn't deal with that all week." Part of me wanted to make it work with Mister OCD so I could invite him to be my plus one, but he wasn't right for me, and I couldn't go another day dealing with his obsessions.

"You're joking?" Kat chuckles.

"Sadly, I'm not ..." I shake my head and shudder, thinking about his routines. I'd feel a little bad about breaking it off due to that alone, but the truth is his control issues weren't just because of a diagnosis.

"Okay. I'm going to need details. It couldn't have been that bad," she insists, eyes glimmering with the prospect of juicy gossip.

I recount his obsession with the light switch – ten times up, ten times down, ten times quickly flipping it up and down, then one more round about ten minutes after getting into bed – and Kat is soon bending over in laughter. The situation is as sad as it is funny – a good representation of my life currently.

"Hi gals." Stacy stumbles onto the concrete stool beside me. "Watch your step there." She adds a drunken wink before continuing, "Anyways, I wanted to let you all know we have a cooking class later this afternoon. Ryan's making me go back for a nap, but we'll meet you there. Just look at the resort's app for the time and location."

"Seriously, how is everyone this drunk before noon?" I wave at the bartender for another drink.

"Because we can rally like it's 1985. Get with it, Dez!" Stacy says.

I don't understand her drunken pop-culture reference.

I begin to respond, but Kat puts a hand on my leg to stop me. "We'll be there," Kat answers, and Stacy happily takes her leave. She continues to relay the same information to Pat, Will, and Taylor on the other side of the bar.

"She shouldn't be anywhere near knives or a hot stove," I say, even though Stacy is a professionally trained baker and does all of the cooking in her and Ryan's household.

"She'll be fine. I think it's easy stuff. But probably best that we don't drink too heavily beforehand so that someone keeps an eye on her," Kat replies.

"Isn't that Ryan's job?" I joke.

"Ha! You'd think!" She takes a gulp of her drink, looking at Ryan. He appears as drunk as Stacy. Kat and I share a laugh and a shrug.

"Screw it. Let's get drunk!" I say as the bartender sets down a second drink for me. Kat orders another as well. We aren't about to be on Stacy's level, but we aren't stopping either.

Our banter continues for another two hours as we soak up the sun and drink delicious fruity cocktails. When the time approaches our cooking class, Pat volunteers to walk me back to my room so I am not obligated to walk with Will and Taylor. A smartly timed finger flip clued him into my request.

God bless him.

He mentions Dale is excited about the couple's cooking class today and I am slightly disappointed that Pat can't be my partner, but I am used to doing things myself. Normally, I would be hesitant to join a couple's class as a single person, but things went well this afternoon, and I truly am content with flying solo.

Even though Will and Taylor were at the pool today, there wasn't any animosity between us. It is only day three of seven, so I'd say things are looking up. The wedding is in two days, and I honestly believe we will all have a great time. Maybe I'll actually enjoy this vacation.

7

David

I GO FOR A run shortly after walking the woman back to her room and crossing paths with *her* man. I need to clear my head and forget about the mysterious woman. She is married, not that I want to be married to or in some sort of relationship with her; I am just curious to know more. Or that is what I am now telling myself. But people don't come to an all-inclusive with their significant other to spend time alone. Which leaves the question as to why she is continually finding her way to *my* daybed?

When I run by the main pool, I see her at the swim up bar with a group of people. They are chatting happily, and she is getting quite cozy some of them. The warmness she displays toward her friends is so unlike the way she has treated me. Her behavior immediately captivates me and takes all sense of my actions away.

I stop at the juice bar located on the far side of the massive pool. While I observe the mysterious woman, I order a drink so it appears I am here for a reason other than to watch her. To avoid wandering eyes, I hide in the shadows of the wooden beams supporting the drink hut, knowing full well I look like a creep, but unable to stop myself.

She is saying something to another woman. The two of them are in stark contrast to each other – a beautiful sight to behold. My mystery woman with her pale skin and light hair, and a woman, who I assume is her friend, with rich brown skin and black hair. They touch arms and lean in while talking. I'd be lying if I said it didn't stir up some resort threesome fantasy in my mind.

Her friend clutches her stomach in laughter at something the female I know says, and I find myself wishing I knew what the joke is about. My mystery woman doesn't seem like the funny type, but I don't really know much about her. Her entire demeanor is different from the one I have been privy to.

The man from her room doesn't spend much time with her. He gravitates toward her occasionally, but he sticks near a few of the other men in the group. By the way they interact, I can assume they are all long-time friends. Another reason why her lounging on my daybed all day long doesn't make sense. Why wouldn't she want to be here with her friends? It looks like she is having a great time.

She turns suddenly, and I duck behind the wooden beam, pressing my back against it and hoping I blend into the golden varnish of the pillar. Here I am thinking she is a stalker, and I am the one acting like one. Before I lose my dignity, I decide it's time to retreat to my bungalow and change out of my sweaty clothes.

After dinner last night, I realize I am missing out on some of the better resort food and want to get lunch at the Mexican restaurant today. Plus, if I know what's good for me, I should stay away from this mysterious woman. I don't even know her name, but it feels like the least important thing I need to know. Whatever her name is, I'm sure it suits her perfectly. It's probably as beautiful as her smile is when she finally lets her guard down.

"Hiding from someone?" The man from the beach walks up, slapping a twenty on the juice bar and speaking to the attendant. "Pablo, same as yesterday."

"Coming right up," the attendant responds as he gets to work on making the juice.

The white-haired man stares at me expectantly. "So?"

"Um … No. I'm not hiding from anyone." I straighten my shoulders and push off the wooden beam, but keep the post in the center of my back.

"If I didn't know any better, I'd say you were watching Blondie in the pool, but what do I know." He shrugs and leans against the counter.

I peer back at the pool and see her – *Blondie* as the old man calls her – laughing again. It does something to me. There is this unfamiliar tug in my chest, an aching need to know what makes her tick. "Yeah, she is a beauty," I agree.

"Why don't you go talk to her? A young handsome man like you has nothing to lose."

"I wouldn't be so sure about that," I say. I have a lot to lose. In fact, my entire life is currently on the chopping block.

"What's the worst that can happen? She turns you down," the old man argues, taking the juice from the attendant. "Care to join me?" He nods in the direction of the beach.

"Sure." I pick up my juice and take one last look. The woman is turned toward the ocean, facing me, holding a middle finger to the sky and shouting something at her husband. My heart lurches at the possibility of her own impending downfall – the end of her marriage. I internally curse myself for thinking something so cruel, and when a smile turns the corners of her lips up and she laughs jovially, I know it's just some sort of vulgar inside joke between the two.

I should feel guilty for wishing she weren't his. But I find myself wishing I could prove how much better I could make her feel than him. Although, some things in life are out of my control – she's one of them.

The old man and I walk toward the beach. He takes a left on the sand, leading us back to the private section of the resort. My assumptions about where he is staying are correct.

We walk in silence before I decide to explain why it won't work with *Blondie*. I'm not sure if the explanation is more for myself or him. "She has a husband."

"That's a shame."

"Yeah. Normally, I'd just move on, but there is something about her I can't quite shake. And she keeps ending up on my daybed," I explain further, making an excuse for watching her.

"That's odd."

"Right? Who comes to a resort with their husband, but spends the night sleeping alone by the ocean? Never mind the fact that she knows it belongs to me." These are the questions that have been plaguing me all morning. The questions with no reasonable answer.

"People usually do things for a reason, whether that be consciously or not."

"I don't want to get tied up in some marital dispute though."

"No, you don't. I've been there and it is not as fun as it sounds," the old man says, laughing fondly.

"It doesn't sound fun," I agree.

We walk in silence for a bit longer before making it into the private section, the area is clearly defined by the separation of beach chairs and cabanas. "Well, this is me," I say, nodding toward my bungalow, the first in line to many more sprinkling the waterfront. "Thanks for the chat."

"Anytime. I'll be around if you get bored and want some company."

"Thanks. I'm David by the way." I shake his hand.

"Richard. See you around, son."

It doesn't take long to change out of my running clothes and into swim trunks and a T-shirt. I plan to eat lunch, then take a swim or lounge by my private pool for the remainder of the day. It sounds like a good alternative to stalking her – to stalking *Blondie*.

The restaurant I choose is nearly empty, but I can still smell red meat smoking on the grills. It smells glorious. My stomach and brain have only one thing in mind.

"Table for one, señor?" the hostess asks.

"Yep." It's always a table for one. I follow the delicious scent with my eyes, but I am not rewarded with a visual of any food. My head feels light. My run and stalking behavior took more energy out of me than I realize.

"Excelente, follow me, please." The hostess weaves her way through what looks like food prep stations on her way toward the bar.

"What's going on here?" I ask, hoping it won't delay my entree.

"A food instruction course. Our bar is open, though," she says.

"Okay. Good."

I don't particularly care what is happening in the background. The menu for this place looks great, and I have worked up quite an appetite. If anything, the food course will provide a bit of entertainment to my monotonous days here. Well, not as monotonous when Blondie turns up on my daybed, but I have a feeling that won't happen again. And I remind myself of the words spoken with the old man: *I don't want to get tied up in some marital dispute.*

The bartender takes my order and I sit back, watching a recent futbol game on the television while I drink a Modelo. I notice people shuffling in behind me, but figure I shouldn't pay them any mind until they are preoccupied with cooking. God forbid someone recognizes me and disrupts the entire event. It happens more times than it should, and I am looking forward to lunch and a show, not *being* the show.

But angry, whispering voices catch my attention through the shuffling of people's feet.

"Miss, you need a partner for this event."

"I don't have a partner, but I assure you I can handle it alone."

"It would be best if you joined another couple for this. It really does require two people working in tandem. Or maybe you can sit and watch."

"I'd rather sit on a stake and die."

I nearly choke on my beer from the level of aggression in the woman's comment. It's not every day you find someone so vulgar and outspoken. I look over my shoulder to witness the disdain that is likely to be on both people's faces, and notice *her*.

Blondie.

Of course it is her.

Would any other woman make a comment so outwardly inappropriate? But more importantly, where is the mystery woman's man? Why isn't he here to be her partner?

My eyes scan the other people lining up at the prep stations. Her man is here, but he is standing behind a table with someone else – another man. Why isn't he partnering with her? This situation is so confusing.

"Please, join another couple, or I must ask you to leave. You must have two people for this event," the hostess says timidly.

The scornful look on my mystery woman's face could turn a person to stone. I have a feeling she isn't often told no. When she starts to spin on her heel, I bolt upright. It is like my feet have a mind of their own as they pull me toward the arguing women. It seems my stomach and brain have been possessed by this new mysterious base need.

"Hey! Sorry, I'm late. I'm here. I'm her partner!" I saunter over to her side and slide my arm around her shoulders, turning her back around. She tenses under my touch, so I tuck her closer. Her shoulders are so slim that I surround her entire body with one arm. I realize this is the first time I have touched her. I shouldn't be touching her, but I like how rigid and tense she stands, despite how small and closed off she is – like she doesn't need the protective shield of a man.

"Okay …" the hostess says and moves aside. "Please find a station."

Blondie shrugs my arm off as we walk down the aisle between prep stations, and I notice the eyes of her friends following us back to the last remaining spot. I straighten my shoulders and avoid making eye contact with her husband. This is probably a mistake. I am overstepping boundaries, but my body is used to instinctively reacting to events when my brain can't decide what play to make. If I were *her* man in this situation, I would have stepped up and told me to back off, but he isn't making a move toward us.

He merely smiles as we pass.

Crazy bastard.

"What are you doing?" she hisses quietly as we take our spots behind the table.

My stomach growls loudly, and she looks down to where the sound came from in disgust. I better not regret this. "Just so you know, I haven't eaten since my run this morning and I just volunteered to be your partner so you wouldn't get kicked out. You should be thanking me, not questioning me."

"I didn't realize you were a toddler and on an eating schedule," she retorts.

Her reply is so perfect. So perfectly *her*.

I laugh. Loudly.

Maybe she is funny, after all; I just haven't spoken to her enough to know. I like this type of humor. The vulgarity, intensity, and anger behind her words is a nice change from the prim and proper women usually trying to win me over. Most women don't make fun of me, at least not to my face. It is a refreshing change. I liked being roasted, especially when it is quick-witted.

"That wasn't a joke." She grabs one of the aprons from the table and knocks mine to the ground.

The tie wraps twice around her small waist, but the fabric stretches around her hips. I scoop up the other discarded apron as if she didn't purposely let it fall to the floor. She keeps giving me side glances, her face contorting between a look of confusion, frustration, and relief – likely from her inability to agitate me. The mix of emotions on her face combined with her harsh words has my head spinning though. This woman is like a tornado – unpredictable and deadly. I have to know what's going on inside that head of hers.

She is looking around at her friends and mouthing silent commands at them, but I can't read her lips from the side. I follow her eyes to each couple, almost all of whom I saw earlier at the pool. Her husband is with another man, who I didn't see though, and they seem very comfortable with each other. No wonder she is avoiding him; he is more concerned with his bromance than her. He even gives her a playful wink to which she returns a scowl.

A short, curvy woman in front of us turns around. The man with her follows. "Dez, do you want to introduce us?" she prods, glancing back and forth between us.

Dez? Blondie has a name.

"Ugh." Dez looks at me expectantly.

Apparently, it has just occurred to her that she doesn't know my name. I didn't know hers either, until now. I was growing used to the name the old man gave her, but its only been a few hours since I've thought of her as *blondie*. Plus knowing one factual thing about her makes me feel like I'm finally stepping into the pocket. One mystery down, many more to uncover.

I reach over the table and extend a hand to the short woman and her partner. "Hi. I'm David. Nice to meet you both." I glance at Dez for a reaction, but her face is an emotionless plain. It seems she isn't as curious about who I am as I am her. Unless she already knows who I am and her cover has just been blown.

The short, curvy woman shakes my hand excitedly and the man with her does the same. They seem nervous. Typical. "I'm Stacy and this is my fiancé, Ryan. We are huge fans! Well, not of your team – you killed us in the national championship a few years ago, but we recognize good players and those can be hard to find nowadays. Not to mention, you are basically a legend!"

Her finance nods his agreement quietly.

Their reaction is very similar to the thousands of other fan introductions I have made. I stifle a groan and put on my best camera-ready face so that I don't offend Dez's friends. Not that it really matters if I offend them, or her, but some part of me doesn't want to make a poor impression.

"I appreciate it, thank you," I say as Stacy continues rambling.

"So, what are you doing here and how do you know Dez? I didn't know she had a partner for this event. Not that I'm complaining."

This time, Dez audibly groans – it brings a genuine smile to my face. I share her frustration; it's a relief to finally be on the same page as her.

"Can we not play the question game right now?" Dez asks.

The "question game" – something I mistakenly subjected Dez to earlier. I make a mental note that Dez isn't a fan of the "question game". I assume that is why she refused to answer my questions. I can understand that. I don't prefer to share things about myself until I am ready either, and when someone prods for information, I am more likely to shut down than open up.

"Ladies and gentlemen, can I please get your attention?" the instructor says over the murmurings of the participants.

"Nice to meet you." Stacy and Ryan give me a smile before turning back to their food station.

"Do you want to explain why my friends know who you are, David?" Dez whispers beside me, keeping her eyes on the instructor.

Apparently, she really doesn't know who I am.

The way she says my name is like an angry anthem, and it makes me smile wider. I love an aggressive opening song to pump me up before a game. My name on her tongue is my new favorite way to get amped. "You really don't know who I am?" I tease, also trying to pay attention to the instructor as she begins picking up utensils, pans, spices, and food, explaining the use for each. It doesn't really matter if I pay attention, though; I know nothing about cooking and I require a more hands-on approach to learning. This meal is about to be a spectacular failure, but for some reason, I don't care.

"Obviously, I don't. Don't make me ask you again," Dez warns me.

Either she knows her defiance interests me, or she legitimately thinks she is intimidating me – both only humor me more. I haven't felt this charmed by a woman in ages.

I turn to answer her and catch sight of her husband eyeing me suspiciously. It brings me back to reality. Letting my smile fall, I answer her question honestly, trying my best not to provoke her or myself further. "I'm the quarterback for the New York Giants, which is a professional football team in case you didn't know. That's why I asked if you were a sports fan. Most people who watch football recognize me."

Dez stiffens slightly, but doesn't say a word. She simply shuffles items on the table, lining them up in a new order. I am not sure if this is nervous fidgeting or if she is just preparing to cook. Cooking is not a skill set I possess, so it's a total toss-up as to what she is doing.

"Are you going to say anything, Dez?" I finally ask as the instructor recites the steps to prepare the first item – guacamole. It looks easy enough.

"First off, my name is Destiny. Only my friends call me Dez. Second off, I'm trying to pay attention, not be distracted by my unwelcome partner."

I don't hear or process anything she says after her name. *Destiny*. This seriously can't be happening. This woman with so many mysteries and complications shows up on my daybed, multiple times, a woman I can't seem to pinpoint as sarcastic, witty, or funny – because there is a difference – who is more challenging to get to know than a set of new plays, name is Destiny. Circumstance certainly makes this feel like destiny.

I catch her husband staring at us again.

Never mind. Nope. No.

There is no destiny at work here. Just a dumbass who can't keep his mouth shut or his mind centered and needs to start minding his own business.

8

DESTINY

I COULD'VE GONE TO the pool and got drunk or found a solo person activity instead of partnering with him. *David.* I like Achilles better. It reminds me of the reason I should stay away from him – he is my Achilles heel. The fact that he was conveniently sitting at the bar and overheard my entire conversation with the hostess feels suspect – at least in terms of his intentions. I was starting to get suspicious about him being the stalker type until Stacy and Ryan uncovered Achilles identity and I deemed our meeting circumstance.

An NFL quarterback. He's freaking famous.

I am going to kill Pat – especially if he looks back at me one more time. That asshole knew all along.

At least now I have an explanation for Achilles' godly body. I am certain many women appreciate that about him. The jealousy that fuels my resolve is like an annoying fly, constantly buzzing past by ear. So I imagine everyone who plays football for a living has big muscles. No big deal. Everyone who builds start-ups for a living have big brains. Like mine – kind of.

Although I think he is a bit old-looking to be a professional athlete, I don't know enough about sports to know what the average age range is for football players. He could be at his prime or near his retirement. I tell myself it doesn't matter, either way; I don't need to know anything about this man – stalking tendencies, women fawning, or anything else.

The fact that he is alone at this resort is still suspect though. He is definitely hiding something. Granted, I am technically here alone, too, but at least my friends are present. I have a reason to be here and a good reason why I am alone.

Add on the fact that one minute he is flirting with me and the next he gets this sour look on his face. He is so hot and cold, it is downright confusing. The man might be successful at his profession, but he is borderline losing it in his everyday life. Famous or not, I suppose he could still be a stalker.

"Are you going to say anything, Dez?" he asks, looking down at me and standing way too close.

My name slips between his teeth like he is sucking ice on a summer's day. It is far too seductive to be innocent, making my defense mechanism – sass and sarcasm – spark to life. "First off, my name is Destiny. Only my friends call me Dez. Second off, I'm trying to pay attention, not be distracted by my unwelcome partner." I put emphasis on *unwelcome*, hoping to emphasize that I don't need some knight in shining armor coming to my rescue.

Although I am a little relieved that I don't have to partner with another couple or sit this one out, he doesn't need to know that. All he needs to know is that I don't need him – or any man, for that matter. At least, that's what I keep telling myself.

David looks down at me like he is having some type of epiphany, but someone in front of us catches his eye, and he quickly straightens and clears his throat before focusing on the instructor as well.

Cold.

His actions only reaffirm my earlier suspicion that he is on the verge of a breakdown, but it appears my curt responses are finally sinking in, which is for the best.

He reaches for the avocados and the butcher's knife, following the instructor's movements as she begins cutting around an avocado. I watch his oversized hand palm the avocado instead of placing it on the cutting board. He slices the knife down the side while rotating the fruit in his hand.

"Whoa. Stop. Stop!" I place a hand on his forearm before he cuts his palm wide open. I am not an expert on sports, but I doubt slicing off a finger would be good for his career. Impending breakdown or not, no one is bleeding all over my lunch today.

David stiffens against my touch and asks, "What's wrong?"

I take the knife and avocado out of his hand, inching closer to him so that I can show him how to properly cut the fruit on the cutting board. He stands stiffly, watching me. His gaze is penetrating and makes my spine tingle, but I do my best to ignore it and teach him the proper technique so that he doesn't expose himself to bodily harm.

"Watch me. Then you can do the second one, and I'll get started on preparing the main dish," I instruct.

"Oh, I'm watching you alright," he says with a wry smile before my glare forces his lips into a thin shameful line.

Hot.

As I turn away, my cheeks instantly heat from his inappropriate comment. Achilles is shameless. An asshole one minute and flirting the next, but I won't let him get under my skin. That is likely his goal – to make me as uncomfortable as possible – but I don't understand why.

Why was he a dick to me yesterday and trying to be my friend today? Why is he here right now? We are literal strangers on vacation. We don't need to make any association whatsoever; we just need to mind our own business.

Picking up the knife and placing my fingers over the top of the avocado, I show David how to cut open the fruit, remove the core, and spoon out the contents. When I hand the knife back to him, his fingers graze the back of my hand and he says, "Thank you" – far too slowly and thoughtfully for my liking.

Hot.

As he gets back to work on the remaining two avocados, we prep in silence. I season the steak and begin cutting herbs for the guacamole. He spoons the avocado into the bowl, and I add cilantro, garlic, and salt. David picks up some Tabasco and adds a few drops. He doesn't know how to cut fruit, but apparently he knows a little about seasoning and likes things spicy.

I like spicy, too.

There is hope for him yet – not that it matters. I just hate thinking a grown-ass man can't cook for himself; it would be a tragedy if he couldn't.

The instructor moves on to the main meal, and I notice David and I are lagging behind the others' progress. "Can you handle the peppers and onion while I do the rice?" I ask David, moving around him. His broad shoulders are unavoidable, and my head bumps into the perfectly rounded muscle. This prep station might as well be made for one of him, not two of us.

"Ow," I say instinctively, scratching my head even though it didn't really hurt.

He reaches up to touch my head, but stops mid-way. "Sorry. You're the boss, just tell me what to do," he says with a genuine smile – no teasing intended.

I like being called the boss because I *am* the boss, but it is odd coming from him. I am not his boss, and he isn't the type of man who seems like he answers to anyone. Yet, he says it to me so naturally and in a tone that makes me feel things in places that haven't felt anything in a while.

I feel my cheeks heat again, and hate myself a little for being flattered so easily. In an effort to punish myself for succumbing to his charm, I bite the insides of my cheeks. If only pain could actually deter the flushed color that exposes my thoughts from making an appearance. David has no problem showing his delight to my response. His lips curl in a knowing smile, and he winks at me.

He actually winks.

Arrogant son of a bitch.

"Okay …" I clear my throat and get back to business. "Do you know how to cut vegetables? I don't want to worry about you chopping off a finger while I'm rinsing the rice."

David leans in with a cocky grin. "Are you worried about me? How cute." His fingers brush the back of my knuckles as he slips the knife handle out from between my fingers.

The slow drag of his fingers across my hand causes my cheeks to go full-blown cherry-pop red and I snap. "I'm worried about you bleeding all over our food, not losing a finger. Your constant stomach growling is making me hungry." Before he can respond, I grab the bag of rice, a pot, and storm over to the sink at the front of the restaurant.

I need space from this man.

When I return, David is slowly chopping the peppers. It is painful to witness. I wince each time the knife slices down, and imagine it slipping and cutting off the tips of his fingers, which are lying flat against the vegetable. He looks up at me as the knife slices down again, just millimeters away from his middle finger. I bare my teeth, waiting for the worst, as the knife rises and, thankfully, reveals all fingers intact.

"Do you want to do this?" He holds up the knife, carelessly flipping it around, and offering it to me hilt first.

I bite my inner lip as I admire the way the knife presses into his palm without piercing the skin. His calloused hands are a thick pad of protection against the sharp edge of the blade, and he holds onto it with ease and unconcern. I hardly ever touch that side of a knife. In fact, I avoid it at all costs possible – the risk of being cut is too high.

"Destiny?" David adds expectantly, shaking the knife. It bobs and bends as he shakes it, taunting me to steady it before it cuts his hand, tempting me to educate David on how to properly cut a vegetable.

This dish is easy; I could have done it alone, but I hate knowing he doesn't know how to slice a pepper. Plus, he should do some of the work if he is going to be eating this food as well. I simply cannot leave here without knowing he won't have an unfortunate accident with a butcher's knife in the future. Teaching him will feel like I did society a favor. His team and fans will be forever grateful – or at least that's the excuse I am telling myself as I near him.

"Here ... Let me show you." I move to stand behind him and put my hands over his, but he is too large to reach around, so I move to his side. I reach under his arm to place my hand over his, but his arm length makes it impossible for me to reach his hands. And now it feels like I am just groping him for fun. I groan in frustration, assessing the situation and trying to find a solution that doesn't involve me standing in front of him. His size is making it impossible.

"Stand in front of me." He opens his arm and motions to the space in front of him.

I stare at the space, in between him and the counter, and think about how close that will put us, and how I will be trapped between him and a hard place again. It is entirely too close for comfort.

"Never mind. Just tell me what to do." He moves back into place, but I react without thinking, placing my palm on his forearm and stopping him.

David moves aside and I hesitantly step in front of him. His warmth radiates against my back as he closes the area around me. His palms rest on either side of the counter as he waits for me to begin. I am effectively trapped. My heart races as I say, "Give me your hands. I'll show you." I turn my palms toward the sky.

David places his hands, palm up, in my open ones. His breathing is steady; I can both feel and hear it against my left ear as his chest is overwhelming close. The brush of his breath causes the hairs on my neck to rise. Shoving the growing nerves at his proximity in my gut aside, I place his hand back on the pepper and the other hand on the forgotten knife. Then, I place my hand over his and curl my fingers around his massive ones.

We pick up the knife and I say, "Let me direct you."

He allows me to puppeteer his hands, curling his fingers into the pepper and positing them high on the knife's hilt near the blade. I bring the knife over to the pepper, resting closely against his curled knuckles, and press lightly on the top of the pepper. With both our hands holding the vegetable and knife, we work in tandem to slice perfectly even strips. Then we cut the onion and two more peppers.

Neither of us says a word as we work together. Our movements relax as we focus on the task at hand. His fingers and mine intertwine and his chest presses comfortably against my upper back. David's steady breaths fan around my face and bring with it a scent of sweetness, mixing with his masculine flavor that smells of the forest in fall – it reminds me of late nights drinking bourbon by a campfire.

When we are done slicing the vegetables and our bodies once again find distance, I feel like I've been doused in cold water. My concentration has been so fully absorbed in what we were doing that I hadn't realized everyone else is already halfway through cooking their meals. Nor have I realized how uncomfortably comfortable it felt to be in between David's arms and touching his hands.

"We need to catch up," I say somewhat breathlessly. My mind swirls in confusion about what needs to be done next. I inhale deeply, focusing on my breath as I assess the situation before me. Cooking is the perfect distraction from my conflicting emotions. I pour oil in two pans and turn on the burners, getting straight back to business. The rice is already simmering in its pot, having caught heat while Daivd and I were preoccupied. "I'll make the tortillas while you cook the veggies. How do you like your steak? I like mid-rare, so we can do that last."

"I'm a fan of mid-rare as well," he says, and adds the vegetables to the hot oil.

They sizzle. Loudly.

Turning away from him and the mocking vegetables, I combine the tortilla mix with water and press the dough into flat circles. I set the tortillas aside while I heat more oil for the steak. The vegetables are nearly done, and we are catching up to the other groups' progress. A server comes around with margaritas, and David grabs two drinks while I heat the flattop to cook the tortillas. There are so many things happening at once and it such a short amount of time.

"Here you go, Destiny," he says, handing me the pale yellow drink.

"Thanks," I say quickly, taking the drink and tasting it. It is delicious and refreshing, just like every other margarita I've had at the resort thus far. Something about being in Mexico makes the margaritas taste so much better.

"What do you want me to do next, boss?" David asks, stirring the vegetables.

Boss.

A shiver runs up my spine. He keeps saying that word, and it is starting to sound like a pet name. "Um … I don't know. What do you want to do?" We only have the steak and tortillas left to cook. I am not sure what else he is referring to because I am clearly already about to start cooking both.

"There are many things I want to do right now. But I'm waiting for you to tell me what you want," he says, his words holding so much more longing than they should.

Hot. Scolding. Fiery hotness.

My stomach twists. There are only two things left to do, but I feel like he is referring to something that has nothing to do with cooking and everything to do with me standing between his arms again. I ignore his insinuation because there is no way he is interested in me. I tell myself, *There is no way.* If anything, he just likes to make me uncomfortable. But there is no coldness between us now, not by the way he looks at me. There is only heat. A lot of heat.

"Why don't you cook the steak and I'll handle the tortillas?" I suggest, dragging my attention away from him as quickly as possible.

"It's a plan," he says, shuffling around me to the other side of the prep station to resume cooking the steak.

As we move about, the energy between us becomes charged and when our forearms accidentally brush, a shock stings my arm. "Ouch!" I place a hand over the stinging spot.

David drops the tongs he is using to turn the steak and moves around the pre-station to my side with impressive speed. His palm rubs small circles into the spot where I was shocked. "Sorry about that. Feel better now?"

I do feel better. A lot better. His hand warms me, warms my entire body, while also leaving my mouth dry and me speechless. He's like the desert in summer, sucking every last drop of moisture out of the air, leaving one desperate and yearning for hydration.

And he is both the desert and hydration.

"You're cold," he says, rubbing my other arm and leaving goosebumps in his wake.

I am so *not* cold.

I wet my lips and swallow the dry lump in my throat, trying to force out words. The statement that comes out is more than I mean to expose about myself. It is an indirect explanation of who I really am. He is odd, but he is also kind, and he showed me that today. I've been rude, ungrateful, hateful, but that isn't who I am. Not all the time. I need to show him I am not only the stubborn, brash woman he met yesterday, but also kind and fun. Even if he isn't interested in me.

"I feel that way, but I'm not."

David makes a curious face before saying, "I'm starting to pick up on that."

I don't know what is happening between Achilles and me, but I feel like the air around me is low on oxygen. How did taking a cooking class turn into arguing, then touching, then feeling something – something weird? He is taking up too much space and depriving me of rational thoughts. I need to get some distance and clear my head.

Today's revelations have reached their maximum. I try to remind myself that he is a potential stalker, but he isn't. It's like my brain has been fried by the sun and the alcohol, because only my body is doing the thinking right now. And the aching need it expresses is growing unbearable.

9

David

When I catch her concern over my cutting form, she is clearly embarrassed to stand in front of me, but she still can't help herself – she has to teach me how to do it right. Watching her try to figure out how to show me was so entertaining and I couldn't resist the opportunity to get her between my arms again, even if her husband is standing ten feet away.

While I could have moved closer to the cutting board and allowed her to stand behind me, I couldn't be completely emasculated by having her stand behind me, as if she were showing a kid how to swing a golf club. Plus, having her between my arms and a hard place is something I am beginning to realize feels nice. She is clearly skilled in the kitchen – a skill I don't share – and it feels good to have someone teach me something new. Normally, I am the expert and always in control. This feeling is unfamiliar, but it excites me to learn a new skill from this bossy woman.

I call her boss because she is the boss of me right now, and it brings out a look of satisfaction that I hope to see on her face more often. She can be my boss any day, telling me what to do and where to do it. Her sassy attitude and angry faces are captivating me, but when she smiles and laughs – like when she was in a foot race against me or cooking – she is mesmerizing. I am so beguiled by her that I have lost all manners and continually forget about her husband two stations in front of us.

Fuck him. This woman deserves the best. The lack of a diamond ring on her finger just reaffirms how mistreated she is. She wears a few golden bands on her fingers, and one with a row of diamonds rests on her ring finger. I'd buy her a rock so big, there'd be no mistaking that she's married to me.

He isn't concerned about her at all, and I am beginning to feel less and less guilty about flirting with her. I don't even feel guilty for touching her again, even if it is just her arms. Destiny is hard to resist. She is hot and cold in all the best ways. When I feel how chilly her arms are, my natural response is to warm her up. I rub up and down her arms, and probably linger too long, but her skin is like velvet. Despite the goosebumps that my rubbing produces, I've never felt skin so soft or luxurious, and I never want to stop touching it.

"You're cold," I say nervously, making an excuse for my lingering hands.

"I feel that way, but I'm not," she says quietly, looking me in the eyes and then diverting her gaze to the ground.

It is a curious thing to say. I can't help but think there is more meaning behind those seven little words than she shares. When we first met, getting to know her was like penetrating a brick wall. She would continually throw ice daggers with her eyes and words, but there is a warmness, a lightness, that creeps through now.

I am beginning to realize her icy demeanor is her defense mechanism, and as I chisel away, bit by bit, the light is seeping through. There is so much to learn about this woman. She doesn't have a chance against me – I am an offensive player, and when I have a goal in sight, I find a way to win. Her statement is proof that I've just opened a gap.

"So, um … I guess we'll all sit down and eat after this. I'm assuming by the sound of your stomach that you'll be joining," Destiny says casually, trying not to make it sound like she is asking me to join, but rather accepting the fact that I will join her either way.

I almost forgot about how hungry I am. Obviously, I am sticking around – for more than one reason. "Are you trying to uninvite me after I just helped cook all this?" I goad her into admitting she wants me to join. Her husband is busy with his friend; she deserves some male attention.

"No. It's just I planned on sitting with my friends, but by the way they are looking at you, I feel like it's going to be awkward," she admits.

I glance at the people I saw from the pool and notice them watching us as they whisper amongst themselves. There are definitely some football fans in her friend group. It may be awkward, but I feel like I am finally seeing underneath the layers of this mysterious woman, and the best way to really learn what she is all about will be from her friends.

"I love awkward lunches with strangers," I lie.

Destiny rolls her eyes. "Right ... So do I," she says.

Those rolling eyes ... Again.

I gather the serving dish filled with our prepared food. "Grab the drinks, will you?" I say, walking toward a long table that seats the whole group.

Destiny grabs the drinks and scrambles after me. Her short steps have to work overtime to catch up. "They're going to be weird about this because I went missing the other day, and now that you're here, they might assume we slept together or something. Pat and Dale love making people uncomfortable, so I apologize in advance for anything they say," she says quickly under her breath before we reach the table.

I have no idea who Pat and Dale are, but I find it odd that her friends would openly discuss who she sleeps with when she has a husband. Granted, between my combating thoughts for the woman, I have been openly hitting on her. I wouldn't mind the rumors of us sleeping together to be true. It sounds like she is in an open relationship. While I am not personally a fan of that situation, it might have its advantages.

I don't think I am going to get her out of my head any time soon. Getting her in between my sheets may be the only way to end my intrigue. Although, I have a hunch that it won't. Not until I fully figure her out. She is my new playbook.

"I'd be happy to give them the details of our little rendezvous," I tease, setting down our food.

"What little rendezvous?" asks the dark-haired woman from the pool, who is seated across from Destiny and me.

Destiny's face flushes crimson. "There was no little rendezvous. He doesn't know what he's talking about," she says, brushing aside the question with vicious ease while finishing her margarita. She presses the ice-filled glass against her neck after emptying it.

"Feeling hot, Dez?" asks the man beside the dark-haired woman.

Destiny shoots him one of her infamous ice-dagger looks and he chuckles. Apparently, I am not the only one who receives those looks, and I am also not the only one who finds them amusing. I feel a tinge of jealousy from the realization that her looks are not reserved exclusively for me, but I shove it to the back of my mind. There truly is something wrong with me for wanting her to save that sassy attitude for me and me alone. We hardly even know each other.

"David, this is Kat and Matt," Destiny introduces her friends, "Michelle and Javier. You met Stacy and Ryan, the couple getting married. Will and his girlfriend, Taylor, are sitting at the end. Lastly, but certainly not least, Dale and his husband Pat."

Pat is the man from this morning. Pat has a husband. I look down at their interlocked hands, and sure enough, both men are wearing wedding bands. The same wedding bands.

I run through the morning and afternoon's events, realizing I completely misread Destiny's situation. "Where's your husband?" I blurt out before I can stop myself. Now that I think about it, there's no way she can be here alone; everyone is a couple. There is still an uneven number of people present, so her real husband has to be somewhere.

"Honey, don't you think you should have been asking if she was single before last night?" Pat asks.

Both Destiny and I flush. I flush because I keep assuming she is married, and now feel stupid for thinking her modest jewelry could pass for a wedding ring. She flushes because her friend is openly calling her out for sleeping with me – even though she definitely has not.

I wish she had.

I realize how this morning must look to an outsider, but Destiny is not the type of woman to be caught doing the walk of shame – even I know that.

"Pat! Stop it." Dale, his husband, smacks his hand.

"Wait! Is that why you keep going missing?" Stacy chimes in from the other end of the table with a twinkle in her eye.

She'd be the type to do the walk of shame and I am certain she'll be pestering Destiny later for details on our meeting. Not that Destiny will tell her anything. There isn't anything to tell, other than how we keep awkwardly running into each other.

Multiple people at the table are busying themselves with their food and politely ignoring this awkward conversation. Destiny wasn't kidding when she said her friends would try to make us uncomfortable. I don't like to be the butt of the joke, nor do I like the horrified look on Destiny's face as she stares down the table at her annoying friend.

"Before this conversation gets out of control," I speak up, getting everyone's attention, "I ran into Destiny this morning and walked with her because I was headed in the same direction. Obviously, I think she's an attractive woman and I'd like to get to know her. Then, I was having lunch here today when I overheard that she needed a partner. It's pure happenstance that we keep running into each other. Nothing worth gossiping about has happened, so please don't speculate."

"Pure happenstance? Maybe it's *destiny*, Destiny," Pat teases.

"Shut it, Pat." Destiny elbows her friend as he takes a drink and he chokes. Her triumphant look makes me feel like I handled the situation well. When she mouths *thank you*, I feel as if we have a secret understanding that she doesn't share with anyone else here.

Lunch continues with more roasting. Thankfully, it is directed at other people. There is the occasional question about my profession. I was right in my earlier assessment – there are quite a few football fans in her friend group.

Destiny orders two more margaritas. She talks in a friendlier tone and even shows affection by reaching across the table and squeezing her friends' hands or side-hugging them.

There is a warmth in her. I just have yet to be on the receiving end. But I'll stick around to receive it. Now that the imaginary husband is no longer a roadblock, when she is ready to make her pass, I'll be there with arms wide open.

10

Destiny

AN ATTRACTIVE WOMAN THAT he would like to get to know? Just yesterday I was verbally and nearly physically fighting with Achilles. It is like he made a total one hundred-and-eighty-degree turn from yesterday.

He asked me all these odd questions this morning, and then, I could have sworn he was flirting with me while we cooked. Of course, his flirtation was confirmed when he mentioned his attraction to me.

I was not expecting him to come to my defense like that. It was so refreshing. But I'm still reeling over his words.

Honestly, I'm not sure why he's drawn to me, other than out of pure boredom or loneliness. A man like him can get any woman he wants, but this is a small resort, so his options are probably limited.

But I don't want to be anyone's consolation prize. I plan to actively date when I get back to San Francisco. I am looking for a man who excites me, who is as independent and mature as I am, a man who knows what he wants long term and is looking for the same kind of commitment as I am.

There is no way David's interests align with mine. The fact that he is vacationing here alone is a red flag. The fact that he is actively pursuing a single woman, whom he thought was married an hour ago, whom he barely knows, at a resort where everyone is bound to return home, makes me question his intentions and assume he is just looking to stick his dick in something.

Do I want to be his broom closet for a night? Maybe. He has this power over me that makes all sense and rational decisions seem like poor choices.

"Can I walk you back to your room?" David asks as we say goodbye to my friends. Everyone is returning to their rooms to freshen up for tonight's dinner.

"David," Stacy coos, pulling his attention away from me before I can answer, "we're doing a drink-mixing course tomorrow afternoon, and Ryan and I would love for you to join us if you aren't doing anything else. We also have dinner reservations tomorrow night, and we could easily add one more!"

David looks at me expectantly, and I realize he is waiting for my invitation.

"Stacy, I actually need to work tomorrow, so I'm not sure I'll make it to the class."

"Really?" Stacy pouts, but nods in understanding. She knows how important my company is to me, and that a business owner never really gets to go on vacation, even while they are technically on vacation.

"I get it. Let us know if you change your mind. David, you're still welcome without this bitch," she says and gives David a wink before walking off, her hips swinging side to side more aggressively than usual.

David laughs and calls after her, "Thanks, Stacy." He seems genuinely happy to have met my friends. It's endearing. I hate it.

I tug on his arm and drag him toward the restaurant exit before someone else can stop us and invite him to hang out.

"What's the rush? Does Destiny not like to wait on people?" David teases, falling into step beside me.

"I just love it when people use my name as a pun." I roll my eyes, which only seems to make him happier. "You know, you're supposed to be offended when I roll my eyes."

"How can I be offended by something so cute?" He looks down at me with a crooked smile that makes my stomach knot.

"It's not supposed to be cute," I reply sardonically.

"Can I ask you something?" His tone turns serious.

"Depends on what you want to ask."

Considering how random his earlier questions were, there is no telling what type of question will come spewing out of his mouth. Some questions need to be off-limits because I need to keep this man at a distance. He is prodding at my personal bubble, and I can't allow a man who only wants to fuck and duck to breach that line of trust.

Men who enjoy the chase don't know how to celebrate the winnings once they get them. They move on as soon as you let them in, and I am not about to put my heart on the line for a chance – no matter how much he makes me feel. And *damn* do I feel it deeply.

"Do you really have to work tomorrow?"

We turn a corner and David's shoulder bumps into mine. My right foot slips on the edge of the sidewalk as I bounce off him. I nearly fall over, but his hand catches my arm and straightens me with ease. I look down at the massive hand surrounding my arm as his eyes trail down to where our skin touches. He slides his fingers across my bare skin. His touch is slow and gentle, yet thorough and inquisitive. It is nothing like the way he rubbed my arms earlier. It is so much more.

"You have really soft skin," he says gently.

"So, I've heard," I say, crossing my arms over my chest and pulling out of his grasp to avoid his touch.

I'm pretty sure all men have rough skin, so they think every female has soft skin. I don't take it as a compliment, but I also can't stop thinking about his hand wrapped around my arm either. This man is so painfully present. There isn't a moment that I'm not aware of his existence and any part of him that touches me makes that presence solidify further and linger on my skin like a second scent that betrays my body's cravings.

"So, are you really working?" he asks again as we walk down the sidewalk once more.

"Probably for a bit," I reply honestly.

I don't want to tell him about my plans to take a sailing lesson tomorrow. I don't want to tell anyone about my plans to sail tomorrow because they will want to join me. Most of my friends are avid sailors and frequently boat on Lake Michigan, but I never learned how to do it. It is a sin to be prideful about something so inconsequential, but I am. Therefore, I am not about to allow myself to be the most inexperienced sailor in my friend group. Stacy and Ryan rented a massive sailboat to take out on our last day in Tulum and I will be damned if I can't hold my own when or if the time comes.

"Well, maybe we'll run into each other again," David says hopefully.

"Hopefully not," I let my thoughts slip. I haven't been overly nice to David since we met, but he's been an enjoyable enough partner today and so kind to my friends, despite their attempts to embarrass and harass him. He doesn't deserve the harshness of my words.

But I'm a little bitter because I don't want to be some woman he screwed on that one vacation. I mean … I want to be some woman he screws on vacation, but I also don't want to be. Nevertheless, I meant to be subtle about my turn down – not downright insult him. But the man flusters me.

David's eyes widen. He didn't see my remark coming, but he doesn't look offended by it – just surprised. "I've never had a woman be so put off by me. I should warn you, I'm not very good at losing."

It is my turn to go wide-eyed at his blatant honesty. I shouldn't expect more from a man like him, though. I suspected he was drawn to the chase and his words now confirm it. Women probably like his honest approach to stating his intentions, but it makes me less interested.

He is so goddamn nice looking and I will likely regret this later when all I have at my disposal is a hot pink vibrator.

"Well, you aren't going to win with me. I know what I want, and it's not this," I say, pointing my finger at his chest and twirling it around to encompass his entirety. He needs to know where I stand, and it is on the other sideline.

His brow furrows and he says, "Seriously?"

"Seriously," I say unemotionally, crossing my arms over my chest.

David steps closer to me, forcing me to step back. He takes another step forward and as I step back again, my heels hit the edge of the sidewalk. I struggle to balance on my toes without stepping into the gardening that lines the pavement. Then he takes another step and I'm forced to lean back, trying to avoid the brush of our chests, but I stumble. The seriousness in his gaze intensifies.

Screw heels and narrow sidewalks and big ass sexy men.

He catches my arms, moving so quickly that I barely notice him coming before he pulls me forward to stand flat on my feet while pressing firmly against his chest. His arm snakes around my lower back.

This is way too close for comfort. Again.

I keep my eyes straightforward, burning a hole into the broad width of his chest. I squeeze them shut as I regain composure, but the proximity sucks the air straight out of my lungs.

David is like a warm, immovable boulder and instinctively I want to climb it, which makes my thoughts churn with indecent images of his shirtless body touching me in ways that are far from competitors standing on opposing sidelines. My traitorous body responds so quickly and easily to him.

My heart continues to race, but I steel my nerves. I tilt my head back and open my eyes. His gaze could melt glaciers. The inferno of desire flaming within his eyes forces his lids to droop lazily as he scans my face. I study the subtle changes in his demeanor – the way his hands soften against my arms and move to my lower back, the way his eyes flick between my eyes and my lips, the way his lips part to say something, but nothing slips out.

Before this goes further than it should, before he can say anything, I shove him away and storm down the concrete path toward my room. I need to get some distance from this man before I lose consciousness from lack of oxygen and the inability to think straight.

11

David

FOR HOW COORDINATED SHE was yesterday, I'm surprised Destiny keeps stumbling. It's a good thing I was there to catch her, or she would have fallen into a cactus. I don't think she even noticed the spiny thorns inches from her legs before she took off. She flew down the sidewalk as fast as my best wide receivers.

If I hadn't seen the conflicting look in her eyes and the way she tried to fight our connection, I would've thought she meant what she said. She may be trying to convince herself that she doesn't want me, but there is at least some physical part of her that wants me. Badly. Except, I don't only want a physical connection. I want to engage with this woman. I want to talk, bicker, tell her the random shit that's on my mind. I don't know why or how this feeling has plagued me so quickly, but it's clear – I want more.

Other women who have come and gone over the years wanted me for my reputation, how much money I make, what I look like, or what I can offer them in terms of connections and advancement, but no one ever wants me for *me*. I am more than a piece of meat with benefits. I want a woman who can challenge me with intelligent banter one minute and sit in comfortable silence with me the next. If she can ride my face in between those two things, then I will have found my perfect woman.

Destiny is tempting me. She is intriguing in all the best ways. However, she isn't being honest with herself. This is a losing game. I know it, and I can't afford it right now. Yet, I can't stay away her. I feel like there must be a way to break through her emotional walls.

When I touch her skin and feel the warmth of her body near mine, something deep in my core yearns for more. I am not trying to push her buttons by being inquisitive. I just want to know more about her and understand why I am so drawn to her, despite knowing this game she plays might hurt me. There's always a chance we discover this attraction is only because our state of minds.

"David!" someone shouts behind me.

I turn around, and find Pat and Dale approaching.

They stop to talk. I am not usually interested in small talk with strangers, but these two men know more about Destiny than I do, and they might have some insightful advice.

"Will you be joining us tomorrow?" Dale asks.

"I don't know about that. Destiny doesn't seem like she wants me to," I say, looking down the path to where she disappeared.

"Don't pay any mind to her," says Pat. "Destiny is known to be unreceptive to men. She's very particular, and she doesn't want to get trapped in another relationship that might hold her back. Thing is, she's the one holding herself back."

I mull over his comment. Pat is giving me more insight in one minute than Destiny has in the hours I've spent with her thus far.

"What do you mean by hold her back?" I ask. I can't imagine anything holding that woman back. Especially a man.

Dale answers this time: "Destiny is a very purposeful woman, and she's spent the last five years dedicating her life to building her company. She's fiercely independent and her last relationship …" He looks at his husband, who nods, before he continues: "Her last relationship with Will, whom you met, wasn't great. He didn't appreciate her dedication to her company and felt that she cared more about ambition than their relationship. Truthfully, I think she did care more about the company, because there were so many other issues between Will and Dez, but she'll deny that. She hates to admit being bad at things or accepting fault for something – she's crazy stubborn. Anyways … Now Will has found someone who is solely dependent on him, which is perfect, and we are happy for him, but Destiny is still struggling to find her equal."

There is so much about Dale's admission to process. First off, I must've been the most oblivious person in the world because I thought Pat was her husband and didn't suspect there was any history between Destiny and Will. I try to recall his face, and as I do, I begin picking out all the reasons why the man is unworthy of her. Second off, I am not sure I believe Destiny's issue is that she can't find her equal.

If she were looking for her equal, she should've seen it in me. I am most definitely her equal and she is running away from me as fast as possible. Stubborn doesn't even brush the surface of her defiance. Yet, she still said I am not what she is looking for. Could she be referring to my mental capacity? I know I am physically her type. Call me cocky or arrogant, but I know when a woman's body is responding to mine. A woman turning me down for my lack of intelligence, now, that would be a first. But it's the only thing I can reasonably assume. Most women I've dated don't want to have deep, philosophical conversations, so they never think of what my brain has to offer, and apparently, it isn't up to Destiny's standards.

It stings. It's not like I have had time to impress her with a big brain in our limited meetings. I make a mental note to show her my depth.

"I feel like this goes without saying, but don't mention any of this to Destiny. She'll be pissed at us and even more so at you if you bring it up," Pat says, patting my arm.

"Of course," I say, shaking my head and tossing over the conflict in my thoughts. "Thanks for the insight, guys. Although, I'm not sure I'll run into her again. Based on our last conversation, I think she'll be avoiding me like the plague."

Dale and Pat share a look, one of those looks only couples who are deeply connected can share and understand, before Dale advises: "Destiny has a way of working things out. It just takes time, and she does it in her own way."

With those peculiar parting words, the two men leave me on the sidewalk – speechless and contemplative. Destiny has a way of working things out … If Destiny heard her friends use her name in a pun, I'm pretty sure she'd punch them. Thinking of Destiny going full psycho on her friends brings a smile to my face. This woman doesn't even know it, but her claws are in deep.

12

Destiny

I WALK INTO THE room and dive-bomb onto the bed. "Ugh!" I groan out loud as if it will make me feel any better. If there is a god, can he or she hear my frustration and solve this problem for me? I would greatly appreciate it.

We haven't discussed the duration of our stays, but I have four days remaining at the resort. Hopefully, David will be gone with the sunrise.

He is entirely too tempting – physically and emotionally. I want to press up against his body as if my life depends on it. I want to feel the hard plains of his stomach pressed against my soft belly. I want him to fight me with his words, to not take my shit like everyone else does.

The way he makes me feel triggers every red flag in my brain. I am on high alert. Everything about this man screams danger. If I know what is good for me, I will stay far away from Achilles.

He has my head spinning with doubt and confusion. I tell myself he is just another man drawn to the chase. This is a game to him. He is a football player – he is an expert at games.

I have found there are many men in the dating world who prefer to play games over having an honest relationship. When I make a man wait for sex or don't show interest immediately, they invest all their time getting to know me – like that is their sole purpose in life. As soon as I fall into their trap and open up, they are gone with the wind.

That is not the type of situation I want to get trapped in while on vacation or any other time. I don't have energy for it. My dumbass, cowardly self will not find its way to David's daybed again.

I can't.

I won't.

I will come back to my room tonight, and put earplugs in so I can't hear Will and his new girlfriend making love for the tenth time this trip. That is the whole reason I ended up in this mess. I ran away from one problem and straight into another.

"Knock, knock," Pat calls from the doorway.

I must have left the door ajar. "In here," I reply. Pat and Dale walk into my room with foolish grins on their face. "What?" I ask suspiciously, making no attempt to get up from the bed as I bury my face into the pillows.

"We just ran into David," Dale says. I feel the bed shift as he sits down beside me.

"And?" I say, my words muffled by the pillow.

"And he was quite curious about you. I think the man is smitten. Although, aren't they all smitten with you, Destiny?" Pat says, sitting on the other side of the bed.

I sit up abruptly, feeling the need to shut down their efforts to play matchmaker before the situation gets out of hand. "He's smitten because he's alone at a resort and there aren't many single women here to choose from. Good grief, we're on vacation. He lives in New York; I live in San Francisco. What could come of this? Nothing! He's just looking for a hookup."

"You could just have a little fun with him … I mean, have you looked at the man?" Dale says, falling back on the bed and fanning his face as if the thought of screwing David makes him hot.

It probably does. It makes me hot, too.

"I agree. Was I not saying the exact same thing to you at dinner last night? You need a good lay," says Pat.

"Yes, you were. But it's not going to happen." I whack Dale's fanning hand and make him stop. I feel like I'm ping-ponging between these two – it's exasperating.

"I can see the cobwebs in your vagina peeking out of your swimsuit, Destiny. Go get laid already." Pat pulls my attention to the other side of the room. He is making his way to my mini-bar.

"I'm trying very hard not to be offended by that comment. And not that it's any of your business, but my vagina has no cobwebs."

"Masturbation doesn't clean house in quite the same way, honey," Dale murmurs, picking at his nails.

"Preach," says Pat.

"I'm going to smack you in the gut next time if you don't watch your mouth," I threaten, pointing at Dale's lower abdomen, where hitting will make him feel the pain deep in his balls, not just in his stomach. If he wants to play hardball, I can too.

Dale covers his stomach and rolls off the bed to stand. "Do that, and I'll walk outside and invite that big ass spider killer in here. We won't give you an option. The deep cleaner is on his way!" Dale retorts as he marches to the door.

"Don't!" I yell at him, jumping off the bed, running after Dale and slamming the door shut before he can open it further.

Pat bursts out laughing behind us as he cracks open a beer. "I love you, baby."

I glare at Dale as he returns to his husband's side to accept a beer of his own. They settle on the small room's settee together.

"And I hate you both right now," I say as I get a beer for myself. They are right – I need a sexual reprieve – but alcohol will have to do for now. It's less risky.

"Well, you're really going to hate us when you find out what we talked to David about," Pat says as Dale puts an arm over his shoulders. They sit united before me.

I suppress my comments. Knowing them, they didn't hold anything back. They could have said anything. They might have claimed I was lesbian or a prostitute, just to see David's reaction. Or they might have said much worse – they might have told him the truth. That I am a sexually frustrated woman in her early thirties who works too much and has ridiculously high standards that will probably result in my being alone forever.

The saddest part is that I'm fully aware of it.

The silence becomes achingly painful. "Spill. Now," I finally say.

"Pat and I might have given him a little information on what you're looking for … Which isn't a one-night stand. We know you – that's not your style," Dale says.

Pat continues, "So if he comes around, looking to spend more time with you, it's doubtful that he's only looking to get in your pants." His brow arches knowingly.

"You don't know that," I counter, refusing to believe David's actions could be anything more.

"I guess we'll have to wait and see," says Dale.

"You're welcome," Pat adds sassily.

While I don't love Dale and Pat sharing information about me, it could serve a purpose that I might be grateful for later. I believe I was abundantly clear about my intentions, but their explanation would leave little doubt in David's mind about what I desire. He knows that I am not interested in playing games. I want more. And there is no man in his right mind, who vacations alone in Tulum, who is looking for more.

My days with David were numbered from the start and while there is a tinge of disappointment in knowing I'll no longer see him after his conversation with Pat and Dale, I am relieved to know my heart is safe from being messed with.

13

Davio

I was up half the night thinking about Destiny. When I went for an early morning swim, I partially hoped that I would find her on my daybed again, but she wasn't there. Last night, I daydreamed about what I'd do if I saw her sleeping there. She is vulnerable when she is asleep but a viper when awake. I wanted to savor those few moments of peace, analyzing the tranquility in her face, before waking her in the worst way possible and exciting her venomous rage in a way that would hopefully result in another battle of physical wills.

She won't juke me again; I'll be ready next time, and there will definitely be a next time if I have anything to do with it. Destiny told her friends she would be working today, but the lack of conviction in her response yesterday makes me think otherwise. I think she is hiding other plans. My goal is to discover what they are.

I finish swimming, take a quick shower, and put on fresh swim trunks, a T-shirt, and sandals. Most activities around here involve water, so I figure if she really isn't working, this will be a suitable outfit to crash whatever occasion she has planned.

Although, as I walk toward the public side of the resort, my steps grow heavier. It is a feeling similar to that pre-game pump-up, when the adrenaline is building and I'm running through every potential play that might occur and planning every counter the defense might make before the whistle blows.

I shouldn't compare getting to know a woman to playing football, but that's all I know. My life revolves around the game, and it revolves around winning. I have never put so much effort into a woman before – I've never had to – which may be why it never works out.

Although, I've also never met a woman worth putting in the work for …

I bought them gifts; I opened doors; I spent time with them and their families when my scheduled allowed. Yet, in the end, it was always the same. I didn't spend enough money on the gifts; I didn't network enough; I didn't have enough time available for them. Simply being there when I could, being supportive, and enjoying each other's time was never enough.

When I was in my twenties, I could understand their arguments, but it is no longer about the money and fame for me. I have more money than I need and more fame than I want. If I can play football, win games, and come home to a family that supports my career at the end of the day, I'll be the happiest man alive. But this lifestyle isn't easy for a lot of people.

Destiny isn't necessarily going to give me all of that right away, but she is the first woman I've met who doesn't seem interested in money or fame, and who seems as ambitious about her career as I am.

I have no idea where she lives and I am fully aware that pursuing a woman while on vacation is cliché but when you meet someone like Destiny, you have to give it a shot. I might be throwing a Hail Mary with thirty seconds left on the board, but I'll be damned if I don't leave everything I have on the field.

That is what it takes.

A woman like her, with curves like that and a mouth that spits fire – she deserves to be worshipped.

But with every step I take, more doubt surfaces. What if her friends are messing with me? What if she really has no interest in me? Showing up at her room unannounced may come off as a bit stalkerish. I've been to her room once, and somehow remember the number – that is a psycho move.

Plus, I am a successful, professional athlete in my late thirties and still single. She probably isn't interested because she sees right through me: I am a football player holding onto my youth, playing a game with guys ten years younger than me, and usually dating women even younger than that.

From an outsider's perspective, it might appear like I have no idea what I want and all I care about is football and fucking.

Suddenly, I don't know what I am thinking by coming to her room. Destiny is a driven, young, independent woman looking for a man who has his shit together. Meanwhile, I am on the verge of losing my contract with no plan of what to do or where to go next. I might be forced into early retirement, even though I know I am in my prime. I am as stubborn as they come, and she probably doesn't want a man who combats her all the time – because I will definitely combat her. We already butt heads, and while I find it entertaining, she might think it is frustrating.

I stop outside her building. I am seconds away from talking myself out of this whole plan. On the one hand, there is no harm in trying. On the other hand, denial will hurt my ego, and that is already in a fragile state. But I don't do things half-assed, even if I am at risk of getting burned.

"Thanks so much." Destiny's voice comes from further down the sidewalk.

I still haven't decided what I am going to do, so I hurry down the pavement in the opposite direction of her voice and duck behind a maintenance shed. If I was concerned about looking like a creep before, I undeniably look like one now. Dismissing my embarrassing behavior, I peer around the corner of the building and watch Destiny.

She is wearing khaki shorts and a button-up long-sleeved linen shirt. It is see-through. I can easily see the two bright pink triangles covering her breasts under the thin fabric. Those aren't the type of clothes you wear to work. I look back toward the building she came out of and notice it is the concierge's office.

Jackpot.

When she is further down the path and out of sight, I jog to the concierge to find out what her plans are today. Based on that outfit, it's definitely not work.

I put some swag into my step and saunter into the office. Randomly running into her at the resort is a much better option than showing up at her room. It will appear like another accidental, fated run-in – totally innocent and not creepy at all.

"Hola, señor. How may I help you?" asks the woman behind the desk. She is wearing in a dark blue uniform, like the employees typically wear around the resort. Her name tag says Rosa.

I sit down across from Rosa and lean in, giving her my most charming smile. "Hello, Rosa. Would you mind telling me what activities the woman who was just in here has planned today?"

The concierge blushes. "Oh no, señor. I cannot share that information. You should ask her if you would like to know."

Her blush is telling enough; I'll get the information I need if I just put on a bit more charm. "Maybe you can't explicitly tell me, but maybe you could recommend an activity for a man who is on vacation alone and who has befriended a woman whom he'd like to make a good impression on and spend more time with." I broaden my smile and wink slyly. Surely, she can sympathize.

Rosa crosses her arms; my charm has the opposite effect than I intend. "I do not think that is a good idea. If you would like to book an activity, I can help you with that," she says, sliding a catalog across the desk to me.

I sigh and pick up the catalog, flipping through the pages dismissively as I debate what activity Destiny might be interested in. Horseback riding, snorkeling, surfing, kayaking, tennis, paddleboarding, jet skiing, and sailing are all listed. Sailing catches my attention though. I haven't sailed in months and the last time I was on the water wasn't an ideal day. The wind died down before I made it out of the marina. I look out the window. It is overcast, and there is a steady wind moving in from the ocean.

While I desperately want to spend the day with Destiny, I am torn on how to best approach the situation. So far, we keep accidentally running into each other. Deciding to let fate determine our next rendezvous, I change plans.

"Sailing sounds fun. What time do they go out?" I ask, setting down the pamphlet.

Rosa clicks her tongue as she types on her keyboard. "It looks like most of our boats are out on the water already, but we do have one boat leaving in twenty minutes. I can radio the instructor and see if he can wait for you."

"I can be there in ten. Where's it at?"

The concierge pulls out another pamphlet from her desk drawer and lays it in front of me. "Follow this path toward the boat docks," she says, drawing a dark black line down the path on the shortest route to the docks. "I'll let them know you'll be joining them soon."

"Great, thanks." I pick up the map and make my way toward the marina.

The resort is closer to the marina than I realized, so I stop at the juice bar for a smoothie. When I arrive at the marina, with several minutes to spare, it is mostly empty, except for a few sailors cleaning their boats. One of the men waves at me so I make my way over to him, walking across the wooden planks of the dock.

"Nice little double-handed dinghy. This will be fun!" I call to the first mate, who is readying the lines.

He replies happily, "Climb on board. I was just explaining the basics."

I don't need to know the basics. A boat like this usually needs two people to manage it, but I've done so by myself on a few occasions – my long arms have many uses. Between the instructor and me, we can explain the basics to anyone else who joins. I round the backside of the boat and climb over the railing. When I duck under the boom and stand fully upright, my day gets a whole lot better.

It turns out the sea isn't the only thing calling my name.

Destiny.

14

Destiny

David. How the hell did he find me here? Also, what the hell, Rosa? I requested a private lesson. This boat is barely big enough for two people. With Achilles on board that basically brings the occupancy to four. Rosa will be getting an earful from me later. It is inappropriate and unprofessional to be disclosing guest activities to strangers. Plus, the last thing I want to reveal is my sailing inexperience to David. He'll be highly amused to find something I'm not good at.

"Destiny. What a pleasant surprise to see you here!" David says after shaking the instructor's hand and introducing himself.

He sits down next to me and pats my hand that is resting on the bench we now share. I quickly fold my hand into my lap so he can't touch it again. His touch is too much, too close and too casual for comfort.

"Alright, guys. Do you have any experience sailing, David?" the instructor, whose name is Alejandro, asks.

"I've been sailing for about fifteen years now, everything from dinghies like this to catamarans and trimarans. I'm in it more for the thrill than the cruise, if you know what I mean," he replies jovially, leaning back against the small boat's railing so casually that it looks as if he owns it.

I am surprised a football player has any interest in water sports. It just doesn't seem right. His body is so large ... He looks like he would sink in the water, not float.

But I suppose everyone needs hobbies. Football may be considered his hobby, but it is also his career. He's allowed to enjoy other things. While I spend most of my time working, I am not a complete psychopath either. I like reading and cooking when my time allows me to do such things.

"I know exactly what you mean. We're going to have a great time today! Life jackets are just behind you. Snap them on and we'll get going," Alejandro says, jumping down from the hull, untying the boat from the dock.

David turns back to me. "Is this what you call working?"

It takes all my effort not to roll my eyes, if only because I don't want him to call it cute again. "I'm taking a break. Are you stalking me or something? I'm seriously starting to get concerned. I didn't tell anyone other than the concierge where I was going today."

The boat begins drifting away from the dock and Alejandro uses a motor to steer us out of the marina.

"I'm not stalking you, although I can see how it would appear that way. I was hoping to see you today, and when I was talking to the concierge about activities, I chose sailing because it's something I love to do, not because I knew you were here. The fact that you were already here on the sailboat is like—"

"Don't say it." I cut him off before he can add my name. I have heard enough puns using my name and I don't need him to stoop to that level. Although, annoying me might be a welcome change from making me feel … other things.

"I was going to say it's like scoring a field goal – extra points!" He chuckles, laughing at his own terrible joke in reference to his profession.

"That is so dumb," I say, unable to resist rolling my eyes at him.

"I know." He shrugs and turns away from me.

David stands as we exit the marina. He holds onto the boat's middle beam and I wonder how satisfying it would feel to see him knocked on his ass by it. But he surprises me as he starts gathering the ropes. "Watch your head and hold on," he says, smiling as he tosses a rope over my head and pulls it taut.

The mainsail starts to unravel and slide up the long metal beam in the center of the boat. Alejandro takes position at the bench across from me. He and David exchange words, but I can't follow their instructions. They grab, pull, and tie ropes. David jumps into the middle of the boat as the main boom flies over the deck.

I do exactly as David says – I hold on and duck.

Our boat launches forward in a rush and tilts to one side. I grip the side railing like a vise and watch as David stands, loosely holding onto a beam. He yells out triumphantly and looks down at me with a broad grin. He looks like a kid in a candy shop – so carefree and unrestrained. This side of him is completely at odds with the man I met two days ago. The contemplative man from yesterday flickers between my first impression of him and today. His temperature gauge is all over the place. Although, it's been a steady stream of temptation since he determined I wasn't married.

After adjusting the ropes a bit more, he sits down beside me, putting his arm along the railing behind my back. I turn in my seat to face him, and try to avoid looking at his muscular forearm resting so close to my shoulder.

"First time sailing?" he asks.

"No," I say, not knowing how else to answer without admitting why I am here today.

"Cool," he responds, leaning his head back and closing his eyes as the wind whips his freshly cut hair around.

The haircut really does wonders for his features. The sharply faded sides make his jawbone stand out even more, especially now that he is cleanly shaved. The longer, tousled brown hair on top makes him look young and wild. It's obnoxiously tempting.

I expect David to talk more, to ask me a bunch of questions like before, to express the interest he said he has in me, but he doesn't. I'm partly glad he doesn't because I don't want to disclose any information about why I am here. But I am also disappointed, because another part of me wants to believe that he isn't just trying to get laid. That this was some elaborate plan to get to know me more.

I laugh internally, thinking about how wrong Pat and Dale are. I would be happier doing this sailing lesson alone. To learn how to sail from someone who won't make me feel inadequate or embarrassed. But it's not David's fault the concierge didn't honor my request for a private lesson.

Instead of letting his presence sour my mood, I decide to enjoy myself and my unexpected sailing partner. After all, yesterday was pleasant. There is no reason today can't turn out the same.

Pleasant.

Good.

Adequate.

Remove the temptation and the day will be utterly perfect. Now that I know David is not looking for more, I can create distance between my mind and body's desires.

The wind beats aggressively against my face as we glide across the rippling ocean water. David's happiness is infectious. He smiles broadly, and it makes me want to smile. The speed of the boat picks up its pace, jerking us in a new direction as David and Alejandro maneuver the lines on their opposing benches. Each man remains seated as the sails go from flapping to pulling tautly.

Since I don't have much experience sailing, I don't realize how much adrenaline it can produce. The feeling is a heady mixture. It causes my cheeks to ache as I fight against the smile that has taken over my face. David grins and laughs at me. Before I know it, I am giggling.

Actually giggling.

The boat takes a quick turn to the left as Alejandro yells, "Duck!"

Even as I remain seated, I am caught off-balance from the sharp turn, and I brace myself as I fall forward. The boat makes a sudden jerk back to the right. I spin in the seat, attempting to regain my balance, but am thrown into David's lap. He struggles to catch me and falls onto the floorboard of the boat with me still in his arms.

The boom swings over us, narrowly missing our heads. "Holy hell," I say breathlessly, looking over my shoulder and feeling the excitement heightened by the near miss.

When I turn to David, our faces are inches apart. From being strangers two days ago, our bodies are strangely familiar with being close. My legs are on either side of his and my knee is resting on …

Oh my god.

Achilles.

My knee is jammed into his crouch. I lift my leg but David grabs the upper part of my thigh. His fingers dig into my flesh.

"That … That's a sensitive area," he stutters as his eyes heat and his hand remains in place. When I don't move, his hand flattens. He runs his thumb slowly down the middle of my thigh, touching me so gently that it tickles.

I choke on my breath as his thumb slides back up. My body shudders. David bites his lower lip and I nearly crumble.

"Sorry," I say, feeling a blush creep onto my cheeks as I scramble away from him.

"You guys okay? Sorry about that," Alejandro says, offering me a hand to stand.

I take the instructor's hand and quickly sit down before the lightheadedness makes me pass out. My heart is racing as fast as this sailboat cuts through the ocean's currents. David gracefully stands and braces himself on the mast. He subtly turns to the side and adjusts himself.

I feel as if the air has been stolen from my lungs.

The middle of his swim trunks is strained. The stretched fabric slowly loosens. But I find myself unable to look away as it does so. Now that I know where his cock rests, I struggle to look away. Because when I look closely, I can still see it there.

All of it.

And there's a lot.

I look away before our eyes meet and confirm that I just shamefully eye screwed the entire, hard length of his dick.

I am certain my cheeks are on fire at this point as my mind burns with the image of his constrained manhood. My body is recalling the position we were just in, my legs tucked into and around his firm body. Our groins perfectly aligned. My core aches, imagining what he would look like without his swim trunks on.

"Now that we're out of the rough water, who's ready to learn how to sail?" Alejandro's voice pulls me from my indecent thoughts.

I clear my throat and say as enthusiastically and nonchalantly as possible, "I am!" My voice croaks.

I am ready for anything to get my mind off the tight pants in front of me. I need a distraction. Otherwise, I may just give in to the temptations that are slowly creeping under my skin.

15

DAVID

IT IS LIKE THIS woman's body was made for mine. Her long legs straddled my thigh for far too long to be an accident and I am instantly pictured those legs around my waist. As soon as the words *holy hell* leave her pouty little lips, I am a goner. Destiny is ill-mannered on her best days; her usage of profanity only turns me on more.

It's no wonder she thinks I'm dense. When I am around her, there is something wrong with my brain. I speak before I think, and my dick reacts so easily, it's only going to get me in hot water. She might have a vulgar mouth, but the look on her face when she notices how her fall turns me on … She probably thinks I'm some sick mother-fucker.

The truth is, I've never been so immediately attracted to a woman. Sure, it doesn't take long to get it up for a hot piece of ass. But with Destiny, it is an instant hard-on. She is so effortlessly herself. And my body responds to that.

She doesn't care what anyone else thinks. She says what's on her mind and doesn't regret it. This is a woman who knows her value and doesn't need anyone else to reassure her. She is fierce, independent, and confident. The air around her vibrates restlessly, as if it can feel her dominant energy taking up more space than it should be allowed.

Alejandro is showing Destiny how to loop the lines around the cleats on the port side of the boat – this is important to learn because you don't want a line to get loose unintentionally. She is following his instructions with an intensity that I only see in the most determined athletes. The ones with drive that has been built through years of dedication and constant adversity.

Although, all the practice in the world isn't going to make a difference when you're trying to teach a bull not to buck when their balls are strapped. Alejandro has moved on from teaching her cleating, and is now trying to show Destiny how to hold the lines while pulling and loosening them in a simple maneuver, but she can't get it right.

She insists that looping the line over one arm and under the other is the right way, yet the lines keep getting tangled because she refuses to listen to her instructor. I stand back, enjoying the entertainment. The only thing that would make this day better would be a cold beer and a bowl of popcorn.

Destiny's eyes snap to mine as if she can hear my amuse-ment. I straighten, press my lips together, and give her a supportive thumbs-up. Clearing my throat, I ask, "How's it going?"

"Are you going to sit there all day and watch, or help us sail this boat?" she says sharply.

I wasn't aware we were ready to start sailing again – and neither was Alejandro based on the look he gives me. But, we both shrug. Now is not the time to disagree with Destiny.

"Are you sure you're ready for that?" I look at her hands that are unconfidently holding the tangled ropes. Yet, her face displays nothing but confidence.

She tightens her grip and locks eyes with me. "You didn't even know how to cut a pepper. If you can do this, I'll be excellent at it."

Having sat watching her for far too long, I stretch my back – twisting side to side, then leaning forward and back – making a show of it. If Destiny wants to sail, we'll sail.

It is time to take this bull by the horns.

"Let's do this." I untie the lines on the cleat nearest me, running through the movements like a pro.

Destiny is in for the ride of her life.

As Alejandro reels in the anchor, I prepare the lines and sails. "Raise the sails!" I shout, moving around Destiny as she frantically looks around, lines still in hand, as if the boat will tell her what to do.

Alejandro jumps into action, moving to the front of the boat while I pull the outhaul and raise the mainsail. I cleat the line while Alejandro raises the jib and cleats the halyard. The boat begins to move unsteadily. Destiny stands there with knees bent, bracing herself for action, while the sails flap in the wind. A strong crosswind snags at the main sail and hauls us forward.

"Cleat your line," I command, realizing Destiny is still holding onto the rope that secures the boom. She's about to be taken overboard if it's not secured quickly.

Despite her unsuccessful previous attempts, she winds the line in a figure-eight around the cleat and looks up triumphantly when the line pulls tight.

There may be hope for her after all. It is time to really test her, though.

"Destiny, tighten the sails, just to your left."

Destiny looks around and points to a loose rope. I nod in confirmation. She pulls the rope, and the reeling sound is like music to my ear. The sails tighten and the wind catches us almost instantly, tugging us forward, the pace quickens as Destiny successfully cleats her second line. But the speed is still too slow. We need a steeper angle to really catch the wind and move forward.

"We did it!" Destiny yells over the deafening whistle of the wind.

I laugh, not only at her excitement, but at her naivety. We are just getting started. Alejandro hops down to my side of the boat – the starboard – and gets in place to begin our maneuver. He's an expert sailor, knowing the maneuver I intend to perform, before I even have to tell him.

"Destiny, why don't you sit on the bow and watch, then you and David can trade places?" he suggests.

She gives him one of her infamous fiery looks but before she can respond, I say, "Dez can sit with me. I'll help her if you take the tiller."

Alejandro nods and moves to the tiller at the back of the boat. Destiny needs to learn how to manage the lines and transition from starboard to port before she can do anything else. I figure she has learned enough from Alejandro, and for both of our sake, I plan to take the lead on this lesson. With a look of condemnation, Destiny settles in to the bench beside me.

Yesterday, she was the boss. Today, I am. I can't help but think the playing field has leveled.

I wrap my right arm around her dainty waist and lace my fingers into hers – like she did when teaching me how to properly slice a pepper.

She tenses immediately and I feel, more than hear, her breath catch. It takes several seconds for her to release it, but she does. "Relax," I whisper in her ear.

Taking her other hand in mine, I lace our remaining fingers and run the line between both of them, getting a feel for the roughness of the rope between our fingers. Her hands are so small that it will be easy to maneuver the ropes like this. I think I could probably do this forever if I had to.

"I hope you're better at following instructions than you look. When I say move, you move," I say as Alejandro turns the boat away from the wind and we are forced to begin.

Destiny's shoulders shiver against my chest before she nods. Her lack of response stills me. It amplifies this moment like nothing I could have ever imagined. She is putting her trust in me. A literal stranger. Although, it doesn't feel like we are strangers.

She is opening herself to learning a new skill from a man she only recently met. A woman who is so clearly guarded and uninterested in trivial pursuits, yet she is allowing me to sit behind her and take control of her body. The pure, raw honesty behind the way she trusts me right now makes me respect her even more.

A small part of me hopes she doesn't pick up sailing easily and will always require my full, undivided attention. Because this feeling … This feeling feels like a gift.

"Get ready." Alejandro turns the tiller toward the boom and the wind catches the sail.

"Duck and move portside," I say to Destiny.

Keeping our hands on the line, I crouch and move us to the port-side bench. A momentary sharp pain pierces my shoulder, but I ignore it. Destiny allows me to move her, not giving any resistance. Our bodies connect and touch in so many interesting ways, but my favorite is the way her backside brushes against my groin.

The mainsail is well over the starboard side of the boat, and we are moving briskly through the water. Destiny still shivers slightly, and I fear that we will need to slow down, but when I lean over to peer at her face, she is smiling broadly.

"Can we do that again?" she asks excitedly.

"Alejandro, tack portside," I direct the instructor. He salutes and pivots the tiller portside.

The boom swerves back toward us. Destiny and I duck under and move back to starboard while the boat shifts direction once more. When we sit on the bench, her butt is jammed between my legs, pressing firmly into me as the force of the boat's movements pushes her back. At this point, my shoulder is on fire, but I continue to ignore the pain. There is no way in hell I will risk her moving from this position. Nor will I allow the pain to taint this experience like it does so many others.

"This is called tacking," I explain, both to teach her and distract myself. "You basically move side to side, catching the wind against your sails to propel forward into the direction of the wind. Does that make sense?"

"Yeah!" she says as her hair whips loose from her braid and whacks me in the face. It smells like jasmine and honey with a hint of sea water. It's transcendent – I think she's my new favorite scent.

We continue like this for several more turns before Destiny requests a break. She sits on the bow of the boat, holding onto the mast as Alejandro and I take the sailboat for a real ride. He is as experienced at sailing as I am, but he is spry and small, so he moves around well, which is good, considering he has to pick up some of the slack for me. The pain in my shoulder is a constant reminder of my healing injury, but I accept that it's just from the awkward movements of sailing, and soon Alejandro and I have the boat seamlessly cutting through the water.

As I look to the bow of the boat, I see the most beautiful sight in front of me. It isn't the wide-open ocean. It isn't the sun setting in the far west, or the expansive white sandy beaches.

It is her.

Destiny.

She is more captivating than the crystal-clear ocean water around us and more radiant than the sun above. Destiny is winning this game. Actually, I'm not even on the field – I'm on her sideline serving water.

16

DESTINY

I AM SITTING ON the bow and watching the water sweep by at an incredibly fast rate. Alejandro and David are behind me laughing and chatting as they sail us through the water. While my original intention was to come here and learn the basics of sailing, I am no longer interested in any of it. I'd rather let someone like David take the reins on this activity. Plus, watching him is far more pleasurable than doing the work.

I have learned the terminology and taken part in the act, but now I am just enjoying the ride and the company. When David wrapped his arms around me and intertwined our fingers, I was a shaking mess. Thank god he couldn't see my face. I was barely able to focus on our task, but he directed my body and helped me learn the movements. Near the end, his arms were barely doing the work as he let me take over. But he didn't stray far.

It wasn't the type of instruction I signed up for today, and while I was originally pissed at Rosa for letting another person join my lesson, I am now grateful. Alejandro wouldn't have been able to teach me half as much as David. Nor would I have had nearly as much fun.

"You want to take over, Dez?" David asks behind me.

I look back at him and shake my head. Hair flies wildly around my face, having snuck out of my tight braid, but I ignore it. The relaxing pull of the boat and companionable laughter has me feeling relaxed and careless.

It suddenly occurs to me that David has called me *Dez*.

I sit up and frown, distaste at the familiarity coating my tongue. Our bodies might have touched and rubbed up against each other in nearly every place possible for the past hour, but that doesn't mean we are on the nickname level.

"Did I say you could call me Dez?"

"No …" he says before looking back at Alejandro, who shouts a command as he turns the tiller. David tugs at the lines and swaps sides of the boat – doing the same thing we had done together earlier. The boom and mainsail swing across the deck and block my view of him.

I crawl under the jig to the other side of the boat and continue scolding David. "Only my friends call me Dez."

"Turning," Alejandro shouts, and David goes back under the boom as it swings in front of my face.

Damnit.

I crawl back under the jig to find David and Alejandro laughing at me as I scramble to sit up. The buttons of my blouse have loosened and my bikini top is close to fully slipping off. Their eyes delightfully absorb every ounce of exposed skin.

"You guys are assholes," I shout at them, adjusting my bikini, securing every button on the top.

They laugh louder at my snide comment, and if bones could grind, mine would be grinding. David pretends to wipe away unshed tears in his glimmering green eyes. They threaten to ensnare me. I flip the two men off and David's smile falters.

For a moment, I nearly regret my actions. But when David and Alejandro return to their tasks, I settle into the front of the boat again, savoring the illusion of privacy.

Eventually, we maintain a cruising speed, and Alejandro takes over steering the boat, letting the sail drift to one side as the boat cruises up the coastline. Without an invitation, David sits beside me on the bow.

"How do you like sailing?" he asks, leaning back on his forearms and squinting out at the ocean.

"I've been before," I say brazenly, feeling the need to shut down any more of David's flirtations.

"That doesn't answer my question."

"I don't like the question game."

"I've noticed. How else am I supposed to get to know you, though? You aren't one for openly sharing," he says, his irritation obvious as he sits up and stretches his arm.

"Why do you want to know anything about me? We're strangers who annoy the shit out of each other, and the freaking universe thinks it's hilarious, so it keeps pushing us together in situations like this," I let out an exasperated breath.

David lets out a frustrated sigh of his own. "I don't think it's some cruel joke that keeps pushing us together—"

"Do not say it's *destiny*," I cut in.

"Why do you keep thinking that's what I'm going to say?"

"Because you seem cheesy, and every cheesy man I've ever met loves to use my name as a pun."

"Noted. I won't ever use your name as a pun … Again." He winks.

"You're insufferable."

David's brow arches.

Apparently, my insult hit home. I feel a little bad. Just a little, but not enough to take it back. He is being a pain in my ass right now and I am not in the mood to waste energy turning him down again. Achilles will forever be a memory of that one vacation, where I met that one super-handsome man, whom I could have slept with, and it might have been life changing, but I chose not to because I'm a rational person.

"Is that really what you think? Because I think you like to sabotage any relationship before it starts because you're afraid of it working out."

I huff my indignation. This man's audacity is unparalleled. I poke my finger in his chest before letting him really know what I think. He looks utterly appalled – like he might bite off the finger I'm jabbing into his chest.

Good.

"You don't know shit about me. Just because I'm protecting my interests doesn't mean I'm afraid of love. Did it ever occur to you that I'm not interested in some random vacation hook-up? That I'm not some floozy vying to sleep with some rich NFL quarterback. Earth to David – the biggest jackass I've ever met – I'm not some cleat-chasing, gaping vagina, whore who wants to suck your dick so I can tell all my friends about it later."

David chokes on his own laughter and begins coughing. "Wow. We are so not on the same page right now."

"You think," I say sarcastically.

I expect him to say *screw you* and we go our separate ways. But he keeps laughing.

"Dez …" David says softly.

My blood boils at the transition in his tone and his use of my nickname. He hasn't earned the right to call me anything other than my full legal name. "I told you not to call me that," I say through gritted teeth. I am two seconds from shoving him off this boat.

"Actually, you said only your friends call you that. You didn't tell me I couldn't call you that," he argues. "And before you start cussing me out and assuming you know what I want or think, let me explain something."

I turn away, not wanting to hear some stupid excuse that has my head spinning, gut churning, and thighs clenching, but David catches my wrist and forces me to look back.

"Please, just give me a minute," he pleads.

"You have thirty seconds before I push you off this damn boat," I say, tugging my wrist out of his grasp and crossing my arms. His touch has a way of unnerving me and I need all the steely resolve I can muster.

"I'd like to see you try ..." he says under his breath before I shoot him another threatening look. "Okay. First off, I never thought you were anything close to the woman you described – the ones who chase after athletes like me. In fact, I know you aren't. If anything, you're the polar opposite. Second, I'm not interested in some random vacation hook-up either. I came here to be alone, not to find someone to bang. Have you even considered the reason I'm here? Do you honestly think it's to get my dick wet? I can do that in New York. I don't need to come all the way to Tulum to get laid! Lastly, I want to find your erratic, stubborn, bitchy attitude unattractive, but somehow, I find myself gravitating toward you the more offensive you become. It makes no sense, but I like it, and I want more of it. Are you so fucking stubborn that you can't tell when a man is actually interested in something more, or are you just that uninterested in me? Because the signs of your body tell me you're interested in at least one thing I have to offer."

What the hell?

No one talks to me like that. Ever. Except, I don't have time to be offended because his words are proof that we want the same thing. Achilles is nothing like the man I imagined him to be.

"Fuck Pat and Dale," I curse.

"What?" David asks. He is breathy and red in the face from his rant – proof of how much he means the words he says.

I want to turn back time and make him tell me something else, something that doesn't make me want to jump in his lap and suck on his face. Already, I can taste the saltiness of his skin on my tongue, and as disgusting as it should be, I know I'll love every bit of it.

"Fuck Pat and Dale!" I yell at the ocean, letting my frustration funnel into the resonation of my voice, hoping they can hear me from the shore.

"Are you okay?" David taps my shoulder. Thankfully, he is not looking at me like a crazy person. Although, he should be.

"I don't like to be wrong," I say.

"What were you wrong about?"

"We're not seriously going to play the question game, right?"

"If you responded with more than five words, we wouldn't have to," he retorts.

He has a point.

"I thought you were just some asshole looking to get in my pants. Which is fine, if that's what you're into, because we all need a release – but I don't want to be some notch on a man's bedpost. In my twenties, I would have been so down with whatever. Even now, I've considered it because … it's been a long time. But ultimately, I am looking for someone I truly connect with. Someone who can challenge me, who cares for me, who respects me. I'm looking for my equal, and it's been a struggle to find. I came on vacation to relax and not worry about life. Then I run into you, and you frustrate me in ways that I can't explain, and I have no idea what to do or how to act around you!" It is my turn to gasp down air. Revealing my internal struggles feels like a weight has lifted off my shoulders, yet it also feels like a new weight is hovering above them. The fear of his denial casts a shadow over me – a giant, leaching reflection of my doubt and lack of faith in men.

"You sound very confused," he suggests.

"Yeah, I am. You confuse me," I add nervously.

"You confuse me, too. For what it's worth. I never would've considered you a notch on my bedpost. You'd be like the whole damn thing," David jokes.

He has such odd ways of describing things, but I under-stand his explanation – he's telling me that I'm more than just a number to him, more than some random vacation fling – and I kind of like it. I kind of like the idea of exploring something more, but that shadow of fear remains.

"Good to know." I smile shyly.

He reaches across the small space between us. His hand touches mine and I jolt back. The lines in his cheeks soften as his smile disappears. Again, he attempts to hold my hand. This time, I allow him.

David studies the palms of my hand, running his calloused fingers over the soft pads, before intertwining our fingers. My knuckles brush the sides of his bony fingers as we settle into place – David leaning back on his elbows, keeping our hands interlocked, while I use the mast to support my weight.

While only our hands touch, I feel an invisible rope wrapping itself tightly around my heart and anchoring me to him. *Achilles* … The name becomes even more appropriate.

17

David

Since her confession, I kept our hands intertwined for as long as possible. I even walked her back to her room with our hands still locked together. She pulled out of my grasp a few times, but my fingers continued to find hers like a dog on a scent. Her hand felt so natural in mine, like it has been holding my hand for its entire life.

Other than our drastically different sizes, the only difference between Destiny and me is that she is clearly scared, and I am ready to dive into the deep end. She might have let her guard down for a moment, but I could already see her walls forming as she closed the door to her room between us, effectively shutting me out. I debated knocking and asking her to dinner tonight, but it's been a long day.

Frankly, I have nothing left to lose. With my career going up in flames and potentially forcing me into early retirement, I don't have much else to look forward to in life.

It's always been about football. Everything in my life has been about football.

Football.

Once, the only thing I found pleasure in, and now, the bane of my existence.

I shove all thoughts of football aside and focus on my Destiny. She is the only thing that has given me some reprieve on this vacation. Jumping on a last-minute flight to the first warm place I could think of has done nothing to distract me like I thought it would. Throwing darts at a photo of my teammates and drowning myself in booze has done nothing but make me sink deeper into my despair. Yet, when she came along – *Blondie*, as the old man likes to call her … a fucking beautiful viper, Medusa reincarnate is a more appropriate title for her, but I digress. She has turned my mood and quite possibly my world upside down.

It's not love at first sight. If anything, it's attraction at first fight.

But that's not even what has me so perplexed. She's like that defensive player who sneaks into your blind spot and slams into you so hard the ball pops loose and your helmet flies off. They hit you so hard and so suddenly that the jolt of the attack makes life seem like it's passing by in milliseconds. The pace of the world around you continues along; the defense has retrieved the ball and scored a touchdown, but you're still laying on the ground staring at the asshole who took you down. And while you aren't entirely happy about the outcome of events, you can't help but respect the player in front of you for their ability to take you down so brutally.

The ring of my cell phone jolts me from my daydream about Destiny. It's my agent, Blake.

"What do you got for me?"

"Good news and bad news," Blake says, getting straight to the point.

I've been waiting on this call, and he knows I don't like when people beat around the bush.

The sound of car horns and motors, doors opening and closing, people yelling at one another, and sirens fill the distant space behind his voice. It's not until now that I realize how peaceful it is here compared to my home of the last fifteen years. Maybe there is something about being in this climate and this place that has opened my eyes to the world around me.

"Can you get somewhere quieter? It's hard to hear," I say impatiently.

"Getting in the cab now. One second." He shuffles around, and slams a door shut. "Alright," Blake continues as if he didn't just give me an earful of him getting into a cab, "bad news is New York is putting you up as a free agent."

"Fuck," I curse under my breath. The news hits harder than it should, even though I knew this moment was coming. It feels like finding out your best friend is screwing your wife behind your back. While you might have suspected it, the news still bruises.

"Good news is I'm talking to the Chargers, and they're very interested in bringing you on. You could be looking at a better deal than you would have got from the Giants to extend your contract. They're confident in your ability and have no issue with age. I didn't even have to give them the whole Tom Brady and Aaron Rodgers speech."

"Los Angeles?" I ask, considering the team and the logistics of the move.

"Yeah. It's different. Different team. Different culture. This has yet to go public, and I think it'd be beneficial to get you in a meeting with management before it does. We need to have a game plan in place. We don't want people talking and putting misinformation in other people's ears – if you know what I mean."

Blake doesn't outwardly state it, but I know he is referring to my injury and the doubt that some teams may have about my ability to recover.

"Agreed."

"How soon can you get back to the States?" Blake asks, his voice cutting in and out between the tapping sound of fingers on glass.

"I can be back in a few days. Try to give me some notice if it has to be earlier." My vacation isn't due to end for another five days, but I've been avoiding this mess for far too long. While I want to stay here as long as Destiny does, some things are unavoidable, just like returning home – wherever home is for both of us.

"I'll do the best I can. Talk soon." Blake ends the conversation with his usual departing words. While he isn't overly polite, he gets the job done.

Blake has managed my career since I entered the league at twenty-three. I trust that he is finding me the best contract and best team possible. I'd be lying if I said it doesn't hurt finding out that the Giants are officially releasing me. I have dedicated so much time and effort to that team – helping build a bond between players that resulted in two national championships. But lately, I can feel the animosity building between my requests and leadership's goals.

They've been biding their time until they could find a solid replacement. My injury only sped up the process. They want someone who doesn't ask questions or push back on strategy. I simply can't help it. When you've been in the game this long, you start picking up on things that coaches can't see from the sidelines. I want a partnership and a place where my opinion matters. Hopefully, that doesn't put me out of a job. Hopefully, the Chargers – or even another team – can respect that.

If they don't, well, Destiny is going to have her hands full because I'll make her my new full-time job. I am a man with a lot of energy, and it needs exerting, but I have a sneaking suspicion she can keep up.

18

Destiny

We didn't talk much after the boat ride, but David's hand didn't stray far from mine, either. It was his way of accepting what I'd said without pushing the topic, while still confirming his intentions. It was confusing.

I am confused.

What type of person finds my sarcasm and profanity attractive? I think he's been hit on the head one too many times and is officially off his rocker. Or – and that is a big *or* – he actually *is* into me.

We don't know a lot about each other. It has only been three days and a few short hours each day that we've spent together. But there is an undeniable chemistry that I've been fighting. Plus, with all my friends coupled up, it would be nice to have someone to talk to while I am at the resort.

He is here alone. I am here alone.

Maybe, we can be here alone together. It's neither a novel nor absurd idea.

"Am I seeing things, or did I just see you and David Green holding hands?" Pat sing-songs behind me as I return from the gym.

After Achilles and my steamy sailing lesson, I needed a release. Something about Will and Taylor in the room next to mine makes me feel awkward jamming a vibrator up my cooch, so I opted for a different type of physical activity that makes me sweat even more.

Although, that one particular itch that seems to act up around David has yet to be relieved.

"You've been drinking. There's no telling what you think you saw," I say, unlocking my door and holding it open for him. Dale is hot on Pat's trail, holding two martini glasses with liquid sloshing over the sides as he attempts to catch up to us.

"I haven't been drinking and I know exactly what I saw," Pay winks as he struts past me. My room has basically become Pat and Dale's second accommodations. I'd gladly swap rooms with them if they asked. However, I have a sneaking suspicion they would find me regardless.

"Is there a reason I can't seem to escape you two?" I ask, walking up to my mini-fridge and grabbing three beers. It is my turn to initiate the drinking today. Despite the two-mile run I just completed, my body aches in places that only booze can numb right now.

"Want to tell us where you were all morning because I know it wasn't spent working?" Dale passes by me, abandoning the now-empty martini glasses on the coffee table and taking one of the three beers.

I open the patio door and motion them out onto the balcony. It connects with the lazy river, which is highly convenient because I desperately need to cool off. "I'd rather not share. Can we just get drunk, and you guys tell me all the funny things that happened today?" I pass Pat a beer as I open mine. "I'm going to change. Give me a minute."

Pat and Dale are already in their swimsuits, so they hop into the pool while I change and put on sunscreen. When I return, they give me their full, undivided attention – obtaining the sole focus of two gay men is never a good sign for a single straight woman.

"For starters, everyone has been asking why you've been so MIA this trip," Dale says, picking at his nails.

"Wait until they find out who you've been spending time with. Stacy might have a heart attack. She wants to invite him to dinner tonight," Pat adds.

"Wonderful," I say, sitting down on the edge of the slow-flowing water and dipping my calves in. The cool water soothes my freshly worn muscles, but it doesn't find its way any further north.

"Kat and Michelle were googling him today. Do you have any idea what he's worth? Oh! And holy shit!" Pat slaps his husband's arms excitedly, "He was on the cover of GQ last month. Girl! Drooling, jaw-on-the-floor, masturbation-worthy content," Pat gushes.

Dale's expression must replicate mine because Pat quickly moves on to more gossip-worthy topics, while I make a mental note to google Achilles' *GQ* cover later. "Also, it sounds like the Giants are going to release him. Not to bring down the mood, but I bet that's why he's here alone … He's probably trying to get out of New York before the ball drops."

An unfamiliar feeling pangs my chest – I hate hearing about David's personal affairs from someone else and not from the source directly. It makes me feel even more like an outsider, even though my hand was just joined to his for the past hour. He's clued me into his intentions – assuming he's being honest – but other than our short conversations, I don't know anything about him. It's not fair for me to presume I should already know the things Pat is telling me. But it still stings, and I feel an invisible protective shield building a wall between my friends, and David and me.

It must be tough constantly having your life on public display and I don't want my friends telling me things about David that he should be telling me himself. "You guys really shouldn't be speculating. Its none of our business, and half of the stuff in gossip magazines is just that – gossip."

"Are you defending the man already?" Dale looks up from picking dirt out from under his middle nail and lifts his brows so high they nearly touch his hairline.

"You know … I don't recall inviting you two into my room. Yet, you keep showing up!" I quip, changing topics and hoping to keep David's name out of their mouths.

"You happen to be one of the more interesting people here. We might be married, but those bitches are more domesticated than we're comfortable with." Pat wraps an arm around his husband's waist and kisses his cheek in not-so-subtle mockery.

"Mm hmm …" I lean back onto my palms, watching them. Pat and Dale love gossip as much as they love match-making. I don't for one instant believe their purpose for being in my room is innocent. They saw David and me walk by, and couldn't resist the urge to investigate some new juicy gossip.

"So …" Pat prods. "Was I right?"

Gossip-mongers.

"Maybe," I reply with a shrug.

"I knew it," Pat squeals as he and Dale high-five.

I deliberately wait for them to turn back to me so I can give them the biggest eye-roll of my life.

"Why are you not happier about this? Dating has been a nightmare in San Francisco. This guy has it all, does he not?" Dale genuinely asks.

Pat and Dale make it seem so easy. I remember the days Pat would scroll Grindr, and within five minutes he had a man rolling up to the bar in a Mercedes. Hooking up came first; then they'd consider if there was something more. It was simple. It was obvious. It was fun.

But I don't operate that way.

"How do you know he has it all? We're in a romantic setting, my blinders are on, and I'm lonely. He lives on the other side of the country. We'll never see each other again. This is a great way to get my heart and my head all screwed up because no matter how this ends, we are going our separate ways. And I'm not trying to date a man on the other side of the country. He has danger written all over him."

The words coming out of my mouth make so much sense. Yet, it feels like another person is saying them. The rational and irrational parts of me are blurring.

"Sounds kind of perfect," Pat says with an overly expressive eye wiggle.

"It's not. I want someone in my city. I'm too busy to be planning trips two time zones and hours of flights away with someone who has as insane of a schedule as I do." I begin to fully think through the obstacles of dating a man long distance, especially one who plays in the NFL. I may not know a lot about sports, but my friends are fans, so I've heard enough to know how it all works. Games are played every week for months on end, and as a former athlete myself, I know that training is a full-time job in itself.

"Couldn't you just get to know him a little and decide all that later? It's not like you've got to put a ring on it in three days, girl. Calm down." Dale rolls his eyes at me this time.

He has a point. I am being a little dramatic and thinking way too far into the future, but that is how my brain works – I'm always measuring the risk versus reward. And Achilles is screaming risk.

I don't even know if he and I have anything in common outside of our competitiveness. There is something physical between us, and it might very well be the only item under the reward list, but it's still a risk. That intense spark will likely result in us either being best friends or hating each other's guts. It might be worth exploring a little further – if only to find out if the reward is as big as I think.

Like Dale says, it's not like we are getting engaged after a few days. I can feel things out while keeping my heart at a safe distance until I determine the risk and reward.

"I guess I could see where things go in the next few days," I decide.

"I told you she'd come to her senses," Pat says to Dale.

"What's that supposed to mean?" I playfully kick water at Pat. The tension I hadn't realized this conversation caused is slowly seeping out of my shoulders. It's like half the stress I've incurred is because I simply can't decide what to do.

Before I receive a response or finish mulling over my inner contemplation, Pat and Dale pull me into the water and push my head under.

Darkness envelops me, and my breath escapes me as the water surrounds me. It feels a lot like jumping into a relationship. All you have is blind faith and a short amount of time before you know if the other person is going to let you sink or help you swim.

19

DAVID

I HAVE NO WAY of contacting Destiny, so I opt for walking around the resort, hoping to run into her. Except, I don't see her or any of her friends. After an hour of searching, I determine it is a lost cause. Plus, my stomach is beginning to complain.

After our sailing session this morning, I ordered room service, took a nap, hit the gym, then showered in hopes of meeting up with Destiny tonight. But it seems my luck has run its course.

Nevertheless, my mind and body are restless. There is a yearning to find Destiny, to spend what little time I have left here with her. I need to convince her that there is something more worth exploring between us, even if we've only just met.

Eventually, I'll go back to New York, or wherever my job takes me, and she'll go back to wherever she lives. I'll be kicking myself if I don't at least try to see what can become of us. Long-distance isn't ideal, and I honestly shouldn't be thinking about a relationship before we get to know each other, but for some reason, I have this gut feeling that there is something special about her.

Now that we are on the same page about our intentions, she's opened up to me. But my window closes every time she's away. I can feel the distance between us growing the longer we are apart. It makes the probability of pursuing something more while long-distance even less likely, but I push those thoughts to the back of my mind and focus on what is currently under my control.

During my idle wandering to find Destiny, I stumble on an Italian Steakhouse located in a small, appropriately themed building beside the main lobby. The pungent aroma of oregano and basil sneaks by my nostrils and makes my taste buds salivate. My stomach is already groaning its approval.

I request a table for one – it's always a table for one. A little sliver of sadness and longing makes my chest feel like it's concaving upon itself as the hostess seats me at a two-person table in the corner of the quaint restaurant. The small rickety table sits directly by the bathrooms.

You've got to be kidding me.

Just when I think my evening cannot get sadder, I hear the flush of a toilet and the clang of the bathroom door. I'm not done cringing by the time the man from the restroom walks by my table sans washed hands. I'm not the cleanest man, but that's fucking disgusting.

I search the restaurant for a better table, but there are only a couple tables without guests. One of which is a large hand-crafted wooden table in a glass-encased room with wine bottles mounted along the back wall.

That's more like it.

As the hostess turns to leave, I speak up. "I'd like the table over there," I say, nodding toward the private room.

"Um …" The hostess looks around nervously. "That table is by reservation only and you have to buy two bottles of wine. It isn't typically included in the cost of the accommodation."

If I have to eat alone, it won't be in the corner by the bathroom like the sad, lonely man I am. "It's fine. Bill it to my room."

The hostess nods eagerly and picks up my menu, steering me toward the glass case. Her doubt is no longer apparent, now that I have agreed to pay for additional items. I hope I haven't screwed myself into spending ten grand, but it's too late to back out now. Plus, sitting in a glass enclosure like some prized game winning football feels appropriate. I'm nearer to that reality – when you become a picture on the wall, a legend, something of the past, not the present – than I've ever been.

After sitting, a waiter greets me. "Buenos días, me nombre es Miguel. May I recommend several bottles of wine for you tonight?"

"I'll take the chef's recommendation on wine according to what I order and a water to start," I respond.

"Si, señor. Any starters?"

I glance at the menu, and my stomach rumbles louder as my eyes scan the never-ending list of carb-heavy appetizers. It's like this menu was made for me. Tonight is looking up. "One of each appetizer." I decide to go all out. The wine might not be included in the cost of my insanely expensive bungalow, but the food is still free.

"Very good, and will anyone else be joining you?" the waiter asks, glancing around at the numerous empty chairs around me.

"No," I say curtly as my eyes catch sight of the old man – Richard – being seated at the bathroom table. "Actually, I'll have one more."

I wave Richard over.

Richard walks over with the ease and fluidity of a much younger man. "How's it going, son?" Only his choice of words, the color of his hair, and the deep lines in his face give away his age.

"Care to join me for dinner? No reason we should both dine alone in the same restaurant at the same time," I joke.

"You've got a point there. Give us your oldest Bordeaux and put it on my tab. The boy and I have some talking to do," Richard tells the waiter before giving me a curious look.

"We do?"

"I saw you and Blondie – holding hands. There's got to be a good story in this …" It occurs to me that Richard is still under the impression Destiny is married.

"Oh, shit." I laugh. "First of all, she's not married – thankfully. That would have been messy."

"You're telling me – a Bordeaux isn't appropriate for this type of conversation." He looks back for the waiter, who is nowhere to be found and likely already retrieving the bottle. "Well, I suppose I could tell you about my own tryst with a married woman, actually, several married women, but only one story is worthy of a Bordeaux. Anyway, let's hear yours first." Richard's quite the talker tonight.

"It's not much of a story …"

"Says who? Come on, entertain an old man."

"You don't look like you're in need of entertainment," I counter. Something about Richard's spirited personality tells me he has lived life to its fullest, and any stories I share will pale in comparison to his.

"I don't know if you've looked around lately, but there isn't much for single men like you and me to do around here other than find kinship in each other, or, if we're lucky, get laid," he says slyly.

"Well, I didn't get laid!" I laugh. "And honestly, I don't even care. Right now, I just want to get to know her more."

"If I'm not mistaken, I'd say you're falling for Blondie, and falling hard, son." Richard jabs.

He's right, but I don't admit it. "We'll see where it goes. I was hoping to get more time with her, but she's sort of busy with her friends."

"I can see that."

"You can?"

Richard looks toward the door as Destiny and her friends are walking in. He continues talking, but I hear none of it. Theres a ringing in my ears as soon as my eyes land on her. My vision is laser focused on her. She looks so goddamn beautiful.

Destiny's hair cascades down her back in loose beachy waves. She is wearing a dangerously short black dress with heels the color of her skin. They blend in with her luminous long legs, making them appear even longer and even more tantalizing. The neckline of her dress stops just below where the curve of her neck begins, hiding every bit of her ample cleavage, and a simple diamond necklace rests on her boney collarbone. The shimmering jewelry catches my eye, but the neckline of her dress stops me from seeing what I desire. It's such a boner killer, which I suppose is the idea, because I can't stop thinking about where those legs should be instead.

Preferably around my waist or shoulders.

Destiny is walking between Pat and Dale, and they are deep in laughter. Her cheeks are flushed as if she spent the day in the sun, and her eyes are a little hazy.

Is she drunk?

The gamble on her level of intoxication begins, and I find myself drawn to know that side of her. Despite all our previous encounters, I've never seen her cheeks flushed from anything other than disconcertment.

Either way – it's hot. She's a vision.

Richard shakes my shoulder and my jaw snaps up. I wasn't aware that it had fallen on the floor. "What?" I ask, turning back to him. It takes my eyes a moment to adjust and see him clearly under the florescent lights – as if looking at Destiny made them dilate.

"I'm going to take my leave. Ask the lady to come over. Bottle's on me." Richard winks and stands.

"Wait. You don't have to go," I say, glancing over as Destiny and her friends are seated. Destiny's backside is now facing me and I'm speechless once again. The black dress emphasizes her curves, cutting in at her petite waist, tightly hugging the curve of her ass and making every voluptuous part of it pop.

She's not just a vision. She's a fucking snack, and I might just lose it right here, right now.

"Son, if I have any advice to give you – it would be to never wait for your chance. Life keeps on moving, and if you don't seize the moment, you'll keep on wondering where it all went wrong. You control your destiny, nobody else."

I am stunned. Not only by Destiny, but by Richard's advice. It's so dumbfoundingly obvious. Yet, it's something I've never really taken to heart. And as I eye Destiny, the realization fully settles – I'd be a fucking idiot if I didn't pursue this.

"Thanks for the advice, Richard."

"Any time. Good luck," he says, shakes my hand and stands as the waiter arrives with our appetizers. Richard plucks a mozzarella stick off a plate and pops it into his mouth, giving me a smile and another wink as he leaves.

At first, I didn't think this vacation was helping solve any of my problems. But in my short encounters with Destiny and my sparse moments with Richard, these two people have opened my eyes. Not only am I moving forward in my career by looking into a partnership with another team – something I hadn't even considered weeks ago – but I have met someone. Someone who … changes other aspects of me. Someone who makes me think about something other than football. And that's never happened before.

I return my attention to Destiny and watch as she converses with her friends. She is an enigma. Her hands are waving animatedly as she talks across the table. Her face is alight with magnetic energy. I want to be sitting next to her, absorbing the warmth radiating from her glow.

Destiny is the total package. Her sharp, witty tongue, her soft curves, and her venomous determination – it is exactly what I need in life. Her and football, and I'll be a happy man.

Who would have though *Medusa* could ensnare me? Although, I suppose she ensnares everyone.

A waving motion catches my attention on the other side of the table – Stacy is gesturing frantically in my direction. This is my chance. I give her a small, brief wave, keeping it nonchalant. She takes it as an invitation to say hello and gets up from the table. Destiny completely ignores her friend.

"Hi!" Stacy's head pops around the corner of the glass door.

"Hey. Nice to see you again," I say.

"You're welcome to join us for dinner," Stacy says, walking up to the dining table and looking curiously at the abhorrent amount of food on display for one person. "Even though I see you've already ordered," she adds, placing a familiar hand on my shoulder.

I stare at the hand before looking up at the woman I want to be touching me. I have her attention now. Destiny's lips are pressed into a firm, straight line. Her eyes burn like lasers and they are directed solely toward her friend.

Game point.
Stacy, the bride-to-be, seems harmless, but her touch-iness clearly disturbs Destiny, and I can't have Destiny doubting my intentions again. It is time to draw a line in the sand and make them clear to everyone, so that when Destiny doubts me again, her friends will remind her not to.

"Why don't you all join me for dinner? The wine's on me – consider it a wedding gift to you and Ryan," I suggest in return, removing her hand from my shoulder.

"David! Oh my god, you are too kind!" Stacy ignores my attempt to create space between us and basically leaps into my lap as she hugs me.

From behind the robust woman squeezing me tightly, I see Destiny's eyes narrow as she sucks in her cheeks. The fury written on her face makes my dick throb in anticipation of the heated words racing through her vindictive mind. I love seeing that fire in her.

Stacy returns to her table and ushers everyone over to my glass enclosure. Destiny's eyes lock with mine, but her expression is unreadable.

Her friends file into the room, taking seats at the expansive table, more than large enough to seat everyone. The men shake my hand and pat me on the back, except for Pat and Dale, who hug me tightly and linger longer than I'd prefer, while the woman in Destiny's group of friends give me a quick side hug

Destiny is the last to enter.

Her eyes never left mine as greetings were made, and a series of emotions skids across her face as she finally approaches me. But then, her face transforms. She smiles at me.

She genuinely smiles.

It is like a sucker punch to the gut – sudden, unexpected, and it nearly sends me doubling over.

The tension in the air between us grows thick. The world around us disappears. My hand longs to be in hers again, so I reach for her. Gently I lift her fingers, and our cold clammy palms press together. Destiny's bottom lip trembles slightly as words fail to find her.

I lean in and kiss her on the cheek as I whisper, "Good to see you again, Destiny."

"You too," she says softly.

We turn toward the table to find Pat shooing Stacy away from the chair beside mine. Destiny giggles, no longer jealous and clearly amused by her friend. When Stacy is back beside her fiancé – where she belongs – I pull out the chair for Destiny and sit down beside her.

It feels right sitting beside her, our shoulders mere inches apart and her legs within touching distance. *Damn.* Her legs are mesmerizing, and her freshly tanned skin glows under the soft golden overhead lighting. My dick is doing all the thinking tonight, no matter how hard I try to calm it.

"David, how kind of you to invite us over for dinner," Pat speaks up before everyone else begins to chatter.

"No problem. I hope I didn't spoil any of your plans. I've got a bottle of wine open here that you guys are welcome to, and I'm happy to order more."

"You don't need to do that. These assholes will drink the cellar dry, and they're more than capable of paying for it themselves." Destiny gives her friends a warning look.

I appreciate her jumping in. It's cute.

"That we are, but the man's offering, Destiny. Learn to say *yes and thank you*, not, *no and I'll have something else*," Pat says sassily, pouring himself a full glass of red wine.

Destiny's cheeks flush an even brighter red. I have a feeling Pat is talking about more than the wine I am offering when he suggests she learn to say *yes* and *thank you*. I would high-five the man if his comments weren't embarrassing Destiny.

"So, David … What are your plans tomorrow night?" Stacy asks from across the table. Her fiancé, Ryan, sits back quietly and watches her flirt with me. He doesn't seem to mind at all, but I do. Whatever she is thinking of doing tomorrow night is not something I want to participate in.

"I don't have plans," I reply warily, glancing at Destiny and hoping she will give Stacy another one of her Medusa-level looks.

"You should come to our wedding!" Stacy claps her hands as if she has just thought of the world's most fantastic idea.

"While I appreciate the invite, it seems like an intimate affair. I wouldn't want to intrude," I excuse myself, being careful not to overstep the boundaries Destiny has drawn.

"Nonsense," Ryan finally speaks up, supporting his wife-to-be. "We'd love to have you!"

"Why don't you give him time to consider it?" Destiny adds tactfully.

"Thanks, Dez," I whisper in her ear. Her hair tickles my upper lip so I tuck the wavy strand of blonde hair behind her ear.

She flashes me a quick grin before her eyes dart away, confirming none of her friends caught the subtle flirting.

"Wine?" I ask, snatching the bottle of wine Richard ordered before her friends finish it.

"Yes, please," Destiny says, moving her empty wine glass closer to me while still avoiding eye contact.

I pour the wine, shifting my gaze between Destiny and the glass. She watches the stream of liquor intently, doing everything possible to avoid looking directly at me. Is Destiny shy?

"Is this okay?" I slide my hand over her exposed thigh at the same time I slide her glass closer to her. I'm pushing the limits, but I can't resist. The possibility of unnerving her makes my dick throb.

If there is ever a time to figure out her true feelings, it is now. I am taking my chance, just as Richard advised. Plus, Destiny's skin has taunted me long enough.

Her skin is so fucking soft.

Even though she brushed off my earlier compliment about her skin and mentioned other men commenting on it as well, I'll never quit telling her how amazing it feels. She truly has the smoothest, softest skin I've ever felt.

"Which part of this are you asking is okay?" She tilts her head, looking me square in the eyes as a confident smirk lifts the left edge of her lip. There is no shyness in her look now.

Damn.

The look on Destiny's face stirs my dick to life. Gone is the cold serpent queen; here is the goddess of desire.

"This," I reply, flattening my hand against her leg and running it across her thigh. My fingertips brush the inner part of her leg, and she squeezes them together, trapping my fingers between her thighs before I explore further. I didn't plan on touching her intimately at dinner, but my fingers can't resist following the trail of smoother skin up her thighs to the place that sits between them.

"Everything is better in moderation," Destiny says, pushing her hand between her thighs and lacing our fingers. She pulls our hands out and places them on top of her thigh. Her hand lingers for a moment before she unlaces our fingers but allows my hand to remain flat against her leg again.

I watch as she straightens her back and diverts her attention to the wine, swirling and smelling it before taking a sip. She swishes the liquid in her mouth, then swallows. The liquid rolls down the column of her exposed throat, and as my eyes move up her long porcelain neck to land on her red painted lips, she licks a droplet of wine from her bottom lip. I swear my dick twitches after watching her tongue move across the soft planes of her plump lips.

"You have good taste," she comments.

"Thanks," I respond automatically, unable to steer my eyes away from her pillowy lips.

"Nonetheless," Destiny replies, glancing at me finally, noticing the intensity of my gaze.

Her cheeks go molten, igniting a carnal need inside me that makes me want to fuck her on this dinner table. I divert my eyes and shift the conversation before my cravings get the better of me. Acting like a horny teenager will not get me far with a woman of Destiny's caliber. "If I didn't know any better, I'd say you're trying to compliment me," I answer, fueling her usual desire to retort my assumptions.

"And if you were more well-mannered, you'd know better than to address it." Her sharp tongue makes an entrance and gives me a welcome lashing.

Fuck. I love it.

I am trying so hard not to think with my dick, but she makes it unable to resist. I lift my hand to her face, tucking the strand of hair that keeps slipping loose behind her ear before cupping her cheek. She sits stiff as a board, but she doesn't stop me as I lean in.

Closing in on the space between us, my lips brush her ear. "If I were more well-mannered, I would've told you how beautiful you look tonight. But I'm not well-mannered, and my thoughts about the way you look would make even Pat and Dale blush."

Counter that, Destiny.

20

Destiny

Holy shit.

David knows how to make a woman's knees weak. While he didn't tell me exactly what was on his mind or what he wanted to do to me, I have a pretty good imagination, and after the way his hand stroked my inner thighs, I know *exactly* how he feels and *exactly* where else his hands want to explore.

Pat and Dale got drunk with me by the pool so I would work up the nerve to walk to David's bungalow tonight and have a deeper conversation about our intentions.

Considering I already have a major lady boner for Achilles, and never mind the fact that alcohol never results in solving problems, does nothing to deter me from consuming more liquor. If anything, the stress relief from overconsumption is helping lull the embarrassment of my sexual vexation.

Every time those forest-green eyes look at me, my toes curl. The combination of his hand, his eyes, and his words are too much for a single woman to handle. I might combust and jump his bones right here, right now, at this dinner table with all my friends to witness.

I keep reminding myself that Achilles and I need more time together – I need to figure out if he's worth pursuing something more with and not just a random hookup. It's clear my feelings are already involved; there is no going back on that front. But there is still a chance to stop this from moving any further sexually. Despite how much my body begs for more.

Showing up at his bungalow later tonight would have been so much simpler than what is happening right now. Having dinner with the infuriatingly handsome, touchy Achilles is not something I anticipated, and it puts me at a total disadvantage, with no time to figure out what to say or do. And this wine is making my head fuzzy – convincing me that my bodily needs should take priority.

David's light caresses and sensual banter have basically made me melt into a puddle – a puddle on the floor that is slowly drifting toward the sewage grate to party with the same type of trash that currently occupies my mind.

On one hand, I could just sleep with him to appease the sexual frustration that is clouding my judgment. Then, I'd have a clear mind to really assess if there is any other type of connection between us. That was Pat's suggestion. Or I could get drunk, lay out all my issues, tell Achilles everything about myself, and see if he is still interested, but not sleep with him. That was Dale's suggestion.

Their final suggestion – on which they both whole-heartedly agreed – was to do both: sleep with him and open up to him. I argued that I could do neither instead. Why go to his bungalow at all? Why not avoid the confrontation with David altogether?

While I'm still debating the options, a small part of me thinks relying on alcohol to decide is the easiest option of them all. People say your truest self and deepest desires come to the surface when you're intoxicated. There is also the possibility that drinking enough booze will put me to sleep early and allow me to deal with this predicament later.

A very convincing part of me thinks the final and best option is to run far, far away, because David's rough fingers splayed across my thigh are growing hotter by the minute and choices are about to be thrown out the door.

Pat would be cheering for that outcome.

"Destiny," David asks, still cupping my cheek with his palm.

His fingers are so long they reach the back of my skull, and I feel him rubbing small circles at the base of my neck. I don't know if he is intending to disrupt my entire being with that one little touch, but he is.

He is cheating, relaxing one part of my body while exciting the other. He puts me in some type of voodoo trance that I am not equipped to fight against – not in my current state nor likely any other.

"Mm hmm …" I respond, closing my eyes and leaning against the pressure of his fingertips. Achilles' fingers knead against my tense spine, loosening the taut muscles in my neck from all of my internal conflict, and I immediately envision what those talented fingers can do elsewhere.

Stop it, Destiny.

As if David feels the same primal desire rising and aversion to it, he jerks away before the situation escalates. I am left feeling empty and deprived.

"While I love the look on your face right now, we should get back to dinner," he says huskily.

I glance around the table to find Stacy, Kat, Pat, and Will staring at us. Stacy and Kat look ecstatic, Pat gives me a cocky grin, and Will is openly frowning his disapproval. The others are busy looking at their menus or engaging in polite discussion. The physical connection between David and me is undeniable.

I've lost myself in him, and that is not a usual occurrence.

Three days ago, we were enemies, standing on opposing sides and readying for a battle neither of us could have fully prepared ourselves for. I'm not sure how or when I changed sides so quickly, but one thing is clear – David is a fierce competitor. If he is vying for my heart, I am in deep shit – if I'm not already.

"So, what's everyone ordering?" I ask casually, clearing my throat and breaking the awkward tension in the air.

"I'm ordering shots because damn, that right there," Pat's pointer finger draws an invisible circle around David and me, "was fire, and I need something to calm me down – if you know what I mean!"

The entire table bursts out laughing, tension snapped, even my well-mannered friends who are actively pretending to ignore the uncomfortable situation. Well, everyone except Will. His face is doing that thing where one eye and the side of lip try to touch. I became very familiar with this look during our break-up. But I won't allow his reaction to make me feel guilty about lusting after David. It's been a year since Will and I were anything more than friends, and he's been all over his new girlfriend this trip. I'd know; I can hear it from my room.

"Shots? Shots? Shots?" Pat points at everyone, asking for a count before gesturing to the waiter and ordering a round of shots for the table.

When the waiter returns with a tray full of short glasses and clear liquor, David and I accept them graciously. I think we both need a downer. Things are getting way too heated and we have just started dinner. I don't even want to think about what might occur afterward if the tension between us is already this thick.

Although, dinner continues without a hitch. Pat and Dale surprisingly keep their mouths shut, refraining from further inappropriate teasing. My other friends are a bit too inquisitive about David's career, but it's not every day you meet a *legend* – as Ryan and Stacy both deem him.

"What are you guys doing after dinner?" David asks the group as we finish our dessert.

"I think we should go to one of the late-night bars. They're playing salsa music tonight," Michelle chimes in; she and Javier are sitting on the far end of the table and have been quiet tonight. She hasn't had enough to drink yet, but will surely be spewing indecent proposals as the liquor starts flowing more liberally.

"Yeah, that sounds fun!" Kat agrees.

"I'd rather go drink in the pool outside our room," Ryan suggests.

Everyone has their own opinion on where we should go and what we should do for the night. Technically, tonight is supposed to be Stacy and Ryan's reception–although they finished the walk-through hours ago–but I will do whatever they prefer. No matter what ideas David's constantly wandering hand has been giving me.

"Do you have plans, David? You should join us," says Stacy, directing the conversation to David. Her heavy-lidded eyes are set on him, like he's a freshly baked cookie, ready for eating.

Stacy needs to get her cleat-chasing mind out of the gutter and refocus on her soon-to-be husband. I get the sense that she and Ryan have some weird arrangement that involves a hall pass or potential threesome. That will not be happening with me around, though.

Not because I am locking David down–he can do whatever he wants.

Or can he?

Honestly, I am not sure how I would feel seeing David with another woman, but I definitely don't want him touching any of my friends the way he has been rubbing my thigh. That action is reserved for me. At least, until the end of this trip, or if I decide otherwise tonight.

"I was thinking about going to the pool at my bungalow, but," David says, looking at me, "I wouldn't mind hanging out with you all. If you want me to?" He phrases his response as a question to me and only me.

That twinge of jealousy and indifference evaporates as soon as his eyes lock onto mine.

"Yeah! Yes. I want to!" I stutter, blurting out a decision before I even process what spending more time with this man could mean. Clearly, the booze has caught up to me, and is making decisions that my lady parts firmly agree with. Only time will tell if it is a good one or not, but I am officially along for the ride.

"Does your bungalow have a private pool? I thought I saw on the website that some had their own pool and jacuzzi!" Taylor says from the other end of the table. She's also been quiet tonight – I almost forgot she was here.

The scowl on Will's face is now directed toward Taylor. He clearly isn't enthusiastic about his girlfriend engaging in conversation with David, but I am thankful his attention is elsewhere – where it belongs. He has successfully distracted her from any dinner conversation that included David until now.

Apparently, Taylor isn't one to be bossed around for too long though. I feel a little appreciation for her defiance, even though I don't like her inquisitiveness about David's accommodations.

"It does. You all are welcome to come over if you want to chill by the pool," David says to the group, not just Taylor.

I applaud him for being considerate of where his attention is focused. For a man who has an entire table of people fawning over him, he knows how to make his intentions clear. It irks me that I was the only one who couldn't see it before.

My friends' brows and lips turn up at the invitation. They wouldn't miss an invite to his place for the world; I know this group too well. They'll be talking about partying with an NFL quarterback for months after this trip ends and will also likely be full of compliments for Achilles.

This man will be the bane of my existence if things go south.

David is the ultimate gentleman – catering to my us all evening, buying bottles upon bottles of wine. My friends would have been satisfied with the house wine, or bought their own bottle, but he insisted. I have a sneaking suspicion he is trying to impress me.

And it is working, but not because of the amount of money he is spending. I don't need a man to take care of me financially, but that doesn't mean I don't appreciate when he is trying to make a good impression or simply being genuinely hospitable.

The only question I have about David now is whether this is really who he is or if he is putting on an act for my sake?

I've run into more than one man who made a good first, second, even third impression before they showed their true colors. It usually comes down to the same issue – they can't deal with my success or schedule. My job competes with their ego more often than it should and often results in a regression of their personality to childlike behavior.

David is a force to be reckoned with in terms of athletic prowess. I don't need to research how many starting NFL quarterbacks there are in the league and how difficult it must be to maintain his position for as long as he has to know he should be taken seriously.

Plus, I am not blind – Achilles is in his mid to late thirties. With my limited knowledge of professional sports and the human body, I know that most players are young. Our bodies can only take the wear and tear of intense training and physical activity for so long. The fact that David is still doing it is commendable.

Based on our dinner conversation and my inferences, he's gained quite a reputation among sports fans over the past decade.

As we stand to leave, David places his hand on the curve in my lower back and steers me to the side of the dining room as my friends exit. Everyone's plan is to return to their rooms, change into swimsuits, and meet at David's bungalow.

"Can I walk you back to your room? I know you know the way to my place, but it feels odd letting you go, only to see you again in twenty minutes," he says.

His gentlemanly act is in full flow – something he didn't seem to possess an ounce of yesterday. "You didn't ask me if you could walk me home yesterday morning and now – after a two-hour dinner with my friends – you ask to escort me?"

David chuckles. "Well, it seemed like it pissed you off yesterday. I thought for sure I wouldn't see you again after that, so I'm trying to do the right thing here and not scare you off. But honestly, if you said no, I'd probably just walk behind you in the shadows anyways. Nothing else to do," he says with a shrug.

The simplicity and confidence in his unusual behavior calls to me like a siren in a storm. Achilles is utterly un-apologetic about his stalkerish tendencies – something that should scream red-flags, but instead has me drooling.

I find it endearing. And sexy.

Red flags or not, his stubborn passion and stalkerish resolve level out his gentility perfectly.

"You know that's creepy, right?" I quip.

"I can get away with being creepy," he states confidently as if he knows how much I like the balance between his polite facade and control-freak tendencies.

I don't allow myself to visibly agree with such an arrogant statement, even though I do.

I really do.

"Is that so? If I had half a brain – and yes, I said half because currently all of my brain is boozed up and not working correctly – I would stay far, far away from you. But I have a feeling that's not what you want." I admit.

We walk toward my room, weaving between palm trees on the dimly lit concrete path. The smile on David's face is a far cry from offended; he's drawn to my combativeness like a moth to a flame.

"Noted. I guess I just need to keep you boozed up, so you never come to your senses." David elbows my side playfully, tickling the sensitive spot under my rib cage.

I elbow him back, digging my bony point into his firm side and grinding it against what I imagine are mounds of muscle. He cackles, jumping away from me and catching my arms, forcing me to stop.

Achilles is ticklish.

Unable to resist, I lunge for his side, fingers splayed and ready to attack, but David is built for this type of game.

He easily skirts aside and traps both of my hands in one of his. Tugging my back roughly to his chest, he secures my arms under his forearm. His fingers nimbly and purposefully dig into my side, tickling me. A hysterical laugh escapes my lips and David's fingers dig deeper. I squirm, swiveling my hips and bucking my chest to get free, but his strength overpowers me.

I love it. I haven't felt this young, carefree, and turned on since I was in my early twenties.

Before I swivel my hips one more time, David's hands abandon my arms, disconnecting our embrace as he interlaces our fingers and continues our walk.

My breaths come in heavy pants as I recover from the stomach pain of laughter and the searing burn of our bodies touching.

Somehow, I recover.

David holds my hand with a gentleness that is so unexpected for a man of his size. My fingers are barely able to wrap around his, grazing just past the rounds of his knuckles. The pads of his hand and the tips of his fingers are roughly calloused – a result of his profession, no doubt – and an opposing force to my unmarred, smooth palms.

"Let me preface this next statement by saying I'm not trying to make a joke about your name," David breaks the comfortable silence between us, "but I get this feeling that we were meant to meet here. I don't know a lot about you.

From what Pat and Dale say, you're an extremely accomplished woman."

I try to ignore his comment about our fates being aligned. My name is Destiny, which makes ignoring destiny difficult at times, but I choose to believe that there is no such thing. Instead, I focus on the latter part of his sentence. I don't know the details of Pat and Dale's education session, but my company is my life, so it is no surprise they would mention my dedication to it and my success. Yet, I still don't understand why David wants to talk about it.

He continues, "You may not know a lot about sports, but I'd say I'm as dedicated to my career as you are to yours. I don't know what your dating experience has been, but mine has been less than sub-par. Women only want me for my money and fame. I'd guess yours has something to do with men being unable to handle your success. Men are proud like that."

He hits the nail on the head.

Yes, they are proud, and, no, they can't usually handle my success. It is refreshing to hear someone understand my problem without having to explain it, but it also feels like an invasion of my privacy. These are things I hold close, things I don't share, and somehow, David seems to already know them about me.

He continues without allowing me time to respond, "I wouldn't be like that. I admire someone who knows what hard work is and is willing to put in the time."

I've suspected as much, but why is he telling me this? He is promising me something without even knowing me. "Why are you telling me this, David?"

"I just want you to know."

"Really? What's the catch?"

I don't believe a word he says. There is always a reason why people disclose their feelings – whether they know the reason or not. Does he want me to say I believe he will be different? I can't say something I don't believe is true.

Not until I know with absolute certainty.

This conversation is broaching familiarity that I thought we would discuss much later.

"I'm serious. I just wanted you to know how I felt about it. Because I feel like you should. I'm sure a lot of guys tell you that when you meet them, so it may not carry any weight, but I wanted to put it out there."

He is being too genuine, too openly honest. It is adorably frightening. Either I have been waiting for this man my entire life, or he is the king of playing the dating game because he's telling me everything I never knew I needed to know.

But he is wrong about one thing. Men never approach the subject early on, because they don't want to think about it until it is so far into their line of sight that they can't ignore it any longer.

"I appreciate it. This is me," I say, turning the corner that leads to my room, desperate to get away from this conversation.

We are getting too deep. He is drifting into a section of my life that isn't meant to surface tonight. I've fully committed to the alcohol numbing my senses and allowing my body to make decisions over my brain, but the further our conversation delves, the more sober and scared I become.

I don't know why any part of me thought going to his bungalow and putting all my dating insecurities on the line tonight would be a good idea because this talk is nearing my breaking point – the point where it all comes out, the point where my heart is exposed, the point where I can't come back from a hookup because my feelings are too deeply entwined.

We reach the room after what feels like walking a mile. My mind is racing, my brow sweating. I am not prepared for where the night has taken me. Although, I have yet to be prepared for anything when it comes to him.

Achilles.

David waits outside the room and allows me privacy to change into my swimsuit. It takes me longer than usual – mainly because I can't decide which suit to wear. A fine representation of how disjointed and indecisive my mind feels. Should I go for slutty or conservative? Who am I kidding? All my swimsuits look slutty. I opt for less is more on bikinis because I hate tan lines. My buzz is dwindling, and with it my nerve to do anything other than run away from the man who waits outside my room.

A knock at the door catches my attention, David says: "Your friends just passed. You ready?"

"Yeah – one second."

I blindly select a swimsuit and decide to accept whatever happens tonight. To not fight my feelings and just allow myself to have fun, to take chances, and to give in to the possibility of a man being able to accept and appreciate all of me. If he turns out to be wrong for me, and just an insecure player, I will write this experience off like I have every other. It will be like firing a bad employee – just rip off the Band-Aid and exit the situation. The answer seems so much simpler than I know it will be.

We meet my friends at the entrance to the private section, and David leads everyone to his bungalow. I have obviously never made it inside the bungalows, but they are nice. Like, super freaking nice.

His accommodation features two bedrooms, two bathrooms, a living room, and a large kitchenette. All expertly styled with lavish furniture and artwork. A mid-sized pool and jacuzzi open to the patio and are enclosed by greenery, giving it a sexy ambiance. I could definitely see myself spending an entire week here. No wonder he was pissed when I invaded his privacy.

As expected, everyone makes themselves at home. They pour drinks, cannonball into the pool, and lounge around like they own the place.

"Sorry about them," I say to David, cringing when Pat runs inside and grabs a bottle of champagne from the refrigerator. Champagne is not readily supplied in our mini-fridges, and Pat has no shame in drinking all the booze provided in David's more upscale accommodations.

David and I are still in the living room, watching the others through the sliding glass doors that lead to the back patio. I'm not sure what has held me behind – whether to avoid removing my cover-up and exposing more of my body to David's touch, or to test the waters of his prying mind and decide if I should run back to my room now.

"I don't mind. It's better than being here alone. Honestly, the start of this trip wasn't great for me. I was in a bad headspace," he says seriously.

I want to ask why, but I am not sure if it is my place and the conversation threatens to go deeper again. Granted, I previously told myself to get to know him before I decide to cut him out completely or sleep with him casually, but our earlier conversation has me shaking.

"Why?" I ask cautiously.

"My team just listed me as a free agent. I could be entering retirement sooner than I hoped," he says bluntly.

"Oh my gosh, David … I'm so sorry." I turn to face him, totally forgetting about my own problems.

I cannot imagine what it would feel like if my investors forced me out of the company. After all, I am nearly to the point where the investors hold as much decision-making power as I do. It's a risk that grows larger by the day. One wrong move, and everything I've worked for could be taken from me.

He is dealing with a life-changing issue and he is putting it all on the table for me bear witness. I was not expecting him to share such personal details about his life, such tribulations, but this man needs a friend right now. I can be that support.

"Yeah. I just got the news about my contract earlier today. It's been rough, but I'm starting to think it could be a good thing."

"Really, how?"

"There're other options for me – career-wise. After being in the game for over a decade, I've made a lot of connections. I actually didn't think there were other options until I met you," he says, rubbing his shoulder shyly.

"Until you met me?" I ask, confused about how I could have anything to do with his career options.

"Yeah. Something about being around you has made me see things differently."

I don't know whether to be flattered or concerned. If David can lay it all on the line, maybe I can too. He isn't trying to compete with me or win me over for an ego boost.

He is looking for a confidant, a friend, a lifeline in this hectic world.

And wasn't that what I was searching for, too?

Interrupting my thoughts, David says, "Sorry to bring the mood down. I just thought you should know. It felt right to tell you … I haven't really been able to talk to anyone else about it, and I feel like I can trust you."

David's need to share with me – someone he can trust – is like a bullet to the heart. It strikes true and it breaks me. If this is his game plan – if he even has a game plan – he is hitting every mark.

21

DAVID

DESTINY WAS DUMBSTRUCK BY my admission. Frankly, I was a little stunned as well. Sharing the event that has haunted me for weeks feels like a weight lifted off my shoulders. And her supportive response is perfect – she doesn't apologize for my situation or feel sorry for me. She doesn't have much to say at all. Instead, she just listens.

Sometimes the best response is no response at all.

The most refreshing part is that she didn't try to relate my issues to her own experiences or change the subject back to herself.

The women who came before her wouldn't have known how to be helpful if it hit them on the head. But Destiny is more mature and self-aware than any woman I've previously dated.

I am still surprised that a man hasn't locked her down. But she is a motivated and fiercely competitive female. While I appreciate the hell out of her spirit and ferocity, other men probably find it intimidating and frustrating.

She is so unlike other women. She is everything they aren't, everything they will never be, and I need more of her in my life.

Throughout the evening, I was making my intentions clear with each subtle touch and humiliating confession. While I am not perfect by any means, I have enough humility to know when it is time to toss in the towel and quit playing the game. I only hope Destiny likes me for more than my physical attributes.

Because she *really* likes my physical attributes.

Her attraction became fiercely evident as I massaged the back of her neck. Her skin pebbled with goosebumps as she sucked in a breath and shuddered. I've never been so in tune to a woman's reactions before, but this sexual tension between Destiny and me intensifying everything, putting me in a state of hypervigilance. As I increased the pressure against her taut shoulders, they relaxed and her eyelids fluttered dazedly ... I'd give anything to see that face again tonight.

"So ... should we go swim with the others?" Destiny changes the subject of our conversion.

While I wouldn't mind learning a bit more about her, there has been enough sharing for one evening. I am thankful for the reprieve. Life stresses are common for adults, but we don't need to focus on them all day.

"Yeah, sure," I say, opening the sliding glass door.

When she walks through the door, her hand finds mine. She tugs me after her, lacing our fingers like I did earlier – while the sensation still pricks my skin with excitement, it is becoming familiar.

Destiny is taking charge. I consider her voluntary touch one step closer to the goal line.

"David! Dale and I are moving into your second bedroom for the remainder of our stay. Hope you don't mind," Pat says, paddling through the deep end of the pool to greet us on the shallow side.

"All yours, man," I chuckle. Pat and Dale are a good time. I honestly wouldn't mind having people like them around to keep my spirits high.

"Woohoo!" Pat pumps his fists into the air, swimming back to Dale.

"I'm sorry about him," Dale says as Pat snuggles into him. They easily each consumed a bottle of wine tonight.

"You guys are welcome anytime," I reply.

Destiny lets go of my hand, so I return my attention to her. She removes the lightweight coverup, revealing the swimsuit underneath. I should politely look away, but *damn*, it's like time slows down.

This is the part where the lineman sacks me.

The hem of her dress skims across every supple part of her body I have yet to touch, and which I desperately yearn to, as she raises it over her head. Suddenly, I realize I've only seen her body through a layer of sheer fabric. It's not the same as seeing her now – bare.

Her legs are even longer when all she adorns is a bikini, and her bikini … It leaves nothing to the imagination.

It's tiny – all strings and four small triangles – and barely covers her ass. I saw her in the pool yesterday, but the water covered all of this. God have mercy on my soul because her ass will be the death of me one day.

She drops the coverup on the patio and flips her wavy blonde hair over her shoulder as if she didn't just knock the breath straight out of me.

"Are you going to stand there and gawk all day or join me?" she teases confidently.

Oh, Medusa – gawking is all I'm capable of right now.

I like this side of her – confident and sexy. She's ready to play.

"I'd be happy with gawking all day," I say, nearly ripping off my shirt as I drop it on top of her coverup. "In fact, I think I'll continue to gawk as I join you. I don't have to stand in one place to do it," I taunt her, licking my lips satisfactorily as I dare her to one-up me.

Destiny's gaze flicks over my chest, right to left peck, then lower. The lines of her jaw sharpen as she sucks in her cheeks, biting down on them before her hyper-focus snaps and the skin on her cheeks smooths back into place.

"Witty. I can't say the same about you," she remarks smartly, turning and sauntering over to the pool as if my bare chest has no long-term impact on her.

Yet, I remember the way her eyes devoured me the first day we met. The fact that they continually do so means there must be some residual effect, some curiosity. As much as she tries to deny it, Destiny notices me.

I follow her across the concrete patio like an insatiably hungry puppy without an owner to feed it. All I can stare at are her legs and ass as it bounces with each step. After having my hand on her thigh all evening, I need to know how soft the back of her thighs are and how the curve of her butt cheek feels cupped in my hand.

Destiny reaches the edge of the pool, gives me a sly grin, and then cannonballs into the deep end, right next to Kat and Michelle.

"Thanks, Dez," Michelle snaps as she dabs at her evening makeup. It's no use – her raccoon eyes came out with the moonrise.

Destiny laughs and winks at Kat, who is unfazed. I'm slowly starting to pick up on her group's dynamic. Previously, I'd have pinned Destiny as the stuck-up, selfish player who refuses to work with her team because someone stole her shower towel, but she's not like that.

I love that she doesn't care about such trivial things, and I jump in after her, hoping to make an even bigger splash while also hiding my growing boner. Everything about this woman makes my dick stand at attention.

She is perfect.

Michelle politely giggles at me, pretending not to care that my splash effectively soaked her hair and makeup.

Typical.

Before I can be any more disgusted by the woman's response, Destiny swims up to me.

She is swimming far closer than I expect, given our minimal clothing, her legs brushing mine as we wade in the water. When her hands slide up my chest to rest on my shoulders, I place my hands on her waist, holding on to her with intent. The proximity of our nearly naked bodies and the casualness in how Destiny approaches me quickly puts me off balance.

Destiny weakens me. She makes me lose sight of the goal line. She tempts me, making me react to the demands of my desires, taking risks to get to the line faster.

Regardless, I pull her closer, and the smile on her face could melt every glacier in the ocean. She is bright and all-consuming. Her legs skim the outsides of my thighs, inches from floating around me.

That is, until her boobs are shoving themselves in my face and Destiny dunks me under the water.

I relish in the feeling of her tits smashed in my face for a moment before releasing myself from her hold. I swim up for air to find her laughing and retreating as quickly as possible.

She's smart to run.

If our first foot race is any indication of my competitive drive, I won't be walking away from this without payback. I swim after her as she enters the shallow end, my long strokes allowing me to reach her in seconds. I grab her around the waist again, only granting myself a second to savor the feeling of holding her, before I toss her over my shoulder.

She is lighter than I expected and her ass – which is planted squarely on my left shoulder – is even jigglier than I thought. The possibilities of an ass that jiggly are endless.

Destiny squeals, struggling to escape my arms. "What are you doing!?"

Keeping a strong hold around her backside so she can't buck off my shoulder, I easily stride out of the pool. Her friends are hooting and hollering behind us as I stalk around the pool and through the gate that leads to the beach.

At this point, Destiny is wiggling in between her screams of protest, unable to form full sentences because I bounce her on my shoulder every time she begins to say something.

She is being a surprisingly good sport about failing to escape me. Although, maybe she didn't want to get away from me. Maybe she wants to be as close to me as I want to be to her.

I jog through the sand, excited by the idea of setting her down and seeing where things go, occasionally tickling the back of her legs with my fingers. The backs of her thighs are as soft as I hoped, and I savor in the sound of her jovial laughter.

This moment is everything – relaxed, spontaneous, and so utterly natural, it sparks a reminder of the connection I once longed for but had since forgotten I wanted. A connection I needed.

We enter the ocean and her laughter turns into full-on screams. "No! No! Not the ocean! It's nighttime, you crazy fucking bastard!"

Her entire body tenses and she fights hard to get out of my restraint. Her resistance is no longer playful. In her fight to break free, Destiny knees my right shoulder and pain laces every nerve ending in my arm, shooting down the front side of my bicep and into my middle fingertip.

I release my hold and lower her into the shallow water. This is definitely not how I saw the night going, but my arm is on fire and Destiny is raging.

"What's wrong?" I ask, rubbing my shoulder, as she trudges out of the knee-deep pitch-black water.

"It's night. Don't you know sharks hunt at this time?" She turns around, her face wrought with concern.

I never thought a woman like Destiny would fear anything, and certainly not a quick jump in the ocean –

night-time or not. All of our progress and connection feels like it is being stretched, tested, and on the verge of breaking.

"Destiny … I didn't know you were afraid of the ocean. I'm sorry," I plead, trudging toward her.

Her lip quirks up in a devilish grin and she sprints at me. Before I can move, she tackles me into the waves, saltwater forces itself down my lungs as Destiny attacks.

For such a small woman, she hits me with all the force of a three-hundred-pound linebacker. We tumble into the shallow waves, Destiny's barely covered body pressed against mine. Despite the throbbing pain in my shoulder, I take the opportunity to grab her, but she quickly slips out of my grasp.

"You sneaky woman!" I choke on water as we come up for air.

I lunge for her again, but she maneuvers out of my way. Laughing.

"You're kind of slow for a football player!" she taunts me, shuffling her feet in the shallow waters and taking up a defensive stance against the waves and myself.

Her taunting is working. I make a fast grab for her and catch her wrist, but before she can slip away, I tug her flush against my chest and wrap both arms tightly around her. I pin her to me.

If she wants to play dirty, I'll play dirty.

Destiny's forearms press against my chest. Smashed between the hard plane of my pecks and the bulging mounds of her breasts, she stares at the body part separating us before her gaze meets mine.

"I win," I say greedily, unable to hide my satisfaction by our nearness.

"You win," she agrees, her eyes flicking between my eyes and my mouth as her arms slide up and around my shoulders for the second time tonight.

Momentarily, I fear it's a diversion.

But it's not.

Our chests touch and an odd mix of sensations hit me. That sickening, fluttering belly feeling that I haven't felt since before my NFL days starts tickling my gut, and my palms clam against Destiny's skin. There is something about this woman that makes me feel calm and unsteady all at once. I can feel my heart beating rapidly against my chest, and when I look at Destiny, not knowing what to expect, her face gives away a new look – a look of resolve.

Legitimate fear laced with a determination to face it carries a heavy weight on my soul, but I press on. And so does she.

Her arms tentatively restrict around my neck as she rises on tiptoes. I slide my hands down to her perfectly round butt cheeks and lift her in a silent command.

Destiny's legs wrap around me – hooking together on my lower back like I've been dreaming about all evening – and I walk us out of the ocean. Our eyes never leave each other's as I approach the daybed. Our faces are inches apart, our breathing heavy, but the distance between our lips remains separated.

"Destiny …" I begin as I gently set her down on her feet, ready to spill my heart out to her and tell her how fucking beautiful and perfect she is. I don't know what the hell is happening to me, but I am ready to word vomit all of my feelings for her. Including the feelings that will make me sound like a love-struck idiot because I want to make her feel good.

I want her to feel good in *so many different ways*.

"Don't say anything. You've said enough for one night," she whispers.

There is uncertainty in her eyes as she battles with something far deeper than I can imagine, but I don't have the same internal battle happening, and I'll take everything she is willing to give me, when she's willing to give it.

She backs up, gently pulling me with her until her thighs hit the daybed and she scoots across the massive lounge toward the middle. I follow her, crawling across the mattress until I am kneeling between her legs. I desperately want to ask if this is okay, but she told me not to speak, so I don't.

I glide my hands over her legs, starting at her feet and curving around the backs of her calves before I find the tender skin on the inside of her thighs. It is as smooth as butter, and I imagine this is what heaven feels like – if heaven could be felt.

My calloused hands don't deserve to touch something so perfect. Jerking my fingers back before they mar her beautiful skin, I place my palms on either side of her waist and replace the trail of my fingers with light kisses, repairing any damage they might have caused.

Working my way from the tips of her toes to her thighs, Destiny shivers under me. When my mouth reaches her inner thigh, that part I crave to touch most, her fingers dig into my scalp, tousling my hair. She tugs softly, grabbing my attention, and I stop my progress to gaze up at her from my spot between her glorious legs. There is so much skin left to explore around that tiny bikini line – I don't want to stop.

And I won't unless she stops me.

"Come here," she rasps.

Like the good puppy I am, I follow her command. As I crawl over her, I keep our bodies an inch apart. If our skin touches again, I might completely lose it. It is already taking every ounce of my willpower to slowly cherish Destiny and not take all of her while my hands are within reach. I want to be in between her legs again, showing her how a woman of her caliber deserves to be treated, but I promised myself to follow her lead and allow her to control the situation.

I position myself over her, my legs straddling one of hers, effectively pinning her to the daybed. Even though our bodies are inches apart, it feels like miles. No amount of space between us should be acceptable. But I keep the distance.

Destiny's hands cup my face as she studies me intensely.

"Is this okay?" I ask, my voice mirroring hers as I inhale her wine-kissed breath.

"More than fine," she says before she pulls me down.

Our lips collide and I collapse onto her. As soon as I feel the velvet-soft touch of her lips, there is no stopping myself.

Apparently, there is no stopping her either.

She lifts the leg between my thighs, brushing against my erection as she pulls it free and wraps it around me. Again.

Destiny latches her legs and arms around my body, clinging to me like a lifeline while our mouths explore each other.

Our connection is undeniable. It is like fire and ice combating in a race to decimate everything in its path. It's a slow burn that feels like my body is simmering in ethereal fluid. It is a chemical reaction that starts in the center of my chest and explodes outward.

It is everything. And it is more without having to deliberately state it.

I grind my hips into her pelvic floor, needing to feel the intimacy on the surface before I internally combust. Her answering moan of approval encourages me to grind harder, letting her feel the length of what I have to offer.

It isn't only candid banter and emotional support that I am offering up. Destiny has a lot more to look forward to in the moments we share behind closed doors. After all, I excel at all physical things.

"Dez! Dez, come back!" female voices call out for Destiny from the direction of my bungalow.

"Fuck!" I curse against Destiny's lips.

She giggles but makes no attempt to move as our heavy breaths intermingle. "We should probably get back. They'll come looking for me."

"Don't they know how to take a hint?" I groan, rearing back and admiring Destiny's swollen lips and pink cheeks. Our kissing was aggressive and needy in the best way.

"They're drunk, thanks to the countless bottles of wine you were buying to win them over," she counters.

She has a point. They are very drunk – no thanks to my insistence to buy more wine and loosen everyone up – and most definitely not picking up on the fact that Destiny's disappearance is a good thing.

"I totally fucked myself in this situation, didn't I?"

"Yep," Destiny says as she pushes my chest and forces me to roll to the side.

When my back hits the mattress, her eyes land on my wet swim trunks. They are stuck to my skin and offer a very clear view of the outline of my penis under the moonlight. Her lips part as if she is going to say something, but instead, she snaps her mouth shut and gulps.

"Did something catch your eye, Destiny?" I tease her, unable to resist the opportunity to receive an unwarranted scolding over her own sexual frustration and admiration of my goods.

"I thought I saw a crab, but turns out it was nothing. Too small to be anything of note." She turns her head away, hiding her smile as she tries to underplay her awe.

Her friends' voices draw nearer as they make their way onto the sand.

"Maybe I should ask Stacy if she sees anything. You know, have her take a closer look around before you dip your toes in the sand. I have a feeling she's the type of woman who likes crap hunting." I laugh.

Destiny's head whips around to stare at me with her mouth gaping. "If you want some woman to worship at your feet for having a big dick and an even bigger ego, then maybe you should be talking to Stacy, not me," she says nastily.

"Whoa. I'm teasing, Dez," I say, reaching for her hand, but she yanks it out of reach.

"Don't call me Dez."

Fuck. She's serious.

My boner instantly shrinks. It is put away in the dog-house for yapping his stupid mouth. Before I can register the scope of my stupidity, Destiny's feet are moving across the sand, flinging it up in her wake, forming a storm cloud, as she heads back to the bungalow.

22

Destiny

Everything was perfect until he decided to open his big fat stupid cocky mouth. Funny how his mouth and his cock are so similar – big, fat, and stupid. It's almost funny. If I weren't so goddamn pissed.

I'm sure Stacy would be more than willing to dip her toes in his sand and dig around until her heart's desire was sated. Moments before, I had been willing to do the same thing.

"Dez, where are you going?" Kat asks as I pass her and Stacy on their way to find me.

"Back to my room. I've had enough fun for tonight." I place emphasis on "fun" like it is a curse.

I thought I'd been having fun. My body certainly thought it was having fun. If it weren't for Kat and Stacy's interruption, I might have made a huge mistake and slept with David.

Well, a one-night stand isn't that big of a mistake –especially in my current sexually frustrated condition – but my emotions are in this. The kiss we shared felt different;

it felt deeper. In fact, the intimacy and the connection were deeper than anything I've ever felt. I nearly panicked when the realization hit me. But it felt so good, so I kept going.

It is the same feeling that ecstasy induces, a euphoric high that makes you feel like you've never known love until that very moment. I was falling into the love trap.

Achilles' love trap.

When our lips connected, I could have sworn his lips were made for mine. And the way he trailed kisses up my body ... he made me feel like a goddess.

That is probably how he makes every female feel, though.

I'm willingly signing up for heartbreak by pursing things with David. That is for certain. There is no reason to take such an unnecessary risk.

"Dez, wait up!" Stacy yells as both women run to catch up with me. "What's wrong? Where's David?"

I ignore her question and round the tropical bushes that encase the private pool. Certain my face tells my friends everything, I avoid their gazes and grab my coverup. David's shirt is tangled in my dress, and when I free the clothes from each other, I decidedly toss his shirt into the pool. It is an immature move, but I'm not really concerned about my behavior currently. The combination of alcohol, hormones, and pheromones is a heady concoction that has no business dictating my life right now.

"Destiny," David says, grabbing my upper arm from behind.

I want to peel away from his touch. It is a reminder of where I let him touch me, not just physically, but emotionally, and I can't handle it anymore.

I've known the man for three days, and I am already a blubbering mess. Yet, I can date men for two months and not feel the same raw emotions or disconcertment. It is unfair how easily he can infiltrate my defenses and disrupt my stable life.

"Can everyone please leave?" David says seriously, more of a demand than a question, while keeping his massive hand on me like I am some sort of possession – not allowed to leave unless he says otherwise.

But, for some odd reason, my feet don't move. I don't attempt to fight him and leave. A part of me knows David will find me either way. He is a competitor, and he will try to win until it is clear he has lost – until I make it abundantly clear that I don't want him in any way.

My defenses are building, preparing for the most vicious battle of my life.

"Dez, are you good? Taylor and I can walk back with you." Will walks up to me with Taylor trailing behind. As much as I want to hate her, she is utterly amiable.

"I'm fine," I say, dismissing them and turning my attention back to the Achilles.

Will leans in to whisper in the ear furthest from David, and I feel David's hand shake against my arm as Will says, "We don't know him. I think you should leave with us."

Will's concern irks me, I've never thought of David as dangerous. This scenario looks far worse than it is, and it is heartwarming to know that Will still looks out for me. But I am a woman, and I can handle this myself, so I steel my features and lie, "Thanks, Will, but I promise I'm fine."

I'm *so* not fine. I'm pissed.

Hesitantly, Will nods. He and Taylor leave with the rest of my friends. When I am certain they are out of earshot, I whirl on the man who thinks he was about to score by threatening me with another woman.

"Screw you!" I say as maliciously as possible.

"Oh, come on! You know I was teasing!" he says, folding his arms across his chest insolently.

We take up our opposing sides.

"Were you really, though? Or is that how you get your way with every woman? You make them feel like there's always someone else waiting, so they need to take their chance now before it's too late. You use jealousy to manipulate them into sleeping with you?"

"Where are you even coming up with this shit? You don't know anything about my dating life. And if you did, you'd know I've literally never had to manipulate or convince a woman to sleep with me," he fires back.

"Oh wow! That's nothing to brag about either. I can't believe I was even considering this," I point between him and me disgustedly.

Granted, as I say the words, I don't quite believe them. One look at the man and there is plenty of reason to consider at least one thing happening between us. But there is more to it than that. David was trying to make me think there was a lot more than just a physical connection between us and that is downright conniving.

"If you were considering this," he repeats my actions, pointing between the two of us, "you would have known I was teasing. Stacy has been throwing herself at me since the day we met. It's comical, considering she's about to get married. And honestly, do you really think I like women like that?"

"I clearly know nothing about you, so yeah, I bet you do like women like that. You certainly don't go after women like me. If you did, you'd know better than to play games." My voice hitches at the end of my sentence. I am losing control of the situation and trying to reassure myself that my actions are warranted.

David is in the wrong. Right?

But as he questions my reaction, my mind becomes frantic – trying to make sense of all his actions up until this point. One comment. One comment, and I felt like everything between us backtracked. Is it really him or is it just me?

"Destiny, I'm not playing any games with you. I made a bad joke because my dick was doing the talking and your friends' interrupting us pissed me off. Is that what you want to hear? That I am an idiot, and yes, even at thirty-fucking-six, I still act like a teenage boy." He throws up his hands and paces while he rants. "You're right. I don't go for woman like you because I haven't met a woman like you before! You are one in a million, can't you see that? I'm sorry about what I said. I've never felt like this …"

He stops in front of me, breathing heavily as he gazes down at me with a look of defeat. Meanwhile, my heart is physically punching my brain. I want to believe this man; at the same time, I don't want to believe him. I want to run away because running away is easier than taking a chance. Whether I am wrong or right, this doesn't end well.

This type of intense attraction never ends well.

My brain doesn't believe it is possible to find something *more* at a random resort in the jungle with some famous athlete. This is the stereotypical romance novel plot that I binge read and cry about because I know it will never be a reality, but it's so freaking beautiful that I can't stop reading.

Things like this – meeting a stranger on vacation and pretending it is happily ever after – simply doesn't happen. Especially for people like me.

"Destiny, please say something," David says quietly. His hands reach for mine, but stop halfway and drop to his sides.

He is waiting. Waiting for me.

I don't know what the right decision is, but I know that I've never felt like this with anyone else. I've never been so scared, jealous, and insecure in my life. Yet, I only feel this way because I refuse to believe his intentions are pure.

What if they are pure?

What if he really did make a bad joke and everything else we have shared is sincere?

Could the fairytales I read about really become *my* reality?

23

DAVID

I WISH SHE WOULD say something. Anything. Her eyes dart back and forth, like a computer downloading new software. I can see the wheels turning behind her eyes, weighing the pros and cons, debating my honesty. There is nothing else I can say or do. Her decision will be final, and I will leave here wondering what else could have been between us.

The way she felt in my arms was so right. Too right to be real. Too easy. It was like I stopped breathing, stopped existing outside of the moment that I was with her. Life became simple.

"Destiny, please say something," I implore her.

She looks up at me, her brows furrowed, and her lips quivering as she wrestles with the thoughts racing through her head.

"Don't call me Destiny," she replies, her lips trembling.

Thank fucking god.

I reach for her, pulling her into my arms tightly and squeezing. I thought I might break until her full name passed through her lips – finally giving me permission to use her nickname.

"I'll never joke like that again. I swear," I say, knowing that I'll never let her doubt her place in my lineup again. She is my number one pick.

"Don't make promises you can't keep," she says warily, as if she thinks I am still not being honest with her.

"If my intentions weren't clear, Dez, I really like you and I really want to get to know you – even after we leave this resort. That is a promise I can keep. Is that okay?" I say as I take her hands and pull them around my back.

She allows me to take the lead, trusting me. For now.

My body naturally envelops hers as we sink into the hug. To think we barely touched before this evening, things progress quickly – maybe too quickly, but I am only getting older, and I have nothing to lose.

The days that I plan counter moves in advance of calling a play are over. I am heading into a new era, and that era is all about acting instinctively. After all, that's what decades of experience are for. There's no need to overthink things; I trust in my ability and so does my team.

"That's okay. Sorry, I freaked out." Destiny bites the corner of her lip as she attempts to hide her smile.

"I think it's called jealousy, not freaking out," I suggest, hoping she will take the criticism lightly.

She does – her smile widens, and she laughs at herself. "It's not just that. But yeah, maybe a little jealousy too …

Jesus Christ. Stacy's literally getting married. What is wrong with me?"

I chuckle and absentmindedly knead the little muscles in her lower back. My knuckles brush the top round of her butt cheeks as I do so. I could stand like this all night.

"Why are you so good at that?" Destiny asks, her voice low and rough as she rests her forehead against my bare chest.

The tips of her wet hair fall forward and tickle my skin, causing goosebumps to spread across my arms.

"Hand control is crucial in my profession. Plus, I just like doing this – touching you, making you feel relaxed," I explain, rolling my knuckles down her lower back and into the muscles that define her upper buttocks. Her bikini bottoms catch on my fingers and roll down. I peer over Destiny's head and see the deep line between her cheeks before I pull the bottoms back into place. Sue me for being a creep – I am a man and Destiny is fucking hot.

"I'm a little cold. Can we go inside and warm up?"

"Sure. We could also get in the hot tub to warm up," I suggest.

Destiny looks at the hot tub, then around the pool as if she is searching for something. I'm not sure what she is looking for, but she asks, "How big is your bathtub?"

My eyebrows shoot up at her question. The answer is big, *very* big. This resort is made for adults and serves copious amounts of liquor; they know their guests expect double occupancy bathtubs. But I didn't for one second expect Destiny to suggest *we* bathe together.

"It's big," I respond.

"Like multiple people big?" she prods.

"Well, it's not the size of a hot tub, but it could fit you and me – if that's what you're asking?"

A sinful expression takes over her face and hypnotizes me. "Obviously," she says.

I bite my lip in anticipation and grab her hand. We can't make it to the bathroom faster.

Destiny sits on the vanity bench and watches me as I fill the bathtub with hot water and bubble bath, turn on the steam shower to heat the bathroom, and dim the lights.

We are doing this. We are *actually* doing this.

"All right. Make yourself comfortable, I'll be right back," I say as I hurry from the room, imagining all of the ways I will get to know Destiny tonight.

If she is giving me another shot, I am not going to screw this up. Destiny will get the royal treatment – or at least as royal as I can make it.

I collect an unopened champagne bottle – thankful her friends didn't find it – and two glasses from the kitchen, a tray of chocolates, cheese, crackers, and other finger foods the staff left in my fridge earlier today. This place definitely has its perks when it comes to setting the mood – something I didn't expect to be taking advantage of at all on this trip.

When I open the bathroom door, the steam hits the cold air behind me and fogs my vision. Using my senses, I walk into the dimly lit room and blindly navigate my way to the tub. As the steam clears from the air around me, I finally see her.

Destiny.

The back of her head rests on the edge of the oversized tub. Her eyes are closed and her blonde hair is splayed over her shoulders, dipping into the water and floating around her. She looks like a goddess.

My eyes drift further down her freshly tanned shoulders, the bubbles halting my view of Destiny's curves, but I notice her wet bikini on the floor, so I know what awaits me.

She is gloriously naked under those bubbles.

Destiny's eyes slowly open, remaining partially closed as a hazy expression takes over her face. "Hi," she says.

"Hi," I reply as I set the food and drinks down on a bench beside the tub. "Champagne?" I ask, lifting the bottle.

She nods.

I open the bottle. The pop of the top echoes in the small space between Destiny and me. The air is rich and heavy with anticipation as I pour two glasses of champagne, waiting for the bubbles to go down so I can top them off.

"Thank you." She accepts the glass of sparkling wine that I extend her.

When she reaches over the tub's edge, the full mound of her breast emerges from the water. Bubbles peak on the tip of her nipple, hiding its perfection from me and making my mouth water insatiably. My creepiness is in full force as I eye Destiny hungrily.

Pretending I haven't nearly cum in my pants at the sight of her breast, I clear my throat. With everything now in place, I realize I don't know what to do next. Destiny merely watches me with interest, waiting for me to get into the tub and making me feel even more uncertain about my next steps.

I am not normally a shy man. Frankly, I never get nervous like this around women, but still, my legs don't move from my position squatting beside the tub.

"Are you going to get in or what?" she taunts, sipping her champagne.

"I am … Should I take off my swimsuit, too?" I ask, deciding to leave my next move up to her. She is naked, and I want to be naked, but something still stops me. I don't want to push her too hard. I don't want her to run away again.

"I'd prefer you don't get all the chlorine and salt from your swim trunks in the tub," she says simply before adding, "should I look away?"

Her words trigger me. I have nothing to be embarrassed about, and I am not about to let her think I do. She knows how to kickstart my competitive side and I'll make her squirm for it. Plus, her little peep show already has my cock at half-mast. He's ready to make his debut.

"No, Dez. I want you to look." I roll the words off my tongue like melted ice and slide my swim trunks down slowly as I stand, letting the base of my cock be revealed inch by achingly slow inch.

Destiny watches intently as my shorts drop lower. She sinks into the bathtub, her eyes wide and the lower half of her face covered in bubbles to hide her expression.

She hasn't even seen the whole show and she is already turned on – just as I hoped. As my shorts lower to knees, my manhood bounces free, now standing perkily straight from the excitement of turning Destiny on. She lifts her head slightly, peering over the bubbles to get a better look.

"Should I join you now?" I ask, giving myself one pump of satisfaction.

Destiny nods and licks her lips, the words dried up with her tongue.

I saunter to the tub's edge, letting my cock bounce with each step, and I swear her eyes don't blink.

Yeah, that's the size of it, baby. Soak it in.

The water is the perfect temperature – hot, merging on painful, but still bearable. When I lower myself into the other side of the tub, I feel under the water for her legs so I can pull her closer. But instead of finding her legs, Destiny shifts and moves to top me. She floats through the water and straddles my lap, her breasts fully out of the water with bubbles sliding down them, and her … *Holy fuck.*

The center of her body glides across my shaft, and it is my turn to go still as I feel a tenseness build in my balls. This is so unexpected. She is unexpected. This woman is Aphrodite reborn, and her touch alone is about to be my undoing.

"Fuck," I hiss, as she slides her sex over the full length of me, grinding hard so I can feel every crevice stroke across my stretched skin. The heat of her body and the sticky substance that is proof of her desire runs along the underside of my shaft, giving me taste after tantalizing taste of her essence.

"That feels good," Dez moans above me, moving her hips faster.

I am not even inside her and I am already about to blow my load. This is so unlike me. Sure, I've slept with plenty of hot women, but they are all the same. They lie back and let me do all the work, which is great and all, but they never take the lead like this.

They never catch me off guard and unprepared.

Turns out, a take-charge type of woman turns me on like no other.

Destiny's hands are all over my body, hugging my shoulders as her breasts move up and down in my face, matching the movement of her hips, while my hands are going numb with how hard I am clutching the sides of the tub to avoid cumming.

"You couldn't keep your hands off me all day and now you refuse to touch me." Destiny arches her brow indignantly, still moving her body.

Fuck it.

I release the tub and cup her breasts. They are better than I ever could have imagined. Her answering whimper is all the encouragement I need to begin exploring them further. I knead the pillowy softness of her breasts. They fit the size of my hand perfectly, not too small or large. It's like they were made for me, like every part of Destiny was made for me.

I suck her right tit into my mouth, tasting the lavender bath soap on her silky skin. This time, it is her turn to still as my teeth graze across her nipple. Her hips move in shallower circles as her hands thread their way into my hair to hold my mouth against her. At her command, I suck harder before releasing her sensitive peak and lapping my tongue over the tip, forcing it to harden.

Destiny quivers on top of me, and her legs contract against my sides, digging into my quads with a force that is equal to her ability to seduce me.

I gaze up at the beautiful woman and know there is no turning back. We have breached the point of no return. We both know it. Our eyes lock and unspoken words – confessions and admissions – pass between us as our bodies align.

Destiny centers herself above me and reaches into the water. When her fingers wrap around my girth and squeeze, I lose all control and thrust upward into her hand. She strokes me as my hips lift and lower, causing water to spill from the tub and successfully riling me up even more.

"If you keep doing that, I'm going to cum," I admit, holding her wrist still as my balls tighten.

"Good. Then you'll last longer when we have sex," Destiny breathes, breaking my hold on her wrist and continuing to pump her hand up and down.

Her nasty words are the spark to my fire, and it takes all my self-control not to combust. "I'm not getting off without you, Destiny," I say, lifting her ass and slipping a hand between her thighs.

She gasps when my fingers dip into her folds.

24

DESTINY

"OH MY GOD." I collapse into David's chest, still holding onto his cock.

It hasn't been that long, maybe a few months or more, but no man's fingers have filled or explored me quite like his do. They aren't just skilled at massaging my aching muscles; they are unequivocally qualified to rub the more sensitive regions of my lady parts.

And to think I was willing to walk away moments before and never look back. My fiery personality isn't appreciated by many – the highs and lows of my mood can be a turn-off – but David sought it out as a challenge. A challenge of equals.

His fingers move in a rhythm that matched the pace of my hand and it spurs me to continue. Shifting my body, I allow myself space to stroke him once more. Because he needs room, and a lot of it, to be fully appreciated.

The girth.

The length.

The entire freaking thing – maybe it's the booze altering my perception, but David's penis is unlike any other I have felt.

My index finger and thumb attempt to touch as I wrap them around the base of him, but they can't – not even at the tip. He is monstrous in the most intimidating, mouth-watering way. The bubbles block my view of his groin, forcing me to rely solely on touch to explore him.

Our hands move in sync, pleasuring each other, and the most unnerving, sexy part about this entire erotic bath is that our eyes never leave each other's. His green eyes turn golden in the middle as if giving me a window into his soul.

David is my match, my equal.

He sees me in a way other men don't. He challenges me while simultaneously appreciating me. This could quite possibly be the best or worst mistake of my life, but I am at the finish line and there is no turning back.

I am one step away from crossing the line that cannot be uncrossed. This ink is permanent, and it is written on my heart, carved into my brain, and stained on my soul.

Once more, his mouth finds my breast, sucking on the tip while his eyes peer up at me and his fingers continue their dance across the fleshier parts of my body. When a sharp sting pinches my nipple, a pressure clamps down on that little aching bundle of nerves that has been throbbing incessantly to be touched.

My entire body clenches – a tension that I haven't felt in a long time taking over. I try to fight it, but it is overwhelming.

The line has officially been crossed.

Skilled as he is at reading playbooks, David senses my impending release. He abandons my breasts to kiss me fervently. His hand shakes against my pelvis, palm pressing firmly into my sex as I ride the electric high coursing through my center. Mindlessly, I pump him faster, fueling the energy of my release into bringing him to his.

He groans against my mouth and tilts my head so our kiss can deepen. David's tongue sweeps into my mouth. Tasting. Exploring. Claiming.

His long fingers curl inside me, while his tongue swirls around my own, licking and tasting every part of my mouth. Our kissing is raunchy and exhilarating. The energy radiates throughout my body, from my core to my fingers, my toes, and my head – expelling a shockwave of ecstasy in a slow hypnotic release as our hands and mouths move with the flow of our climax.

When the high slowly disperses, my whole body trembles and collapses into the water, bringing me flush against David's chest. The warm water around us does nothing to cool the heat that transpired between us, but it is a welcome, soothing sensation.

At this point, I'd usually clean up, feeling self-conscious and uncomfortable with the aftermath of our intimacy, but

I don't want to move. I feel weightless. David's arms are wrapped securely around my back, holding me against his chest. The only movement comes from the heavy breaths he and I take, causing the water to ripple soundlessly as it settles.

His head rests against the lip of the tub while his eyes remain shut and a satisfied grin is plastered across his face. He looks as pleased as I feel. Not only that, but he looks different to me now. Over the past three days, I struggled to hate him, to find some flaw in his image or behavior. In all that time, I continued to notice how handsome he was, but I never fully realized it. Until now.

He is beautiful … Achilles is beautiful.

The rich golden color of his skin seems to glow, despite how dehydrated my own looks from the sun and saltwater exposure. The features on his face are as hard and angular as the muscles lining his arms, chest, and abdomen. If a marble statue of Greek gods could come to life, David would be the living, breathing result of it.

"What are you thinking?" he asks, opening his eyes and catching me assessing every centimeter of his perfect face. The tiniest bit of black stubble lines his jaw, just enough to be visible, but not enough to feel rough.

"Nothing," I lie, feeling the blush creep up my cheeks.

"Want to know what I'm thinking?"

"Yes, please," I slur, exhaustion from a day's worth of day-drinking and a much-needed orgasm beginning to weigh me down.

"I'm thinking that's the first time I've cum from a woman giving me a hand job in like ten years. Actually, probably like fifteen years." He chuckles.

Achilles might be beautiful, but his mind is filthy.

"You're lying." I feign shock, even though I secretly relish the knowledge that no other woman has done what I have achieved. At least, not in the majority of his adult years, as he claims.

"I'm really not!" He laughs again. "Honestly, I probably would have come without you even touching me. God … When you straddled my lap. Fuck. You're amazing." David drags me further up his body so our faces are inches apart. He kissed me softly.

When was the last time a man spoke to me so honestly and vulgarly? Admitting his own unabashed attraction and how it impacts him – how I make him feel. David is hitting every mental check box right now. I am so screwed. It doesn't make sense that this man is single, that he can't find a worthwhile woman who will continually praise him.

I pull away from his kiss. "Why are you single?" I ask the question before the sensible part of my brain can stop me.

David's shoulders stiffen as he breaks eye contact with me. Still, he attempts to answer. "I don't exactly have the best taste in women. Being a star quarterback living in New

York City … Let's just say I've had more than a lifetime worth of fun. Along the way, I think I just fell into the same routine because it was familiar – even though I knew it was wrong. Each year is tougher. I realize more and more what I want, but I can't seem to find it."

His words are like ice running along my bones. A tinge of jealousy spikes from his reference to fun and the unknowing knowledge of who was involved. Yet, at the same time, I feel a desire to ease the pain of his longing. I understand the frustration of being unable to find what you are looking for. I've been searching for someone for a long time, too – falling into failed relationship after failed relationship. The only true success in my life and the only thing that I've committed myself to completely is my business. I can always rely on my business because its success depends solely on me.

"Why are you single, Destiny?"

I don't want to answer his question. He explained it earlier – most men's egos are unable to deal with my success or cope with my busy schedule. Although, there is more to it, and based on our prior conversations, I think the other part of my dating failure is the answer David is looking for.

It is a subject I hardly feel equipped to approach myself, but something about David makes me want to try. Even if there is a minute chance of something *more* happening between us after we leave this resort, I owe him a little bit of honesty after everything he has shared.

"I think … I think I've never felt like I could depend on the men I date. And so, I don't fully give myself to the relationship. I've always prided myself on being fiercely independent, so I didn't think it was a bad thing if I couldn't depend on the man in the relationship. But I'm starting to realize it would be nice … To not feel like I have to do it all myself. It would be nice to be on the same team, rather than fighting through life alone."

It hurts to voice the words that have hidden themselves deep in my subconscious. It is like swallowing dry bread – it scratches your throat the entire way down, despite how much water you attempt to wash it down with.

"Do you think we could be on the same team?" David asks, sliding his hands down the spine of my back to rest on the top of my butt cheeks. His hands continually find their way to that spot.

"Maybe."

He doesn't return a response.

Nothing about how Achilles and I met is normal. Nothing about where we go from here is either. While things with David didn't start traditionally, I hold onto the hope that it doesn't matter.

25

DAVID

MAYBE. IT WASN'T A no, but it also wasn't a yes. I need to know what is holding her back because I am putting it all on the table and serving it up with a side of secret sauce. If she can't already tell, the ball is in her hands. Her extremely skilled hands. Nonetheless, it still makes me anxious. I need her to give me a chance like I need the promise of standing under those stadium lights again.

Although, the way she rubbed my cock – her grip was like a vise – made me forget about almost everything else that matters. But it wasn't that alone that sent me over the edge, cumming like a horny teenage boy who has never been touched by a woman. It was the look on her face when her orgasm hit and the way she fell against me, giving herself completely to the feeling I elicited from her.

I made her feel that way.

And I want to do it over and over again.

"Let's go to bed," I suggest, sitting up and feeling my flaccid cock rub against her center.

Almost immediately it starts to harden, even though I am not trying to push for sex. We both had our release tonight, both physically and emotionally. All I want to do is cuddle her until the sun rises. I want to touch her bare skin for as long as I can, especially in her most vulnerable state.

There is something about knowing a woman can fall asleep next to me that brings out a sense of pride – it means she trusts me. This will be the ultimate unspoken test. Does Destiny trust me? Does she think I am worthy of being on her team permanently, as an equal, not a subordinate?

"Okay," she says, taking my hand and standing from the tub. I wrap a towel around her curvy frame then she leads me to the bedroom.

She only has her bathing suit and cover-up here, so she doesn't have any clothes for bed, but she seems unbothered by the nudity as she drops the towel and climbs under the covers. Her naked body will be a slight problem for me, though, so I grab two boxers from the dresser – one for me, one for her.

"Here." I extend the boxers toward her and Destiny's brow furrows.

"Is something wrong?"

"No," I say, still holding the boxers she refuses to take. They awkwardly hang between us.

"Are we not going to continue what we started?" she asks dubiously.

Destiny doesn't need to ask me twice; we can definitely continue what we started. Although, I don't want to push her limits or make her think I expect sex after fooling around – I am happy with whatever she grants me.

"Whatever you want, Destiny. I'm yours," I reply like a sappy puppy willing to do anything to please its owner.

She worries her bottom lip as her eyes soften. I drop the boxers on the floor, no longer thinking about how to calm myself down around her naked body. My nerve endings are triggered and buzzing, ready to be set on fire by the heat within her.

I waste no time. I sweep the blankets aside and crawl over Destiny's silky body, peppering kisses along the supple curve of her waist. If we are going to do this, I need to taste her and get her body ready for my entrance.

While she may not realize just how much I will fill her, I do. Only two fingers were inserted earlier, and she gripped those with ridiculously strong internal muscles. My cock will require a lot more room, and I don't want to hurt her.

"Tell me what you like, Destiny. Tell me how to please you," I whisper across her skin as my lips travel down her abdomen to the soft spot between her legs.

"You already know how," she says breathlessly, throwing her head back against the pillows as I go down on her.

Her words hold more meaning than they seem to – or at least I think they do. But it still doesn't make sense as to why she is holding back. If I knew how to please her, in every way possible, what is her hesitation? What is her fear?

This may not be the typical way two people meet, nor the most romantic. We are two lost souls, alone at an all-inclusive adults-only couple's resort, but it doesn't mean there isn't a chance for us.

Either fate or circumstance brought us here, but I hope it was the former. Without hesitation, I give Destiny what she wants. My tongue delves into her dewy lips and tastes her sweet, tangy nectar. It truly is the nectar of the gods – an indecent and intoxicating juice that my tongue slurps down languidly. This is a task meant to be savored, and feasted upon slowly.

Destiny writhes below me as my tongue and lips explore her crevices. With a total lack of control, I flick my tongue furiously across her clitoris and watch as her back arches, pushing her breasts to the ceiling. Her womanly body only beguiles me more.

I hungrily drink in her delectable arousal, before pulling away to watch her sex pucker in thirsty abandon. The image of her surrendered beneath me, begging for more while her juices coat her thighs, representing her heady arousal, will forever inhabit my fantasies. Destiny – *my Medusa* – is provocative in nature and irresistible to mankind. I am trapped in her allure, willing to do whatever it takes to please her.

"David," she wines, needy and desperate.

I am compelled to comply, and my mouth engulfs her once more. Destiny rolls her hips under me, grinding her pelvis into my lips as soft moans slip past hers. My dick throbs restlessly, but I shove down the desire to be inside her and plunge my fingers into her instead. Her response is irresistible – her entire body goes rigid and quakes under me.

Destiny stiffens and squeezes around my fingers, so I plunge them deeper, spreading them apart and pumping them faster. I accelerate the pace of my hand and my tongue, eager to devour her pleasure when it comes.

When her hands find the back of my head and hold me down, I feel her climax soil my hand and taste the sweetness of it in my mouth. While other men might have qualms about consuming a woman's cum, it invigorates me, and I tenaciously ravish her while she rides the waves of her orgasm and spirts onto my fingers.

Above me, she pants heavily, coming down from her orgasm. I slowly retract my fingers, licking and kissing the areas of her body covered in cum. When a long sigh escapes her, I take my leave.

I crawl over her body, letting my rock-hard erection settle between her legs, close enough to feel the heat emanating off her body, but not close enough to touch. Not yet.

"Ready for more?" I ask, anxiously awaiting the moment my dick will be inside her.

Destiny nods, but says, "I feel like I should return the favor first."

It isn't necessary. In fact, I don't want her to. The only thing on my mind is the warm space between her legs and how cozy it will feel when I am tucked inside it. "It's not necessary."

"But …" she protests, licking her lips.

Apparently she is as hungry for me, as I was for her.

"Destiny. We have time for that later if you really want, but right now I'm dying to be inside of you," I admit, my testicles swollen and hammering their indecent proposals against my brain while it warns them to be patient.

"Okay … Condom?"

"Right. Shit," I say, jumping off her to find a condom. My patience is dwindling. My control waning.

There has to be a condom around here somewhere. I never have sex without one. Cleat chasers are known to beg for a cream pie, full of promises to take Plan B after. Fortunately, I've never been caught in that trap. Not that I think Destiny would ever do such a horrific thing, but I'm shocked I didn't think of using a condom at all.

I search through every bag, drawer, and cupboard in the two-bedroom bungalow and can't find a single condom.

In my defense, I wasn't planning on coming to this resort and getting laid. Having sex with someone was the last thing on my mind with all the drama that has been unfolding in my life. But damn, do I regret not preparing for this.

"So …" I start saying as I walk into the bedroom, running a hand through my hair. Destiny is sitting up with her back against the headboard, the covers pulled under her armpits – she looks cute and shy, maybe a little nervous. It is uncanny how quickly she can go from writhing below me to hiding her body from me, even though I still have the taste of her cum on my lips, and there is no forgetting how she looks, feels, or tastes.

"You couldn't find one," she finishes knowingly.

I shake my head.

"I can still …" she offers, looking down at my exposed cock, still standing at the ready.

"No," I cut her off. I don't want an obligatory blowjob. While I might have accepted her offer a moment ago had I known there was no condom, the moment has passed. "Let's go to bed," I say, tossing the forgotten boxers on the bed beside her.

If we are going to sleep in the same bed with no immediate access to condoms, we need to cover our genitals. Destiny doesn't seem like the type to take unnecessary risks based on her hormones, but if she begs me hard enough, I'll cave. It's a scary thought knowing I would give in to her. I never give in.

Never.

But I've also never wanted a woman this badly in my life. It is going to be both a pain and a blessing falling asleep beside her tonight.

26

Destiny

As my eyes squint open, morning light floods through the massive glass windows, causing agonizing pain to shoot through my skull. "Ugh …" I press on my head and squeeze my eyes shut, but it offers no relief to the hangover that I signed up for after day drinking yesterday.

"One second," a sleepy male voice says behind me, the weight of an arm removes itself from me as he gets up.

Moments later, the light behind my lids fades, and despite the thundering drum beating against my brain, I dare to look at the man. Strands of light peeking through the blinds search for him, casting him in an eerily sensual shadow. The mounds of his muscles highlight in the soft hue, while shadows cut the muscle deeper, emphasizing his masculinity.

Achilles.

"Good morning," he says, stretching his back before sitting beside me on the edge of the bed.

"Morning," I reply, unsure what else to say, nor able to think about much more than the tight pressure compressing my cerebrum.

David is unmarred by the morning-after awkwardness. He is seemingly at home sitting beside me in his little cotton briefs that leave nothing to the imagination. Last night was something else. The image of his mouth buried between my legs flashes through the searing headache, offering a momentary reprieve from the pain while making me ache in other places.

"Are you feeling okay?" David asks casually, tucking a strand of hair behind my ear gently and expertly avoiding the brush of our skin.

His touch is paternal, devoted. Yet, somehow it is also suggestive. He was spooning me only minutes before. The warmth of his arm still comforts my bare stomach and the reminder of his breath against the back of my neck … "I'm fine," I lie, shoving away the memory and the feelings it entices. The warmth that blossoms in not only my loins, but my chest.

As I sit up, a wave of lightheadedness rushes over me, forcing me to wobble dizzily. Hangovers are not something I frequently encounter – I am usually too busy with work to binge drink. Although, my nerves and my senses got the better of me yesterday and I went into full-on party mode.

The success of said day drinking is to be determined.

It might have been a blessing in disguise that David didn't have a condom last night. The way he made me feel – it was something else. Something *more*. Something far scarier than I realized until now. Now that I am fully sober, the weight of my feelings for him crash into me like a wave barreling onto shore.

I don't regret what we did, but I regret being slightly intoxicated when it happened. Last night everything seemed clear. My feelings. Emotions. Our connection.

It was as if our souls connected, but I know that isn't true. Things like this simply don't occur. Not this quickly. Feelings like this are the result of infatuation. This is danger-ous territory, and I must tread carefully because intoxication leads to believing in false realities.

"You don't look fine …" David says.

His genuine concern makes my heart ache with appre-ciation, but I shove the feeling aside and will myself to think rationally.

"It's just a headache. I drank too much yesterday," I admit.

"I didn't notice … Wait here. I've got a remedy for this." David jogs out of the bedroom.

My sarcasm meter is currently incapacitated, along with many other parts of my brain, and I debate whether David really didn't notice I was buzzed last night. If he had, would it have changed what happened?

"Any allergies?" David pops his head around the corner, holding a phone to his ear.

"No," I say, using the moment to quickly gather my wits and determine a course of action.

David's voice fades, but I hear him ordering room service in the other room. As he does so, I assess the current situation. Last night, David told me about some very private and potentially life-changing news. The admissions delved past getting to know someone on a friendship level. He put himself out there in the most vulnerable way possible. I don't know if I would have been so forthcoming without a little liquid encouragement.

He quickly ruined our moment of closeness with a bad joke. My reaction might have been a bit exaggerated, and we recovered quickly, but there is now a feeling in the pit of my stomach that I am not sure will ever go away. There's a slice of doubt that taints my opinion of him.

It might have been jealousy, or it might have been intuition. I've never had to distinguish between the two. In any other circumstance, I would simply run away and label the man's actions a red flag for making me feel such insecurity.

But there is another feeling. An indescribable feeling that paralyzes me.

"Smoothies are on the way. For now, swallow these," he says, placing two Advil in my hand, and setting several pink tablets on the bedside table with a bottle of blue water. "Chew the pink ones and drink all of this."

"What is all this?" I look suspiciously at the blue liquid in a bottle plainly marked as filtered water.

"Just vitamins and electrolytes. I take this daily, but it'll help your hangover. It's a beautiful day, you wouldn't want to waste it!" David takes a long swallow of his own blue concoction.

"Thanks."

"So do you have plans today?" he asks.

I swallow the tablets and try the blue water; it tastes like artificial blue raspberry, which I hate. "Gross," I mutter, chewing the pink tablets quickly and drinking more of the sour liquid.

"It doesn't taste the best, sorry. But it'll help, I promise."

"It's fine. I need to recover."

"So ... About today, I've got to make some calls and I need to workout—" he begins.

It occurs to me that David is trying to get me to leave. He's nursing me back to health so I don't overstay my welcome because the man has shit to do. And what did I think anyway – that we would spend the day cuddling in bed?

I cut him off before the rejection sinks in further. "I should really get back to my room."

I swing my legs over the edge of the bed, doing my best to ignore the feeling of my brain bouncing around in my skull.

"At least wait for the smoothie. You should eat something," David suggests, placing a hand on my elbow to steady me, but his eyes shift lower and narrow.

I follow the direction of his gaze to my breasts. "Sorry," I cover them and search the room for my clothes.

He probably thinks I am flouncing around naked, wearing only his boxers, to get his attention – the thirsty little whore I was last night would certainly pull something like that. My drunken brain lacks any modesty. But I am back to my usual sober and rational self.

"Don't be sorry." David follows me around the room, grabbing my wet bikini and cover-up from the floor before I reach them. He cradles them like a football to his chest as he says, "I can loan you a shirt."

Of course, he can. Anything to get me out of here faster.

"No. It's fine." I rip the clothes out of his grip and quickly make my way to the bathroom.

He is right on my heels, and I am not sure why, but I slam the door in his face to halt his advance. If he is trying to embarrass me further, there is no need. I've officially sunk to my lowest low – I am about to perform the walk of shame.

What was I thinking throwing myself at an NFL quarterback? He can have any woman he wants. When he saw me sober this morning, he probably realized it, too. No. He probably realized it last night when he tossed those boxers on the bed and refused to go any further.

I stare at my reflection in the mirror – my hair wild and knotted, my skin red and dry. I pale in comparison to him. To his perfection on the other side of that thin white door. Freshly risen from bed and he still looks utterly screwable.

There is no way I can compete with the type of woman he usually sleeps with. He claims he's never met a woman like me, but that isn't necessarily a good thing. And it's probably not even true. At this point, I can't even remember what else he claimed; my self-loathing reaches its peak and encompasses all my thoughts.

"Destiny? Are you okay?" David calls from the other side of the door.

Why is he following me? Probably to make sure I leave as soon as possible without rummaging through his stuff. He is keeping an eye on me, so I change as quickly as possible.

"Coming," I say shakily.

Before opening the door, I take several deep breaths to steady my emotions. The embarrassment is overwhelming, but I won't let it show. I won't be defeated. I won't be this impacted by a man.

Why would I think the morning after with him would be any different than with other men? That he would continue to pursue and impress me. That he would prove he was the type of man I need – I've read too many romance novels.

I open the door, and David stumbles back.

"Hey!" he says excitedly, running a hand through his unruly hair. He keeps doing that, making the awkwardness impalpable.

Forced to face the truth, I turn the tables before he can fully turn them on me. "Thanks for last night. It was fun, but I need to focus on Stacy and Ryan's wedding. Maybe I'll see you around. If not, it was nice meeting you," I say casually as if the sharing of our souls and body meant nothing.

Because it didn't. It was all in my head.

Without giving him the opportunity to answer, I pull my shoulders back and walk past him toward the front door.

"Destiny?" he says behind me, but I fling open the front door and keep moving.

David doesn't chase after me this time. And even though I knew he wouldn't, it still hurts.

27

DAVID

"DESTINY?" I YELL AFTER her, but she is already through the door and down the path.

One minute we are fine – or so I thought. The next, she is rushing through the place in last night's wet swimsuit and avoiding eye contact with me. The only reason I'm not running after her is because of her words: *Thanks for last night – it was fun. Maybe I'll see you around.*

Last night had been more than fun for me. It meant something – or at least I thought it did. But Destiny from last night and Destiny from this morning are two completely different people. Has our connection really been completely in my head? Or is Destiny closing herself off because it is easier than admitting how strong our connection is? I want to believe the latter because she's stubborn as fuck.

Although, she was a little drunk last night. She might regret her decisions. It makes me sick to think she regrets what we did because I certainly don't. I loved every minute of it and I want more. Thinking she might feel differently makes me nauseous. It is the worst kind of rejection. While her leaving abruptly this morning affirms my worst fears, I won't allow myself to believe her actions are sincere.

Destiny won't defeat me. Not like this. Not yet. We are only at half-time.

I dress quickly and take the beach-side route to the main resort. It is too soon to risk a run-in with Destiny. If there is any hope for us, my plan to convince her otherwise must be solid.

I'll have to perform some evasive maneuvers. And the best way to do that is by talking to her friends.

While there is a small chance this method will piss her off, there is as much a possibility the plan will be a success. Granted, that's if her friends don't think I am a total prick after last night.

"David? There you are! Destiny isn't answering her phone," Stacy says, walking briskly over to me from one of the bar side carts. Ryan follows, holding two juices.

"Hi, guys!" I feign excitement to see them. Pat and Dale are the two friends I hoped to find and ask for advice, but Ryan and Stacy will have to do.

"I'm not sure if you remember, but we are getting married tonight!" Stacy gushes, giving an eyeful of appreciation to her husband as he passes her a juice. *About time.* "Anyways, we'd love to have you there if you don't have any plans. It's a little ceremony and will be super quick. The important part is the party afterward! Obviously. And we'd love to have you join!"

"Right, how could I forget today is the big day. Congrats, man!" I shake Ryan's hand as a grin that has nothing to do with my happiness for them and everything to do with the convenience of this invitation spreads across my face.

"Thanks," he shakes my hand and quickly places it on his fiancés back.

"So, you'll be there?" Stacy asks excitedly.

You bet I'll be there.

"Wouldn't miss it for the world," I reply.

This is my opening, but now, I need to plot the rest of my way past Destiny's defenses.

"Great!" Stacy squeals.

"See you tonight, man," says Ryan.

As they walk away, I can't help but think this has been too easy. Fate may have a plan for Destiny and me after all. I can only hope it's on my side because showing up at her friends' wedding unannounced is sure to ruffle her feathers – something I rather enjoy witnessing, but she rather doesn't enjoy happening.

I debate the plan as I aimlessly walk around. This morning, as I watched her sleep, I planned an entire day of activities for us, but her quick retreat nullified any hopes I had of spending the day with her. Part of me considers finding her, regardless. Another part of me – the sensible part – is worried about over-enthusiastically pursuing the woman.

Women don't usually respond well to desperate men. Granted, I've never been a desperate man, so I wouldn't know first-hand, but I've witnessed it happen to others and I don't want to end up a failure like one of them.

Yet, that yearning feeling to find her and be with her doesn't decrease. The longing only increases the further away she feels.

After an hour of wandering around the expansive resort, I circle back to the centrally located main pool. Destiny's male friends – minus Ryan – are taking shots on the edge of the pool. I spot Pat and Dale.

It is now or never.

Putting my best foot, and face, forward, I turn on the charm and walk to their side of the pool.

"What's up, guys?" I say crouching down beside Pat and Dale.

Pat gives me a skeptical look before Dale shoots him a warning glare. They know I have ulterior motives.

"Destiny wasn't in her room this morning," says Pat. "Either the night ended well for you both or she passed out on the beach again. If it's the latter, you better run fast."

I choke on a laugh at the skinny man's threat, then realize he is entirely serious and would probably do some damage before I restrain him. Personal threats – to the people you love – carry more weight and hold far more potential for danger.

"Sorry. Um … I said something stupid and that's why she got pissed, but no, she didn't sleep on the beach last night. Things went great. Well … until this morning," I explain.

"What do you mean *until this morning*?" Dale asks, crossing his arms on the edge of the pool and leaning in, ready to hang on every word of possible gossip.

The other men are pretending not to listen and making clipped conversation behind Pat and Dale.

"I'm not sure how to explain it, but she just up and left. She said she wasn't feeling well, and when I came back with aspirin, she fled. It was like a completely different Destiny."

Will laughs and joins our conversation. He is the last person I want advice from. Mainly because I don't want to think about him ever having touched Destiny. Jealousy is not an emotion I am familiar with, and avoidance is the best way to never experience it.

"Typical Destiny. She doesn't like people taking care of her. Runs from the first sign of potential dependence," Will says.

"We all know how independent she is, but I highly doubt David bringing her an aspirin triggered the response. It doesn't make sense," Dale says in Destiny's defense. I like him even more for it.

"What exactly happened last night? Maybe that's why she left," Pat adds curiously, but he's fishing in empty waters.

"Last night …" I begin, glancing at Will. Telling Pat and Dale is one thing; disclosing what happened last night to Destiny's ex is another. "Last night we had a really good conversation. There's nothing that indicated she felt differently."

As much as I want to fully explore the details of last night to determine when Destiny decided I wasn't worth her time, now isn't appropriate.

"So, you didn't sleep together?" Pat says, backing up and crossing his arms.

Will and Dale glare at him but don't jump in to save me. Instead, they all shift their attention to me, waiting for a response. I'm used to this type of talk in the locker room. In fact, I've taken part in it plenty of times when I saw women as sexual conquests. But Destiny isn't a conquest.

"Um. No. We didn't. And I don't think I should be discussing that with you all." I stumble over the words as I feel heat creep up my cheeks.

"She probably thinks you don't like her." Javier drifts over in the water, joining our conversation. Matt lingers in the distance, staying quiet and drinking a beer.

Now I have all her friends weighing in on the events of last night. This is straying from the original plan and I'm starting to fear how Destiny would react if she knew what we were talking about.

"She'd only think that if you denied her …" Dale trails off, giving me an arched brow in an unspoken question.

"Jesus Christ …" I curse under my breath. These men are digging for way more details than I want to discuss.

"I don't need to be here for this conversation. Come on, guys," Will excuses himself, swimming past Javier and Matt toward the pool bar. Javier shrugs but follows Will.

Matt says, "Good luck, man," before following them as well. He doesn't say much and I begin to appreciate him more for it. Luck might be all I have right now.

"I see how it is, Will, conversation gets tough and you leave the girls to handle it." Pat winks at me, then turns serious when the other men are out of earshot. "So?" He crosses his arms on the edge of the pool by his husband. They both lean in.

Now that the other three males are gone, the air feels less dense and I can finally speak freely. "I didn't have a condom. But I promise I didn't deny her other things," I say, thinking about how my hands and mouth devoured her body. God, it felt good. There's no way she could doubt *my* intentions after that.

"Sounds like she's just not that into you," Pat says matter-of-factly.

My heart sinks. It can't be true. I refuse to believe it until the words come from Destiny's mouth.

"Pat!" Dale scolds his husband, so Pat explains his thoughts.

"Tell you what, we'll talk to her. The girls are getting ready in Stacy and Ryan's suite, and they invited us – the token gay guys – to join them for drinks."

Relief rushes through me. If anyone can convince Destiny to keep an open mind, it's Pat and Dale. "Thanks! That would be amazing. You guys are the best."

I extend a fist to them both and they bump knuckles with me before chuckling at the purely masculine gesture. This is how we respect one another on the field, and I respect the hell out of Pat and Dale, especially since they are willing to help me.

Destiny, here I come.

28

DESTINY

"Shit!" I curse at myself as I frantically gather my things.

After the awkward morning with David, I passed out in my room for a solid three hours. Stacy, Michelle, and Kat have been calling me non-stop but I slept through it. It is the day of the wedding and we are supposed to be having brunch then getting ready together.

The men are doing their thing, and we women are doing ours. Michelle, who is Stacy's maid of honor, arranged the entire day. I've apparently already missed brunch and they are not happy with me – mainly because, according to their text messages, they have no idea where I am and if I am okay after last night.

I understand their concern. I'd feel the same way if I left my friend late at night chewing out some sexy oversized man. But I loathe all the questions they are bound to ask. My answers likely won't be satisfactory.

No, I didn't sleep with him.

No, I'm not going to tell you about his dick.

No, I doubt I'll see him again.

Granted, it is a small resort, so there is a strong possibility that I will run into him, but I only have two days left of this trip and there's still a chance I can avoid David until then.

After stuffing my dress, toiletries, and makeup into a bag, I barrel out of the room toward Stacy's suite. Better late than never.

The resounding pain in my head has subsided in my panic, but it is slowly coming back in full force the closer I get to the chattering woman. Right now, the last thing I want to do is talk about David. Yet, my late arrival has basically signed me up for an hour of questioning. It is inevitable. No matter how much it pains me.

The knowledge of his rejection bites like that of a flea, and I can't simply lie about that. I threw myself at him. How many women have thrown themselves at the insanely handsome, incredibly fit, ridiculously successful man?

I am *so* pathetic.

I was smitten and acted like a teenager in lust – no rational thoughts, just need and greed. No consideration of the consequences of my actions or the opposing feelings of the two parties involved.

And David. David Green. He has this quiet confidence, a steely resolve that makes the rejection burn harder. It was like he was completely unaffected. But why should he be? We only just met. He probably has a line of women waiting to date him in New York City. And after that GQ spread of him, the line likely spans much further than one city.

The worst part: I knew it. I knew it all along – that he would be my Achilles heel.

As I reach Stacy and Ryan's room, I hear animated discussion. It sounds like Stacy's mom and sister are inside – they all have the same midwestern accent. I send a silent prayer of thanks to whoever is listening for the. My friends won't be asking me dick questions with family members present.

"There you are!" Pat sing-songs behind me.

So much for the help.

"Hi …" I say, swiveling around to face Pat and Dale who are fresh from the pool, swim trunks still dripping chlorinated water.

"Don't worry. We aren't going to ask about last night. We already got the details," Dale says, picking at his nails.

"What? What details!" Not that I want to share the details myself, but I sure as hell didn't want my friends hearing another side of the story – the side where I am embarrassingly rejected.

"Just that you ran off as soon as you woke up. You're really putting that man through the wringer, Dez," Dale says.

"Excuse me?" I cross my arms, shocked that Dale is blaming me. If anyone should be blamed, it's David, for making me feel the way he did last night and then this morning giving me excuses about all the things he needs to get done today so that I would leave. He is in the wrong, and I am determined to make it known. "Don't you dare—"

"Shh, shh, shh." Pat places his index fingers over my lips to silence me. Heat explodes across my face as my anger rises to infinitesimal levels. No one shushes me. "My husband is usually so much more tactful. Aren't you, Dale?" Pat scolds Dale.

Dale's mouth opens and closes in an effort to defend himself, but he fails to find the words.

Before I bite off his finger, Pat continues, "Why don't you tell us what happened last night? Because we ran into David, and that man has it bad for you. Like, he might be in love with you. Actually, I'm almost certain he's in love with you. But as soon as you tell us what he did wrong, we'll threaten to kick his ass if he comes near you again. Pinky promise," Pat winks, removing his index finger from my lips and hooking his pinky finger in front of me instead.

The childish promise tempers my anger – if only momentarily. What doesn't help my anger is that David spoke to my friends this morning and that he made it seem like he is in love with me. What kind of game is this man playing? Because I don't play games of the heart. Especially not on my goddamn vacation.

He wanted me gone this morning. Not the other way around.

"Last night was fine. But I think you've got your facts wrong. David is absolutely not in love with me. That's absurd. I don't think he's even interested, nor am I at this point." I turn on my heel to enter the room behind us, but Dale shuffles around me clumsily. "What the hell, Dale?"

"Don't hate me for saying this …"

"I can already tell whatever you're about to say is going to make me hate you." I tense up, awaiting his advice.

Dale places his hands on my shoulders, forcing me to tense more, but effectively holding my attention and my fury. "From what we can tell, David is really torn up about your exit this morning. He said he thought last night went really well and was confused when you left this morning. He thinks you're not into him, which I'm sure is a real eye-opener for the man. I mean … I doubt he gets denied often." I scoff at him, and he shrugs unapologetically. "It probably makes him want you more honestly. So, if that's your game plan, then you're killing it, girl."

"My game plan? I have no game plan," I say, pushing away Dale's hands.

There is no way in hell David feels like me right now. It isn't possible. I am sure of it. Like Dale said, David probably never gets denied by women. This is exactly the type of behavior that fuels the desire to chase what you cannot have. David wanted me gone this morning, then whines to my friends about my leaving. His actions don't make sense.

But another part of me wonders, what if he really was just trying to make me feel better this morning with no ulterior motive, like getting me to leave him alone? If that were the case, what would it change between us? Nothing. Or maybe, everything.

I have a sickening feeling that my defense mechanism – in place to protect my heart – is self-sabotaging David and mines connection. I've never met a man so worthy of my time or my heart. I've known David for just a few days. Yet, in that short amount of time, I feel something different with him. It is like I don't have to hold anything back. My emotions flow freely, my words even freer, and all of it is received without judgement.

He allows me to be angry, happy, sensual, and with no abandon. The only thing I reserve, the only thing I hold onto, except for my momentary blip last night, is my heart. It caged itself in iron long ago, guarding against those who weren't worthy, protecting me from wishy-washy sub-par men whom I can't depend on. Last night, the iron cracked. This morning, it exploded. And I ran.

David *is* dependable. David cares. *Fuck me*. David is all the things I have been looking for, but I don't want it to be true. Because we are on vacation. We are living a fantasy. If I give my heart to him, it will be crushed as soon as we leave this place. There isn't a future for us. We live on opposite sides of the country, multiple time zones away.

The truth is David and I can't work anywhere else.

"Dez, are you okay?" Dale asks.

An overwhelming sense of self-preservation clashes with my longing to be loved. The internal conflict is too much, and my best option is to ignore it, to move on and forget about everything that has transpired between us.

"Yes," I say, although my voice is far shakier than I'd like it to be.

Pat wraps his arms around me and snuggles my back into his front. This comforting act is too much. "Babe, don't have regrets in life. Follow your heart – it knows best. If I hadn't listened to my heart, Dale and I wouldn't be together, and that would have been a damn shame because I've never been happier."

Dale nods his agreement and hugs me from the front. Both men kiss my head as one salty tear slides down my cheek. I feel like shit and not just from the hangover. I came here to celebrate love, not fall into it.

29

David

She's just not that into you. Denial hurts regardless of what form it is delivered in. I've gotten used to the feeling lately, but Destiny's denial – that is something else entirely. It is like a sucker punch to the gut. Over and over and over.

I hold onto the possibility that Pat and Dale will change her mind. And if she really isn't into me, then so be it. I'll move on, I'll endure, and I'll recover. I am agile like that because I have to be. At least, I'll have no regrets in this respect.

Not this time.

Since Destiny will be busy with wedding day activities and I have hours before the ceremony begins, I decide to take my frustrations out in the gym. There's no problem a good burn can't resolve.

At least, temporarily.

I hope to be so exhausted from the workout that my brain will shut off completely and only be able to focus on one thing – breathing. All my worries will be left on the gym floor covered in sweat. Just the way I like it.

Thankfully, no one is in the small room that barely qualifies as a gym to witness my physical release. It is empty most days. People visiting an all-inclusive resort tend to care about the other available activities, which I don't blame them for, but the gym is my home away from home and I'll be here regardless of the other temptations – excluding Destiny, of course.

The recent strain on my shoulder is proof that I need to continue therapy. I need to repair the torn shoulder muscle before next season. It's in a good place, but any sign of pain is a bad omen in my mind.

I start the workout with a three-mile run which feels like it takes ten times longer than usual. My brain simply won't stop replaying the last twenty-four hours. I recount every second, every word, and every touch between Destiny and me, trying to figure out where it went wrong. Unfortunately for my workout, my thoughts keep skipping back to how beautiful she looked lying beneath me – her face twisted with pleasure.

The taste of her still lingers on my tongue. Brushing my teeth this morning was a challenge; I didn't want to lose the flavor of her, but I am hopeful for another chance to devour her. To please her. To make her quiver. *Fuck*. I'd tear down heaven and hell to hear *Medusa* moan my name.

Sweat drips down my brow and off the tip of my nose, landing on my upper lip. The salty taste reminds me of Destiny's ocean water-covered legs. I'd give my next paycheck to have her long legs wrapped around me as I grind myself into her. As I let her feel my promise of pleasure.

This workout is doing nothing but increasing my desire and running with a half chub is painful, so I swap exercises. I load three forty-five-pound plates on each side of the Olympic bar, gearing up for squats. Squats use the largest muscle group in the body and exert maximum energy when performed properly. They will be my saving grace – letting my mind finally empty itself.

As I warm up my legs, squatting down and feeling the full stretch of my muscles before exploding upward, I sense Destiny. It is like she is near, but I know she isn't. It's like the more I use my body, the more my body craves her.

The quick beat of my heart and increase in body temperature are another reminder of how I feel when around her. There is no escaping her, like her aura has permanently attached itself to me.

I wish it actually had. Instead, she ran away from me before it could. The only thing keeping her close is my overactive imagination – something I never struggled with until now.

I'm not safe from her anywhere.

Not even here. My safe haven has been infiltrated by reminders of her. I am unable to clear my thoughts. Meditation is a curse, no longer a reprieve, because all I am aware of is how every thought drifts back to *her.*

She is everywhere. She is everything.

I rack the weight bar and pace in front of the squat rack, frustration leaking from my very pores, replacing the sweat that should be there.

I am a lost cause. I have it bad.

This is a fool's game. A losing game.

Yet, I still play.

And then, out of nowhere, I see her.

Destiny is standing outside the gym, hiding beneath the shade of a nearby tree, watching me. I divert my gaze quickly from the window, unsure whether I should acknowledge her yet.

How long has she been watching me? Maybe, I can sense her after all. More importantly, did she see the contemplation on my face? Does she know the thoughts that haunt me? Did she come back – for *more*? There is no telling what she thinks, but she is here for a reason, and I don't think it is because she is just passing by.

In my peripheral vision, I watch her as I return to the squat rack. She doesn't look at me like she did this morning. Her face is softer, yet somehow more anguished. To anyone else, she looks as if she might be sick, but I know better. I recognize that face – it is the same one I currently wear.

But resolution settles over me as I make the discovery. Destiny isn't simply walking by; she is looking for me.

And I am about to give her a show.

30

Destiny

For a moment, I thought he spot me and I nearly ran away, but he looked onward and then continued working out. His brow glistens, his light blue cotton T-shirt darkened by his sweat. The man is strong; there is no denying it. The thick corded muscles in his thighs flex and his shorts ride high against those bulging mounds as he easily squats three hundred pounds.

No wonder he barely needed a breath after carrying me across the sandy beach. I am like a feather compared to the massive weight bar he is squatting over and over. Just when I think he can't do another, he surpasses my expectations and does five more. His facial features are pained as he exercises, but his body shows no indication of it slowing him down.

The dedication. The perseverance. It's sexy as hell.

If Pat and Dale are right, the pain reflected on David's face may be more internal than external. I hope they aren't right. But I also hope they are. Because if David is experiencing an iota of hurt from my leaving this morning, that means he was never planning on rejecting me. In fact, it would mean I nearly sabotaged everything with my assumptions.

As much as I hate to admit it, I've often used avoidance as the easy way to deal with a problem in my relationships. My heart was in danger and I chose the easy way out.

If I confront David now, there is no turning back – I knew that last night and I know it now. I've already crossed the line. Sex or no sex. The moment I kissed him, all hope of my heart remaining untarnished was lost.

Achilles. He is *my* Achilles.

Looking at the man, no one would blame me. If he hadn't been a professional athlete, he would have been a model or CEO. He looks like the perfect poster boy. His golden skin and hazel green eyes are painfully mesmerizing. I envy every woman who has thought the same and seen those glowing eyes between their legs. It makes me want to run. To hide. To deny this attraction, this uncontrollable longing for something more.

There is no turning back time, though. We can't walk away from the experiences that shape us or the people in-volved. But we do determine our future. The decisions we make in the present should harness the mistakes of our past to ultimately better our lives. Or so I tell myself.

I will take the risk – making the harder, but presumably better choice. Despite the mistakes David and I made in our past, this could be the moment we make the right decision.

It is a noble thought and much easier to envision than to execute, but I decide to try.

David turns his back to me; his shoulders rise and fall with labored breaths. I seize the opportunity, rounding the corner of the building, heading straight for the gym door.

It is now or never. I need to explain my behavior this morning and find out what his intent was for us today. It's time to clear the playing field.

When I fling open the door, David is standing on the other side of it. My footsteps falter.

"Hey," he says, pulling up his shirt and wiping the sweat from his brow.

"Hi," I reply, savoring every inch of his exposed abdomen. My earlier resolve evaporates in my lustful admiration.

David chuckles. "Feeling better, Destiny?"

Each syllable of my name slides off his tongue spicily and I recall the other things that tongue can do. A shiver runs down my spine. It unnerves me how quickly David's presence impacts my mind and body. This is why I ran – he makes me feel a base level of desire that can be described as borderline animalistic.

"Destiny?" he asks again.

"Ya …Yes. I feel better," I say, watching his eyes and lips move slowly, turning up into a cocky smile.

"I was worried after this morning …" he drawls, running a hand through his sweat-laden hair.

"About what?" I ask, my insides turning excitedly as I wait for his admission. Nothing about this conversation is going according to plan.

The door grows heavier against my body, the air-conditioned gym chilling my front, while the hot Tulum weather heats my back. The comfort level of this interaction is becoming oppressive. David's eyes glance back and forth between my own as he debates his response. I shift uneasily under the weight of his gaze and the uncomfortable silence.

This is the moment of truth.

My feet brought me here without a second thought. I dropped my stuff in Stacy's room and left without an explanation. The need to make things right before it is too late overtook all rational decisions and prior obligations. I need to know if David really does have feelings for me, and if it is simply *me* who hinders chance for something more. Something real, raw, and life-changing.

"Well … After you left, I thought I did something wrong. Or that you weren't interested anymore." David attempts a smile, but his lips quiver slightly. "I'm still not sure how you feel."

"Me?" I ask, dumbfounded. He really thinks I am the one who isn't interested.

"Yeah, you." He laughs nervously this time, all hint of arrogance gone.

"I thought you weren't interested," I explain.

"Me?" His brows shoot up in surprise. "What made you think that? I'm more interested than ever. Last night was amazing!"

His candid honesty catches me off-guard. It is as if the air is lighter around us. I'll never know why it took Pat and Dale chastising me to realize what needed to be done, but matters of the heart aren't easy. Although with David, it is easy. It is easy when I let myself be open with him. With communication and an open heart, it can be effortless.

"It was … I just thought I was a burden to you this morning. Being hungover is so unattractive and I figured you'd want privacy."

"Privacy is the last thing I want from you. And you were cute this morning – hungover or not. You snore a little when you sleep. It's the cutest sound I've ever heard," David admits, reaching for my hand.

Our fingers intertwine and it feels like the world's axis has been righted. "No one thinks snoring is cute," I argue meekly.

"Normally I wouldn't, but there's something about the way that you do it that's perfect." He pulls me into an embrace, placing my hands on his shoulders and wrapping an arm around my waist. "Don't run away from me just yet."

"Okay," I promise shyly as his lips brush mine.

31

DESTINY

I'M NOT SURE WHAT came over me, but after our lips connected, I got the sudden inclination to invite David to the wedding. Hopefully, Stacy and Ryan don't mind. After all, they drunkenly invited him last night. David gladly accepted my invitation, claiming he wants to spend as much time with me as possible. His assertive dedication is unbearably hot.

I never understood how someone could be both cute and sexy at the same time until now.

His intentions are clear, and now my interest is, too. Risk of heart break still lingers in the back of my mind, but I keep repeating Pat's advice to follow my heart. This situation is odd. I can either fight it or roll with it, but rolling with it sounds a lot more fun. Scarier. But more exciting.

I return to Stacy's suite feeling a hundred times better and my happiness doesn't go unnoticed by the woman.

"Better late than never I suppose," Stacy calls from her place at the small dining-room table. Hors d'oeuvres and drinks are set out next to a spread of makeup. The room is littered with beauty supplies and clothing, and smells of copious amounts of hair spray.

"Sorry, what did I miss?" I say, sitting down at the table and accepting a mimosa from Kat, who plops down on the chair beside me.

"You missed Pat and Dale. They stopped by before heading back to party with the guys. Apparently, they spent the morning drinking by the pool. I swear to God, if they are too drunk to make it to the reception, I'm going to lose my shit."

Michelle laughs from her place lounging on the couch. "Chill, Stacy. The guys will be fine. I already told Javier to have the bartender water down their drinks."

"Let's hope it works," Stacy murmurs.

Kat and I share a knowing look. The guys will definitely be drunk. Hopefully, Ryan has a little more sense on his wedding day though.

"So … Should we even ask?" says Kat. "Because Pat and Dale had a few things to say about last night."

I glare at her. Kat isn't normally one for gossip. I guess she drew the short straw among the group, being forced to ask. And with a little liquid encouragement, they'll be pestering David when they see him later if I don't share now.

"I don't even want to know what they had to say, but last night was good. David's … David is really nice." I say.

"Really nice?" Michelle scoffs. "That's all you have to say? We already know he's really nice."

"Tell us something we don't know, like how he was in bed," Stacy purrs.

Of course, Stacy wants to know how he is in bed. Although, that throbbing ache inside me wants to know, too.

"We didn't sleep together," I admit.

Everyone's eyebrows raise suspiciously. I wouldn't believe it myself either, if it weren't true. The man is panty-dropping handsome. Fortunately, tonight I'll have another opportunity. Although, that means I have hours to imagine the event and second guess my every move before it happens. After last night, I discovered David is talented at more than just sports. I don't have the same experience, and I hope I won't be a disappointment to him. This will truly be a test of his continued interest.

Taylor walks out of the bathroom. "Am I hearing this right: you didn't sleep together? Damn, girl, you've got some serious self-control."

Great. Even Will's new girlfriend is stunned. At least she assumes I am the one who denied David, not the other way around. In reality, it was a tiny piece of latex that forced us into abstinence. And after tonight, we – or more likely I – might be forced back into abstinence based on my ability to perform.

"Well, we didn't have a condom …" I say quietly, hating how much detail I am sharing, but I don't want anyone to think I am a prude or that David might have been uninterested in me. Call it pride, but I'm still trying to convince myself that he really wants me. The women snicker at me. "What?" I ask acidly, cheeks flaming.

"Seriously? Why didn't you just text one of us? We all have boyfriends here – someone is bound to have a condom," Michelle says.

As if I was going to text them in the heat of the moment. My mind was solely on one thing, and it wasn't any of my friends. "Yeah. Maybe next time." I busy myself with surveying the food on the table and snag a strawberry.

As I place my lips around the pointed end, my mind flashes back to David's lips locked around my nipple and I feel them peak at the memory before taking a large bite of the juicy fruit. The sweet strawberry nectar slides across my tongue and my mind wanders further, imagining David feasting on various parts of my body.

"I've got some in the room. We can stop by later. Matt won't mind," Kat says, pulling me from my lustful thoughts.

"I'm sure David can handle it … If he wants to do … *that*." I try to come up with an excuse for declining Kat's offer. David is significantly above average, and I don't want to offend anyone's significant other's package.

"Best to be prepared for anything, Dez," Stacy warns.

"Yeah. It's no problem. I have a feeling you'll want to borrow some of mine … Sometimes it's hard to find the right *kind* at the convenience store and we don't have a lot of options around here." Kat winks.

"Huh?" I ask, unsure what she is referring to. If I were having constant sex, then I'd be pickier about the type of condoms too, but just about anything will get the job done tonight as long as it's the right size.

"Well, if the size matches the package, you're going to want something extra-large." Kat giggles.

The realization clicks and the image of Kat's boyfriend, Matt, having a gigantic dong makes my cheeks go molten. "Oh my god!"

"Oh my god!" Stacy and Michelle repeat, coming to the same realization.

"Damn, girl … Good for you," Taylor chimes in, sending us all into a fit of laughter.

"How did we not know this before?" Michelle asks, sitting fully upright on the couch and ready to hear more about Matt's penis.

"Because it's none of your damn business," Kat replies sassily, but a playful smirk gives away her amusement. I'm thankful for the distraction.

"Whoa, whoa. Back up … I didn't hear a denial from Dez. Does that mean the size matches the package?" Stacy interrupts.

God help me. Stacy is relentless. And her constant interest in David is pushing my buttons. Wedding day or not, things need to be set straight. "We didn't sleep together because we didn't have a condom, but that doesn't mean we didn't do other stuff." I eye her seriously, but her eyes only light up.

"And?" she insists.

"And what?"

"Details …"

"Jesus Christ. I'm not sharing every detail with you Stacy. Be concerned about the man in your bed tonight, not the man in mine."

The room silences with my rebuke. I might have pushed it too far.

Stacy's answering glare confirms as much. "David Allen Green has been my hall pass since the day Ryan and I got engaged. Forgive me for wanting to at least know the spicy details since obviously it's never going to happen for me. One, I love my future husband and would never sleep with anyone else – hall pass or not. Two, I love you, too, and actually think you guys are really cute together. Yes, I know I have been flirting with him! But I've had a crush on the man since the day I saw him play the Bears. You just now found out he exists. I've been a football fanatic for life."

She stands and storms out of the room, slamming the bathroom door behind her.

"Damnit …" I groan, taking a massive gulp of my mimosa.

"I'll go talk to her." Kat stands, rushing after Stacy. "Don't worry. She's just emotional today."

Michelle leans back on the couch and adds, "We told her she nearly ruined your chances with him last night and she felt awful. I think she is just trying to make sure she doesn't actually ruin it by ensuring everything works out between you and David. You know her … She's more embarrassed than anything else. You guys will make up when she comes back out."

"Yeah. Right …" I say, biting into another strawberry, the sweetness goes sour on my tongue.

32

DAVID

THAT KISS. IT LINGERS, just like everything else about Destiny. She isn't with me physically, but she leaves little pieces of herself behind to tease me. If the torment weren't so gratifying, I'd be in more pain. These blue balls are happy to wait though – no matter how long it takes.

There is no expectation for things to progress physically between Destiny and me tonight or the remaining nights of our vacation. But I'll be prepared if she wants it to. Based on the way her tongue hungrily explored my mouth, I'd say Destiny wants more.

Her intoxicating scent and sex appeal is my new higher power. If she allows it, I'll worship her until she's torn from my grasp. And I have a firm grasp. Her mind, body, and soul will be overflowing with appreciation from the attention I give it.

Just the thought of giving her the treatment she deserves, worshiping her like the goddess she is, excites me. It has been so long since I felt this motivated to know a woman.

This is more than going through the motions, like my other relationships and job have been.

Being with Destiny, learning her ticks, quirks, passions, and peeves is only going to be more fun. I'll explore her and appreciate her in ways no other man has. Or I hope no other man has. I want everything between us to be new and unique. Not a replica of her life with anyone else. Including our sex life.

The night she allows me between her legs will be a test. A very important test. If I do anything to make her uncomfortable or to remind her of another man, she might decide I am not the right fit.

So many people think sex is a small part of what makes a relationship successful. That if the sex isn't great, you can work as a couple to make it better. But they are very wrong. If it isn't great the first time, it will never be good. And a relationship with incompatible sex is a friendship, not a partnership.

There is no way in hell I am being friend-zoned.

I must read Destiny carefully. Figure out her signs and tells. Whether or not she can take me is another problem entirely. Destiny was so deliciously tight around my fingers. I couldn't stop myself from wondering how long it has been for her to be so tight.

My presence will no doubt shock her. I'll stretch her and make her sore – a fact I delight in yet hate at the same time. Because she may not like the lingering pain. There is so much on the line tonight. It feels like overtime in the playoffs. One wrong move and everything is over.

I drop onto the fluffy comforter covering my freshly made bed. Shortly after the gym and my run-in with Destiny, I ate lunch and showered. I have several hours until the wedding starts, and nothing to do but bask in my nefarious thoughts.

My phone buzzes on the bed beside me, and I see my agent's name appear on the screen.

"What's going on, Blake?" I say, propping myself up on my elbows.

"David, my favorite client, have I got some news for you, my man. Chargers are in! They want to meet with you Friday, so get your ass back to New York and pack your bags. The offer is being drawn up as we speak, and while I can't give you an exact number, I can tell you it's big!" Blake says, the usual sound of heavy New York traffic surrounding him.

"You know it's not all about the number," I warn him.

Early in my career, the dollar value of my offer was everything. I'd been a poor kid who had grown up on the wrong side of town and needed money to help support my mom and sister. This far into my career, money is no longer an issue. I wouldn't be playing football anymore if money were all I cared about.

Blake's voice changes an octave as he fumbles to reassure me. "Of course, of course. These guys are long-time fans of yours, David. They understand this is more about a partnership and good working environment than a dollar figure. You know I'm going to get what you're worth, though. I don't want you being underpaid."

Of course, he doesn't. After all, as my agent, Blake is getting a cut of this deal.

"Make it clearer. I'd rather retire early than deal with more political bullshit that results in losing games," I demand.

"Whoa … Retire early? Your mindset on retirement was totally different a few days ago. Now it almost sounds like you're threatening the possibility. Should I be concerned?"

"Not at all. I've just decided that I'll no longer settle. Settling is never going to make me happy, and it only distracts me from the better option. If the Chargers can't meet my demands, another team will," I state, feeling the truth in my words. Because I am experiencing it currently.

I have settled on women my entire life – going with the flow and accepting the type of female around me as high quality. Yet, when I exited my stale life, I found the spark I've always needed. Fuck me for taking so long to figure it out, but different is good.

My old team is wrong for me. The person I was ten years ago fit in with that lifestyle and team dynamic, but I've grown. The things I need now are completely different and probably have been for a while. I just didn't realize it until now.

"I'll see what I can do before they send you the offer. No promises, but I think they'll want to make it work. Keep your phone nearby." Blake hangs up before I can get another word in. He knows my demands, though. We talked about them extensively.

Knowing I'll be visiting Los Angeles by next Friday means I have a lot of work to get done. Should the negotiations go well, and based on the timing of the off-season, I need to move as soon as possible, so I message my real estate agent.

I have visited LA numerous times. The weather there is ideal, especially for my favorite extracurricular activities. Being close to the training facilities and the ocean is a must for my next property. I text my real-estate agent my wish list and she replies, saying she will have tours set up for Saturday morning.

Things are moving along smoothly.

It will be weird going back to the real world and to a potentially different life. Hopefully, that life will include Destiny, but I am not sure how it will work. We can take it one day at a time. But if I lock myself into a contract with LA and she is based on the East Coast, things could become difficult.

My heart says we can make it work. My brain, however, is wearier. The ultimate test may not be sex after all; it could be geography. It could be that we only fit here, in this place, and not in the real world.

There are too many unanswered questions about our lives that we have yet to discuss, and tonight isn't the right time. I don't want to spoil our evening with future concerns. Hell, I may scare her off with thinking too far ahead. It seems like Destiny is on the same page, in terms of looking for a serious relationship over a fling, but talking about the details could make her rethink her decision. And we still need time to get to know each other.

So much is at stake. While one couple makes the commitment to spend their lives together – sailing through the unknown as a team – Destiny and I will be navigating temperamental waters, capable of tipping the boat at any time and separating us for good.

33

Destiny

"Sorry about earlier," Stacy says as the wedding planner steers us toward the temporary tents that will serve as the waiting area for Stacy and Ryan's first look.

"No. I'm sorry. I was being jealous and caddy. It's your big day and I know you're kind of obsessed with football. If Chris Hemsworth were at this resort making eyes at you, I'd be doing the same. It wasn't right of me to get snappy. You love Ryan. I know that! Honestly, I've never been that weird, possessive, jealous woman before. I don't know what came over me, but it was wrong to snap at you."

Stacy laces her fingers in mine as we walk. At the end of the day, we are best friends and have been for years. The distance created by living in two different cities is more than mere miles; our friendship and ability to interpret the other's feelings has suffered, too.

"Thanks for being here. And if I'm being honest … Please don't kill me or lash out further. It is my special day after all," she gives me a stern look, "I think you're feeling those things because you're not being honest about your feelings for David. Maybe you should give him a chance."

"I guess it's a good time to tell you that I invited him to the ceremony tonight." I wrinkle my nose, waiting for her reaction – she's either going to squeal happily or start cussing me out. I don't think she remembers inviting him last night, so I basically just added a plus one without the bride's permission.

She laughs. "Dez. Ryan and I talked to him this morning. He was coming all along, silly."

"What?"

"Yeah. He said he wouldn't miss it." Stacy lets go of my hand and walks into the tent as the wedding planner holds back the thick white curtain for us.

Michelle, Kat, and Taylor are already waiting inside, having walked ahead of us to usher the other guests away and ensure Ryan is nowhere in the vicinity. The first look and capturing it on camera is incredibly important to Stacy so we all have a part to play in guaranteeing its success.

I sit on a small, padded bench and replay David and mines conversation in my mind. He gave me no indication that he'd already confirmed he was coming. That man is sneaky as hell. I really have been completely wrong about him.

Even though I ran away this morning, basically telling him I never wanted to see him again, he still planned on showing up tonight. What was he planning – to court me? It's the cutest possible thing he could have done.

A small part of me regrets making up with him so soon, if only so I could have witnessed how hard he would have tried to win me over. It would have been fun to watch him tiptoe around me, pulling out all the stops. I wonder what kind of moves David has? What kind of charm he is capable of? If it's more than I've already been privy to, I'm not sure I'd be able to resist him for long.

"All clear, we're ready for the first look. If you ladies would please follow me, I'll take you to the reception area. Stacy, I'll be right back for you. Sit tight." The wedding planner directs us out of the tent before I can contemplate David's actions or ask Stacy more questions about when she confirmed his attendance.

It is time for the wedding. My mind should be on celebrating my best friend, not fantasizing about some man. Some crazy fine, equally aggravating, and sexually stimulating man.

"Not that I doubted his abilities, but David cleans up nice," Kat says and nudges my side as we approach the other wedding guests who are waiting to be seated.

David is standing with Pat and Dale, dressed in dark linen slacks and a matching button-down shirt that stretches against his muscular upper body. It looks like the resort store didn't have a "big and tall" section, but damn am I glad they didn't. One tug and I can rip that shirt right off him.

"Yeah," I agree with Kat, my mouth going dry.

'By the way, just in case," Kat reaches into her clutch and discreetly passes me a condom.

"Kat – not now!" I hiss, tucking the small foil packet into my clutch before anyone notices.

She rolls her eyes and says, "You can thank me later."

If tonight pans out the way my vagina hopes it will, then I will be thanking her later. But I am still torn. While I want to see what this thing – this connection – is between David and me, sex makes everything more complicated. If it is good, like really good, I'll never be able to forget it. If it is bad, like really bad, I'll never be able to forget it.

Something in between would be most satisfactory, but not ideal either. Honestly, really good sex is something you don't find often. People's sexual preferences vary, and I am not into super kinky shit. David has probably seen some things – a lot more than I have. And the chances of his tastes aligning with mine are questionable.

"Hi," David says breathily as I approach him, his lower lip drooping.

"Hi," I mimic his tone. It feels like the air around us is charged. A buzzing heat pricks my skin as if one move from either of us will ignite that charge. This is a feeling I am becoming all too familiar with when I am in his presence.

"You look stunning."

"Thank you. You do, too."

His lip quirks up. "Thanks. I had to buy clothes from the store here. They don't make much for guys my size …"

"I noticed!" I say, pinching his bicep.

David's arm twitches and flexes under my touch, straining against the fabric. Last night I felt so much more of his body, but I had been lost in the heat of our exchange and unable to focus on what that touch meant. Somehow, this small exchange feels so much more sensual.

"Glad you noticed," David's voice is husky and low.

I suck in my lips to avoid the smile that is creeping across my face at this new form of conversation we are discovering. There is so much sexual tension between us.

After inviting him to the wedding, all I have thought about is what will happen tonight. What he will look like. What he will say. Would we dance? Would we sit together? Would we or should we act like we are each other's date? The answers are obvious, but they still play like a movie reel on repeat in my mind.

"Are you two going to act like teenage virgins all night? Because if so, Dale and I are swapping seats. This is a show I can't miss," Pat says, dousing the tension between David and me with an invisible bucket of cold water.

The sexual tension evaporates – something I am not entirely grateful for. "Very funny, Pat." I lace my arm in David's and turn us around. "Let's get drinks before the ceremony starts."

"Sounds good." David gives Pat and Dale an obligatory shrug. He seems to enjoy their teasing.

We walk toward the bar and order two whiskeys neat. There is only one way to lessen the tension between us and that is to get a little buzzed.

"So … When were you going to tell me that you were already planning on coming tonight?"

David takes a large drink of his whiskey, gulping half of the glass to avoid my question. "It didn't seem right to spoil the moment earlier. Plus, I wouldn't have come without your permission anyways."

"Is that right?" Little does he know, I like the idea of his coming to the wedding without my permission and trying to win my favor. Sue me. I am a sucker for rom-coms, and while I don't believe those things happen in real life, David is giving me hope. My sappy heart deceives me.

"Yeah. I mean … I might have stopped by to see how you were feeling after this morning. But I would have left if you didn't want me here." His lying tongue gets more confident with each word.

"I don't believe any of that!" I laugh at his failure to hide the truth.

David smiles and leans into me, throwing me off balance as his gaze narrows on my lips. "What if I told you I planned to come all along? Especially after you left today."

"I'd say you were being honest."

"And what if I told you I planned to do anything it took to convince you to give me another shot?"

"I'd say … Anything?"

His grin widens and he says, "Anything."

I return a devious smile, all sorts of wicked things drifting through my mind. *Anything.* He would do *anything.* Except all I want him to do is drop to his knees and kiss his way up my legs again. Something we, unfortunately, can't do right here, right now.

"Not that kind of anything. Damn … Destiny." David reads me so well.

The sensual heat from earlier returns with a quick snap.

"This way. Please take your seats, everyone." The wedding planner passes by, motioning us toward the white wooden chairs on the beach.

Once again, David and I are presented with a momentary distraction from the impending situation we'll later face. Butterflies fill my stomach, but I invite them.

Tonight will be the test. It is officially scheduled. If only I had more than one little foil packet.

34

David

As if I am not already struggling to keep my mind out of the gutter, Destiny's sensual expressions of promise are making my balls turn to lead. And to make matters worse, she is constantly touching me. If we weren't at a wedding, I'd shred this shirt so we could be skin to skin already.

The long, flowy lilac dress she is wearing is also doing nothing to help my growing desire. It loosely hugs her curves, moving with the wind and the sway of her hips. She looks like a goddess walking across the white sandy beach, her blonde hair and luminescent skin blending in with the haze of the setting sun. Several small braids adorn the low ponytail she wears her hair in, and a dainty necklace skims her collarbone. I've never seen a woman look more classically beautiful than Destiny. It almost makes me forget about the viper lurking beneath the surface.

How had I not noticed the vastness of her beauty the moment I met her?

Granted, her skimpy bikinis are a far cry from the modest woman before me. But I realize it is the perfect balance.

Destiny is both sexy and beautiful. She is both intelligent and funny – in her own way. She is what we, in sports, call a well-rounded player. She doesn't bring one or two things to the field; she brings ten. She is an asset and someone you do everything in your power to hang onto. Because she will have no trouble finding something or someone better if you give her the opportunity.

"Let's sit here," Destiny says, leading me by the hand to the third row of white wooden chairs.

Her other friends are also taking their seats, along with people who I assume are Stacy and Ryan's family based on their resemblance to the couple. The wedding planner is running around adjusting flower arrangements and directing people to the empty seats. Ryan and the officiant are standing under a simple wooden altar.

Any moment now, I'll be watching two virtual strangers get married. Except, I don't feel like as much of an outsider as I actually am. I haven't spent much time with the group, but sitting here beside Destiny feels right. It feels like some small part of me has always been in her life and will always be.

In order to be a bigger part of her life, though, I need to know more about her and her friends. I need to know this will be worth the effort when I leave Tulum.

"So, when and how did Ryan and Stacy meet?" I ask.

Destiny shifts in her seat, letting her knee touch mine as she faces me to respond. "We all worked at the same company right out of college. They met that first year so … When we were only twenty-two. It's kind of crazy seeing them finally get married. They acted like they wouldn't for a long time, but things sort of changed when we all hit thirty."

"How so?"

I know how things change when you hit thirty, though. For a minute you feel like your life has been a complete failure and waste of time. Then, when you get over that, you realize there is so much more to life. There is so much more to discover and celebrate. Instead of getting fucked up and finding temporary happiness, you begin to focus on the things and people that bring you happiness. The kind of happiness that lasts a lifetime, not a night.

"It just seemed like all our priorities changed. We used to hang out constantly, going out to bars and kicking off the weekend with bottomless mimosas at brunch. Always planning trips and fun events. But when we reached a certain age, all of us started focusing more on our careers or family. It's just a new life stage," she says.

"I get that."

"What about you?"

"What about me?"

She fiddles with the skinny gold bands on her fingers. "I don't want to assume your age, but I'm guessing you're older than me … Why haven't you settled down?"

Her question catches me off-guard and I can't help but laugh at her assumption about my age. "Do I look that old?" I tease her.

"No! I just feel like you're older than me, but not like too old."

"What would be too old?"

"Um … How old are you?" she deflects my question.

I sling my arm around the back of her chair, letting my fingers skim her shoulder as we talk. "I'd rather know your age limit, so I make sure I'm within it before answering!"

Destiny's laughter makes the sun stop setting. "That's not the way it works! Anyways … You're within the range, I can assure you. Just tell me."

"I don't know … I could be in my forties or fifties with three kids already. You don't know," I continue taunting her.

Those piercing blue eyes roll slowly. "I know you're joking. Quit deflecting the question."

"Fine …" I smile, putting my full palm on her shoulder while I rub small circles into her skin. Destiny doesn't even flinch from my touch. Instead, she leans into it, awaiting my response. "I told you why I haven't settled down already, Destiny. Are you doubting my previous answer?"

"No. Maybe, I need a reminder," she says bashfully.

Destiny is being cute. She wants to hear me say no woman has stood a chance. No woman has been anything like her. No woman has successfully trapped me so thoroughly and willingly as her. *My Medusa* –I will happily give her the answers she is searching for.

"Well, there are two reasons. One, I was a player for a long time and didn't want women who intrigued or challenged me. Two, when I was looking for more, I had poor taste in women. Having always been surrounded by the same type of females, I didn't know what to look for or where to look for it. When I thought I found someone worthwhile, they tended to disappoint me. In big ways. And eventually, I realized that I was never really dating anyone different."

"That's sad," she says, looking down, offering a small bit of sympathy.

"Okay. Shit on David hour is over." I joke, wanting to forget about the past and focus on the future.

Destiny gets my drift and grabs my hand before facing forward and stating confidently, "I failed so many times before my company took off. I think we need to go through shit before we succeed. Because if you don't, you'll never appreciate what you have. Too many people think there's always something better out there, and they miss what's right in front of them. The people who had it hard, who failed and got shit on, they don't miss it."

This woman continues to surprise me in the best ways. She is more right than she knows. It might have taken me thirty-six years and a lot of failed relationships, but I notice what is in front of me and I am not missing my chance.

Not this time. Destiny doesn't speak of fate. She speaks of wisdom and experience. And I respect her more for it.

Before I can respond and tell her I whole-heartedly agree, the music begins playing. Hushing sounds spread throughout the group and Ryan's back straightens at the altar. It is time.

I can only imagine how Ryan feels standing there. There is no fear in his eyes, only joyful anticipation. He rubs his sweaty palms on his pants, not from fear of regret or making the wrong choice, but from the excitement of what is to come after. I can't help the jealously that stirs within me.

One day, I will put a ring on my wife's finger. One day, I will feel the same pride Ryan feels as everyone admires my future wife walking down the aisle. And then, one day, I will put a baby inside my wife and watch her be the best mother in the world.

My destiny needs time, but one day, it will all happen and *more*.

35

Destiny

The ceremony was beautiful. Ryan cried as Stacy walked down the aisle, Stacy balled through her vows, I cried watching them cry. And David silently held my hand the entire time, rubbing small circles on the space between my thumb and forefinger.

When I look over to see what he is thinking, his expression softens into understanding. There is so much love and happiness in the air – even he feels it. Weddings, no matter who or how many people are present, are a momentous occasion. This is a moment Stacy and Ryan will never forget and will cherish forever. And we get to be part of it.

My heart could not be fuller.

Weddings are the ultimate proclamation of love, a legally and soulfully binding contract between two people, and something I wasn't sure I would ever experience personally. But a tiny bead of hope is slowly forming that one day I might.

My gaze absentmindedly finds Will and Taylor. Will's arm is around Taylor's shoulder, and she rests her head on his. They are a good match, much better than he and I were.

Pat and Dale, Michelle and Javier, Kat and Matt. Everyone is here. Everyone is happy. Everyone sits with their significant other, embracing each other as they watch their best friends' union. In this little group of friends, only I came alone. Yet, somehow, someone found me here and I'm not alone anymore. In the most unexpected place, with the most unexpected person, a connection has formed.

David *Achilles* Green.

My younger self never would have believed that I would one day be holding the hand of an infamous athlete. I was the nerdy girl in school, and jocks didn't look twice at my stick figure, big glasses, and splotchy complexion. Maturity hit me later in life, gifting me with a small backside, perky boobs, and contact lenses. A little weight gain over the years has added some roundness to my curves, while the constant work grind and forgetful eating has blessed me with a flat stomach.

Not that appearances matter much to me – I have always been attracted to intelligence over looks. I've dated attractive men, but athletes are a lust of the past – something my teenage self-longed for, but my mature self passes on because she is too smart to date players. Although, intelligence clearly hasn't been enough to win my heart because even some of the smartest men I dated still had self-confidence issues.

The man beside me has more than mere athletic ability, though. I can see the intelligence behind those piercing inquisitive eyes. He is a play-maker at heart and his mind is always spinning. But I still pegged him wrong before – when I thought he was some selfish, brooding asshole and then when I assumed he could never be interested in someone like me.

Men don't fall into one genre based on their profession; people place them there. Just because David is an athlete doesn't mean he fits into the typical narrative of a player. In fact, almost everything he has shown me would signify that he is far from one.

As Stacy and Ryan walk down the aisle, hands clasped with their arms raised, David lets go of my hand to clap and cheer with everyone else. For a moment, I am mesmerized by him, forgetting about the celebration. The hypnosis doesn't break until he turns his cheerful face to mine and says my name.

"Destiny?" David asks, extending his hand expectantly.

"Yes?" I place my palm in his.

"You ready?"

"Of course."

He laces our fingers and leads the way to the reception. The reception is taking place in a massive white tent sitting just off the edge of the sandy beach. The view is impeccable, the mood down-right dreamy.

The sun is setting, casting a cool spring glow over the area. Tiki torches are being lit by staff, while the bartender is already being bombarded with drink orders, and the wait staff is walking around with appetizers. Soft classical music filters through the air as if the ocean wind were carrying it, not the surround sound speakers hoisted on tent posts.

"This is pretty sweet. I've actually never been to a wedding like this. And I've been to a lot of weddings," says David.

"Oh yeah, how many?" I ask, grabbing a piece of bruschetta from a waiter's serving tray as they walk by.

David grabs one as well, popping the entire thing into his mouth in one bite. "The quarterback gets invited to all the weddings. Considering all the teammates I've had over the years … At least fifty."

"Wow! That's so many wedding gifts," I joke.

He laughs. "You have no idea. And football players are the worst. Everything on their registry is outrageous. It's not just expensive – it's pointless shit because they already have all the stuff a couple usually needs."

"Well, now I know I need an example. What was the weirdest gift you purchased?" I ask.

"You really want to know?" David arches his brow playfully.

Now I do really want to know. "Yes."

"One of my old running backs – loved the dude, he was a good time and absolutely hilarious, but he had no filter or shame – he asked for a sex swing. All the guys on the team picked numbers for who had to buy it and you're looking at the lucky winner!"

I laugh picturing David purchasing a sex swing and signing his name beside the gift receipt. "Who asks someone to buy them a sex swing? Or anything having to do with sex! That's so ... so private!"

My cheeks instantly heat as I realize how prudish I must sound, but David doesn't pick up on my blunder.

"Like I said – no shame. Although I've got to hand it to the dude, he's still married, has five kids, and I know for a fact he's never cheated. Never even once looked at another woman since he met his wife. In my industry, that kind of commitment deserves respect."

"Really?" David's words trigger all my warning bells. When we return to our lives, will I have to worry about him being faithful?

His shoulders stiffen, and a frown appears as he realizes his mistake. "Destiny, I shouldn't have said that ... There are a lot of faithful men in my profession. And a lot of players. If you're worried about where I fall, you should know I've always been faithful to the women I date. Even when I was a quote unquote 'player'."

I cringe at the mention of his player days. I don't want to imagine David's rolodex of woman. I don't want to picture beautiful women, with far more to offer than me, holding his hand like I have been. Or doing far more with him than I have yet.

"Don't start second guessing this. Please." He grabs my hand and kisses my knuckles with such affection that it beguiles me how quickly his reassurance comes. "There's a connection between us. A strong one. And one that I am fully invested in. As long as you'll let me."

I swallow the jealous lump in my throat because I know that my fear will be the biggest hinderance to us. "I know, I believe you. I just don't know what life will look like after this …"

"Me either. Try not to worry about it right now. Let's just take it one day at a time."

It is so much easier said than done, but he is right. Worrying will only make matters worse. "You're right. Let's enjoy tonight!" I agree.

We walk toward the bar and join my friends, who are already taking celebratory shots.

"Bets on who is next?" Stacy says, pointing to each of the unmarried couples, including David and me. She gives me a wink before continuing, "I think Kat and Matt are next!"

Kat rolls her eyes but Matt tries to hide a smug smile. They are the logical choice for who will get engaged next. They have been together for four years. Matt is in his mid-thirties, probably a similar age to David, and Kat is the same age as me, thirty-one. She talks about wanting a family. If that is still on the table, marriage may not be far off – assuming they want to get married. Based on Matt's expression, I'd say he is planning on it.

"Speaking of engagements," Pat interrupts, "I believe we have an engagement with these shots! There's no time like the present, bitches, bottoms up!" He holds up his glass and we all toast Stacy and Ryan before throwing back the tequila shots.

It burns my throat, but the warmth of the liquor soothes the pain it elicits. I hate tequila, but Pat is right – there is no time like the present.

The DJ's music turns up, blaring a dance beat over the speakers.

"What about dinner?" I ask Ryan, knowing I'll need food or else I'll turn into a drunken mess by the end of the night. And tonight is one I need to remember.

"Appetizers will circulate all night and food will be set out buffet style in about an hour. After we've had time to get nice and toasty." Ryan does a jig in place, apparently he is already feeling toasty.

My friends are crazy.

"Your friends now how to party!" David says cheerily.

That is an understatement. "They know how to do something …" I refuse a shot from Ryan as he passes more out.

David accepts the shot and takes like a pro.

"Want to dance?" he asks.

David's upbeat, carefree attitude makes me second guess everything I know about him. I quite like the broody, arrogant man from the beach, but I suppose I kind of like this side too – the playful, happy side. I look at the empty dancefloor and remind myself *there is no time like the present.*

"Hell yeah!"

We walk onto the dancefloor, and I let the music take the lead. My hips sway to the beat, perfectly in tune to the rhythm. The ladies join David and me. Either the effect of alcohol is in full force already, or Michelle and Stacy's immodest dance moves are a show put on just for David.

David makes a motion of retreat, signaling that he is going to grab us drinks. Instead, he finds the guys and gets sucked into conversation. In his absence, Michelle and Stacy's movements only become crazier – I determine it was the alcohol after all and the former was just my usual warry thoughts.

Even though my friends just met David, he fits in seamlessly. And already, he is comfortable doing his own thing while I do mine. Yet, I know he would be happy to stand by my side if I needed him to.

The night quickly becomes a blur. Not from a drunken loss of time, but from having so much fun that I forget time is passing. Granted, there is a bit of haziness from the liquor. And a lot of another kind of haziness after dancing with David.

Stacy told the DJ to turn on ass-grinding music and he complied, playing some sexy beats that made me want to rub up on David. And rub I did.

Eventually, the songs turn into slow grooves, and the guests start trickling out back to their rooms. David and I say goodbye to those remaining before taking the beach path to his bungalow.

36

DAVID

"THAT WAS FUN," I say, holding Destiny's hand as we walk along the water's edge.

"It was," she agrees.

"So … We're walking toward my place. Pretty sure we passed yours a while ago."

She knows we passed her room, and I have no plans of going there, nor taking her there tonight. Not with Will and Taylor next door.

"Yep," she replies casually, as if nothing about getting closer to my room and closer to finishing what we started last night fazes her.

Good.

"Would you like me to walk you back?" I foolishly ask, taunting her, forcing her to tell me what she wants tonight.

"No, David." She giggles.

My heart beats rapidly. "Are you sure?" I ask one last time, desperate to hear her say she needs me as badly as I need her.

"I'm positive, David," Destiny says with defiance, refusing to tell me what I yearn to hear. Instead, she pulls my arm around her waist and places my palm low on her side, letting me feel the curves that ground against my raging hard on all night.

I had to tuck my dick into my waistband so no one would see just how turned-on Destiny makes me. Even in public, I have no control. My blinders are on and the only person I see is Destiny. The way my body reacts cannot be controlled.

We arrive at my bungalow shortly after her silent proclamation of desire. I open the glass doors that face the beach and she saunters inside. Her confidence strengthens with every step she takes and it unravels me. This confident, sexy woman is mine. To have and to hold ... At least for tonight. And hopefully for longer.

Destiny walks straight for the bedroom, and I follow her. No words are exchanged. Mainly, because I don't know what to say, and if I speak my voice will likely betray my dwindling control. My heart pounds against my chest, beating faster the closer we get to the bed.

She stops at the foot of the bed and faces me. Her hands slide up the back of her dress, unzipping the garment and letting it fall to the floor. My brain instantly turns to mush under her radiance. White satin underwear clings to her frame – it looks as soft and luminescent as her skin. Her delicious sun-kissed legs scream to be touched.

I drop to my knees in front of her, kissing her inner thigh and receive a rewarding moan of relief. "Destiny …" I begin, planting a kiss on the edge of her panty line. Arousal already coats the bottom of them. How long has she been wet for me? The thought makes my dick spasm.

"My purse," she breathes heavily, as affected as I am by the anticipation of being together.

"What about it?" I peer up at her, gaping at her ethereal beauty. *My* goddess. If being on my knees already doesn't tell her that I worship her, I will have to find another way to show her.

"I brought a condom," she interrupts my drifting thoughts.

She brought a condom?

I already prepared – purchasing a box when I was getting clothes for tonight, but I adore the fact that she prepared for tonight as well.

She wants me.

"I got some, too," I say.

A sly smile spreads across her face, and she sucks in her bottom lip. Her white teeth nip at that full lip, and I spring to my feet, stealing the lip from her mouth. We fall back onto the bed, kissing and sucking like this is what gives us life.

"Now, David. Please …" Destiny squirms underneath me.

At some point, her legs have found my waist and I have been grinding against her because my cock is achingly hard. Her skin is red and flushed from the friction – just the way I like her to look. Knowing I'll be inside her soon, I tear myself off her and jog into the bathroom to retrieve the condoms.

I peel off my clothes, leaving them in a pile on the bathroom floor, and return to Destiny with a condom in hand. It isn't romantic, but her pleading eyes tell me she doesn't want romance.

She just wants me.

Last night was romantic. Tonight will be something more desperate and primal.

"Got it," I say, holding up the foil package. I stand at the edge of the bed and fist my cock. Ripping open the package with my teeth, I roll the latex down the length of my shaft. Destiny watches me intently as I crawl across the bed and center myself between her legs.

"Are you sure?" I ask one final time. In no life, this one or the next, do I want to stop what is happening, but I will give her one last chance to change her mind.

"More than sure." She smiles and pulls my lips to hers.

As we kiss, I prod at her entrance. While my fingers slipped into her easily last night, this task will be harder, much harder. I debate stopping and readying her with my mouth, but the teasing tonight has me nearing release already. I need to be inside her.

The tip enters but is halted by her tight entrance. Destiny sucks in a breath as I push further, shoving the girthier parts of myself into her. Her quick, panting breaths fan my face and her brows pinch together.

"Relax. Breathe," I coach her. This won't be the first time she feels like this, nor the last. A fact I typically relish, knowing she'll feel me for far longer than I am inside her.

"David. Oh. My. God," she responds in short, strangled gasps.

With one final push, I cleave through her walls and slam into the back of her cervix, finally feeling her. Destiny eyes go wide and her mouth drops open as a gasp escapes her.

"David!" she cries as her hands latch onto my forearms.

"Are you okay?" I ask as her nails pierce my skin and my hips still.

I have no pride in causing her pain, but there is a lot of pride in seeing how shocked she is by my size and feeling how tight she is around me.

"Yeah. It's …" Destiny's body shakes as she attempts to relax. "It's a lot more than I expected." Her throat bobs with the words.

A laugh escapes me, but I lock my lips together when I see her brows furrow again. She doesn't realize there's still more. "There's a lot more, Dez," I say, lifting my body slightly off hers and looking down at the space between us.

There is *a lot* more.

"Oh my god," she says as that shocked expression fills her face again.

"Just relax." I kiss the side of her mouth, swiveling my hips to open her further.

Millimeter by millimeter, I am gaining space and my dick is purring with delight as I feel her moisten. It won't be long until my balls are slapping against her ass and being coated with her juices.

"Let me get on top," she says.

"Are you sure about that?"

The look of defiant determination that takes over her face speaks volumes. She doesn't need to tell me twice. As long as she's sheathing me, she can do it however she chooses.

I roll over, holding her close, but remaining inside. The movement forces my shaft in another inch before Destiny's walls clamp down, halting me. "Fuck, Destiny. You're tight."

"I know," she says.

Slowly, she lifts herself into a sitting position, allowing me to watch as she takes deep breaths and closes her eyes. Destiny is fully focused on the task at hand. At her own pace, she lowers herself onto me. It is an erotic sight, watching each inch of my cock disappear into holy her. When her pelvis hits mine, my penis is snuggly wrapped inside her.

"Good job, baby," I say proudly, sliding my hands up the smooth skin of her thighs before grabbing her waist. "Do you want to ride me, Destiny?"

She smiles as arrogantly as I feel. The timid female who didn't think I would fit is gone. The goddess of desire is back.

"The question should be, do you think you can handle it, David?" Destiny counters, grabbing my hands and pinning them above my head.

Show me what you've got, Destiny.

37

Destiny

Challenge accepted.

His cock is nice. Better than nice, actually. Honestly, I didn't think it was going to fit, but I found my body easily adjusting after realizing how good he feels inside of me. I could adjust to other men as well, tighten around them to experience more pleasure. But with David, I don't need to focus on the contraction of my body because he fills me to the brim.

Last night's proud display of his manhood replays in my mind. It was both a turn-on and a challenge. Tonight, I will show him what I have to offer. It is a test after all, to see how well we fit. And I find myself desperate prove my worth.

I lean forward, holding his hands above his head while I buck my hips. The length of his cock seems never-ending as I lift myself to the head and drop back onto him. His penis slams into my cervix each time he plummets into me. He is so much larger than I realized. His cock looks normal against his body. But when it's moving in and out of me, it looks absolutely enormous.

As I learn the length of his member, I speed up, moving my hips faster and finding a steady rhythm to stroke the tingling sensation building deep in my belly. Each time I drop fully onto him, the head of his dick plunges into the space that is further than any other man has explored.

"Destiny, slow down," David says through gritted teeth, grabbing my hips and slowing our pace.

"No," I moan, leaning my head back and dropping onto him once more. The sensation of him filling me is too good to stop.

"I'm going to cum if you don't stop," he warns.

I halt. Selfish as it is, I want more of this, so he needs to hold off a bit longer.

"You like it, don't you?" David says, relaxing his hands against my sides.

"Clearly." I shift my hips and pull my legs forward before leaning back and using David's muscular thighs to hold myself up. This is an entirely new position and it hits even deeper. I arch my back and the tip of his cock protrudes under my stomach. A moan of pleasure escapes me as a groan of satisfaction escapes David.

"Hold on," he commands, sitting up and sweeping me off the bed in one fluid motion.

Our groins stay connected. One thing is certain – the man is a master maneuverer in bed. I wrap my legs around David as he turns our bodies and lays me down on the sheets in a more intimate position.

"How deep do you want me to go, Destiny?" David asks, thrusting in and out of me slowly.

The pace is unnervingly satisfying. But his question isn't solely about my satisfaction; it is a challenge of wills. How deep can I go – emotionally and physically? How deep will I *allow* David to go? I am not sure, but as far as right now, I am willing to test it. Because tonight is the ultimate test.

"Show me and we'll see what I can handle," I decide. David flips me around, letting me land on my stomach with an *oomph*. "I didn't mean show me like …" His cock plunges inside me and a squeal silences my words.

He plows into me with fervor, rocking my body and molding a hole made specifically for him into my center. In hindsight, all sex I've had before now is immeasurably awful. The way David's cock pleasures me is a sweet, sensual torment that will be burned into my nerve-endings forever.

Sweat coats my brow as I clutch the pillow for dear life and exhale my gratification into it. My whole body shakes, not only from his movement, but from the overwhelming amount of humming energy lighting tiny fires throughout my body. The frenetic copulating stimulates my pleasure, and just when I think my reality is fragmenting, David slaps my ass and growls.

My release surges to life, tearing through my senses in a wash of euphoria that sends me flying into oblivion. Time and space are nothing. I am fully submersed in David's realm and have given myself over to him completely. Copious amounts of morphine have nothing on the way my body falls apart and slowly molds back together. I am left without a thought or a feeling.

There is only the sound of heavy breathing beside my ear. With a final thrust and groan, David releases himself inside me, the condom capturing his cum. I wasn't willing to take a risk on not using a condom last night, but *damn* do I want to feel him let go inside me. The question of how deep I want David to go answers itself with my apparent base level desires making requests.

"Oh, Destiny," he says, finding my lips with his.

We kiss. One kiss turns into three. Three kisses turn into more and more and *more*. He pulls himself out of me, only to flip me over and wrap his arms around me. Our lips find each other again and we kiss like it's a slow dance. This moment makes me lose all sense of doubt.

Something has happened. Some mutual understanding of what this is between David and me has finally come to light. I sensed it forming all evening. The warm feeling in my chest only growing hotter with each passing moment. David continues to surprise me in the best ways possible. And the sex … The sex is mind blowing.

It is that life-changing, unforgettable kind of sex. The kind of sex that you often wondered if it even existed. And when you get a taste, if it is taken away, you ended up an old, angry hag always in search of it.

Fuck me.

I am doomed.
Doomed – and maybe, very possible, falling for Achilles.

38

David

Destiny and I fell asleep while kissing so I wake up with the used condom still on my dick. While partly disgusted by the crusty cum stuck to my flaccid penis, the elated feeling I have from drifting off with my lips on hers remedies any feeling of discontent.

The sex test wasn't even a test at all. We're cut from the same cloth. I never should have thought otherwise. From day one, everything about this woman captivated me. When she took control and got on top of me last night, I nearly lost it. She leaned back, her whole body on display so I could watch as she rode me, and I've never seen a more beautiful sight.

The only way I was able to last long enough for her to find her release, too, was to flip her over and take back control. Now that I have had a taste and a release, though, I'll give her the chance to ride me again. And for a lot longer – so we both can enjoy it. Next time, she'll find her release multiple times before I find mine.

When I slip back in bed, Destiny stirs, turning over to face the wall, pressing her backside into me. I'll take whatever side she gives me, but especially this one. Her shapely ass rests needily against my groin as I spoon her, and my mind imagines being inside her again. My body reacts naturally, my shaft hardening between her butt cheeks.

It was a late night and I only slept a few hours, but I am already ready for round two with Destiny. She sleeps soundlessly, though, and I can't bear to disturb her when we haven't been asleep long, nor do I want to push her before she is ready. Last night was all about quenching our deepest desires. The sexual tension between us grew too heavy, like a storm cloud nearing its bursting point, there was no stopping what progressed between us. But today we have shit to discuss and not much time to do it. When Destiny wakes up, we need to talk. Then, we can stop thinking and keep enjoying each other.

For now, I need to clear my mind and plan our day. If there is ever a time for sealing the deal, it is now. I lie with her for another hour, studying every curve of her face, every imperfectly perfect feature, committing her image to memory so that I can dream about her when she isn't nearby.

I feel both lost and found when I am around her – lost in a sea of infatuation, while my north star shines brighter than ever. But it is more than simple infatuation. I knew that from the moment she shocked me with her lewd tongue, and it was only further confirmed at the wedding last night.

When the first tear slid down her cheek during the ceremony, multiple feelings of protectiveness, then admiration overwhelmed me. The feelings I have for Destiny aren't mild or flighty. They are intense and abundant. They have become the roaring mantra in the back of my mind – constantly steering me toward *her*.

At the first sign of that wet droplet, I wanted to massacre the reason behind what made her cry, until sense struck me and I realized they were just tears of joy. Tears of joy, not for herself, but for someone else. I admire the hell out of her ability to feel so strongly for others' happiness, and not just her own.

She is one of a kind. A fucking keeper.

As the sun rises, Destiny continues to sleep, so I decide to go on a morning jog before she wakes. I plan to visit the concierge on my way back to the room so I can schedule a private sailing excursion and candle-lit dinner on the beach for Destiny and me later today. There should be plenty of time for us to talk during these activities.

Hopefully, she doesn't have other plans today. If so, I'll adjust to her needs. But right now, the timing and mood feel right to start making plans. I only hope she'll agree and be receptive to furthering this relationship.

With the soft thud of my feet hitting the ground, reminders of my achievements flash through my memory and bring me back to thinking about the woman waiting in my bed. The only thing I have yet to accomplish in life is a successful relationship. I long for the life-long commitment Stacy and Ryan entered into last night.

Everything that has happened until now pales in comparison to my future. While some people look back on their past achievements and wish to revisit them – to change them in some way – I am happy to leave them in the past. The person I used to be reveled in the limelight, the crowd, the cheering, the notoriety. The person I am now wants a quiet life.

A life that allows me to slow down and appreciate the important moments is all I yearn for. But those moments will mean nothing without the right person beside me. Call me a hopeless romantic, a love-struck fool, an infatuated, idealistic dreamer. I don't care what anyone thinks. All I know is that this feeling I get when I'm with Destiny is different, and I am starting to see a brighter path to my future. An achievable, happy life is within my grasp when I look outside of my usual life – my comfort zone.

I knew from the moment I met her that something was off about Destiny. It took a couple of meetings until the realization dawned. She is different because she is my perfect match. The missing piece to my puzzle. As cliché as it sounds, it is true. We are equals – combating and complementing each other's strengths and weaknesses perfectly.

Tonight, we will talk about how to make it work in the real world. We will discuss how to make it work in the short term if we live far apart. My life is still in turmoil, on the brink of collapse if LA doesn't meet my demands, and that doesn't even account for the details of Destiny's life.

I need to find out where she lives, and then I can make my game plan. Maybe she lives on the East Coast. If so, would I turn down LA and retire early instead? Owning a company would make moving her life a lot more difficult than mine, but we may be able to make long distance work in the short term until we find a solution.

The questions and solutions are endless, the weight of their importance unmeasurable. I have yet to meet with the Chargers, so nothing is set in stone, and tonight's conversation will help me make those decisions – assuming she wants to make this work as much as I do.

My phone buzzes as I approach the concierge's office.

"It's David," I answer before looking at who is calling.

"David, it's Blake. Got a minute?" my agent asks.

"For you, always."

"Great!" he says, missing my sarcasm, "I relayed your concerns ... And they want to meet before sending over the contract."

"Okay." The concern in Blake's voice seems misplaced. We already planned to meet with the owners and coaches before I sign the contract anyway – so why is he calling?

"They want to meet today," Blake cuts to the chase.

"Today? I can't meet today. I'm in Mexico. Did you tell them that?"

"Of course. But then one of the owners said his daughter was also in the region and offered you a ride on his private jet to make it work … They'll be at the terminal in an hour," Blake says.

Clearly, he already agreed to the arrangement and I can't cancel without severely harming my chances of negotiation.

Declining a lift from one of the owners could seriously offend them. In these guys' minds, they're meeting me halfway. The meeting is today, regardless of what I want – unless I want to kiss my chances at a career goodbye. While super last minute, considering I am a five-hour flight and multiple time zones away, they are providing me with the means to arrive on time. Excuses – like I have an important discussion with this hot-ass blonde, whom I'm obsessed with, but just met on vacation – won't fly.

You win some, you lose some.

But in this case, I lose nearly everything.

I am two days from leaving the resort. That only gives me two days with Destiny. Two days isn't nearly enough. And now football is stealing all of that time from me and *my* Destiny.

"You have to be fucking kidding me, Blake," I curse.

"Look, I'm sorry. The situation got dicey, so I did what I could. You can't miss this flight. Do so, and you could be kissing your chances of a comeback goodbye."

"Who said anything about a comeback?"

Blake snaps back, "Do you want to retire early?"

I think about it. It isn't the worst idea, not since I've met Destiny. It would make life easier – I could go wherever she needs me. I could sail more. I could read something other than playbooks. But ultimately, I don't want to end my football career. Not yet. If I can have both Destiny and my career, life will be golden.

"No," I admit.

"Then get your ass on that plane. You have ten minutes to pack and leave. I've got a car waiting and details are … sent. Check your phone. Daughter's name is Regina. Try not to screw her."

"You should be more worried about me firing you than getting with some random chick," I warn him.

Blake has ruined everything. I hope Destiny will understand. And maybe, just maybe, I can convince her to come with me. It is a slim chance. After all, she is on vacation, too. Who would ditch their friends on vacation to fly to LA with me to attend a business meeting? No one, that's who. But I'm still going to ask. If she feels an inkling of the connection I feel, she'll take the chance.

Blake laughs. "She's trouble, Green. Don't say I didn't warn you."

I hang up the phone, check the details Blake sent, and sprint back to my room. The last thing I need to worry about is some cleat-chasing whore. Destiny is the only woman I have my sights set on.

39

Destiny

When I wake up, the bed is empty. I roll off the edge of the bed and pad through the bungalow looking for him, but he is nowhere to be found, so I slip on one of his cotton T-shirts and walk out to the beach.

The first day we met, David was returning from a swim in the ocean. He is likely out there now.

His body seems to be immune to the effects of alcohol and the symptoms of hangovers – *that lucky, physically perfect bastard.* My heart aches when I think about his perfection.

The sun is bright, having risen fully over the horizon as I slept in. I squint against its blinding rays, searching for David amid the shifting ocean water. Still, I cannot find him. Only the white rippling waves and occasional seagulls breach the surface of the cerulean water.

I return to the bungalow and realize I don't have any-thing to wear today. After last night, I am confident David will be back soon and I want to look my best. Plus, I want to spend the day with him, I don't want to run away and screw everything up like last time, so I need to be prepare for anything. I don last night's dress and trek back to my room.

After arriving, I shower quickly and braid my hair to avoid drying it. I dress in a sage sundress and sandals but stuff my bikini and some casual clothing in a beach bag. Regardless of what we do, I don't want to spend a second away from him today, so I pack extras, tossing sunscreen, makeup, and several toiletries into the beach bag as well.

With a pep in my step, I take the beach-side route back to David's room, excited to see what is in store for today. I hope I run into him on the way there. Otherwise, I'll wait for him on the cabana bed where we first met. It would be cute to replay our first meeting, but with a little more touching and less glowering.

40

DAVID

Destiny isn't here. The bedsheets are thrown to the side and there is no trace of her. Even her dress, shoes, and handbag are gone. I left for less than an hour and she is *already* gone.

Panic ensues me.

I have ten minutes to pack and get to that car. With the time it will take to walk to the main entrance, find Destiny, and convince her to come with me, I am left with two minutes to get out the front door of this bungalow.

I run through the rooms, throwing my shit into a suitcase, and not caring how it fits or if I leave something behind. I only need the essentials for today's meeting. Nothing else, except for finding Destiny, matters.

Carrying my suitcase under one arm and a backpack over my other shoulder, I jog to her room. I convince myself she will be there. She must have gone back to clean-up for our day. There is no way she ran away from me again. Last night was perfect. I know it was perfect. I *know* we are on the same page now.

I knock on her door, but no one answers.

I knock several more times, to no avail.

The guest room doors lock automatically and can only be opened with a key fob, but the back doors don't, so I run around the unit to see if she is sitting out by the pool. There is no sign of Destiny, but Will and Taylor are lounging on their patio.

"Hey! Have you guys seen Destiny?" I ask breathlessly from across the lazy river that flows between us.

"Haven't seen her. We just got up, sorry, man," Will says. He and Taylor are in their pajamas, sipping coffee, their hair still disheveled from whatever nightly and morning activities they enjoyed. That is what Destiny and me should be doing.

I glance at my watch and note three minutes to spare. I have to leave now.

"Alright. I'm headed out. Enjoy your vacation, and nice to meet you both!" I say to them, receiving a skeptical look from Will as Taylor waves goodbye.

"Take it easy," Will says eventually.

I speed-walk to the lobby, rushing to the receptionist so that I can leave a message for Destiny. It occurs to me that I could have mentioned something to Will and Taylor, but it's too late to second-guess my decisions.

"I need to leave a message for a guest," I say quickly, looking out the glass door entrance.

The black suburban Blake instructed me to find is waiting outside. The chauffeur is holding a sign with my last name on it as he glances at the watch around the opposite arm.

I am running out of time.

"Yes, señor, what is the message and who for, may I ask?"

"Her name is Destiny. She's in room 315. Tell her …" I think about what to tell her. How do I explain my abrupt departure? There is so much to say, but I can't express it in one message. I need to talk to her.

"David! Leaving already?" Richards says as he claps his palm on my back.

His sudden approach causes me to jump. "Richard," I respond briskly. The receptionist looks at me expectantly, and for a moment, I am at a loss for words as I glance between her and Richard.

Last night was undeniably one of the more memorable moments of my last five years. It could very well become one of the most memorable moments of my life. While I berated Destiny for running away from me, I am doing it to her now. But not for the same reasons.

"You okay, son?" Richard asks as he adjusts the leather strap on his shoulder. A tan leather bag is slung over his right shoulder, matching the roller luggage sitting on his other side.

"Are you leaving?" I ask.

"Yep. Time to head home."

"Oh." Words escape me.

"You want to take a seat?" Richards asks.

I look at the receptionist, finally pulling myself back to the present. It feels as if I am simply going through the motions – on the outside looking in and not entirely in agreement with what I am doing.

"Can I get a pen and paper, please?" I ask the receptionist.

She places a notepad in from of me. I set down my luggage, feeling a slight twinge of pain in my shoulder as it rotates to release the bag, but I ignore it and write: *Call me. I can explain. 212-458-2903 – David.*

Unease creeps its way under my skin, but I slide the paper over to the receptionist. She replies, "I'll make sure to pass it along."

"Thanks."

"So how did it work out with Blondie?" Richard asks, not hiding the fact that he read my message.

"It went well, but I've got to get back to the States for a meeting. I wasn't able to talk to her this morning, so I'm not sure how she is going to take my disappearance."

"Hmm ..." Richard murmurs, rubbing his chin as we walk toward the lobby front doors.

They automatically open and the driver identifies me. He opens the trunk of the black SUV and I pass him my baggage.

"In my experience, you can often resolve business when the excuse is personal, but you can't often resolve personal matters when the excuse is business."

He sounds like a fortune cookie. Regardless, my stomach drops because his words are painfully true. "I have to go, though. She'd understand if I could explain."

"I'm sure she will," he says as his own driver walks up and takes his luggage. "Well, best of luck, son. If you ever need anything, here's my business card." He pulls out a patent-leather card with silver embossed lettering. The logo of a very well-known airline is imprinted on the bottom right corner and *Owner and CEO* sits under his name.

"Fancy title." I shake the card. It's no wonder Richard never commented on my profession – he's a legend in his own right and one of the wealthiest men on the planet.

"So I've been told. Good luck with the meeting. You'll make the right decision – I'm sure of it." Richard winks and slips on a pair of dark shades.

As he climbs into his transport, I climb into mine. The driver speeds away from the resort, only giving me a moment to look back at what I am leaving behind.

Everything depends on whether Destiny receives my message. I hope that my future can have both a career and a relationship. I hope I didn't just make the wrong choice.

41

Destiny

Where is David? It has been over an hour since I arrived at his beach – happily lounging on the daybed as I wait for him – so I attempt to enter his bungalow, but it is locked and no one is answering when I knock.

I knock again.

Again, no answers.

I knock continuously.

But still, no one answers.

At this point, the speed of my heart and the intensity of my knuckles rapping on the door are in sync. My patience is wearing thin as panic sets in and I begin to think something terrible has happened to him.

Looking around for all available options of entry, I decide to try the back door. My patio door only locks from the inside, so it might still be unlocked from last night. As I round the building and enter the patio area, I notice the back door is slightly ajar. I instantly feel relief.

This gives me all sorts of wicked ideas about what to do before David returns. I sneak inside the bungalow, looking around for any sign of him. It occurs to me he might have fallen back asleep. I hope he's receptive to my sneaking under the covers and initiating some morning fun. Because, after last night, I am ready to go again.

I walk quietly toward the bedroom and notice someone has cleaned the living room. He must have come back.

I crack open the bedroom door and slip inside. This room is unusually clean as well. Like really, really clean. Like no one is even staying here clean.

Outside of the bed covers piled on the floor, there is no sign of David.

Absolutely no sign of David.

His clothes, his electronics, his toiletries are all gone. I pace around the room, opening closet doors, drawers, turning over the goddamn bed because I can't believe he isn't here.

Is this some sick joke? Where has he gone? Did I imagine last night? Is he a figment of my imagination?

Although, I know he's not.

Last night was real. It was too overwhelming to be anything less than physical. But how does a man just disappear in under an hour? And, most importantly, why would he leave like this?

Why would he leave *me*?

Something in my chest fractures. An unfamiliar feeling that I do not want to acknowledge – the reason I told myself to stay away from David in the first place. I never wanted to feel this ache again.

It is the type of feeling you get when you're both ashamed because you finally opened up when you knew better, and devastated because someone stomped on that vulnerability.

I feel stupid.

I feel mad.

I feel lost and betrayed.

What type of sick joke is he pulling her? Is this retribution for my leaving the first night?

My knees hit the floor beside my already discarded bag – packed full of supplies to spend the day with David. But he never planned on spending the day with me. No. He planned to fuck me last night, then leave.

He has always known when his vacation would end. Apparently, that day is today.

David *Achilles* Green is a goddamn bastard.

Before his actions can make me feel worse, I pick myself up off the ground. I reach for the unshed tears pooling in the corners of my eyes and wipe them away before they can fall.

Achilles doesn't deserve my pain, nor my pleasure.

I collect my things and leave David's bungalow. On the verge of becoming a fond memory, it could burn for all I care now. Just like the daybed should have burned that first day I met David *Achilles* Green.

His name is a tasteless poison on my lips.

I won't waste another moment of my life on him. This was a temporary distraction. Something I knew better than to get involved in. Yet, I was out of my comfort zone – alone in a romantic setting. I was vulnerable, and that vulnerability wanted to believe in fairy tales. But reality is no fairy tale; happy endings are only tragedies.

So, I chalk this experience up to what it is – a temporary distraction, a life event, a blip in time, an inconsequential "makes for a great story" memory. David *Achilles* Green will become the story of my once-in-a-lifetime vacation rendezvous with a famous playboy athlete – nothing more, nothing less.

And I sure as hell won't be doing this again.

On the way back to my room, I rebook my flight to depart today. My friends will understand if I tell them I have to leave for a work-related issue. I can't bear to tell them the truth. It hurts too much to admit. They will have too many questions, and my answers will only disappoint them and embarrass me.

I am on the next flight out of Tulum. It is time to get back to work. Love is for fools, and my destiny is of my own making.

42

DAVID

"You must be David." An attractive woman, whom I presume is Regina, the owner's daughter who lent me a ride, greets me from her oversized leather recliner as I duck under the airplane doorway.

Four women, including Regina, who appear to be in their mid to late twenties, lounge around the private jet. I take a seat in the open recliner closest to the doorway, not wanting to walk through the middle of them. Their eyes are already scanning me intently, too predatory to be innocent.

Even though I feel like shit for leaving without talking to Destiny, I swivel in my seat to face Regina and put on a good-ole boy smile. She is the owner's daughter. It can't hurt to make a good impression. I made my choice – I sure as hell don't want to regret it because my dickish attitude fucked up this opportunity, too.

"Nice to meet you … Regina?" I extend a hand, and she shakes it firmly.

"That's right! And these are my friends – Trish, Becca, and Lizzie." She points to each one of her friends, and they give me flirtatious smiles before returning to their phones. They are trying to act casual, but their continual glances over the edge of their phones tells me they are messaging one another and far more in tune to my actions than they let on.

"Nice to meet you guys." I place emphasis on the word *guys*, hoping they will take it for what it is – a reminder that I don't see them as conquests, but acquaintances at most.

I don't have time to fuck around with some cleat-chasing groupies – because that's exactly how they look. The twenty-five-year-old me would have turned this flight into an orgy, but those days are in my past. Now, my thoughts are consumed with only one woman. And that woman has a bite as sharp and quick as the metaphorical vipers that rest on her shoulders.

No matter how young or beautiful another woman may be, Destiny will still be my number one. She haunts me in the best damn way possible.

These women on board are beautiful. Without a doubt, the type of chicks you'd peg as models on the streets of Los Angeles. Most guys in my position would be asking what they are doing tonight and taking down their numbers. But there is only one number I want and that is Destiny's.

Destiny. Destiny. Destiny.

The mantra repeats itself every time one of the women looks at me, and then at one of her friends. Destiny is all I will think about. She consumes me, and the further I get from her, the more my obsession grows.

Hopefully, Destiny doesn't try to contact me while I am flying. If I miss her call because I am out of range, she won't know, and I'll have no way of reaching her because the call will never connect, giving me her return number.

I didn't even get her last name. I feel so stupid for not prying some useful contact information out of her. I didn't ask the name of her company or what city she lives in. There are so many questions that I planned to ask today so that I could ensure I wouldn't lose track her when we returned to our lives, and I never got the chance.

Timing is a bitch – a mother-fucking inconvenient bitch.

"How was your vacation?" Regina asks sweetly, breaking the awkwardness that is sure to follow from my eventual rejection.

"Uh … Good. I needed it. Where are you all coming from?" I don't want to talk about my vacation with them. I don't want to tell them about the woman I left behind without a word in order to save my career. I don't want to ponder if Destiny received my message, or if she will understand why I left. That woman jumps to conclusions faster than my center can snap a ball.

And just like that, my worry escalates.

"We're coming from a shoot in Brazil. Were you alone in Tulum?" Lizzie asks.

Regina chimes in before I can respond, "First, it's none of our business if David was alone. Second, if he was, that's okay too. Sometimes people need alone time, Liz. Tulum is a great place for a solo getaway." She gives me a soft smile and reaches across the aisle to pat the top of my hand.

Her touch is kind, but unnecessary. I can't quite figure Regina out, but I am not sure making small talk is helping clarify intentions between us. There's no risk of me straying. But I do find her defense of me kind and cute. Mainly because it makes me wish another blonde was here, coming to my defense about vacationing along.

Destiny would hate the kindness Regina extends to me, though, and she'd hate Regina's symmetrical face even more. If she knew I was on a private jet with four models, she'd think I was exactly who she feared – a player. I groan and lean back in the plush chair, shutting my eyes.

I chose wrong.

I should have declined this meeting. I should have made the owners wait. I should have stayed with Destiny. Richard's words haunt me: *You can often resolve business when the excuse is personal, but you can't often resolve personal matters when the excuse is business.* A man with his success and experience would know better than most.

"Are you okay?" Regina asks, reaching across the short aisle between us and patting my shoulder. Her fingers brush the spot that has begun throbbing since I left the resort. The spot where scar tissue from my previous injury still remains.

I shrug off her touch, dismissing the pain. Her friends are busying themselves by taking posed photos as we taxi down the runway.

"Yeah, I'm fine. Just a long day."

It is considerate of her to ask, but she barely knows me. The only person I want to talk to isn't here. Venting to Regina won't make my situation any better, nor will it satisfy my wishes.

Regina laughs and narrows her eyes at me like a mom who, despite your best efforts, knows you're lying. "The day just started, David. You look like something is eating you alive right now… Do you want to talk about it?"

I don't want to talk about it.

Thinking about it only makes me feel regret. It tortures me – not knowing if Destiny received my message, not knowing if she will give me the chance to explain why I had to leave after the amazing night we just spent together. It was meaningful. It was *more*. It was making love – something I'm not sure I've ever even done before.

"I'm a really great listener …" Regina continues.

Either I have to be a dick and shut her down now, or I am going to have to tell her something. Because of her last name, being a dick isn't an option.

"I had to leave in a rush, and I didn't get to say goodbye to someone," I say, keeping my explanation short.

Her eyes light up. "Ooh la la, who was it?"

It's seems Regina is as incapable of reading people as I am of making solid decisions.

"Her name is Destiny … She was at my resort for her friend's wedding. We didn't really like each other at first. She stole my alcohol and fucking juked me on the beach when I tried to get it back." I laugh, feeling my heart warm and mood improve just remembering that first meeting. It feels good to talk about Destiny, like it somehow brings her closer to me.

"You're a professional athlete and some random chick got the better of you? Damn. She's a keeper," Regina jokes.

I instantly like Regina more when she compliments Destiny. I realize her touchy behavior is more gentle and motherly than flirty. I suppose it wouldn't be the worst thing to get another females opinion. "Yeah. She is."

"Well, if there really is a connection between you two, I'm sure she'll understand why you didn't get to say good-bye," Regina says.

Her doe eyes convince me that she is right.

"Yeah. Thanks!" The jet engines roar, and I feel the pull of gravity as we begin to lift into the air. "Also, thanks for the ride," I yell over the sound of the engine.

"It's no problem! But to be honest, I was really excited about meeting you …"

"Really, why?" I ask curiously.

I just determined Regina was chill and told her I fell for another woman on vacation. Surely, she isn't about to hit on me. But the fear remains.

"I'm a huge football fan. Obviously! I come from a football-obsessed family …" She giggles shyly. "You're a legend! I'm fan-girling so hard right now!"

I laugh at her admission – it's a relief. A fan, I can deal with. A thirsty hoe, I cannot. "Honestly, I didn't even notice. You contain yourself pretty well."

"Well, I didn't want to scare you off by being like 'Oh my god, can I get a photo with you?'"

"It's fine," I say, turning away. Out of my peripheral vision I notice a frown forming and realize she means to take a photo now. Right now. "You want a photo?" I ask, hating this situation, but feeling obligated for the sake of my career.

A smile spreads across her face, and when I expect her to turn the camera around for a selfie, she jumps out of her seat instead while we are still climbing to a cruising altitude. Turbulence hits at the exact moment she steps toward me, and she falls sideways. My instinct surges and I catch her before her head smacks into the side of the plane. The pain in my shoulder spikes as I am forced to balance the fallen woman amid the turbulence.

"Ow!" Regina clutches her head.

"Fuck. Are you okay? Let me see …" I shift her weight to relieve the strain in my arm while moving her hand to inspect her wound. There is a red mark the size of a baseball forming on her forehead.

"Is it bad?" she asks, looking up at me through thick black lashes.

Her face is inches from mine.

My stomach knots.

Regina is way too close.

She is so close that I can smell her – like lavender bath salts. I swallow that anxious feeling rising in my throat, remembering another lavender scented female. I think about what Destiny's reaction to this situation would be. It wasn't purposeful, but another woman should not be in my lap. Especially not another woman who Destiny would deem as a threat.

In my mind, no woman is a threat to her. But I am not about to fuck up my chances with Destiny by making her think otherwise. By making her doubt again.

"Um. Maybe you should buckle up and we can take that picture later," I suggest, taking Regina's hand and helping her back to her seat.

"Yeah, thanks," she says sheepishly, still holding her head.

"Regina, are you okay?" Trish asks, leaning forward and looking over her friend.

Her friends' attention is solely focused on us. I hadn't noticed they were watching before – I assumed they were still on their phones. It wasn't like anything happened, but I get this strange feeling from the way their eyes shift between us that something is amiss.

"I'll be fine. Don't worry," Regina says, rubbing the knot on her head. "Sorry about that, David. I hope I didn't make you feel uncomfortable."

Her words reassure me. They are as honest as she seems kind, and I believe I can trust her. At least, for now. "No worries. I just hope your dad doesn't kill me for getting his daughter hurt." I make light of the situation, hoping to make her feel better.

"It wasn't your fault! I was overly excited!" Regina returns – a silent promise that she won't let me take any blame for the massive bruise on her head. "Plus … maybe you could do me a favor?"

"A favor? I was already going to take a picture with you." I joke.

"I heard you were looking for a place in LA," she cuts straight to the point.

"Oh! Regina should be your realtor!" Becca suggests animatedly behind me.

I stifle a groan. There *was* something amiss.

"I have a realtor. But you're correct – if I move to LA, I'll be needing a place."

Regina crosses her legs and puts on her best professional face. "I'm getting into realty, and I could really use someone like you as a client to help my reputation. People don't take models seriously … I know you probably already have a realtor, but I swear I know LA better than anyone! Especially the kind of properties you'll be looking at."

"Look, I don't know how today is going to go, but I'll keep you in mind," I promise, knowing it will make her father happy if I employed her as well.

She squeals and claps her hands. "You're the best, David. Seriously. I'll owe you big time for this!"

"Yeah, no problem," I say with a shrug, looking out the window as I feel the plane level itself.

Here I am, making plans for my future, but none of those plans hold the one certainty whose presence I desire.

With each passing second, another mile takes me further away from her. There is no land in view now, only the vast ocean and its unpredictable currents. They are as untamable as Destiny, which only makes me worry more.

43

Destiy

I am back in the office and ready to work. Grace, my assistant, was apparently not ready for my return because she is scrambling to re-organize my desk.

"Grace, what the hell is this? I left for one week," I complain, picking up an empty coffee cup with mold growing inside the rim and tossing it in the trash bin.

"I'm sorry. You know I can handle all the day-to-day stuff, but setting everything up for the new office is killing me. This is a two-man job, Dez. I don't know how you do it!"

Grace is a good assistant, and I don't give her as much credit as she likely deserves, but that is how you push people to be better – you make them work harder for the credit they will eventually receive. Plus, she's getting a fat bonus at the end of the year.

I left her in charge of managing my daily emails, responding to what she could, and filing the rest for me to review later. But I also asked her to review vendor contracts for our next office location in Los Angeles on top of all her other job duties.

After seeing the countless red mark-ups on the papers strewn across my desk, I realize she took that task very seriously. Which is good, because it means I have less work to do, but also bad, because it left my office in complete disarray.

"It's okay. We'll tackle this together. Get me up to speed and we'll make a to-do list. Oh, and schedule a lunch meeting with Kendal. I want the latest on our release schedule."

I begin stacking papers and putting my mind into work mode.

"Yes. I'll be right back." Grace rushes out of my office to schedule the meeting.

She is a frail-looking woman. All skin and bones, jet-black hair cut into a jagged bob, and pale skin. But I've personally seen Grace chow down a half-pound burger in under a minute, so I don't let myself be overly concerned about her health or ability to perform. Her metabolism is simply as speedy and efficient as her. By the look of my desk, the past week has been a bit too much to handle – for her and me both, honestly.

But I shouldn't have expected Grace to handle the same workload as I do. *She* has a life. Unlike myself.

Grace is married with twin toddlers – her hands are full enough at home. Piling two people's worth of work onto her already-busy schedule is unreasonable. I easily spend seventy hours a week working because I have nothing better to do.

As her boss, I owe her an apology and a well-earned vacation.

Grace returns. "Done! Kendal will be here at noon. I'll order in lunch for you both."

"Thank you. Grace, let's sit down." I motion to the two chairs on the other side of my desk. Her face pales as the change in my tone turns more serious. It's not often I express gratitude, so she's in for a surprise. This isn't a conversation consisting of constructive criticism. If anyone needs that conversation, it's the part of me that lacked proper decision-making skills in Tulum. But based on my experience there, I feel it necessary to commend Grace for her work.

She sits in one chair and I sit in the other. "I'm sorry for dumping all of this work on you. I should have pulled someone else in to work on the new location. But I really appreciate your hard work."

I insisted we keep the new location a secret until we secured the location and vendors. The insistence on privacy was deemed necessary so I could finalize the budget and have a solid plan in place before announcing the move to our shareholders. I still hold a majority of the shares in the company, but things like this still have to be communicated carefully. Yet, it's no excuse for overwhelming my favorite employee.

Grace starts shaking her head. "No, no. I can handle it. It's fine."

I stop her by placing a hand on her thigh. "No one should be responsible for this much work."

"But you do …"

"True," I admit. "But I also don't have a life. And that's not a healthy way to live anyways."

Grace's brows rise. "Dez, you have a life." Her voice is soft and caring, like a concerned mother refusing to believe her child could be lacking in any way.

Technically, Grace and I are the same age, but based on familial life experience, Grace is a lot older.

"I don't have a life, Grace. It's okay. You know I don't – you can agree!" I say.

She laughs timidly. "Well … Maybe work is your life."

"Clearly!" I toss up my hands and look around at the room that has gone from orderly to chaotic – a good representation of my life pre- and post-vacation – before I lean back in the chair and sigh.

"How was Tulum?" Grace asks, changing the subject.

How was Tulum? Awful. Then amazing. Then heart-wrenching. So, ultimately, awful.

But how can I tell her all of that without looking like a fool? I am known as the boss, expected to have all my shit together, but I feel far from someone who has nearly a hundred employees' livelihoods depending on her success.

"Fine." I look away from Grace's inquisitive eyes.

"I'm sorry for asking."

I glance back at her, hating how this difficult line between employee and friend forces our conversations to strain. We aren't the typical type of friends who do things like go out to dinner or watch movies together, but we are friends in our own way.

In the way where you spend your entire day working together and care about each other's happiness because clipped conversation over the years has somehow exposed you to more personal information about a co-worker than you should professionally know. And frankly, more than you even know about some of your so-called friends.

"Don't be sorry. It just ended differently than I thought it would."

"What do you mean?" Grace leans forward, placing her elbows on her knees, her chin in her palms.

She gives me her undivided attention as if the mess around us means nothing compared to my personal problems. Cleaning my office and diving into work is the distraction I need to clean up my life. But Grace will see right through my actions. After all, she is a mother – they have good intuition when it comes to these things. And, as far as people to vent my problems to, she is likely the only and best option.

"Do you watch football?" I ask. If she is a football fan, I'll need to ease her into this news. I don't want her taking sides too soon.

"No."

Thank God.

"Good!"

Grace's brows pinch together and her head quirks to the side.

"So, I met this guy …" I begin to say and her eyebrows shoot up. "I'm going to skip all the details and just say that he left without a word. He just disappeared one morning. No note, no message. Nothing! Poof. Gone," I say.

"Gone? How? Was he staying at the resort?" she asks, not missing a beat over the details I skipped.

"Of course. He was there most of the week and we hung out a lot! He even went to Stacy's wedding. Everyone loved him. But then, after I spent the night with him, he just disappeared. Packed up his room and was gone!" I breathe out a lengthy sigh, letting my frustration leak through every molecule of released carbon dioxide.

Gone. Just like that. *Poof.* I'm still in disbelief.

It pains me to think about how easily he fooled and evaded me. Because it doesn't make any sense. Achilles was so convincing.

Part of me longs for a reasonable explanation so that I can forgive him and we can return to how things were in that moment. The moment where it felt like he was the only person on Earth who really saw me. Feeling seen like that … it broke me. And yet, it made me feel whole at the very same time.

"That doesn't make any sense. Wait. Why did you ask if I was a football fan?"

I rub my temples, feeling the anger rising toward David and his stupidly perfect body and face and everything else. Just thinking about him makes my blood boil.

"Because he's a football player."

"Who?"

"David *Achilles* Green." Grace's fingers are already typing furiously on her phone as I say his name. I'm thankful she doesn't think twice or mention anything about me replacing his middle name. "What are you doing?" I peer at her phone.

"I want to see who he is," she says.

I lean over to watch as she opens his Instagram profile. I never even thought to look him up online before. Outside of his *GQ* spread, shown to me by Pat and Dale, I've basically ignored the fact that David is a public figure and anything I want to know about him will be on the internet.

He has over a million followers – while I am not personally on Instagram, my business is, and a million followers is something to write home about. His influence and reach truly knows no bounds. I shouldn't be surprised. Someone with an ego as large as his needs many followers to keep it in tact.

Grace scrolls through the never-ending football photos, but one photo in particular snags my attention.

"What is that?" I lunge for Grace's phone.

"Dez." She pouts, but I pull her phone in front of me and click.

An insanely attractive, fit, blonde female stands by David's side. Apparently, he has a type. He is dressed in his football uniform, and she is wearing a crop top with his number on it. The crop top and low-cut jeans show off her abs, and there is no stopping the jealousy that rages within me. David was right – I am nothing like the other women he has dated. Outside of the blonde hair, we are totally different.

His hand rests on her waist. Those long fingers spread across her abdomen like he is claiming it. The deep well that I shoved all feelings into begins spilling over the brim again.

"Who is that?" Grace asks, leaning over my shoulder.

"I'm assuming an ex," I say acidly, tasting the disdain, jealousy, and anger on my tongue. I breathe deeply and will that well of emotion to retract. While also doing my best not to wonder why he hasn't removed the photo.

"She's hot."

"Thanks, I didn't notice!" I retort, giving Grace a warning glare that instantly makes her grimace.

"Go back to his photos," she directs me. I go back to his feed. "Look, he barely has any other photos with her. If he liked her that much, he'd have tons with her. Plus, it's like two years old."

Her words don't reassure me. "Mm-hmm," I say, handing back her phone.

She refuses it and points at the screen. "Go to his tagged photos. That's where you'll see who he's really hanging out with."

Curiosity replaces the anger and jealousy. What has David *Achilles* Green been up to? Not that Instagram would confirm the reason for his disappearance, but it's worth a shot. A reason – such as his untimely death – would soften the blow of his rejection.

I click on his tagged photos, and my blood goes from boiling to vaporizing.

"What the hell!?" I grind my teeth together. Yesterday, I'd been angrier at myself than David. Angry that I gave him the opportunity to hurt me. But today. Today, that bastard would be better off dead than dealing with the rage that encompasses me.

David better hope he never sees me again.

"Dez …" Grace says, hesitantly pulling the phone from my hand before I crush it.

Yesterday, shortly after leaving me, David was tagged in a photo. A photo in which some *other* hot blonde – not the previous one in his photos or myself – is sitting in his lap while he looks adoringly into her eyes, tucking a piece of hair behind her ear.

The incriminating evidence tells me all I need to know. David *is* a player. Always has been, always will be.

And I got played.

"I'm so sorry, Dez …" Grace says, her voice empathetic.

I feel pathetic.

I remind myself that work is all that matters. Had I been ashamed of my lack of life just minutes ago? Yes. Had I been jealous of Grace's family and happiness? Yes. Had I just been reminded of the reason why I choose work over relationships? Hell yes – every goddamn mother-fucking time.

"Handle my inbox and pack the contracts. I'll visit the vendors myself. We have a deadline to open by month end and I've got work to do," I say, stuffing my laptop in my tote.

"Since when do we have a deadline?" Grace asks, jumping up and gathering papers.

"Since now. Book the last flight to LA tonight. Also, have a list of the vendors on my desk before my lunch meeting with Kendal. And please book a hotel on the westside this time, Grace. Downtown was too far from any acceptable locations. I don't have time to be stuck in traffic for hours."

I've been out for a week, and we are behind. Work is where my focus now lies – all my focus. I can see by the contracts on my desk that the vendors need a talking to, and when I am in bitch mode, I get shit done.

Plan initiated.

Los Angeles, here I come.

44

David

"Just look at these floor-to-ceiling windows and the massive balcony! I know you're not used to this in New York because the weather is awful half the year, but in LA you'll have these windows open every day. Plus, these two," Regina motions to the center windows, "slide open completely, allowing you to walk out onto the balcony."

Nothing about the windows impresses me. Nothing about this apartment impresses me. Plus, I don't really care about my living space.

Based on my meeting with the owners and coaches, my contract will only be for one year. I debated renting a place, but my financial advisor suggested I buy now. The market is on the rise, and he is confident I'll get a decent return, even if I don't hold onto it for more than a year.

"Looks nice," I say, crossing my arms and leaning against the kitchen island.

The condo is modern, with an open concept design and impeccable views of the ocean. What more can I ask for?

Oh, wait. I could ask for a call from Destiny, but I have yet to receive one and I don't know why.

It is eating at me.

If she received my message, she would have called. I'm convinced she would have called.

Although, a tiny part of me fears the worst – that when I returned to my bungalow the morning I left Tulum, Destiny left me. Not because she was going to change to spend our day together, but because she had no interest in pursuing anything more with me. Because what we shared wasn't a strong enough connection for her to stay. *Or* to call.

"That's what you said about the last five places," Regina pouts, walking toward me and swaying her hips far too obviously.

The more appointments we attend, the more flirtatious she becomes. It's like she thinks flirtation is going to sell me faster, but it has the opposite effect.

This woman is a completely different one than the innocent fan-girl from the private jet. When we arrived at the stadium for the meeting, she immediately told her father I'd agreed to let her be my realtor. I hoped to talk my way out of it or at least speak to my realtor first, but her father was so happy that I agreed to work with her, I couldn't then refuse.

So here we were, on day two of looking at places, and on the cusp of me losing my shit.

When I say a place *looks nice*, Regina insists on showing me another property. At this point, I don't fucking care where I live. I am ready to make an offer.

If only the girl would initiate the damn negotiation. It's like she thinks I have to love a place before I actually buy it. But I can't love a place when I know Destiny isn't a part of it.

"All the places are great, Regina. We've looked at ten equally great options in the same five-block radius I suggested. At this point, let's make the offer."

"I want you to love your new home, David! If you don't love your home, you won't love your team or your life."

Here we go again. "I bought my place in New York unseen, and I've been there since the day I started playing in the league. Trust me, they're all great. I'll be happy."

My words don't convince her. Probably because they come out sharper than I mean for them to sound. Regina is exhausting me, though. I don't enjoy buying new running shoes – something I use daily. Why the fuck would I enjoy house shopping for two days?

"Oh, David … You don't understand because you've been living in New York too long. People are different here."

It's comical that Regina thinks she can convince me otherwise. We don't speak the same language. No matter how many words in the English language she mutters, it all comes out as gibberish.

But I play along because the last thing I need is to piss off my new team's owner. "How so, Regina?"

"Well, first off, people are never home in New York, so they don't care about where they live. Second, it's all about aesthetic and vibe here. We need to make sure you fit into the place, and so far, none of the places we've visited have a very good energy when you're in them. I think we just haven't found the right one yet."

"Shouldn't I be the one to decide the appropriate *vibe* for *my* house?" I counter, crossing my arms.

Regina steps closer, placing a folder on the counter behind me before she skims a hand over the forearm I have tucked across my chest. I uncross my arms and place my palms on the counter behind me so she won't touch me again.

She has quickly crossed the line from a fan girl to a cleat-chaser, and it is taking all of my control not to bitch her deceitful ass out.

"I'm just trying to look out for you, David. Let's try one more. Then, I promise we'll pick one!"

Her pouting makes my stomach turn. Not to mention, nothing about my decision to buy a home should involve her opinion. She keeps saying *we*, like she is going to influence my choice in any way.

"One more. That's it. Let's go."

We leave the condo, heading toward the elevators. Regina's hand continually skims the back of mine as we walk, despite the hall being wide enough to fit four people shoulder to shoulder. Every time I move away or change the pace of my steps, she follows me. We reach the elevator, and I punch the down arrow button, letting some of my frustration out on the little defenseless green light.

"Don't break the place before you buy it, David," Regina says cutely.

Her comment doesn't even deserve a response. Right now, these steel elevator doors are looking a little too shiny. Punching a dent in them would be most satisfying.

Especially, if it offends Regina.

It doesn't help that it's been two days since I last saw Destiny. The frustration of not hearing from her, Regina's annoying nagging, and the constant regret I have about leaving the resort without speaking to *her* is weighing on me. I could rip apart this entire damn building right now with no regret for my actions because of how frustrated I am with myself. Leaving was the wrong choice.

I am in the wrong place with the wrong goddamn woman.

The elevator chimes and the doors open.

I step inside and lean against the back wall, planting my hands wide on the railing behind me so that Regina can't stand too close.

Elevators have an air of intimacy about them, and I don't want Regina getting any closer than she has been. Every minute I spend with her feels like I am tempting fate. It feels like I am falling back into the same routine – allowing worthless individuals to consume my time and energy.

Yet I am unable to change the situation.

Any other man in my position would take full advantage of this beautiful young female coming on to them. But I am not just *any* man, and I don't want just *any* pretty face.

"David?" Regina asks, looking bashfully through those long black lashes.

I am not falling for her act. Regina showed me her true colors when she posted that photo lying across my lap on the airplane. Her and her thirsty wannabe-model friends probably planned the whole thing for media attention.

My PR team is already working on keeping the photo out of the headlines and will hopefully force Regina to remove the photo from her social feed soon. I can only hope Destiny didn't see it.

Destiny doesn't seem like the type to be stalking me on social media, though.

"What, Regina?" I close my eyes and let my head fall back against the elevator wall. I want to slam my head into it, over and over, but I can't allow my resentment to be that obvious. Keeping my cool is part of the job, so I count to ten in my head.

One. Two. Three.
"David?" she whispers into my neck.

Four. Five. Six.
This little vixen is getting braver.

I open my eyes and begin to outwardly deny her, making myself and my intentions abundantly clear for the thousandth time, but she is already moving. Her fingernails snake up the front of my shirt and wind around my neck.

Seven. Eight. Nine.

I grab her forearms, attempting to gently remove her as I say, "Regina. Please, this is not …"

The elevator doors open.

Ten.

My arms are still on Regina's when my eyes land on two people waiting outside the elevator.

"Destiny?" I say.

45

Destiny

Mother. Fucker. Pure rage wells inside me.

I imagine launching myself at them, clawing that bitch's eyes out and repeatedly punching his beautiful face in.

Fuck him.

As soon as his deceitful green eyes lock with mine, I break out in a sweat. I never expected to see him again. Especially not here. Not now.

It doesn't take long to remind myself why I never wanted to see him again, though. The blonde from his tagged photos is pressed against him, her arms wrapped around his muscular neck.

"Regina," Christian, my real-estate agent and long-time friend, says acidly. Apparently, he isn't a fan of her either.

Wait. Christian knows this woman.

"How do you know her?" I ask Christian before Achilles and *Regina* step out of the elevator.

The woman with her hands all over David turns, smirks at me, and saunters up to us. "Hello, Christian. What are you doing here?"

"What do you think I'm doing here, you dense bitch?" he retorts, crossing his arms, and cocking a hip while completely ignoring my question.

The blonde – *Regina* – is curvy in all the right places and slim in others. She has an aura about her that reeks of confidence and money. If I knew more about the beauty industry, I might be able tell if her perfectly pouty lips were natural or injected, but I don't, so I have to assume she is simply naturally perfect.

I instantly hate her.

I am distracted by Christian and Regina's bickering, so I don't notice David sneak up behind me.

"Destiny ..." David says my name like it's a distant echo.

His fingers skim my exposed collarbone and I recoil from his touch. That one light touch feels like scalding hot water spilling across my skin. "What?" I hiss, refusing to turn around and give him any of my attention. Instead, I focus on the battle in front of me.

Christian and the blonde are mimicking each other's sass – flipping hair, cocking hips, and making jabbed remarks about the others appearance.

I love that he despises her as much as I do – whatever his reason. I've never hated a stranger as much as I do her, and seeing my friend talk endless shit to the woman helps ease my suffering. A little.

The pain of seeing David with her, however, is not so easily dulled. It's the confirmation I didn't want, nor need. David was done with me; he saw a better opportunity and left.

The connection we had was nothing more than mere boredom and slight attraction.

"Why didn't you call?" David's voice sounds wounded, which only angers me more because his ability to appear genuine is astonishing.

"What the hell do you mean, why didn't I call?" I spin around to face him. He'd be a wonderful actor if his football career ends.

"I left my number with the front desk. You were supposed to call me. Also, what are you doing here? Do you live in LA?" His voice perks up like the possibility of our being in the same city will improve his chances of playing with my heart again.

The nerve of this man.

He seriously thinks he can continue flirting with me, like nothing momentous happened between us, right after I catch him embracing some other woman.

If my dress had sleeves, I'd be rolling them up and handing Christian my purse to hold while I slap some sense into Achilles' thick skull.

"I checked out two days ago and they didn't say anything about a message, David. Save your lies for someone who can't see through them. Oh, wait!" I glance at Regina and Christian. "Looks like you've already found someone. So fuck off. You know how to do that, right? I'm pretty sure you said those same words to me when we first met. Come on, Christian."

I grab Christian's arm and pull him into the elevator.

"Destiny, wait! It's not what it looks like."

The doors close before David can vomit more bullshit. I know how crafty his silver tongue can be and I won't allow it the opportunity to transform his actions into something less culpable.

Christian and I both let out a huff of angry air. "What just happened?" I ask him.

My heart hammers against my chest as the shock of running into David finally hits me. I thought he lived in New York. Never in my wildest dreams did I imagine I would run into him. Not here – thousands of miles away from his home and hundreds away from mine. Just two days from last seeing him.

But I suppose that is how we met the first time, too. Thousands of miles away in the most unexpected of places.

"No idea! But I hate that woman, and by the looks of it, you hate David Green – America's sweetheart. When were you going to tell me about this?" He laughs.

I laugh with him, if only because laughing feels better than punching these elevator doors. And it definitely feels better than crying. The situation I got into with David on vacation feels like a dream. I don't know how I got there, or here. It's like my life has taken a sudden turn and it doesn't know how to get back on track, so it keeps following the same blind rocky path.

"Fuck them," I say finally.

"Yeah, fuck Regina. I hate that bitch. I'd say fuck David, too, but honestly, I'm a fan. Unless he did something really awful … Tell me he did something really awful? Also, how do you know him? I should have heard about this already," Christian rambles as he presses the button for the second floor.

We are looking at the commercial property on the second floor. I had vendor meetings this morning and was able to finalize most of the details. The last step is finding a location. Fortunately, Christian and I go way back – all the way to freshman year of college – and he had a list lined up for me by the time I touched down last night.

Since I already vented to Grace, I don't feel the need to explain more about David. But I do want to know how Christian knows the bitch who had her claws in David's neck. "I wouldn't say I know him. Actually, I don't know him at all. How do you know her?"

"She and I used to be friends – years ago. But she's a lying, back-stabbing snake of a woman and I don't associate with people like that. Did you hear her trying to figure out what we were looking at today? She thinks I'm trying to steal her sale. That stupid bitch knows I only deal in commercial properties, but I told her we are looking at the only unit for sale in this building just to piss her off." Christian smiles wickedly.

"Cute," I say, stepping off the elevator as the doors open to my potential future office space. "Wait. Steal her sale … What are you talking about?"

While I don't particularly want to know more about the woman who was lounging in David's lap on a private jet, I *want* to know more about the woman who was lounging in David's lap on a private jet.

Christian waves his hand dismissively and starts walking the perimeter of the empty office space. "As I said, we used to be friends. She bitched about me working too much and not having enough time for her, so I told her to get a real job instead of living off daddy's money. It started this huge fight. She became a real-estate agent to spite me and has been trying to sabotage me since. Except I now specialize in commercial, and she has no chance of selling commercial properties. Not when she hasn't made a single residential sale. The bitch can't keep a client to save her life. I mean, come on … You can see why. She's an arrogant, spoiled bitch, and she hits on her clients. Plus, she doesn't know shit about real estate."

Regina is a real estate agent? Apparently, or maybe, David's real estate agent – who he is also screwing? *Wow.* David Green really is a piece of work.

"She clearly sucks." I act as if the information Christian just dumped on me didn't just seep into my bones and chill me to the core.

He sighs. "I showed you mine; now you show me yours, Dez," Christian says.

"Um, what?" I look at him, pretending not to understand his question.

"How do you know David Green?"

"Nope, not going there. Where are the offices?" I change the subject, walking away.

Christian speeds up, walking around a large column and cutting me off as he continues pressing the subject. "I'm not going to stop, and we have three more tours. And who knows how much traffic will be on the way. I can drag this day on forever if need be."

He will. Christian is as persistent as they come. That is the very reason I enlisted his help in finding me a property. I trust he'll get me the best deal. If I were better at pretending, I would have ignored David completely and I might have had a chance to avoid this conversation. I motion him forward so we can get through this tour.

"We hooked up in Tulum," I say finally. Christian stops abruptly and I run into his back. "Christian!" I shove him.

He turns around. "I cannot believe you failed to share this information when I picked you up at the airport, when I took you out to dinner, or five minutes ago when I asked about him! Hooked up in Tulum – the Tulum where you were two days ago!?"

"Yes, Christian. Is something confusing about that?"

"No, bitch. I just can't believe you're only now telling me this. Why didn't you call him? That man has puppy-dog eyes for you! Plus, he's hot!"

I roll my eyes. He sounds like my Chicago friends, the ones who actually met David, but they were easily fooled – just as easily as me. The proof is in the pictures – and in the fingernail prints that likely line David's back from hooking up with Cruella de Vil.

"If you weren't so caught up in your drama, then you would have heard me say he never left me his number or message as to why he left. And in case you forgot, he and Regina were quite cozy in the elevator."

Christian laughs mockingly. "Cozy? Are you joking? I don't know what you saw, but I saw a bitch trying to sink her talons into a gorilla. David was about to flip out on her. Like I said, she hits on her clients. She doesn't have a professional bone in her body. She only knows how to lie on her back to get what she wants."

"He was holding onto her, Christian. And it doesn't matter anyway," I argue, hating everything about this conversation. I am here to focus on work, not be distracted by David. Again.

David *Achilles* Green is a mistake. A little vacation fun and nothing more.

I was never supposed to see him in real life, but it seems fate has an evil sense of humor. An evil sense of humor that wants to constantly remind me of where David's hands have been – like on the waist of one blonde and on the arms of another.

"I bet the only reason he hasn't told her off is because she's the Chargers owner's daughter. He got released last week. Seeing him here, with her, looking at condos, confirms it – he's changing teams!" Christian gets lost in his own excitement, forgetting the fact that I am clearly not a fan of David *Achilles* Green.

"Christian, if you want me to buy this place, you better start chanting *Fuck David Green*, not *Go Chargers*," I warn him.

I am getting sick of warning people. The harsh, cold part of me that has shut David out is starting to shut everyone else out with him. This isn't who I want to be. But David's betrayal broke a part of me, and I need time to mend that broken part. It would help if my friends understood.

"Girl, I've got your back. Don't worry. But … just so you know, Regina's a caddy bitch who has slept with half the team's roster. I don't know what kind of guy David really is, but he messed up letting you go. That I know for sure," Christian says, throwing an arm around my shoulder and leading us back toward the exit.

"Thank you."

This is the support I need.

David messed up. But I messed up, too.
I fell for his trap. And it won't happen again.

46

DAVID

I turn to her – the woman who now blocks my path to Destiny. If I thought I felt rage before, it has nothing on what I feel right now.

"You," I seethe.

Regina tosses her hair over a shoulder. "Me?"

"That was Destiny!" I point at the closed elevator door as if someone as dense as Regina would even remember me telling her about Destiny.

As I expect, Regina has no clue what I am talking about. I instantly regret letting her know about that sacred part of me, but am thankful for her miniscule amount of brain cells.

"Who?" Regina asks, shaking her head like an idiot.

"Who was the guy you were talking to?" I say, transitioning into my new game plan before my irritation with her gets the best of me and I say something I'll later regret.

"Ugh. Christian Ortega? He wanted to be in my friend group, but when he insulted me, I quit talking to him. He's a back-stabber and a terrible realtor."

"He's a realtor? So, they were looking at the same property?" This has promise. I can work with this.

"Yes, David. Christian is a realtor – like me. He said they were looking at the same unit. Except one of the girls in the office told me he's doing commercial properties now, so I'm not sure why he's showing a condo," she says.

Light bulbs of inspiration shine brightly in my head.

I spin on my heel and walk out of the building without another word. Regina's heels click on the floor as she hurries to keep up with me. "David? David, didn't you want to see the pool?" She is still on the topic of viewing the property, but I've moved on.

Just as I suspect, a massive sign advertising a commercial property for lease is on the front entry windows.

Touchdown.

Destiny is here on business. It seems fate has a plan for us, after all.

"David?" Regina says, irritated. She is holding the door open while motioning me back inside.

This woman really doesn't know how to read a room. I am done with her and her facade. All my time and energy has been drained by her, only to be rejuvenated by the prospect of seeing Destiny again. Touring condos and putting up with Regina's bullshit is over.

Destiny is in my line of sight again.

"Get me Christian Ortega's number," I tell her.

"What? Why? Are you serious right now?" Regina plants a hand on her cocked hip, forcing the door to fall into her side and knocking her forward. Teetering unsteadily on her pointy heels, she says, "You are not about to agent swap me. I will tell my father!"

It takes every bit of willpower I possess not to give this immature female the reality check she deserves. "Regina. I'm buying a property through you. Not because you're a good agent – because *you're not* – but because I don't want to piss your *daddy* off. And you'd be smart not to complain about me because I'll tell him about all the players on his team you've fucked."

My assumption is a shot in the dark. I have no idea whom she's slept with, but by the way she cozied up to her father's business partners in our meetings, I'd guess she's slept with a lot more than just the football players.

Regina's lower lip drops.

Fuck yeah. Extra points.

"Get me Christian Ortega's number and buy this fucking unit. Got it?" I repeat, my tone far more threatening than professionally acceptable, but I am desperate to finish this.

"Um … Okay," she stammers, opening her phone. Her fake fingernails click against the screen. "I sent you his contact."

My phone chimes and I check the message. Looks like Regina has one use after all.

"Tell the sellers it's all cash. I want a fast close – no inspection, no appraisal. Offer ten percent under. I want a counter by tonight or a final decision in two days. Can you handle that?" I ask, anxious to seal this deal and get in contact with Christian already. This isn't the first property I've purchased, and nothing is official until the papers are signed anyway.

I am moving on to bigger, better things.

Still, I am not taking any chances on this property. If Destiny chooses this as her new office building, there will be no escaping me. The possibilities and opportunities to get her back between my arms are endless when we are within close proximity to each other. Without the proper distance to separate us, Destiny is bound to accept our chemistry.

"Yes. I can do that. Thank you, David." Regina recovers, no longer looking stupefied as she steps away to call the seller's agent.

I leave her without a goodbye and walk to my rental car. After climbing in, I connect the Bluetooth and open Christian's contact information. If I call him now, he'll still be looking at the property with Destiny. I need to wait until they exit the building, and then I can tell him to walk away discreetly.

That is the plan.

A loose, somewhat chancy plan, but a plan, nonetheless.

If he refuses to walk away and instead tells Destiny I am on the phone, things might go to shit. Sitting in a car across the street and watching her is a bit too close to stalking than I am comfortable with. But I've come to realize I'll do a lot of desperate things for this woman. And my stalking behavior has become somewhat of a habit around her.

It takes fifteen minutes for Destiny and Christian to leave the building. His arm is slung over her slim shoulders, although it doesn't come off as intimate. Destiny doesn't lean into him the way she leans into me. She smiles at him warmly, if not fondly, but not passionately. I deem that he is not a threat. Hopefully, he will be my confidant.

I dial Christian's number and watch as he fishes his phone out of his front pant pocket. He signals at Destiny to give him a moment. As he steps away, she busies herself with her own phone.

This may be easier than I thought.

"Hello, this is Christian Ortega," he answers smoothly.

"Hey, Christian, it's David Green." I watch as the short, skinny man's steps falter and he sneaks a glance over his shoulder in Destiny's direction.

Don't do it.

Christian quickens his steps, placing more distance between himself and Destiny before responding. "How can I help you, David?" He says my name with familiarity.

Someone has been talking. After getting the sense that Christian has already been filled in on the events that happened between Destiny and me, I jump straight to the point.

"Is Destiny leasing the property in this building?"

"I can't say – we have several more to look at."

"Which one's the best?" I ask.

"Why are you calling me, David?" Christian replies suspiciously.

I sigh, expressing as much of my emotions into that one sigh as possible. Sue me. I am not above manipulation. I'll pander to Christian's emotions by showing him my desperation. Although, nothing about my desperation is actually an act.

"Because I've got to get her back," I say.

"I knew it!" Christian condescends quietly. A smile so wide I can spot it across the street spreads across his face.

Apparently, I have a fan. A fan who appreciates that I am a sucker for the gorgeous woman in a fitted cobalt-blue dress standing twenty feet behind him.

She is breath-taking. It momentarily distracts me from the reason I called Christian to begin with.

"What's the plan? And you better have a good one, because she thinks you're into that she-devil Regina. Ick, by the way," he adds, leaning against the building and picking at his nails.

He reminds me of a cross between Pat and Dale with his nail picking and flagrant disregard for diplomacy. Even in our short time together, I find myself missing their banter, too. It seems that not only Destiny but also her friends have seeped their way into my empty life, fulfilling it with *more*.

"I'm buying a unit in whatever property she chooses. Can you give me the other addresses?" I ask, hurrying to get the information I need to ensure Destiny doesn't get away from me again.

I'll make an offer on every available residential property near her top three choices. When she picks a property, I'll pick, too – choosing the one nearest her. My financial advisor will not be happy with me, but losing some earnest money is more than worth it.

Christian's brows furrow and then unfurrow as he debates his response. "I can do you one better. I'll make up stories about the other properties to ensure she doesn't choose them. Honestly, I liked this one best, and she probably would've, too, if not for running into you."

"Great!" This is turning out to be easier than I thought. "You wouldn't be able to tell me where she lives, would you? I need to show her that I meant what I said in Tulum."

"What did you say in Tulum? She mentioned something about that." Christian's shoulders straighten as he checks on Destiny.

Destiny is off her phone and walking toward him now.

"Nothing bad. I swear. She's coming back … I appreciate your help, man. Whatever you want, it's yours!"

His wide smile falters before it curves up at the side. Something tells me I will regret offering him *whatever* he wants.

"It's a deal. Be in touch."

The line goes dead.

47

DESTINY

"I THOUGHT I WAS your top priority today?" I joke. While David and the *blonde*, Regina, are still in the back of my mind, I am not going to let it distract me or ruin my day.

Christian's face when he hangs up the phone tells me all I need to know – he is keeping secrets from me, too. And I am going to get to the bottom of it.

"You are my top priority, love. Let's head to the other showings."

"No, you don't. I showed you mine, now show me yours."

He rolls his eyes. Christian's his sass-o-meter is off the charts. Which means his bull-shit-o-meter is too. I glare at him.

"What do you want to know?" he says.

"Who was on the phone?"

"A client." Christian crosses the street and I follow closely as we approach his car.

Fortunately, we carpooled, so he can't escape my questioning. I love giving him a taste of his own medicine.

"What were they calling about?"

"A property, Dez. That's what clients call about."

"Mm hmm …" I mutter, opening the passenger side door of his posh-looking BMW.

He waits for a car to pass before getting in the driver's seat. The silence between us is barely palpable and he seems content on letting it rot.

"Come on! I told you about hooking up with David. Who are you hooking up with? I know you were talking to a man."

Christian chokes on a cough while clearing his throat. "That was so not who *I'm hooking up with,* Destiny. Please, don't jump to conclusions, love."

"What was that stupid look on your face for then?" I don't believe him. He is hiding something. Christian had the best hook-up stories in college, and I need a good alleyway blow job story to improve my day.

"Because someone with a lot of connections now owes me a favor. Again, I am *definitely* not having sex with them." Christian presses the car's ignition. The fancy vehicle purrs as it turns on, and he pulls into the street, heading to our next destination.

I can't help my curiosity – it keeps my mind occupied – and I now want to know who owes him a favor. Los Angeles is as posh as Christian's car. Being owed a favor by someone with influence can get you far in this town. I may not follow celebrities on social media, but I know the business people who reside here, and a favor from one of them could do wonders for my company.

"Who owes you a favor?" I ask.

"Are we playing twenty questions? You know I don't like playing these games. Sometimes shit is confidential in my line of work, Destiny," he spits back at me.

Twenty questions.

"Whatever," I sigh, looking out the window.

David asked me twenty questions. He wanted to know more about me and I refused to tell him. We were only going to be in Tulum for a short time, and I didn't want to get my hopes up or have expectations about a man I just met, so we didn't get to the important stuff – like phone numbers.

But he did try once. I just didn't let him get far. I thought we had more time.

Yet, the world couldn't be any smaller because lo and behold, David Green and I still ended up in the same city, in the same place, only two days after last seeing each other.

Playing twenty questions wasn't necessary to ensure we found each other again. But I didn't want to find him. He left without a word. No explanation. He claims to have left me a message, but nothing about his disappearance convinces me he did.

Even if I received *said* message, I do wonder – would it have made a difference? Would we have still gone our separate ways and run into each other later? Or would I have been the woman in the elevator?

My friends didn't mention anything about him leaving. They texted me to ask why I left and when I told them I had to get back for work, they said they understood. They didn't ask about David's absence – like they didn't even notice he was gone or anything was wrong.

Twenty questions and the missing message. How could the world be so cruel as to separate David and me through such unusual circumstances, only to bring us back together?

Grace calls as we drive to the next property. Her call gives my spiraling negative thoughts a break. Unfortunately, she isn't calling with good news.

My Chief Financial Officer, Angie Marks, emailed her resignation and Grace wants to know how to respond.

The last thing I need this week is for my CFO to quit. I tell Grace to schedule a meeting with her tomorrow. I'll listen to Angie's concerns and do whatever it takes to keep her because I don't have time to find a replacement for such a prestigious position.

Angie is the backbone to opening this new location. She reviews, approves, and manages the budget alongside our balance sheet. Plus, she manages the reporting for our investors. I'll be on the afternoon flight back to San Francisco tomorrow to convince her to stay, which means I need to secure a location tonight.

"Give me the low-down on our next properties and take me to the best one. We don't have time to visit them all today. I have to move my meetings to tonight and leave tomorrow," I tell Christian.

He looks at me understandingly. After all, he heard my entire conversation with Grace. The panic and frustration in my voice isn't easy to hide – especially not from someone who knows me as well as Christian.

My world has been falling apart since I met David Green.

"Honestly, the best property was the one we just left. It's in an ideal area that's still growing, so the lease is low for the square footage. The rate locks in for five years and it comes with a fully furnished business condo upstairs. You'll save thousands a month on short-term leases and hotel bills with that perk alone."

Saving money on a personal property would be extremely helpful. I was going to take the travel expense out of my personal funds to make it work with the company budget, but it is hard to pass up free accommodations.

"You're certain about this?" I ask.

"Have I ever steered you wrong?"

"In college … many times! Since then, not that I can recall," I half-heartedly joke.

Christian switches into business mode. "I'll send the contracts tonight for your legal team to review."

"Great, thanks." I look out the window as Christian makes a U-turn and heads back to my hotel. A thought arises. "Oh, and Christian?"

"Yes?"

"Make sure David Green is not purchasing a property there. I refuse to work or live anywhere near that man."

Small world or not, I control my life and running into David with his hands on a different supermodel every day, or week, or whenever, will ruin me.

Fate can screw off, and so can David Green.

"Sure, Dez. Whatever you say," Christian replies.

He drops me off at the hotel entrance, and I give him a quick hug with promises to be back next week. Living in Los Angeles was not part of my long-term plan, but I'll be here often while getting the new office up and running.

I take the elevator to the tenth floor and kick my heels off as soon as I make it inside my room. There are no messages on the phone. Not that I expect any when everyone who matters has my cell phone number.

But I check, nonetheless.

For people who don't matter and don't have my phone number, it is pretty easy to leave messages on hotel room phones. Especially when you have the person's room number. But I purge that thought from my mind because no one knows my current room number. So there will be no messages and no changes in my life plan.

48

DAVID

"WHAT DO YOU MEAN you can't tell me?" I yell at Christian over the phone.

He agreed to help me. He made a deal, and now he is backing out. Nothing sets me on edge more than a man without integrity. And there is no one better at making a man lose his integrity than Destiny.

She got under his skin. I know it with every facet of my being – she got to him. She is good like that. Really good. Destiny truly is the ultimate opponent.

"This company is her life. I'm not betraying my friend's trust for a man she loathes. Like wants-you-dead level of loathing. And you better not buy that condo. I'll come up under Regina's offer and screw you both over if you cross me on this."

"Cross you? Like you're crossing me? I'm buying that fucking condo!" I threaten, my knuckles turning white against the car steering wheel.

It hasn't even been an hour, and Christian is already pulling out of our agreement. After our last call, I was on cloud nine, singing to some pop hit song on the radio. Life was looking up. Now, it feels like my back is against my own team's goal line.

My life is unraveling. It doesn't matter that I secured a contract with a new team. It doesn't matter that they are meeting all my demands.

What matters is that Destiny doesn't know the truth about why I left abruptly, and she assumes the worst about the reason why. After the night we spent together, what else could make her hate me so much?

"David. Be reasonable," Christian says.

"I *am* being reasonable!"

"Destiny doesn't want anything to do with you. Just leave her be."

If she knew why I had to leave and if she received my message, she would want *everything* to do with me. I refuse to believe that our time together was a fluke. There isn't a moment in the past few days that something doesn't remind me of her, and I am convinced she feels the same.

I must haunt her like she haunts me. Or else this connection between us was all in my head. If my ego has become so inflated that I can't see the truth behind her feelings, then I seriously need help.

"Is that what she said? Were those her exact words?" I argue, knowing something isn't right.

Christian sighs. "You and I both know her words were much nastier. I'm putting it nicely."

"Then put it not so nicely," I say, desperate to know what she really said.

"Fine! She said verbatim, *'Make sure David Green is not purchasing a property there. I refuse to work or live anywhere near that man.'* Happy?"

Damn. I was prepared to be relieved by *my* Medusa's vulgar words – as I normally am – but these words hurt worse than a head-on sack. It's like when she said *by the looks of you* – there was something so true in her assessment of me. These words represent the ultimatum fixed in her mind. Her ferocity is unparalleled. I know changing Destiny's mind is like moving a bull, yet I hold onto hope.

"No. I'm not happy."

All of the fire I felt before dwindles. All of the hope gone. But I refuse to accept defeat. No matter how discouraged she makes me feel. No matter how unlikely I am to win her back, I won't give up until she lets me explain.

"What did you tell her in Tulum?" Christian's voice is softer now, as if he can empathize with my pain through the phone.

"What do you mean?"

"When I was talking to her, she mentioned you told her something in Tulum, but then she quickly played it off like you were a smooth-talking liar ... Then on the phone earlier, you mentioned something similar."

Destiny thinks I am a smooth-talking liar – a player, a manipulator. It's not easy to come back from these labels.

Her mistrust and rejection hurt so deeply, mainly because it is so displaced.

But how can I blame her? Those labels were confirmed if she saw the picture Regina posted and then further confirmed when she saw me with Regina in the elevator. Obviously, it isn't what it appears, but without an explanation, it looks bad. Really bad.

"Christian … I realize how this looks."

"Do you?" he says sarcastically.

I resist the urge to yell at him again because I need him on my side. "Yes. I do. I had to leave Tulum last minute and I tried to find Destiny, but I couldn't. I left a message with the receptionist telling her to call me. It's as simple as that. Nothing has changed between us."

"Continue," he says, indicating I have a lot more explaining to do before he roots for me.

"Regina's father owns part of the team, and they gave me a lift to LA. She manipulated this whole situation to fall in my lap, then had her friends take a photo for her social. And then she told her father that I agreed to let her be my realtor. I couldn't very well deny it in front of all the owners, who appear to love her. The whole situation escalated, and after looking for properties, she started coming on to me more and more. But I swear, the most she even touched me was in that elevator. I was literally in the process of shoving her off when the doors opened. I'd never touch a woman like that."

"I wouldn't say you'd never touch a woman like that ..." Christian counters, referring to the many women like Regina whom I had been seen with publicly.

He's right about my past. But the person I used to be is nothing like the person I am now. They say your past will always haunt you, it's true, but they forget to add that it will define others perception of you as well. There's no escaping the choices I've made in life. All I can do is tell the truth and hope destiny is on my side.

"In Tulum, I told Destiny she was different ... I tried to tell her she was everything I've been looking for and never realized I needed. I'm not sure if she understood or if she even wants to know how I feel, but I need to tell her this before she gives up on me completely. I need to make my intentions clearer because it's obvious she doesn't trust people easily and she's pushing me away before giving us a chance," I plead.

"Yeah. She does that ..." He pauses, "God damnit! She's going to kill me," he says with a heavy sigh. "Sending you her contact info now. Don't mess this up. For my sake and yours."

"Thanks, man," I say, seeing my phone light up with Destiny's information before I disconnect the call. I rush to review it, her name lighting up my screen. I feel a tiny bit closer to her, even though all I possess is a means of contacting her virtually.

Her name, cell phone number, work number, personal and business email, plus her LinkedIn are all attached to her contact information. Christian is a meticulous man. For which I am currently very grateful.

My fingers hover over her phone number. He said she was busy; he advised me not to bother her. I debate listening to his advice. Maybe I should gauge her mood before contacting her. I decide to call the work number as an anonymous caller. Work phones always get weird incoming calls, so the New York City area code shouldn't give me away if I hang up before replying.

"Hello?" a high-pitched, semi-frantic female voice answers.

"Um. Is Destiny there?" I say, wondering if Christian gave me outdated information.

"Destiny is out of the office until tomorrow. This is Grace, her assistant. Can I take a message?"

"You said she'll be back in the office tomorrow?" I ask dumbly, hoping to garner some sort of useful information from this conversation.

"Yes, she'll return from Los Angeles in the morning. Maybe around ten am. You can call back, but it's usually better to leave a message so she can return your call."

Destiny will return from Los Angeles? My curiosity is piqued. "Sorry, can you remind me where your office is again? I want to get my time zones straight," I lie.

"We're on pacific time, same as LA. May I ask who is calling?" Grace is getting suspicious, and probably two seconds from hanging up.

It is a shot in the dark, but I am taking chances like crazy lately and they seem to be working out. Since Christian's support is hanging on by a thread, I shoot my shot.

"It's David Green," I say.

Grace gasps.

49

Destiny

The business meetings are over, and I am successfully drained. I don't have energy to do anything but order room service. Tonight, I will be eating and drinking my stress with a cheeseburger, fries, and an entire bottle of white wine.

Because, why not?

On the business front of my life, things are falling into place. Outside of the issue with my CFO quitting, the vendors are sending new contracts this week and the lease terms will be on my desk tomorrow.

Work problems are something I can deal with. There is always a solution, a workaround, a second, third, or even forth back-up plan to solve the issue. The type of issues that can't be solved as easily are matters of the heart.

As much as I want to pretend David doesn't exist or that I didn't run into him today, I can't. He has been present in almost every thought I've had that isn't work related. After running into him today while looking for properties, he has now successfully infiltrated my work thoughts with fear that

I may be running into him more often if he purchases a condo above my new office.

I know Christian has my back and will do everything he can to ensure David isn't living in the building I lease a floor in, but there is only so much Christian can do on that front. Empty threats only get so far, and based on what I know about David, empty threats only encourage him more.

Memories of David permeate far too many of my late-night thoughts. Especially at this hour and with my current stress level.

All I want is have alone time and to find a release, but as soon as I think about the feeling of letting go, memories of David's hands on my thighs, his lips on my neck, and his cock shoved deep inside me flood my senses.

This unusual mix of desire and heartache make me feel sick. It has only been a few days, but it feels like I spent a lifetime with the man. The things he told me spoke to a part of my soul that had tucked itself away for fear of never experiencing what it most desires. Giving it a taste is like giving a child a lollipop and taking it away after the first lick.

It's a cruel torment.

Everything spoken and unspoken was so right between David and me. Even when we first met and argued about who had a right to the daybed and the bottle of liquor, we sensed our kindred spirits and we were able to give each other the support we needed in that moment.

It was fueled by the need to release our frustrations, and once we did, we offered each other companionable silence. I felt so much better after that day, even though I thought David was the strangest man I'd ever met.

There were no expectations about anything happening between us. But when we kept running into each other, something *more* blossomed.

I take another drink of my second glass of wine. Combined with my exhaustion, my head is feeling thoroughly buzzed and heavy. I flip through television channels as I drink the wine, stopping on a sports channel when I see David's picture displayed in the upper right-hand corner of the screen.

There is no escaping this man.

The sports reporters talk about his transition from the Giants to the Chargers. I wonder if it is too late to choose a different location for my second office. But I can't let a man dictate my business decisions.

Los Angeles is the second biggest city in the United States. The chances of running into him again are slim. At least, I hope it is improbable, because I am not sure my heart can handle that kind of torture.

My phone buzzes, so I check the message, pulling my attention away from television David, only to be bombarded with more of his beautiful face. The message is from Stacy, and it includes a picture of David and me dancing at the wedding. Her message reads: *Not sure where you two disap-*

peared off to, but I hope you're having fun. By the way, you make a great-looking couple. Xoxo

I didn't think it was possible to hurt more than I currently do, but it is. David and I do make a great-looking couple, and the way he is looking at me looks like a hell of a lot more than the way he looked at Regina in their photo.

It is all in my head, though. I want to believe David feels more for me than any other woman because I'm competitive and jealous. But he doesn't.

The sports reporters on the television continue to talk about David's stats and debate how he will fit into his new team. They discuss some old injury and his ability to bounce back, but I dismiss it because nothing about the way David moves indicates a lingering injury.

I would know.

There is no juicy gossip about whom he is dating – or sleeping with for that matter. This channel doesn't seem like a gossip platform, but I still listen for it. And while I tell myself I listen for another reason – to find more things to hate about the man – I only learn more about his professional career and about how respected he is in the industry.

If the professional in me didn't respect success so much, I'd hate him more for his accomplishments.

The reporters say he is a *standup* guy with lots of potential remaining, despite his age. Days ago, I couldn't have agreed more. But that was before I hated him.

I push all thoughts of respect for him aside and remind myself that, regardless of the things David told me, he is a player at heart. A manipulative man who is only interested in playing games and getting laid.

It is time to set the record straight.

Destiny: *Thanks for the photo. It's cute, but I don't think David and I are going to work out. Hope he didn't spoil your wedding photos.*

She texts back immediately.

Stacy: *Don't worry about my wedding photos. What happened between you guys? Everything seemed good the last time I saw you.*

I don't want to respond, but I know she won't stop texting me until I convince her I am doing okay.

Destiny: *He's a player, Stacy … Just check his Insta. It's fine, honestly. He was a good lay and I needed that before getting back to work ;) It was a great stress reliever.*

My words are unconvincing, even to me. He wasn't *just* a good lay, and it *isn't* fine. It is so far from fine, but everything will be okay eventually, and that hope is what I hold onto.

Stacy: *Just checked … That's messed up. I really thought he was into you, Dez. Did you ask him what that was all about? Maybe the photo was from before he met you.*

If I hadn't seen David with Regina earlier today, Stacy might have convinced me that the photo was from before he met me, but I know the truth. The photo is recent, and he is still seeing Regina – in whatever capacity or agreement they have going on. Real-estate agent or not, hands were where hands should not be.

Destiny: *It's not. It's recent. Let's not talk about it anymore. I've got super early meetings and then a flight back to San Francisco. I'll call you this weekend. Have fun on the honeymoon!*

I need to shut this conversation down before it makes me spiral out of control. My second glass of wine is empty, and if Stacy keeps asking questions, my third glass will be full of tears instead of wine. I held it together all evening; Stacy isn't about to be the one to break me.

Stacy: *Love you, girl. I'll take care of this!*
Shit.

Typical Stacy – always involving herself. While I know her efforts will be in vain, there's nothing more satisfying than thinking David is about to get a tongue lashing from her. She is a fairly agreeable person – I am the mean one in the group – but cross one of her friends, and Stacy can be malicious.

Although, I fear hearing from one of my friends will make David think I am suffering and desperate. And there is no way in hell I want him to think that. This is a losing situation.

Destiny: *Stacy, please don't.*
Stacy: *xoxo*
I love Stacy, but in situations like this, I wish she were different.

Destiny: *Stacy?*

No response.

I put my phone on silent. I'm sure Stacy will be sending screenshots of whatever nasty messages she sends to David, but tonight I can't handle seeing anything else about him. The more I try to escape him, the more present he becomes.

I turn off the television and pour another glass of wine as I recount my time with him, trying to reaffirm my anger, but doubt still lingers.

Nothing David does makes sense.

And because of that, a tiny part of me still holds onto the possibility that everything isn't as it seems. My brain screams at my heart for allowing the possibility to remain, but it can't be helped. Eventually, with time and distance, the feeling will fade, and David Achilles Green will forever be a memory.

Right now, I need a little hope, though.

Admitting I allowed myself to be betrayed by a man only crushes my spirit. Sometimes, lying to yourself is the best option to keep yourself whole.

So, I hold onto hope that David didn't betray me. Because if he did, that hope is gone and there is nothing keeping me from plunging into a dark mindset that will never believe in love again.

While I drink my wine in the silence of this sterile-looking hotel room, the feeling of being utterly alone continues to grow, and I weep for future I'll never have.

50

DAVID

"I DON'T THINK I should be talking to you ..." Grace says wearily.

"Please, I need your help."

"Why should I help you? I heard what you did. I saw that picture."

I appreciate Grace standing up for her boss while still hearing me out. Either I am one charming son of a bitch or the people in Destiny's life know how stubborn she can be.

"That picture isn't what it seems. She fell in my lap during turbulence and had one of her friends take a photo. She hit her head and I was making sure she wasn't bleeding. Also, I left a message with the front desk to have Destiny call me, but apparently she checked out the same day and didn't receive it," I explain the miscommunication for what seems like the hundredth time. I've been repeating the explanation like a chant, Destiny's mantra egging my efforts on.

"And why should I believe you?" Grace asks.

"Would a lying man try this hard to get a woman back?" I counter, knowing if Grace has any experience with men whatsoever, she'll know I am telling the truth.

"Depends. Some men like the challenge." She sounds like Destiny, and I wonder if she is repeating Destiny's words.

"Are you with Destiny right now?"

She laughs, but not vindictively. "No. I'm not. I still have the office number forwarding to my cell from when she was out on vacation. You're actually interrupting movie night with my husband. Would you like to say hello to him because he's giving me a very irritated look right now?"

"Sorry ... to both of you." I instantly feel guilty. I also now realize my stupidity in calling Destiny's work phone. Of course, no one is in the office right now. It's ten pm.

"What is it you think I can help you with, David?" Grace's tone is strictly business.

"I ... um..." I start to explain but stumble over my words. The reason I called this line was to hear Destiny's voice. I hadn't actually planned what to say or do if someone else picked up. "I think I should just call her."

"No!" Grace blurts out.

"What? Why not?"

"It's late. I know her schedule, and by now she's exhausted or very possibly still working. It would be a bad time to call her. She's flying back to San Francisco tomorrow and has a storm to deal with when she lands. Honestly, you may want to wait to call her until this weekend."

"I can't wait that long." I say.

"Why not?" Grace's voice echoes my annoyance.

"Because the longer I wait, the more she'll think I'm exactly who she thinks I am."

"Which is?"

I sink down onto the bed in my hotel room, sighing. "A player."

Her silence is confirmation. I need to show Destiny that the only woman I am interested in is her.

"Can you send me her flight info?" I ask.

Christian already declined sharing her address with me, so I doubt Grace will share it either, but something more public may be likelier to garner a response.

"You want her flight information?" Grace asks, confused.

"Yeah. Just so I don't call her when she's in the air … That would suck to choose that specific time to call and then not get an answer. There's been enough miscommunication already, don't you think?" I lie.

"That, there has," she agrees. "Before I share anything with you, though … Why are you pursing Destiny so hard, David?"

The question is something I asked myself countless times after I met Destiny and the answer never changes. The woman frustrates and confuses me so thoroughly that I've become infatuated with her. But it is more than infatuation. After that first night together, it became *a lot* more than infatuation.

"Easy. I've never met anyone like her. I admire her – everything about her. From her obstinance to her devotion, there isn't a thing I'd change about that woman. She makes me want to be a better man. She makes me think about the future. Destiny makes me believe there is a higher power at work in this world because no one – and I mean no one – has ever made me feel like this before."

"Feel like what?"

"Like I am missing a part of myself when I'm not with her and like I've found it when I am." The words come to me without thought, completely on instinct. I realize their significance as soon as they escape me which only makes my desperation become more abundant.

Grace's voice is gentle and shaky, as if my words are something she understands personally. "If you really mean it, you better be ready to fight for her."

"What do you think I'm doing?" I lean forward on the bed, placing my head in my hand while holding the phone to my ear with the other.

"Okay … I'll forward you her flight info."

"Seriously? Thank you, Grace! You are a life saver."

"We'll see about that. Good luck, David."

Her message comes through shortly after the call ends, along with a notification from my social media. I receive messages constantly and don't usually check them, but I need an emotional break, so I open the app. Messages from aspiring football players asking for advice are the best pick-me-up, and I need a pick-me-up before figuring out what to do with Destiny's information.

But the latest message isn't from an aspiring football player; it is from very angry, recently married woman.

Stacy: *You piece of shit! What kind of man convinces a woman they are in love with her and then posts photos humping some rich Botox-filled slut the very next day? I thought you were a good one, but it turns out you're the worst kind of man. At least be honest about being a fuckboy. You're one hell of a liar, I'll give you that.*

Attached is a photo of Destiny and me at the wedding. We are dancing. We are smiling. And we are looking at each other with such admiration it makes me ill thinking I might never experience that again. This is *more*. It is clearly written across Destiny's face. As is it on mine. It makes my chest concave.

David: *Stacy, that photo was a publicity stunt, and I wanted no part of it. I've always been honest with Destiny. In fact, I'm doing everything I can to get her back. She's in LA and so am I. Can you help me?*

It is worth a shot, no matter how far off the goal line. Stacy rooted for Destiny and me all vacation; there is a good chance she will now, too.

Stacy: *Fuck off, fuckboy.*

Convincing Stacy may be a lost cause, but I try anyway. I'm getting used to this emotional roller-coaster ride.

David: *I'll prove it. Here's Regina's number. Ask her whatever you want.*

I attach Regina's number in my message to Stacy and send Regina a quick message.

David: *You might get a message from a friend of Destiny's. Lie and you can kiss that commission goodbye.*

There is silence on both ends of the conversation. I am taking a chance, trusting Regina to respond to Stacy truthfully, but I am out of options. Regina has nothing to gain from lying.

While I wait for a response, I look up Destiny's flight. Her airline reminds me of something. I rifle through my bags for Richard's card, and sure enough, I confirm she is flying on his airline.

The stars have just aligned.

Then, my phone buzzes. It's Stacy.

Stacy: *One chance. You better have a good plan.*

Regina is slowly redeeming herself, one good deed at a time. I respond to Stacy.

David: *Call me? I want to bounce this idea off you.*

51

DESTINY

I ARRIVE LATER THAN intended and must speed-walk through the airport to make my boarding on time. The second group is already boarding and my gate is at the far end of the terminal, which is a solid ten-minute walk farther.

This morning's meetings ran late, but they served as a perfect distraction.

Last night did not end well.

After finishing the bottle of wine, I cried myself to sleep and woke up with dry crusty tears, mascara halfway down my cheeks, and swollen eyes.

It feels like I am fifteen again – a hormonal, insecure mess. It is so unlike me. This thing with David has officially shaken me and it is going to take a while to recover.

My phone buzzes, and I pull it out of my pocket to check the message. There are a number of things to complete on my to-do list still, but the first one is getting back to San Francisco and meeting with my CFO, Angie.

But it isn't Grace or anyone else from work. Stacy's number appears on the screen.

Stacy: *Call me.*

Shockingly enough, she didn't message me last night or this morning. I fully expected a report on how she ripped David a new one, but all I received was silence.

Until now. I am intrigued to say the least. And a little nervous.

I dial her number while continuing to dodge people lounging against the railing of the moving walkway. People are insanely lazy, it irks me. Some of us have places to be and things to do. Some people need the moving walkway to get to their destinations faster. Yet it seems like only lazy assholes who have perfectly capable legs use the walkway as a means to slow other people down.

"Hi!" Stacy says uncertainly on the other end of the phone call.

I keep my reply short. "What's going on?"

"Are you at the airport yet?"

"Yeah. Why?"

"Just checking."

"Okay." My patience is wearing thin.

There is a long pause on her end of the phone, and the silence pricks at my skin. I prepare myself for the worst and ignore the sinking gut feeling that has followed the chills spreading over my arms.

"So, I talked to David …" Stacy says.

My heart drops into the deepest pit of my body, deeper than is physically possible. I expected our conversation to revolve around him, but the mere sound of his name makes me want to curl up in bed.

"And … ?" I encourage her to continue, but my breaths are short and choppy, my voice wobbly. I walk faster. I don't think the sweat that begins beading on my forehead is only from the quickening of my steps.

"Dez, I think there's been a misunderstanding. You need to talk to him."

I stop walking.

A young couple on the walkway give me a sideways look. My heart is palpitating, but not from an internal attack. I was fully prepared for Stacy to tell me she confirmed David is screwing Regina and that he never really cared for me, that I was just another conquest. Although, I'm not sure her defending David is a relief either.

Stacy continues, "I know you don't give people second chances. But you never let David explain why he left Tulum. And I'm not taking sides here, but you should hear him out – put yourself in his shoes and ask what you would have done in the same situation. I think you'll find that you two aren't that different."

Apparently, Stacy completely failed to reprimand David last night. He has a way of getting under people's skin. It makes me hate and like him more. Regardless of what Stacy says, David and I might have had an amazing connection on vacation, but in reality, it would be much different.

We are two different people, living two very different lives.

It doesn't matter that a small part of me holds onto hope. That fluttering I feel in my stomach is a caution sign. I must think rationally.

And maybe thinking that he possibly didn't betray me will make it easier to push him away. It is as if I am the one who decided not to continue things, instead of being forced into the decision by his choices.

"Why should I hear him out? Stacy, it was a fling. We were on vacation, having fun and forgetting about life – but we can't live in a fairytale. This whole thing should stay where it belongs – in the past."

"You'll never know if it could be more unless you hear him out. That's all I'm saying. You're the most stubborn person I know, and somehow you've found the most stubborn, persistent man on the planet! Eventually, that man is going to give up though, Destiny. Don't waste this opportunity. He might just be your match, girl." Her voice is pleading, and it makes the vein in my forehead pulse irritably.

From the very first moment David and I met, he was as forward and competitive as me. Most people would be turned off by such brashness, but it fueled a fire in me that hasn't been lit before. He infuriates me like no one else; yet, for some reason, I yearn for more of it.

The feeling is entirely too irrational for me to base a decision on though. I need to stick with the rational choice.

I need to, but my words and actions continue to conflict with my wavering thoughts.

I sigh into the phone. This struggle is wearing on my mind, body, and soul. "I don't know Stacy. What if we're all wrong about him?"

"If you never give love a chance, you'll never find it, Destiny. You might be wrong, but what if you're not?"

She has a point.

It is so much easier to push the hard stuff away before it threatens to break you. And if it doesn't break you, it only makes you stronger. The risk is high, and the reward is even greater. For a woman who spends her life calculating risk, I am doing a poor job managing this situation.

"I'll think about it," I say finally.

"Think quickly. I love you, Dez," Stacy says and hangs up.

As the walkway ends, I step off and continue my quick advance to the gate. At this end of the airport, more people rush about. It seems like everyone is running late.

Everyone is rushing toward something.

"Last call, boarding for San Francisco flight 1034. Last call, boarding closes in ten minutes," the boarding attendant announces over the loudspeaker system.

Shit.

I break into a jog, running a hundred yards down the terminal, taking a sharp turn to the right. Shortly ahead is my gate. There is a crowd of people waiting – it doesn't appear as if I am the only late passenger.

But as I join the line, it seems most of these people are lined up for some reason other than boarding. Loitering for the next flight I suppose. I push through the group and approach the boarding attendant.

A man whose voice I will never forget says my name behind me as the attendant reaches for my boarding pass. But I am unable to move.

The small paper shakes as it hangs between the attendant and me.

"Destiny!"

His voice has said my name in so many different ways, but somehow the way he says my name right now holds every emotion he's ever felt for me in it.

Suddenly, my conversation with Stacy makes sense. I feel my body tense with nerves, knowing there is no escaping him. I can run onto this plane and beg them to shut the doors, but if he can find me here – he can find me anywhere.

I hold it together the best I can as I turn around to face him.

David slips through the parting crowd. Adoring fans shake his hand and pat his back, but his eyes never leave mine. The crowd folds in as he passes through them.

"Destiny, can I please explain?"

The people close in around us, trapping David and me. It's now or never.

So I nod.

Every emotion until now halts in his presence. They wait with bated breath on his next words before they choose how to emerge because I now realize the lengths this man will go to for me.

It may be a bit stalkerish, but it's more than most men will do. If there weren't already doubt lingering in the back of my mind, I wouldn't hear him out. But there is doubt.

Now, there is a lot of doubt.

Because what kind of man – especially one who can have any woman he desires – goes to this much trouble to win *me* back?

"There has been no one else since the day I met you. I tried to find you the day I left, but I couldn't. I planned on asking you to come with me, even though that sounds crazy. Like, what woman would leave her vacation early to fly across the country with a man she just met because he has a meeting?" David laughs, running a hand through his disheveled hair as he rambles.

He looks more haggard than the first day I met him. Frankly, he looked better unshaven and getting drunk on the beach a week ago than he does now. Dark circles line his under eyes and I struggle to accept the reason why.

"What meeting?" I ask quietly, but my heart and my brain are listening intently, and no matter how loud he speaks, I hear every word.

"With another team …" He glances back at the crowd. "It's not something I can openly discuss here, but I'd like to tell you about it – on a date, if you'll give me another chance?" He gives me a cocky smile.

"Give him a chance!" someone from the crowd shouts.

I become keenly aware of the mass of people watching us, as if we are their favorite reality television show. I am not a person who enjoys this type of attention – not like some people. Not like Regina.

"Why are all these people here?" My sharp tongue makes its debut. I shoot the onlookers a dirty look, encouraging them to leave.

My life is not for their entertainment.

David's eyes widen. "I didn't mean to draw so much attention – it's part of the job …"

"Is posing with models across your lap part of the job too?" I say, feeling the unwelcome heat of the crowd pressing in around me and causing my anxiety to spike.

"That's not what happened. You're looking for a reason to push me away without even hearing me out!" David argues, his hazel eyes narrowing on me.

His stance shifts. His shoulders square. His chest puffs.

I see what he is doing.

This fight has been days in the making.

"Then you better talk fast," I say, waving my boarding pass between us and stressing the small amount of time he has left.

David smirks and says, "I have a better idea. Let me compete for a second chance."

"Excuse me?"

"You heard me. If I get that plane ticket out of your hand, you owe me a date. If I don't, I'll leave you alone. Forever."

I laugh mockingly. "You could just wrestle the damn ticket out of my hand. That's a losing game for me."

He arches a brow. "You didn't seem to have a problem with the bottle of whiskey or in the ocean."

I roll my eyes. "Fair." His bating works. "Let's do this." I set my purse on my luggage and push it behind me.

"Final call for boarding to San Francisco. Gates close in five minutes," the announcement sounds over the intercom system.

"Come and get it." I motion him forward, waving the boarding pass in the air tauntingly.

"My pleasure," David says as he paces around me.

We circle each other. I keep the boarding pass between two fingers hanging at my side.

David assesses me, looking for any sign of a trick. "Best two out of three," he suggests.

Smart.

He may be an arrogant bastard, but he isn't pegging me as a weak competitor this time. David learns from his mistakes.

"It's on," I say.

Although, I am not sure if I want to win or lose this competition. Because winning means I'll never see David again, and I am not sure that will feel like a win at all.

52

DAVID

"IT'S ON," DESTINY SAYS, her eyes alight with mischief.

I can see the fire in her eyes. It sparked as soon as I turned our conversation into a competition. This is the way to speak to Destiny's heart.

She needs physical proof of my efforts to win her back. Words can be pretty and inviting, but they mean nothing without the actions to back them up. My actions provide confirmation of my intent and my commitment to Destiny.

"Bring it on," I jest.

She lets out a huff of indignation as she gives the crowd one last evil glare. Thinking her focus is broken, I lunge for the boarding pass, but she anticipates my movements and spins around me at the last second.

Destiny holds the ticket in the air triumphantly after we swap positions.

I planned on giving her one win, but not the first one. If she gets lucky like that again, I can kiss this entire plan goodbye.

"All luck," I say.

"You wish. Get on your toes, quarterback!" She smirks knowingly.

She is quick – I'll give her that. But this isn't the first time we have played this game, and she will not have the advantage of surprise on the next round.

"Again," I say, rolling my shoulders back and getting into a defensive stance.

The crowd shuffles further away, giving us room to maneuver while watching the spectacle play out.

Destiny shifts from foot to foot, bouncing on the balls of her feet. She attempts to distract me by leaning over and flashing her cleavage, but I am in this for the long game. A temporary flash of breasts won't distract me from the real prize – Destiny.

She feigns to the left, just like she did on the beach the first day we met. I expect this and lean into her feign. When she throws her bodyweight hard to the right, I am already moving. Before she can spin around me again, I grasp her waist, lifting her off the ground and pulling her close to my chest, as I swipe the boarding pass from her fingers.

My arm pins her against me as I set her down on two feet. I savor the closeness of our bodies after days apart. I lean into her ear, nuzzling her hair, and inhale her deliciously sweet scent.

It has only been four days, but I miss the smell of her already. I didn't even know I missed it until I caught scent of her hair and the memories of her became as fresh as if they were from this morning.

Destiny stills. As do I.

"Destiny," I whisper.

A shudder runs down her spine as she pushes my arm away from her waist. I reluctantly release her. When she turns, her face is flushed and not just from the physical attempt to get around me.

She feels it – she feels the draw between us – no matter how hard she tries to deny or hide it.

My heart beats wildly. The gates that have been holding my pain and longing at bay burst open.

Destiny is mine.

"One, one," I say breathlessly, even though I know this game is over.

She nods and presses her lips together in a thin line. Her eyes search my body and the surrounding floor, looking for a weak spot as she pretends to ready herself for the last round.

"You won't find one," I tell her, shaking my head confidently.

She is mine.

Destiny is mine.

"How can you be so sure?" Her words are uncertain, and the inflection in her tone holds so much more meaning than that one question can portray.

"Because wherever you are, I am," I promise.

Her face grimaces. Destiny looks away from me, picking up her purse and luggage.

"What are you doing?" I ask, panicked by the sudden change in her response. This isn't part of the plan.

Destiny eyes softening, yet they glimmer with unshed tears. A faint smile lifts the outer corner of her supple lips. I stare into her eyes, shifting from left to right, looking for any sign of what will come out of her mouth next because she is frightening me.

Breaking the silence, she finally says quietly, "You win."

"I don't feel like I've won," I say uncertainly.

"Me neither," her voice is shaky.

All of the anger and resentment in her eyes has long faded. Instead, only pain remains.

"Destiny …" I say her name once more and reach for her hand, but only our fingertips touch. "There's never been anyone else. Not since you. And maybe, not ever again."

Our voices are hushed, barely audible, so the crowd that is slowly being dispersed by airport security cannot hear.

"How can I be sure?" she asks, looking up at me through defeated eyes.

I hate the pained look on her face. That feisty female whom I deeply admire has given up on love because of me. It is the worst feeling in the world. I never want to be the cause of her grief, and I promise myself I never will be again.

"Give me a chance and I'll show you. One date." I say.

"Gates closing for boarding to San Francisco." The announcement for boarding sounds over the intercom system once again.

Destiny glances at the gate, then back to me.

"I have to go," she says.

"Let me walk you." I wrap my hand around hers and she accepts it. My insides hoot and holler when she doesn't reject me – further affirmation that everything is going to be okay.

One step at a time, I will repair what broke between us. And I sure as hell will never leave her behind again.

I walk her to the gate and the attendant scans her boarding pass. Destiny's doe eyes skim the ground as she searches for the words to say goodbye.

But I planned for this, too.

I extract a boarding pass from my front pocket and the attendant scans it. Destiny's eyes widen, and she attempts to say something, but I simply re-lace our fingers.

"Come on," I say.

Her face is still in shock as we walk down the jet bridge. Destiny could win an academy award for that expression.

I step through the door of the airplane and lead Destiny to her seat.

"David," she protests.

"This is your seat, right?" I point to the window seat in business class.

She looks at the numbers over the seat, then at her boarding pass. "Um … Yeah." Destiny sits down and I sit beside her. "What the hell is going on?" she finally asks.

I laugh. I can't hold it in any longer. "You said I won … So, I'm cashing in on that first date."

Her right lip quirks up while her right eyebrow quirks down in the cutest expression I've seen on her face to date.

"This is an airplane," she says indignantly.

"Yeah. I can see that." I look around with a nonsensical grin.

"How did you do this? How did you know?" She is befuddled by my actions, but I can tell she approves.

We began taxiing down the runway and I buckle Destiny's seatbelt. She is too perplexed with my ridiculous plan to do anything else.

As I tighten her seatbelt, I say, "I wasn't losing track of you again, Destiny. Fortunately, I now know your name and your phone number. Careful what you say, because I'm taking notes in case you run away and I need to stalk you again."

Destiny laughs and the sound tickles my soul.

She says, "You are the craziest person I've ever met!"

"Funny, I thought the same thing when I first met you!"

Epilogue

Destiny

"Would you quit fidgeting?" Christian smacks my hand as I adjust my hair for the umpteenth time.

"I'm not fidgeting. I'm fixing my hair," I argue, reaching for the updo style once again.

It isn't like me to get my hair and makeup done for an event, but today is important and the last thing I want to worry about is looking picture-perfect. Because there will be pictures – lots of them.

"From back here, you are doing the opposite of fixing it," Pat says behind me. He and Dale are in the back seat.

"See?" Christian says. He laces our fingers in an attempt to dissuade me from *fidgeting*.

I focus on my breathing instead – inhaling for three seconds, then exhaling for three seconds. The action calms me momentarily as the driver maneuvers the car around the building to the back entrance.

"Can I get you a Xanax or something, love? You seriously need to chill. Your nervous energy is making *me* nervous now. *Certain* people do not need that kind of mojo messing with their head today," Christian says as he massages my hand.

He is right. Certain people do not need this nervous energy today – including me – but here we are. "I'm fine. Just make sure to keep my drink full. Otherwise, I can't be held responsible for my actions."

This isn't the first time we've done this. Today, however, is far more important than any other day before.

"It'll be fine, Dez. All you have to do is watch," Dale suggests, rubbing my shoulders.

"Exactly. I am not good at standing on the sidelines," I say.

The driver stops outside two heavy metal black doors. People are bustling around, finishing last-minute preparations. We exit the car quickly, heading for the entrance.

Christian and I smile and wave at the familiar staff as we walk through the black doors. Pat and Dale follow us, since it is their first time here.

Six months ago, I didn't know this world existed. Now, it is like my second home.

"What's the plan?" Christian asks, knowing I have likely already formulated one.

"David first, drinks second," I respond, knowing Christian's main priority is getting drunk and planting his ass in the best seat in the owner's box.

"David and drinks – my favorite double Ds!" Pat jokes as we round a blind corner.

The hallways under the stadium are cold and barren, but it is the safest and quickest way to get around. Speaking of cold and barren, when we round the corner, we run into Regina. The hallways offer no shortcuts or diversions, which forces us into passing her.

"Oh my god. Hi! How are you?" Regina dismisses the suited men she is talking to and saunters up to me and my friends.

"Regina," Christian greets her coldly.

"Hi, Regina," I say mildly. "These are my friends, Pat and Dale."

"So nice to meet you all," Regina coos, shaking their hands while ignoring Christian.

I am still not a fan of hers, but David asked me to be cordial. Apparently he threatened her into helping him win me back. The scenario is kind of funny, but he feels bad about being so harsh to her. To her credit, she hasn't hit on him since.

"Are you guys going to the field? Can I walk with you? Everyone is so grumpy today. Like, I was just trying to get some extra Gatorade delivered to the sidelines and this worker flipped out on me. They told me to do it myself! Do I look like I can do it myself? I'm in five-inch heels. It's like they don't know anything." Regina flails her expertly manicured hands as she talks, then pivots on her dangerously high heels, expecting us to follow.

"Yeah. I doubt they understand the … struggle of carrying things while wearing *five-inch* heels." I wink at my friends as we follow Regina down the hallway.

After countless interactions like this, I've learned Regina isn't purposely a bitch. Granted, sometimes she *is* purposely a bitch, but right now she is just being a spoiled rich woman who was never taught any better. I'd pay good money to see her thrown into the real world and told to survive without a penny to her name.

"They really don't. Anyways, I better not be blamed for the lack of refreshments. Deshaun can only drink red Gatorade. When he drinks the other colors, something bad always happens."

Regina always finds some way to bring up her boyfriend and make excuses for his mistakes on the field. He doesn't make them often, but when he does, she notices, and she draws everyone's attention to them.

I'd feel bad for Deshaun if I weren't so grateful for his distraction. Regina is so focused on him, she doesn't even glance in David's direction anymore.

Things will get rough on and off the field if she ever paws at my man again.

"Really – red Gatorade? That's the worst flavor. How does anything good happen when he drinks that shit?" Christina says, taunting Regina.

"Not today, please," I say quietly.

Pat and Dale are giggling behind me. Apparently, the show has already started.

Regina turns into the hallway that connects to the field. She flings her hair over her shoulder before giving Christian her best side-eye glare. "It's a subconscious thing, Christian. Look it up. It's totally possible. I'm sure Deshaun wouldn't find you joking about his condition very funny."

She's wrong. Deshaun would think it is hilarious. He's well aware of this *Red Gatorade* myth. But he's too big of a sweetheart to tell Regina any different, and while Regina and Christian hate each other's guts, Deshaun and Christian love each other. When Regina is busy sucking up to her father and his friends for god only knows what reason, Deshaun always finds his way to David, Christian, and me for company.

Deshaun is a wide receiver, so he and David work closely together. Through their friendship, Christian and I became friends with him as well. Regina's presence is an unfortunate consequence of the friendship, but it keeps life interesting. She is never short of drama and entertainment.

"I think Deshaun would be even less humored by the fact that you're telling people he has a condition," Christian murmurs.

I elbow him in the side, warning him against continuing the argument. The last thing we need is Deshaun in a bad headspace because his girlfriend had a petty argument with her ex-best friend. Christian and her are set on labeling each other as such, and frequently make a point of telling everyone around them how they are mortal enemies.

"I'll see you guys in the box," Regina says tightly, refusing to turn around as she steps onto the field. Her heels sink into the turf, but she makes a pointed effort to play off the imbalance.

"Nice going," I tell Christian as we head in the other direction.

"Someone needs to shut her and her ridiculous self-diagnoses up!" he argues.

We stop in an open area to the left of the team benches. I scan the field looking for those familiar broad shoulders. Both teams are warming up, only a few fans have taken their seats. It is still early. The game won't start for another hour.

If it weren't for the pesky pre-game jitters, this would be my favorite part of the evening. David says it is his favorite part. He uses this time to focus. He says there is something about the deafening silence that allows him to think best. Frankly, it only makes the night feel more daunting to me.

Finally, my eyes find him. His eyes are already trained on mine as he jogs our way.

I never get used to seeing him like this – in his team colors, running around the field. He is a marvel to behold. His shoulders are tight, yet relaxed. His movements are loose and free, yet calculated and deadly. The contemplative man who caught my eye in Tulum is a far cry from the person I thought I would end up with. But that's one thing I love so much about us – we are unexpected.

David's eyes don't leave mine for a second as he approaches us.

"Destiny!" he says, grinning broadly as he lifts me into a hug.

I squeal when he squeezes me and kisses my neck.

It is so unlike me, and by the look on Pat and Dale's faces, I know it shocks them. It doesn't surprise David, though. Achilles brings out the giddy female in me. He knows how to make my heart flutter and my lady parts sing.

The man is perfect.

He sets me down but keeps his arms around my waist. "You look beautiful, baby." David kisses my lips lightly so he doesn't mess up my lipstick. He is always thinking ahead about things like that.

"Thank you," I say as my heart beats rapidly.

The proximity of our lower bodies puts me into heat like a dog. I thought my attraction to David would dwindle the longer we dated, but it has only increased as my feelings for him grow.

"Stop that," he says with a knowing chuckle.

I laugh and bite my lower lip. "Sorry," I lie.

"Get a room!!" Christian groans beside us.

"Please don't, I am enjoying this," Pat adds.

"Agreed," Dale says.

David and I ignore them, instead basking in our embrace.

"You ready for today?" I ask.

"I am now."

"Oh, come on … Tell me the truth."

"I'm serious. As soon as I saw you, it's like all my nervousness vanished," he says, tucking a stray piece of hair behind my ear.

I nod my understanding. Recently, I gave a TED Talk at a conference. I was a nervous wreck backstage, but David surprised me before I went on and it felt like the world's axis had been righted again.

"I have to make pleasantries before the game … Do you want to join me?" David asks.

"If you want me to." I cringe inwardly.

The whole reason I prepared so heavily for today is because of the numerous cameras present, but I didn't think I would be near them so soon. Even though I sit on the sidelines or high up in a private box, gossip magazines and journalists have found David and my relationship to be the next best headline – following us around everywhere we go in LA.

David chuckles. "It won't be bad. I'd happily swap places with you, though. You can answer the questions and I'll stand there looking pretty. What do you say?" he teases, turning me and wrapping a muscley arm over my shoulders.

"Pat, Dale, glad you guys could make it!" David shakes their hands before we walk toward the press room.

Usually, David does this on his own and I watch from the television in the box. Today, however, isn't like any other day. Even though I am only standing against the wall, watching David answer reporters' countless questions, being present gives him support. As invisible as it is, I know how far that minimal amount of effort can go. And today he needs extra of it.

"You're going to do great," I say.

"We'll see …" David says, not really paying attention to me. He's putting on his game face.

"Don't worry." I snuggle into his side. "Whatever happens, I'll always be there."

"I'm not worried about the game, Dez," David says as he cups a hand around my shoulder.

I look up at him as we walk, arms wrapped around each other. "What are you worried about, then?"

"This and that. You know …"

"No, I don't know." I laugh. It's not like David to be worried about something other than the game on game day.

We turn the corner, and Richard is waiting outside the press room door.

"Richard! I thought you weren't going to make it!" I shrug off David's arm and hug the old man.

Richard has become a close friend of David and mine the past six months. Apparently, he arranged David's airline reservation the day we got back together. Richard didn't know me at the time, and hardly knew David, but still he helped us. And he's been coming around ever since.

"I wouldn't miss this day for the world, young lady. Just had to make a quick trip to France. You know me – always working," he says, letting me go and giving David a handshake.

"Good to see you, old man," David says fondly.

"We'll wait inside." Christian opens the door to the press room, and he, Pat, and Dale head inside.

"Everything go okay?" David asks Richard.

"Perfectly," Richard says, winking at me.

I don't know what David and Richard are talking about, but they are often up to something. Richard has a passion for aviation, while David has a passion for sailing. The two have been giving each other lessons. It's cute. They're probably secretly buying some new dangerous toy and waiting to break the news to me.

"I'll wait in the press room, too," I say.

I enter the faintly lit room and take my place standing against the wall that says *No Press*. It is designated for coaches, photographers, and other support roles, leaving space for the reporters who sit closely together in the middle of the room.

Shortly after taking my place, Richard comes to stand next to me as David takes the stage.

David's shoulders are tighter now, and the vein in his neck twitches every time a camera flashes.

Journalists and photographers are in a frenzy to ask questions and take unflattering photos – which I recently found out is impossible for David to do. He looks good in every photo.

A mediator hushes the crowd. They begin selecting individuals to pose their questions. Considering the importance of today, I expect questions about strategy and preparations, but the first reporter jumps straight to the personal stuff.

"How do you feel about contending against your old team today? Not only is this the first Super Bowl you've been to in five years, but it's against the men you once called your teammates, possibly even your friends. How will that impact today?"

David's features are as still and calm as a mountain pond. It is as if nothing can touch or faze him. When he looks at me before answering, I know nothing can shake him.

He wasn't shaken when the pain in his shoulder became too much. He wasn't shaken when we talked about what it meant for his career. And he wasn't shaken when he watched another man take his place as quarterback.

He will not be shaken now.

"New York will always hold a special place in my heart. I will forever be grateful for the experiences and the people who shaped me while I was there. But here ... in Los

Angeles … I've found my home and my purpose. Nothing is more gratifying than finding your place in the world. Today's game is just like any other. The only difference today is that I have Destiny by my side."

Looks of confusion spread among the crowd as they mull over David's words, not yet understanding the *Destiny* he is referring to.

He continues, "I've never felt more settled. The trivial worries I frequently encountered in New York are a thing of the past. As you've seen all season, with Xavier as quarterback, we have the speed and agility the Giants aren't used to contending with. And with me as the strategist behind our plays, they don't know what they're getting into. I know their game because I lived it for far too long. And I owe it all to one woman – Destiny. I am a stubborn man. If it weren't for that stubborn woman making me see the other value and skills I possess, I'd be on that field tonight. And I would have been the reason we lost. Instead, I'm going to be the reason we win."

David looks in my direction and all eyes follow his. He's never spoken about me in an interview before. There are photographs of us together and lots of speculation about who I am, but otherwise, he never publicly mentions me. I prefer it that way, as does he. Until, apparently, now.

He waves me over, and without fully processing his motives, I walk along the side of the crowd toward his position at the front. I pause before entering the space below the bright lights.

David notices my hesitance and stands. He takes my hand and pulls me into the focus of everyone's cameras.

He picks up the mic and says, "Ladies and gentlemen, my girlfriend, Destiny."

The crowd of reporters and staff snap photographs, awkwardly awaiting David's next words.

"Can I go now?" I whisper to David through a clenched smile.

"One second," he says, with a sly grin.

David is up to something.

Only he would make a plan to put the focus on someone else during his big day. He is actively redirecting the limelight. And I'm certain he is getting so much satisfaction about catching me off-guard – just like when he surprised me at the airport.

I enjoy his ability to surprise me far too much.

"While I am fairly confident in the outcome of today's game," he pauses, looking from the crowd to me, "I'd like to secure at least one win before stepping onto that field tonight."

The crowd is silent and the room grows dark as we all wait for David's next words.

He sets the microphone on the table and turns to me.

"Destiny?"

"Yes?" I say, utterly confused, but finding his unpredictable nature adorably amusing.

"This morning, you said today was about me. You said you didn't want me to do so much as lift a finger until I got to the stadium." He licks his lips in remembrance.

"Uh huh …" My cheeks flush as I recall our morning and how I snuck under the covers to wake him up. I hope the entire world did not just hear I sucked David off this morning.

"Well, there is one finger I'd like to lift today …" David smirks and kneels.

"What?" I say.

My heart stops.

David is on one knee.

He reaches into his pant pocket and pulls out a small black velvet box.

"David?" I say in disbelief.

It is unexpected – as unexpected as David coming into my life. Yet, in the grand scheme of things, it makes sense. Because your life partner isn't supposed to be someone you spot a mile away. They're supposed to come into your life so unexpectedly and suddenly that you don't have time to self-sabotage it – like I almost did.

"Destiny. You came into my life like a tornado. You destroyed everything I thought I knew about women and relationships. You obliterated every other thought in my head, and filled it with thoughts about you and you alone.

You have consumed me unlike anything before. If you asked me to leave the stadium right now, I'd do it! You give me more happiness than the game of football ever has, and I've spent my life dedicated to the game … It's taken me a long time to figure out how to become my best self. When I met you, it's like I finally saw the light. I finally found my home, and with it, I found peace. And happiness. And love. You are *my* destiny."

David opens the box and extends it out to me. He takes my shaky left hand in his and pinches slightly. I glance at the simple diamond ring, perched on a bed of silk, and my vision blurs.

This is actually happening.

We talk about marriage and children frequently. We often plan our future together, but we've never explicitly talked about an engagement. I knew it would come naturally one day, and didn't think twice about when or how. Especially not today.

But it is happening. It is *actually* happening!

"Destiny, will you marry me?" David asks, smiling.

He already knows the answer.

Six months ago at the airport, he defeated my defiance once and for all. Ever since he tore down those walls, I've fallen deeper and deeper into his trap.

Achilles' love trap.

I'll continually fall for him. Day after day, I'll fall deeper into that trap.

"Just name the time and place, babe," I say, and he slides the ring down my fourth finger.

Author's Note

Rendezvous is the first contemporary romance I've written. I wanted to get away from writing smut for a minute—even though it's my favorite genre—and focus on the more emotional aspects of attraction. Destiny and David are similar in many ways, but their major difference is David's resilience. He's at a different point in his life, so it's expected he has some hardened mentality on challenging situations. If they had met at any other time in their lives, I don't think these two would have been compatible, which speaks to the saying *right time, right place.*

This transitionary point they are each experiencing brings a new perspective and outlook on life that is necessary for a strong, lasting relationship, which I hope is reflected in the pages of this book.

Dating isn't easy, convenient, or without its challenges. We have to communicate and make an effort. Destiny and David exercise control and dedication in every aspect of their lives, other than dating. They accept that you can't have it all. But in those moments we least expect, when we are being our most authentic selves, honest connection can be found. At least, that is what I hope and what D&D experience.

In some ways, Destiny and David's love story is much like how I imagine, or hope, my own will be. But fate tends to work in mysterious ways, so I expect nothing will pan out the way I believe.

This book is for all my notoriously single third wheelers, my hard-on-the-outside, soft-on-the-inside secret hopeless romantics, my career-driven friends who do not settle, my dreamers and believers who never give up, no matter what life throws at them! It's not always about the depths we go or the fancy words we say. Sometimes, it's merely about giving in to intuition and being true to yourself. I hope you enjoy this book as much as I enjoyed writing it!

D&D will reappear in several of my upcoming novels, so you can find out how their time in Los Angeles has been. This book is the first in my LA Archive series, which is a series of standalone modern-day romances with a twist. All the main characters reappear in other novels as supporting characters or merely individuals being referenced. The drama spans novels, but you won't discover whose husband is shagging whose sister until the last book. Get ready. It's going to be wild!

About the Author

Sam Marie is a contemporary fiction author who loves writing everything from spicy romances to science fiction. When she's not reading or writing, she walks her fur child along the beach, hosts dinner parties, and travels often.

Her love of storytelling started at a young age. Sam often entertained her family on road trips with long-winded stories about wild adventures in make-believe lands, and her love affair with writing only grew from there. She wrote her debut novel, Foreign Desires, in one month, publishing it on a popular online reading platform, Inkitt, as she completed chapters. The community engagement surrounding her stories led Sam to leave the corporate life behind and pursue her passion for writing full-time.

Sign up for her newsletter to stay current on Sam's book news. You can also follow her here:

Website: authorsammarie.com

Instagram: @author.sam.marie

Tiktok: @sammarieofficial

Linktree: linktr.ee/sammarie.author

Sam's Titles

Find all of Sam's titles and the latest information on upcoming releases here:

www.ingramcontent.com/pod-product-compliance
Lightning Source LLC
Chambersburg PA
CBHW031200010826
48971CB00013B/1083